HOLLYWOOD
Scent

Nick Winters was born in Australia and grew up in sunny Queensland. He discovered his love for stories and writing at an early age. Nick studied drama and writing in Australia, New York, and Los Angeles, where he developed a strong affection for Hollywood. He has traveled widely in Europe and the United States. Nick loves movies, mountains, beaches, music, animals and traveling.

HOLLYWOOD
Scent

NICK WINTERS

Wintertime

Typesetting by Kirby Jones

Published by Wintertime, Queensland, Australia.
ISBN: 978-0-9943767-2-5 (paperback)
ISBN: 978-0-9943767-3-2 (epub)

For Malcolm,
Catherine, and Brian

ACKNOWLEDGMENTS

With sincere thanks to:

My father and Australia, for giving me a wonderful life.

America, for the memorable times, adventures, and the many good friends I've made there.

Hollywood and New York City, for inspiring me with movies and magic since childhood.

Everybody who contributed to this book.

Writers and their stories, known and unknown—all of you.

And to music, for always being a friend, comfort, inspiration, and the soundtrack to my life.

The wind was building fast; leaves began to swirl and scatter across the sidewalks and streets. The trees rustled, as if whispering rumors of the deadly battle about to unfold. A full moon peeked down through the clouds, turning the night sky into a blanket of silvery gray. High in the hills, a pack of coyotes unleashed their bloodcurdling howls, sensing the pending showdown of good versus evil. And the Hollywood Sign stood majestically, watching over everything.

—N.W.

PROLOGUE

HOLLYWOOD

She stood, knife in hand, her crystal-blue eyes glazed with pure murderous intent, as the unconscious girl lay on the bed before her. The most beautiful woman in Hollywood, she had the world at her feet. Yet here she was in a seedy hotel room about to take the life of yet another innocent. She had experienced it all over again now—the taboo sex, the luxury lifestyle, the adoration and attention. It was all so perfect. She had been granted a second chance by the dark powers to claw her way to the very top of Hollywood, and she would *not* be cheated a second time.

She cried aloud the words of the spell. Eternal youth and beauty would be hers once again. Soon her precious perfume bottle would be replenished with the crucial scent she required for her own macabre self-preservation. For Lillian, murder was a necessity.

CHAPTER 1

BEACHWOOD CANYON

Helen Elliot sat on her back deck in the perfect morning sun, gazing up at the towering white sign sitting high on the mountain, an icon to the entire world: HOLLYWOOD. Thousands of hopefuls arrived here every year because here, anything was possible. This was the place where dreams come true, where a waitress or a cab driver—anybody—could become a movie star.

Shadow purred softly on her lap as she stroked his soft, jet-black coat; with the phone to her ear, she listened carefully to the charismatic voice from the psychic hotline. "But when will my true love come?" Helen asked. "You said he was coming months ago."

"I promise you your time is coming, Helen; the universe takes the time it needs before manifesting your wishes. Just be patient and know what you truly want. Visualize it, go somewhere that's special and spiritual for you, and declare your wish aloud. The universe is always listening, but you have to ask with all your heart. Only then will it hear you and grant your wish and change your life."

"Okay, where should I make the wish?"

"Only you can answer that. Choose somewhere that makes you feel special, then ask with all your heart."

"I will, I promise. I have to go to work now. Thank you, goodbye."

She ended the call. The psychic hotline had cost her a small fortune over the years, but it was better than talking to nobody.

With Shadow tucked under one arm, Helen headed back inside the tiny cottage she had inherited from her mother and aunt. She had never known her father, who had died before she was born. The home was a shrine to the golden days of Hollywood: movie-star posters covered the walls, and display cabinets throughout the house were crammed with Hollywood memorabilia. Many years of studying the classic films and Hollywood history had made Helen quite the expert.

She pulled on her dress, frowning into the mirror at her ample five-foot-two frame. She'd been a size twenty since she was nineteen, and now at forty-one, she had almost given up on her dream of losing the weight and having the movie-star body she'd always dreamed of. Though she had always been happy with her pretty, round face and delicate nose.

Moments later, she was dressed and ready for work. Helen swept her shoulder-length brown hair into a ponytail and kissed Shadow goodbye. She popped a pair of large sunglasses over her pale-green eyes and headed off in her little car through the narrow winding streets, carefully avoiding the early morning joggers and cyclists.

* * *

Helen loved her neighborhood. This was Beachwood Canyon, a picturesque community tucked away in the Hollywood Hills, right under the Hollywood Sign itself. The sign drew swarms of tourists to her neighborhood from all over the world every single day, all longing to bask in its legend and have their photos taken with it. Beachwood's eclectic blend of houses—tiny cottages and vintage bungalows mixed with mansions—always made her smile. The area backed onto a vast park that acted more like a nature reserve, where coyotes still roamed the hills, sometimes even venturing onto the streets under cover of darkness. Red-tailed hawks soared the skies, and owls watched over the neighborhood at night like majestic nocturnal guardians. Beachwood was a special place, and there was nowhere else quite like it. Once you had been there, you never forgot it.

* * *

Helen parked her car, then headed up the escalator. Pausing on the little outside walkway that connected the stores, she looked down at the Walk of Fame. She loved working on Hollywood Boulevard. It was quiet at this early hour, but soon the area would be crammed with tour buses, street performers, and dozens of unemployed actors dressed as past and current movie stars, hoping to earn a few dollars posing for photos with tourists. She headed inside the shopping center for another day's work.

Helen took out her keys and unlocked the door to the little costume and alteration store she had worked in for years. She stepped inside and flicked on the switch; fluorescent lights buzzed to life. Fancy-dress costumes lined the walls and hung from display mannequins, many of which Helen had made by hand. From Dracula to disco to ancient Rome, the store had a vast range of outfits. Stepping behind the counter, she smiled at a sleek black designer suit awaiting pick-up.

"Good morning, dear."

Helen turned to see Ashley, her tiny, stick-thin employer, a woman with a permanent smile and a bounce in her step that defied her sixty years. Her coiffed silver hair, cut sharply at the neck, gave her an elegant look of wisdom.

"Good morning," Helen replied.

"Looks like we've got quite a few things going out today."

"Yes, last week got busy," Helen agreed.

Ashley glanced at the suit. "I see Mr. Perfect is coming in today. Going to ask him out to dinner?"

Helen giggled. Daniel, the new shopping center maintenance manager, stepped into the store. Easily forty, his average height suited his stout build and large arms. His work uniform strained to hold his generous stomach. He nervously brushed back his thinning hair with a cheery grin on his round, friendly face.

"Good morning, ladies. There's going to be some work done on the escalators later in the day. I'll have some signs up—just letting you know."

"Well, thank you, Daniel. How are you settling in?" Ashley asked.

"Enjoying it very much, thank you."

"Wonderful! Everyone's saying you're doing a great job."

"Oh, that's great to hear. If there's anything you need, just call and I'll get onto it right away." He left with a wave.

"I think he likes you," Ashley teased.

"Oh, stop it. He's just being friendly."

"You never know. Besides, he's too young for me." They laughed, and Helen returned to the alteration job she'd started the day before.

After a busy morning, Helen sat in the corner of the café, waiting for her burger to be cooked while flicking through the pages of her favorite book, *Hollywood Stars of Yesteryear.*

A loud clunk startled her as her lunch was slapped down before her. "Oh, thank…" The waiter was already halfway back to the counter. Helen shrugged; she'd been ignored by men all her life. No big deal.

Back at the store, she stroked her finger gently down the silky-smooth pristine designer suit, lost in a daydream.

"All finished?" asked a deep voice behind her.

She spun around to see Peter Jameson standing at the counter, flashing his brilliant smile. His stylish sandy hair and friendly blue eyes, set in his tanned movie-star face, always made her heart skip a beat. At forty-three, he could easily have passed for thirty.

"Oh, hello, um, I mean…er, pardon?"

"My suit. It's ready for me to collect, I presume?"

"Oh yes, Mr. Jameson. Let me just get a cover, sir."

"Please, call me Peter. I've been coming here long enough. I don't believe I've ever caught your name?"

"Uh, Helen."

"Well, Helen, you always do a fabulous job with my suits. I'd never go anywhere else."

With a racing heart and a goofy grin, Helen handed him the suit and then watched his athletic body glide off across the shopping center, still glowing from his compliment. His talent agency was on the lower level of the building, so she spotted him several times a week.

* * *

The rest of the week flew by, and soon enough Helen found herself pondering her usual Friday evening entertainment: watching old movies alone, after she had cleaned and mopped the store floors, of course.

After locking the store, she got in her little car and headed home, wishing she had an exciting night on the town planned with a boyfriend, or any friend. Her only real friend, Tisha, had left town five years earlier to marry an older man in Miami.

She parked her car and closed the garage. The old front door creaked loudly as she stepped inside. Shadow welcomed her with loud meowing from his favorite spot on top of the display cabinet.

"Hello, my lovely." She scooped him up for a cuddle. This little cat was her everything; she had adopted him from the animal shelter where she'd volunteered in the past and had fallen in love with the scrawny abandoned kitten at first sight. She switched on the radio, then checked her online dating inbox—empty as usual. After cleaning and mopping, followed by a nice hot shower, Helen settled down to watch her favorite classic film with a large bowl of ice-cream and Shadow snuggled next to her.

Helen spoke aloud with the actors for most of their lines, as she did with most of her favorite films.

After the film ended, Helen slipped on her tracksuit and sneakers and stepped outside. Moonlight soaked the streets, and a gentle breeze floated down from the hills, winding its way into all the exquisite little roads that made up Beachwood Canyon. Helen popped in her earphones and hit play as she began striding up Hillwood Drive.

She loved walking in her neighborhood; these hills were full of amazing stories and memories. Many old-time stars had lived happily in Beachwood Canyon over the decades. She turned the corner onto Beachwood Drive and continued up the long road, staring up at the Hollywood Sign high on the mountain ahead of her. She headed past the stone arch gates and Beachwood Market, puffing her way up the hill with the cool breeze tickling her face. Helen loved the night's darkness. It swallowed up everything she didn't like about herself. All her insecurities were lost in the shadows; the night's darkness gave freedom.

Twenty-five minutes later, Helen stood high on Canyon Lake Drive, gazing down at the twinkling lights of her neighborhood below.

Catching her breath, she turned and looked up at the towering Hollywood Sign which had sat up here on Mount Lee since 1923. Helen loved those fifty-foot-high letters. She took her earphones out, remembering how her aunt Janice had once told her that thousands of aspiring actors had traveled to this sign over the decades to make wishes, and she knew many still did, along with the throngs of tourists. She could almost hear them: *I want to be famous. I want to be rich. I want the world to know my name.*

And why not? Life was short, and this was the land of dreams.

She remembered the talented—but depressed and lonely— actress who had climbed up then leaped to her death from the sign in the 1930s. The story was legend now, and many claimed to have seen her ghost around these hills and even to have caught the scent of her trademark gardenia perfume, wafting on the mountain breeze.

Goosebumps broke out along her arms as the words of the psychic echoed in her mind, and instantly she knew she had found her special place. The mountain seemed shrouded in silence, except for the cool breeze. The sign emanated a commanding reverence. A strange feeling swept over Helen: a wave of confidence, magic, and adventure, somehow fused. She felt compelled to do something she had never done before, and with a deep breath, she opened her arms to the Hollywood Sign, offering herself to it.

"I don't want to be lonely anymore. I want some magic in my life…I want happiness. I want to be *beautiful* and to be loved. I want the world to know I'm alive. I want to find my soul mate!"

Her voice, echoing loudly off the hills, startled her. It sounded different up here, stronger, with a clarity she had never heard in it before. A chilling wind embraced her and seemed to be coming from the sign itself. Strange images rushed through her mind, each lasting only a split second: a silver dress, diamonds, stiletto shoes, a flash of long blonde hair.

An incredible scent then flooded her mind. She gasped, stumbling backward as the wind intensified. The trees swayed and rustled, and leaves swirled up high into the sky as the wind powered its way down the mountain.

Then, as quickly as it had begun, the wind died away.

Helen lowered her arms. She felt good, adrenalized. She stared up at the sign, popped in her headphones, and headed back down the hill. Something powerful had happened up there on the mountain. She could feel it; something very special was coming to her, and it was coming soon.

CHAPTER 2

VINTAGE TREASURES

Saturday morning, Helen rose at dawn and sipped a coffee with Shadow on her lap while scouring the local yard sales online. Many of her rarest pieces of memorabilia were found this way by getting up early and hunting down the bargains. It was slim pickings this morning, though, only one yard sale listed on her side of town, at Silver Lake. She finished her coffee and left half an hour later, experience having taught her that most yard sales began very early.

She arrived at the house and parked quickly to rush over and hunt for bargains. Laid out on blankets across the front yard was an array of typical items—an old washing machine, a bar fridge, vases, ornaments—but nothing that caught her eye. A few other people arrived and began browsing. Helen then spotted a row of dresses hanging from a rack. They were all old—from the fifties and sixties, she knew at a glance. There were easily twenty of them crammed onto the hangers. She flicked through them with no real interest, but then…

Right at the very end, she spotted something that took her breath away. A long, shimmering silver dress. A flash of déjà vu struck, and one touch of the silky-smooth fabric made her fingers tremble. It was a beautiful piece, with perfect shoulder straps and a long seductive split up one side.

It was clearly designer. Helen snatched it up and draped it over her arm, smitten. There was no price tag, but she didn't care; she was great at bargaining and happy to pay top dollar for such a dress. Thrilled with her find, she looked around and noticed a long table inside the garage attached to the house. Many items were laid out on it—china tea sets, old hats, pots, and pans—but nothing she wanted.

As she stepped inside, she noticed many old movie posters covering the walls of the garage. All the great stars from the golden era of Hollywood were there. Helen was impressed, and planned to ask if these, too, were for sale. She continued browsing with no real interest in anything, until she spotted something astonishing. Come hell or high water, she would have it!

The antique jewelry box stood two feet high and was crafted from dark-stained wood and shaped like a pyramid. Her heart pounded as she slid a finger gently down the gleaming lacquered finish. She counted the little drawers—twenty in all, each adorned with a little ornate silver handle. The intricate detail of the box impressed her beyond measure. Handmade, no doubt about it. A warm glow filled her belly, one she only ever felt when she had found a genuine treasure.

Sliding open the bottom drawer, she caught the tiniest trace of a captivating scent, which was strangely familiar. She stood there, transfixed.

"Lovely, isn't it?" a rusty voice said. Helen turned to see a kind-looking old man standing behind her. A worn brown blazer and a pair of faded black slacks hung from his gaunt, fragile frame. Thick silver hair swept back across his head, and a pair of soft blue eyes enhanced his warm smile.

"It's a beautiful old piece, that one. Belonged to a movie star a long time ago, you know."

"Really? Which movie star?"

He pointed to a large poster on the wall. "This movie star."

Helen looked up at the poster. A voluptuous blonde in a striking white gown was chained to a large wooden cross before a Count Dracula–style man. Above them was the title: "*Mistress of Evil*, starring Lillian Kelly."

Helen gazed at the woman's seductive features: pouting red lips; a large, heavy bust; and captivating blue eyes. Long, thick golden hair reached almost to her waist. Helen had never seen this actress before.

The old man extended his hand. "I'm George."

"Helen," she replied, shaking the proffered hand, then pointing at the poster. "Lillian Kelly. I've never heard of her."

"She's still largely unknown," George explained. "I only worked on two of her movies, but I worked on movie sets all over Hollywood for forty years. Lillian was the most beautiful woman I've ever seen, and I worked with some of the most beautiful leading ladies in Hollywood."

"Wow, really?"

"Yes, I did," George replied.

And Helen believed him. She stared at the poster. "She certainly was beautiful."

"Yes, she was very tall too. When that movie came out, it made her. The audience loved her; Lillian was the new silver-screen goddess of horror films."

"Did she do many movies?"

"No, only a few horrors, which she soon got tired of—she refused them to focus on romantic comedies. But it wasn't to be."

"Why? What happened?"

George shrugged. "I guess Hollywood couldn't see her as anything but a scream queen. Nobody would touch her. She was still young—only late twenties—but horror films weren't hot anymore. She found herself unemployed and typecast. She was used by many directors who lied to her and promised her big parts, like they did to so many naïve starlets in those days. Most had no intention of giving her parts in their films; they only wanted to sleep with her. Lillian spiraled into deep depression and avoided the public spotlight for many months. It was very sad."

"Clearly, you cared for her, and you know so much about her," Helen remarked.

"During the time we worked together I became very fond of her, and Lillian grew to trust me. She told me about her life, her childhood, and her plans. It was sad seeing her end up nearly broke."

"Goodness! Where did all her money go?"

"She never made as much as you'd think, and her agent was a horrible man—a drinker and gambler. He lied to Lillian. Instead of investing her money like he promised, he gambled it away. Bled her dry. The pain of a failed career crushed her."

"Oh, that's so sad."

"Yes, it made her a bitter person, so different to the sweet thing she had been in her younger days."

"What did she do next?"

"She vanished for a while—years, in fact. Some say back to Europe. Nobody really knows for sure."

"Did you ever see her again?"

"She resurfaced out of the blue in Hollywood one day. An old friend of mine called and told me Lillian Kelly was back in town. I was very surprised. I saw her interviewed on TV a few days later. It…it was as though she'd turned back time. She was exactly the same as when I first met her—young and perfect. It was unbelievable. Everybody was spooked…but also fascinated by her appearance. She even got herself a big part in a new movie due to all the hype, playing an air hostess, if I recall right."

"Was the movie a hit?"

George cast a gloomy look at his shoes.

"No. filming was canceled after a few weeks and never finished. The main actress was found murdered."

"Oh God."

"It was a dark time in Hollywood."

"Did Lillian get any parts in other films?"

George gazed up at Lillian's poster. "No, she didn't," he whispered. Sadness flooded his eyes.

"Lillian died in a house fire not long after, and they canceled the film."

Helen gasped.

"I got the news and drove out there late the night it happened. I wandered through the burned-out remains after the fire department and the crowds left. I was so upset. I found the jewelry box down in the basement, hidden up on some concrete beams, and I kept it. I knew it was hers; I recognized it from her studio days. That dress you're holding—it was Lillian's."

"My God, was it really?" Helen was stunned.

"It sure was. I already had her other belongings she left at the studio when she disappeared years before. Management asked me to take them; they knew she had no family. There were hats, scarves, a few coats and things. My daughter used it for plays and fancy-dress parties. I guess she lost it or threw it out over time. But this box and that dress? I never parted with them…till now."

"Oh, George, you must keep them."

George grinned. "I liked you as soon as I saw you. You're a true movie fan, aren't you?"

"I am. I collect anything old-Hollywood."

He chuckled. "I just knew somebody like you was coming today. I love these items, but the thing is I have cancer. I don't have long to go."

"I'm so sorry to hear that."

"Don't be. I've had a good run. I had a wonderful wife who loved me for forty-four years. She died a while back, but I have a beautiful daughter and a darling grandson. I've treasured every moment. It's just my time to go, that's all. I want you to take these things, my dear."

"I don't even know how much you want for them."

"Nothing. Just promise me you'll look after them."

"I can't! They're too special."

"I insist. My daughter's married to a wealthy man. She needs nothing from me. And any money I make here today will go to charity. Like they say, you can't take it with you."

"George, I…don't know what to say."

"I hope you look up Lillian's movies sometime. But they sure are hard to find. She was wonderful."

"I promise I will." Helen hugged him. "Thank you for being so nice to me."

"You take those things home and enjoy them, dear."

"Goodbye, and thank you so much."

She headed to her car and placed the jewelry box in the trunk and laid the dress across the back seat. She was about to drive off when George tapped on the glass. Helen rolled down the window.

"Here, take these too." It was the rolled-up poster of Lillian, a shoe box, and a video cassette of *Mistress of Evil*.

"Oh, George." Helen placed them on the passenger seat.

"I almost forgot I had them. Goodbye, Helen."

As she drove up the road, Helen looked down at the shoe box. Curiosity got the better of her, and she pulled over to the curb on the next street. She opened the box and stared down at a pair of incredible silver stiletto heels. The sides were encrusted with tiny diamonds, and there was a large single diamond on top of each shoe. *Oh, my…*The shoes were clearly old but looked many years ahead of their time. She headed off, smiling happily, to her do her grocery shopping.

* * *

Once home, Helen packed away her groceries then placed her precious new items in her bedroom. She set the jewelry box on her dresser and hung the silver dress by her bed, next to display mannequins that wore three other beautiful dresses she had made herself. Lillian's poster soon hung proudly above her bed, right next to her other posters. Helen placed the shoe box in her closet. After some housework and tidying in the yard, she worked for the rest of the day in her little sewing room on yet another new dress she had designed for her own collection. Apart from old Hollywood, her other love was dressmaking. She had made dozens of dresses and costumes over the years, and she had often dreamed of having her own clothing store, just a little place where she could buy and sell secondhand clothes and her own creations. Sadly, though, she felt it would only ever be a dream.

After an early dinner, and with the lights dimmed, Helen curled up with Shadow and a large bowl of chocolate ice-cream, about to watch her first Lillian Kelly movie. She shivered with excitement as the first scene began. A large dark castle dominated the skyline at sundown. The scene then cut to a forest trail, and there, on a large white horse, wearing a pristine white cloak, with her long blonde hair streaming out behind her...was Lillian Kelly.

"Oh, you were so stunning. Look at you!"

Lillian's character stared nervously up at the castle. As her horse approached the drawbridge, a huge wooden door creaked open. She had come seeking work as a maid but wound up the hapless victim of the evil Lord Zhargon. He soon had her under his spell and enslaved in his cult of devoted followers.

As in many old Hollywood movies, Lillian's white knight soon arrived to save the day and free her from the castle.

Tears slid down Helen's cheeks as the final scene unfolded, Lillian riding off into the sunset, sitting sidesaddle on her hero's black stallion.

Helen clapped at the end. She truly loved the film and thought Lillian a marvelous actress. She was now Lillian's newest fan. She switched off the movie, went to her bedroom, and stood before Lillian's poster.

"I just watched your most famous movie for the first time, and it was fantastic. I cannot believe I've never heard of you before. How sad it is you are so forgotten."

Helen felt compelled to speak to Lillian; those ice-blue eyes called to her.

"God, to see you in the flesh all those years ago…What a sight you must have been."

She then searched online for information about Lillian Kelly; she was surprised how little there was. A few brief articles and old pictures, but with more digging she found a news report about her life and death. It was quite lengthy and told the story of Lillian's beginnings. She was born in Germany, her father had died in an army training accident, and her mother then married an American soldier and they moved to New York. She then lost both parents to a car accident when she was just seventeen. She moved to Los Angeles to pursue acting. She trained hard with acting lessons for a few years, earning small parts in plays and productions before eventually cracking her first big film role in *Mistress of Evil*. A few more low-budget films followed, but her career had soon ground to a halt. She'd then had a string of failed relationships with several wealthy high-profile men, who were mostly possessive and abusive. The article described how she had then moved back to New York to try to break into Broadway productions, to no avail. It was also known she drank and smoked heavily. Some newspapers printed pictures of her, and she had aged badly.

She wound up living in a tiny run-down apartment in the backstreets of Brooklyn. After that she had simply vanished for years, only to return to Hollywood looking remarkably younger than her age, which sent the press into a frenzy, chasing her all over town. Helen read that—just like George had told her—Lillian did indeed get a part in in a big-budget movie, *Flying in Love*, which was canceled after lead actress Taylor Brannigan was murdered. Helen read how Lillian had perished when the mansion she was living in burned down. It was owned by the wealthy hotelier Lillian was dating; he was overseas on business at the time.

The article described her as little more than a B-grade scream queen attempting a comeback in Hollywood. Helen searched for more information, but there was little to find. It was almost as if Hollywood had deliberately forgotten her. The story truly saddened Helen. She looked at the jewelry box sitting dominantly on her dresser. She began putting her own meager jewelry collection inside the box's many drawers, still marveling at this incredible gift from a stranger.

* * *

Outside, darkness had fallen over Hollywood, and the lights of Los Angeles shimmered like glitter sprinkled across the city. A full moon hovered serenely over the Hollywood Sign, and all over Los Angeles people were getting ready to go out clubbing, schmoozing, and partying. It was Friday night, and the town was getting ready to come alive again. The celebrities would be out, limousines would be prowling the streets, and hundreds—even thousands—of wannabe actors, singers, and dancers would be trying to be seen, hoping for their piece of the spotlight. After all, this was Hollywood…the land of hopes and dreams.

But in a little house in Beachwood Canyon, none of that mattered for a second. Something incredible was about to happen.

CHAPTER 3

HIDDEN SECRETS

Helen placed her last few items of jewelry inside the box. She slid open the large bottom drawer and was about to place her mother's beloved pearl necklace inside when she spotted a cut in the velvet lining. It was barely noticeable but was clearly made on purpose. She slid the drawer right out and saw a small rectangle cut into the bottom of it. How odd.

She pried at the crack with her thumbnail, and it began to lift, further…further…until it popped open—to reveal a false bottom. A small object lay there, wrapped in a white silk cloth. With trembling fingers Helen lifted it out, her mind racing with possibilities of what it might be. Diamond jewelry? After all, Lillian was a movie star. It could be anything. It had clearly been there a very long time. As she unraveled it, a fine layer of dust drifted gently off the cloth as the object was revealed. It was a tiny crystal perfume bottle. It felt eerily cold in Helen's hands. It was the old-fashioned type with a squeeze bulb, the base of it looked to be solid silver, and there were foreign words engraved on it. There was a very small amount of dark red liquid inside it. She noticed there was also a folded piece of paper that had been laying under the bottle, yellowed with age. She opened it up—foreign language was written on both sides, similar to those engraved on the perfume bottle. The handwriting was exquisite. Helen folded it up again and placed it back in its hiding spot.

She held up the tiny bottle, admiring its exquisite detail, and sniffed the nozzle, catching the faintest scent of the perfume. She was the first to do so in decades—and it stunned her. Instantly, she recognized it as the scent she had smelled when she made her wish at the Hollywood Sign. It was completely intoxicating, rocking her mind and body.

"Oh!" She stumbled back and sat on the edge of her bed, a bizarre feeling overpowering her. Her eyes closed, and her mind ran amok with high-speed images: crowds, a red carpet, hundreds of flashbulbs exploding all around her…old-style limousines and men—tall, handsome men smiling at her. She saw the diamond-lined stilettos and the silver dress, which clung to a perfect body, moving like a second skin. And then a glimpse of Lillian Kelly's face.

Startled, she took a deep breath, and suddenly the visions ended. Helen opened her eyes and looked down at the tiny bottle, adrenaline tingling in her veins. She turned to Lillian's poster.

"Oh my God. I saw you…your life…It really was you."

Helen sat on her bed, confused, her mind still reeling with images of glitz and glamor.

"How did it feel? To be so stunning, to be in front of all those cameras…Your life ended sadly, but my God, when you lived, you really lived, didn't you? Why did I see your life? Did you show it to me?"

The bottle seemed to tingle in her hands; the urge was overwhelming. An inexplicable tug-of-war raged inside her, and she had no idea why. She raised the bottle to her chest, then hesitated nervously.

Why not? Just this one time…

Helen felt giddy with excitement; it was almost like an unknown force was compelling her to wear the perfume of the late Lillian Kelly. She surrendered to it. Sliding her gown off, her fingers trembling on the pump, she glanced at herself in the mirror then closed her eyes and *squeezed*, just hard enough to spray a small chilling mist of the dark red liquid which disappeared quickly across her skin. Nothing could have prepared her for what was about to happen.

It hit her like a bombshell. The exotic scent filled her nostrils. Her skin buzzed. The perfume felt intensely cold as it penetrated her flesh with an incredible energy. Again, snapshots from Lillian's life streamed into her mind. Cameras were pointed at her and people screamed her name. "Lillian!" She actually *heard* them. Next, she was in the back of a limousine with a gorgeous man in a dark suit seated next to her, kissing her while holding a glass of champagne.

Helen could taste the heavenly liquid on his breath. Her entire body shook. Next, she was at a lavish party in an enormous mansion surrounded by impeccably dressed people, men in tuxedos and women in ball gowns. Waiters swept around with silver trays heavy with cocktails and champagne.

It was old Hollywood grandeur on a scale she could never have imagined. Flashbulbs exploded as all the big Hollywood stars of the fifties walked in the main entrance. People clapped and cheered, and the crowd parted as if by royal order. Helen tried to stand but could not.

Her legs trembled and her heart pounded. Another image then took over—she was in a large sedan, traveling up a steep, winding hillside in the dark of night, surrounded by thick forest. A chauffeur was driving with a large silent man seated next to him. She was alone in the back of the car. She looked out the window to see a large castle, eerie and somewhat dilapidated, standing on top of the mountain they were climbing. The lower windows were softly glowing amber; somebody lived there.

The car pulled down a long stony drive. Suddenly, she was standing in an enormous dark room in front of a fireplace. A slender, hunched-over figure stood before her in a long black hooded cloak; he was chanting softly in a foreign language. The chilling raspy voice sounded from beyond the grave. In one withered hand he held the tiny perfume bottle. It was open, the nozzle unscrewed. In his other hand was a large silver goblet. From it, he poured a dark red liquid into the tiny bottle. A small white vapor began to form above his hands, and though the smell was extremely pleasant, something felt very wrong.

In her bedroom, Helen trembled and shook; beads of sweat slid down her face. She wanted out of this dream, this vision…whatever it was. It had been glorious at first, but not anymore. There was no glamor and no handsome men. Just the frightening figure chanting before her.

The white vapor disappeared into the perfume bottle and the man screwed the lid back on. The hooded face looked up at her. Helen's breathing quickened. She did not want to look, but she had no choice. She felt the crystal bottle being thrust into her hand and she readily took it. A grotesque, ancient face stared up at her, heavy with wrinkles and scars, two piercing black eyes shone with a youth that defied the creased, withered skin. Despite his frail appearance, the man emanated great power.

He stroked her chin softly with a cold, clammy finger.

"Younger," he whispered, through leathery old lips.

* * *

Everything suddenly rushed from her mind like a wild tornado finding its way out of a long, dark tunnel, but she could not move a muscle.

Something was *very* wrong.

A bizarre numbing feeling then crept its way over her chest, like pins and needles but much stronger. It spread down into her legs and over her body like a separate entity trying to embrace her.

The feeling spread up her arms…right through to her fingertips, flooding every pore of her body. The sensation intensified; the feeling became warmer, then unpleasantly hot. Helen shook and squirmed, but the power had her firmly in its grip. Wind began to build outside, all over Beachwood Canyon. It blasted into her bedroom window, and she could hear coyotes howling from high up in the Hollywood Hills, but still she sat frozen, unable to move. The feeling was now unbearable. Whatever this was, she just wanted it to stop. But it didn't stop; it became stronger. She screamed, but there was nobody there to hear her, just Shadow, who cowered under the coffee table in the living room.

Then Helen's body began to shrink. She sat frozen on her bed, her eyes refusing to open. The power slammed throughout her entire body and hurt so much she almost passed out. She let loose a long, mournful scream that reverberated through the entire house.

Everything was changing.

Blinding pain clawed its way through her body as she shrieked in agony. Her arms and legs were now thin, slender, and sleek…like those of a catwalk model. Her shoulders were toned and shapely. Helen sat there, helpless, her upper body naked. The pain continued. Long blonde locks sprouted from her head, slithering their way down her back, and stopping at the base of her spine. Her breasts, once flat and unnoticeable, now expanded, large, heavy, and full. The agony struck her face now.

She could feel everything changing—her teeth, her lips, even her cheekbones. She screamed as the merciless pain pulsed through her face and skull, begging it to stop, but it wouldn't. The power would finish when it was done with her, and no sooner.

Finally, the pain began to dissipate. Whatever force had just charged through her body with lightning speed and fury had completed its task and was leaving her. She began to regain her senses. It was calm now; the wind died away. Everything seemed quiet, except her heartbeat, which throbbed in her ears. She sat with her eyes closed until her breathing slowed to normal. Helen felt very strange.

Slowly, she opened her eyes, only a fraction…but it was enough to see her reflection in her dresser mirror. For a moment she couldn't comprehend what had taken place. What was happening? What was she seeing? She tentatively lifted her left hand to her face and was astonished to see her reflection do the same. It was *real*. Tears of shock and joy trickled down her face from the most beautiful crystal-blue eyes she had ever seen.

Lillian Kelly's eyes.

Her heart raced, but she calmed to a serenity she had never felt before, allowing her to understand and accept what had just happened to her. After all the years of loneliness, all the dreaming and wishing for acceptance, to be loved, respected, beautiful, and admired—somehow, her prayers had been answered. She stood and took a step toward the mirror. She stood six feet tall, bare-footed. Her skin was like silk, incredibly smooth and flawless, with a surreal glow that only movie stars seemed to possess. Her face was simply perfection: two piercing blue, almond-shaped eyes with long, thick lashes looking back at her from the mirror.

Her nose was strong but delicately positioned above her full, plump red lips. And her hair was truly from heaven… thick, lustrous blonde hair hung almost to her waist. She touched it; it was divine. *Nobody should have hair this soft and beautiful,* she thought. She stood dumbfounded, staring into her mirror at the blonde goddess…the movie star she had become. Was she dreaming? Was this real?

Her hand slid down to her cleavage, her breasts so large and full, sitting proud and high. Never had she seen a bust so perfect—and it was hers. She turned slowly in the full-length mirror on her wall and gasped at her perfect figure. Her legs were impossibly long, perfectly shaped, with rounded calves and thighs that traveled up into the most seductive, curvy buttocks she could have ever dreamed of possessing. Her stomach was sleek and flat. She ran her fingers down it, amazed at the perfection of it all. She shook her head, awestruck at the effect of her hair swaying across her back.

Helen whispered in astonishment, "I...I'm beautiful."

She began to laugh, first softly, then loudly and euphorically, but it was not her voice that filled the room...it was Lillian Kelly's: deep, husky, and seductive. She understood now why beautiful women spent so much time grooming themselves in the mirror. It was thrilling to be so gorgeous.

She turned to the silver dress hanging on the mannequin. Her lips peeled back into a delighted smile, revealing dazzling white teeth. She slipped into it, loving the silky-smooth material stretching against her body, and instantly she knew this dress had indeed been made for Lillian Kelly. The fit was perfection.

"Oh, look at me...I'm Lillian Kelly...I'm a movie star!" She spun around, delighted at how gracefully she could move. She looked down at her bare feet. "Oh, the shoes!" She took them from the box and put them on, marveling at how well they, too, fit her. Now she was truly a towering blonde goddess...a living, breathing movie star from the fifties, here, now, today. Whatever had caused this miracle, she didn't care; she only knew that her prayers had been answered, and it was real. This wasn't a dream; it was real.

She walked to her dresser, pleased at how easily she could move in the stilettos. Everything looked different now that she was so much taller. Her bedroom looked smaller. She slid open a drawer and took out a makeup kit she'd hardly ever used. She looked at Lillian's face in the poster and began. In no time she had applied eyeshadow, mascara, and the darkest red lipstick she had. She was complete, ready…perfect. She gazed at herself, still speechless.

* * *

It was time to go out now. Hollywood was calling, and she would answer. She strode up and down the hallway a few times, getting used to this divine new body. She paused in the living room. "Shadow…Come here, baby." But he wouldn't come. She spotted him crouching high atop the bookshelf, his ears folded back, trying to hide from her. She moved over to him. "What are you doing up there, darling? Come here to Mommy." She reached out to him, but he hissed and moved away from her touch. "Oh, baby, it's me, Mommy."

He leaped off the bookshelf and vanished down the hall. "Wha—oh, baby, I'm sorry." She stepped outside onto her back deck, where a pool of moonlight swirled on the floorboards. She stepped into it and looked up at the Hollywood Sign, its white glow gently illuminating the darkness around it.

"Thank you," she whispered to it.

Helen picked up her purse and headed out, locking the front door behind her. She climbed into her little car, sliding the seat back to accommodate her new height, and pulled out into the street, eager to get to Hollywood.

She rounded the corner onto Beachwood Drive; the Saturday night traffic was in full swing with partygoers heading to the Sunset Strip. Helen parked a few blocks back from Hollywood Boulevard in a backstreet, deciding to walk the rest of the way. She stepped out, locked her car, and headed down the street toward Hollywood Central. Passersby stared at the towering blonde goddess sashaying along the sidewalk.

As she continued toward the bright lights, a large limousine cruised past. It slowed down and pulled to the curb fifty feet ahead of her. A back door opened, and a tall, dark-haired man stepped out; a sleek black suit covered his slender, athletic physique. Thick black hair tumbled down over his forehead onto his handsome, chiseled face. He stepped into the middle of the sidewalk, staring at her with a gorgeous smile. A perfectly groomed light beard complemented his large dark eyes.

He took two steps forward, closing the gap between them. Helen stopped and stood before him. He extended his hand to her, and Helen took it. He kissed her hand, sending ripples of excitement up her arm.

"Forgive my intrusion. I am Carlo Genisi, film director. My friends and I are heading to dinner. May I…offer you a lift to wherever you are going? Or perhaps you would do me the honor of joining us for dinner?"

Helen's stomach swirled with butterflies. She knew who he was; she had seen him in some of the gossip magazines.

He looked at her with adoring eyes. She peeked inside the limousine and saw another handsome man sitting next to an attractive brunette in a black dress, both smiling at her.

"I'm…not sure where I'm going," Helen stammered.

Carlo shot her a puzzled look. "I'm sorry?"

She realized how strange her reply must have sounded. "I mean…I'd love to have dinner with you, thank you."

Carlo beamed. "Wonderful!"

He took her hand and helped her into the limousine. He sat very close to her. The other man and woman stared at her. Even the chauffeur was stealing glances at her in the rearview mirror.

"May I ask your name?"

Helen was quietly startled. She knew her name all right, but tonight…just for tonight, she did not want to be Helen Elliot. No, tonight she would be Lillian.

"My name is Lillian."

"A beautiful name. Forgive me. These are my dear friends, Christina and Sebastian."

"Sebastian is assistant director on my current film, and Christina works in marketing at the studio I work for."

Sebastian took Helen's other hand and kissed it gently. "A pleasure, Lillian. This is my fiancée, Christina."

The woman smiled, impressed. "Hello, Lillian. I must say, that's an amazing dress. And those shoes—wow, I've never seen anything like them. Did you find them on Rodeo Drive?"

Helen thought fast. "Oh no, I've had them for years. I think I purchased them in Europe somewhere."

Christina nodded appreciatively. "Europe, of course. They're just divine."

"Thank you."

"Why were you walking along the sidewalk like that, Lillian? Were you looking for a cab?" Carlo asked. Helen turned to him as she quickly thought of a reply. His face was only inches from hers, and his pupils were wide. She was thrilled at the impact she was having on him.

"I…was looking for a cab; I ended up being too late to have dinner with my friends, and I had to cancel. So…I decided to go out for a drink on my own as I was already dressed for a night out."

"I think you made a very wise decision," Carlo said. Helen had barely noticed he had placed his arm around her shoulders. It felt natural—*wonderful*—to have a man's arm around her.

Helen found herself handling this crazy, unexpected situation perfectly. Only she knew who she really was. She felt a power like nothing she had experienced, here in the back of a limousine with glamorous strangers adoring her. In some bizarre way, she felt as if she belonged here, as if she had the upper hand. These beautiful, wealthy people were clearly in awe of her. She could see full well the effect of her beauty, and the night was still young.

CHAPTER 4

LIVING THE DREAM

The driver pulled up outside the hotel. Carlo helped Lillian out of the limousine. Sebastian and Christina stepped out, and the driver closed the door after them.

"I imagine we'll be a good few hours," Carlo told the driver. "I'll call you when we're ready."

"Yes, sir."

A doorman opened the hotel doors for them, bowing respectfully. Carlo placed one arm gently around Helen's waist and led her inside. A suited middle-aged man rushed over to greet them—clearly the hotel manager.

"Mr. Genisi, always a pleasure, sir. And you have such beautiful company." He flicked his eyes at Christina, but his admiration of Helen's beauty was obvious. "Your usual table, sir?"

"That would be lovely."

The manager led them through the foyer and into the restaurant. A pianist was playing a tune Helen recognized from an old movie. The restaurant was elegant and lavish. Helen looked across the room at the large windows over the tables;

the view of Los Angeles was breathtaking. She had never seen it from this side of town before. She was about to have dinner at the famous Star Tower Hotel. This place was the stuff of legend; movie stars and celebrities dined here often.

The manager ushered them into their seats as a waiter hovered nearby. Helen gazed around the room, noticing every man in the place staring at her, along with several women.

"Are you happy with the table, Lillian?" Carlo asked.

"It's fine, thank you."

"This view is to die for. I never get tired of it," Christina said.

The waiter handed out menus.

"I'll have my usual meal," Carlo announced. He turned to Helen. "The swordfish here is superb." Turning back to the waiter, he added, "And my usual champagne while my friends select their meals, thank you."

"Yes, sir."

"Honestly, Carlo. That champagne costs five hundred dollars a bottle. Why don't you just order a cheaper one?" Christina asked.

Sebastian chuckled. "I think he just likes the name."

"Guilty," he exclaimed loudly, while smiling into Helen's eyes. "I would have nothing else poured for the exquisite company I am fortunate enough to keep tonight."

"Hear, hear," said Sebastian.

"What would you like to eat, Lillian?" Carlo asked.

Helen had never even seen a menu like this before. She ran her eyes down it and spotted a Waldorf salad. She pointed to it with a long, perfect fingernail.

"Ah, a perfect choice," Carlo enthused.

Soon everybody had ordered their food and the champagne was flowing. Carlo was an entertaining storyteller, and he kept them in stitches. He sat very close to Helen, often touching her arm.

"Lillian, please tell us about you. Did you grow up in Los Angeles?"

Carlo's eyes burned with curiosity. A tinge of panic spread in Helen's belly, but her face didn't show a trace of it. What could she say? That she grew up in a tiny cottage with her mother and her aunt in Beachwood Canyon? And during the day she worked in a fancy-dress and dry-cleaning store? No, she knew that would sound insane. No woman who looked like her worked in a dry-cleaning store. She decided to recall the life story of Lillian Kelly as best she could, but with a few changes. All eyes at the table were on her.

"I was born in Germany, in Berlin. My real father was killed in an army training accident when I was a little girl."

Carlo's eyes oozed sympathy; he stroked her hand.

She continued, "My mother and I moved around Germany, and then Paris, so she could find a job waitressing— anything—but work was scarce. We finally settled in Vienna, as she had a brother there. It was a lovely place to live, and we settled in okay, but then my mother met an American soldier, and they fell in love. He married her, and we moved to America. We lived in Upstate New York for years, until both of my parents died in an accident.

"I was young and frightened, with very little money. I found myself in a depressing relationship with a controlling older man. He intimidated and frightened me. I lived in his shadow for many years—until I left him recently. I decided to move to Los Angeles and…start afresh, as they say. And now here I am."

Her dinner companions were spellbound by her story; she could see it in their eyes. Helen was surprised how easily the story came to her. It simply flowed, as if she really did know the life story of Lillian Kelly, had lived it, and she just added extra bits to suit her. In Lillian's body she felt she knew exactly how to make people believe anything she told them.

"What a remarkable life," said Christina.

"Yes," Sebastian agreed.

"Germany's loss is most certainly our gain," Carlo added.

The food arrived, with superb presentation. Gleaming silver trays, ornate cutlery, and fine porcelain soon covered the table. Helen had never tasted food like this, had never even eaten in a place like this. She shuddered to think what the bill would be.

After some more amusing stories from Carlo's and Sebastian's younger days, Christina stood up. "I'm going to the ladies' room."

Helen stood too. "I'll join you."

The moment Helen rose, almost every male in the crowded restaurant turned in her direction—even the bar staff stared at the magnificent blonde in the silver dress. Carlo and Sebastian stood respectfully as the women left the table. Christina led the way. Helen felt all eyes upon her as she moved across the room. She followed Christina into an alcove with two gold doors, clearly marked "Gents" and "Ladies."

A handsome young man stepped out of the men's room, momentarily blocking their path. He looked at Helen and froze in his tracks. Christina giggled as she stepped around him and held open the door to the ladies' room. "Uh… hello…I'm Donovan." He held out his hand to Helen.

Helen gently touched it. "Well, hello, Donovan. I'm Lillian, and I'm going to the ladies' room."

"Oh, yes, of course. Could I buy you a drink later? It would be my absolute pleasure."

"That's very sweet of you, darling, but I'm here with company." Helen said.

His face dropped. "Well, whoever he is, he's the luckiest man in LA."

"You're too kind," Helen replied. "I'm sure there are plenty of lovely girls out in Hollywood tonight who would love to meet a man like you."

"Not like you, there aren't."

Helen smiled. "You have a lovely night, darling."

She stepped into the ladies' room, giggling. If this was what being beautiful was like, she was certainly enjoying it.

Christina shook her head.

"Wow, everybody loves you! And why wouldn't they? Look at you."

Helen blushed on the inside.

Back in the restaurant, the band was in full swing and a few couples had taken to the dance floor. The bar area was filling up as Helen and Christina headed back to the table. Helen caught the aroma of tobacco. She spotted a few people smoking out on a balcony. The urge to join them briefly overwhelmed her. Christina noticed Helen had paused; she touched her arm. "Lillian, we're back over this way, honey."

Helen snapped out of it and followed Christina back to the table. Carlo and Sebastian both stood.

"Ah, the two most stunning ladies in Los Angeles," Carlo declared.

"More champagne, ladies?" Sebastian asked.

"Why not?" Christina replied.

Helen nodded. She was already tipsy, but it was so divine she knew she wanted more. In fact, she felt like she could drink it all night. In moments, she was halfway through another glass, with Carlo whispering in her ear and smothering her with compliments.

Christina and Sebastian stood. "We're up for a dance," Christina said.

"Time to show these people how to really cut a rug."

Helen and Carlo watched them take to the dance floor. Helen realized at once that they were both adept dancers. *Wow*, she thought, as she admired the upper class of Hollywood happily dancing. *It's just like a scene from one of my old movies.*

Never did she think she would have a night like this: this luxury, this splendor, French champagne, a handsome man showering her with affection, strangers flattering her with compliments…It was *unbelievable*.

She felt Carlo's fingers gently turn her face to his. He leaned in close.

Helen closed her eyes. Carlo's lips covered hers. They were surprisingly soft. The kiss was deep and passionate. Helen's stomach did backflips. Her body shivered at the hunger she felt emanating from Carlo, one of his arms firmly around her waist while he gently stroked her hair with his other hand. She was aware of nothing else in the room—nothing but his silky lips smothering hers. Helen was amazed at the desire she felt for him.

The kiss ended, and Helen's eyes fluttered open. It was as if somebody had hit a play button and all the noise of the real world suddenly filled her ears and flooded her senses again. Carlo was smiling with satisfaction. "Thank God I saw you walking along the road tonight. Please…dance with me?"

Helen should have been nervous, even petrified. She had never learned to dance in her life, just a few silly tangos in the living room with her mother and her aunt, but she found herself taking Carlo's hand and rising to the challenge, completely unafraid. The crowd parted as Helen and Carlo strode onto the dance floor. Soon men swooned at Helen's figure moving lithely to Carlo's lead.

Helen immediately knew that Carlo was an experienced dancer, but surprisingly, she discovered herself also moving beautifully. He led so perfectly, she felt she could almost read his mind, one moment finding herself spinning away from him only to be snapped back inches from his face within seconds. It was *glorious*, like a movie, except it was *her* starring in this real-life fantasy…it was Helen Elliot being treated like a movie star.

I am a movie star…from a long time ago…but nobody knows that here. Right now, I'm just a beautiful, mysterious stranger who men desire.

As Helen and Carlo dominated the floor, numerous couples stopped dancing to clap them on. The band stepped it up a notch and broke into a salsa number, and the excitement on the floor picked up notably. The music thrilled Helen. She could feel it pulsing through her body. Her eyes closed, Carlo's hands slid down her back. It was sublime. They continued dancing.

A male voice spoke close to Helen's ear. "May I cut in?" A hopeful stranger trying his luck.

"No. This magnificent lady is dancing only with me tonight."

Helen glowed at the reply from Carlo, yet the stranger persisted.

"Would you mind letting the lady answer instead?"

Helen felt Carlo's back stiffen; he had given the man a hint that had not been taken.

"I have spoken for her, and that is all you need to know," Carlo growled in a firm tone to the handsome man with fair hair and Nordic features.

Helen knew from a glance the stranger wanted her badly, but there was no way Carlo was giving him a shred of opportunity. The tension between the two men instantly thickened. The stranger stepped in closer to Carlo with a look of defiance. Carlo quickly but gently moved Helen to one side and stepped in so close to the man their noses were almost touching. Carlo's fists were clenched tight; he stood like a coiled snake, ready to strike at any second.

"It appears to me that you could use a lesson in manners. Perhaps you'd like to step outside so I can teach you some?" Carlo snarled.

The stranger stepped back quickly at the abrupt physical challenge. Nevertheless, Helen felt the need to help calm the situation. She placed her arm around Carlo.

"I'm sorry, but I'm only dancing with dark-haired men tonight—this one in particular."

"You are truly blessed. Forgive me," the man said to Carlo, as he nodded and moved away.

Other males on the dance floor watching the confrontation were at ease now, but Carlo's message to the room was clear: Lillian was with him, and only he would be dancing with her. He held her close and kissed her.

"Darling, I would fight to the death before any other man touched you in front of me tonight." He spun her in a tight circle; Helen was thrilled at how protective Carlo was over her. Never had any man given her the time of day, let alone warned off other contenders. She was surprised, however, that such a sweet gentleman had become so quickly aggressive. It appeared Carlo Genisi had a bit of a temper.

They kept dancing. Whatever this experience was, this… transformation…was a dream come true, and Helen hoped it would never end. The music became faster and louder. A strange sensation swept over her, and she felt her self-control fading. She could see and hear, but somehow…She suddenly felt like a helpless bystander watching herself.

She slipped away from Carlo and began to gyrate to the music, oozing sexuality. Before she knew it, the dance floor had cleared. Helen Elliot realized she was no longer in control. It was Lillian Kelly who was dancing now. She slithered low, turned, spun, and twisted…Every move was provocatively sexy.

Every male eye in the room was on her, and she *loved* it. Carlo stood watching her with surprise and lust in his eyes, admiring the towering blonde goddess moving like nothing he had ever seen. The lights shimmered off her hair. The diamonds on her stilettos sparkled and shone. But the long, silver dress that clung to every perfect curve of her voluptuous body stole the show. Wrapped around a figure like hers, it looked as if hand-stitched by an angel.

She moved close to a solidly built man who was standing by the bar and danced inches from his face. She then ran a finger slowly down his chest, to the clear displeasure of Carlo, who moved swiftly over and led her away. He placed his arms around her waist, but Helen spun her way out of his hold and back to the center of the floor. She had no choice—it was Lillian who was putting on this show, and Helen felt powerless. In her mind, Helen wanted to move back to Carlo, yet she felt a strong resistance. She imagined herself *trying* to move back to him, but there was a strange tug-of-war going on inside her. Lillian's grip finally subsided enough for Helen to regain control. She stopped dancing and returned to Carlo. She put her arms around him and he was thrilled.

Helen sighed with relief; it had frightened her for a moment, the sudden power that had briefly seized her. It was as though Lillian had given her a small warning. But how far would she go? A chill crept through her, and she knew then that somewhere, deep inside her, there was a wild, seductive creature lurking.

Sebastian approached them. "How 'bout we blow this joint and get some cocktails?"

"Can we go to High Bar?" Christina asked.

Carlo turned to Helen. "What do you think, darling?"

"Sounds wonderful."

They left the hotel, the manager waving them off. He knew women like Lillian were fantastic for business. Stunning women drew big spenders, and Carlo was one of his biggest.

Outside High Bar, the queue trailed down the street. Helen had read about this exclusive club in the gossip mags for years. It was favored by celebrities and was extremely hard to get into, especially on Friday and Saturday nights. The doormen were turning people away in droves.

Carlo led Helen straight to the entrance, sidestepping the line with Christina and Sebastian in tow. A large doorman stood before them.

"Hello, I'm Carlo Genisi."

The doorman's face showed recognition. "I will allow you in, of course, sir. It's just very busy right now. The manager told me to hold the door until more people leave."

Helen stepped into view. The doorman's eyes moved up and down her body with approval.

"We were just hoping to have a few cocktails; surely you could be a sweetheart and squeeze us in?" Helen asked.

He unclicked the velvet rope at once. "Absolutely, Miss. Welcome to High Bar."

Sebastian and Christina exchanged an amused smile at how the Lillian Effect had worked its magic. A loud whistle erupted from further down the line as Helen stepped up and into the bar's entrance.

They headed into a large open area where crowds of people stood chatting around a large rectangular swimming pool, all sipping wine and cocktails and competing for attention. Helen looked out at another breathtaking view of Los Angeles. Camera flashes were going off nearby; local media were snapping away at Hayley Duskins, the latest "it girl" in Hollywood. She was partying hard with a large group of friends.

A waitress led them to a booth in the VIP section, large glass screens separating them from the wind and the jaw-dropping view below. After ordering cocktails, Helen and her new friends were soon laughing at Carlo's and Sebastian's seemingly endless supply of stories of times they had shared during their long friendship.

A photographer with a media logo on his shirt approached Helen at the table. "Miss, is there any chance I could take a photo of you and your friends for the social pages?"

Christina piped up. "Absolutely." She huddled close to Helen. Helen found herself automatically arching her back and smiling seductively at the camera. The photographer was loving her. He snapped away, asking Helen to turn her head this way and that. Helen obliged, loving the attention. Carlo looked happy about getting his photo taken with her.

"Great, folks. Thank you so much." The photographer turned to Helen. "Miss, is it possible to get a shot or two of you standing on your own? I hope you don't mind; my camera just loves you."

Helen looked at Carlo, giving him the satisfaction of her appearing to ask his permission, which pleased him. He nodded and stood to let Helen step out from the booth. All eyes were on her as she stood poolside.

She changed her poses as the photographer kept snapping. Finally, he stopped and approached her. "Thank you, Miss. May I ask your name?"

Helen was about to say "Lillian," then hesitated. Somehow, she felt it might not be a smart move. Especially if these photos wound up in the gossip mags. "Angela," she replied.

"And that's it? Just Angela?" he asked.

"Yes."

"Where are you from, Angela? I've never seen you before; you're the kind of lady that stands out a *lot*."

"I'm from New York."

"Okay, and to what do we owe the pleasure of this visit to LA?"

"I'm just here visiting some friends."

He turned to the others on the lounge. "Thanks, everyone."

Helen sat back down next to Carlo.

"Angela?" Carlo asked, puzzled.

"Oh, I'm just worried about my ex-partner in New York hearing about me living in LA, that's all," Helen lied.

"Darling, if you are worried at all, I shall see to it with one phone call that those pictures are not published anywhere."

"Thank you, it may be for the better." Helen kissed his cheek. "I'm just off to the ladies' room." She walked around the pool to the bathroom, making her way through the crowd as men stared at her. As she entered the corridor, she was suddenly confronted by the young starlet Hayley Duskins and four of her friends, who were chattering away. Helen recognized her from magazines.

"Hi. I saw you getting your photos taken. You're totally beautiful," Hayley said.

"You're too kind," Helen replied, noticing all the girls were eyeing her up and down appreciatively.

"You really stand out," Hayley remarked.

Helen could only smile politely as she stepped into the ladies' room. Hayley and a young blonde followed her inside.

"We're having a party later at my place—it's a penthouse not far from here. You're welcome to bring your friends if you'd like to come."

The blonde stepped in close to Helen and stroked her hair gently. "You're so gorgeous. You really should come, you know. We have such great parties. Lots of guys and girls." The gleam in her eye made Helen a tad uneasy. The girl trailed her finger down Helen's dress, almost tracing the side of her left breast. From somewhere within her, Helen felt a strange impulse to touch the girl, to respond…but she resisted it.

"Thank you, but we're heading downtown."

"Another time maybe," Hayley said.

Helen moved away, quite aware now that women, too, were attracted to Lillian's body. When she returned to the table, Carlo stood and took her hand.

"Darling, I was hoping you would join us for drinks at my place in Beverly Hills?"

"You must come, Lillian. Carlo has the most incredible house," Christina enthused.

"Oh, stop it," Carlo said, laughing. "Will you come, Lillian?"

"How could I refuse?"

Carlo took Helen's hand and led her out of the club. They climbed into the limo and headed off. The vehicle's seats were rich leather, soft and comfortable. And there was even an LCD screen above them, along with a minibar.

Carlo gazed at Helen. "Lillian, have you done any modeling or acting? I might be able to get you a small part in my latest film. It's set right here in Hollywood. You would be perfect for it. There are lots of scenes with beautiful women. I know you would look incredible on camera."

Helen felt her face break into a smile. *Good God*, she thought. *Can this night possibly get any better?* It had been the greatest night of her life, and now here she was being offered a part in a *movie*, by a real film director!

"I've never really acted before," was all she could utter.

"It doesn't matter, darling. It would only be a very small part, non-speaking. I could arrange a little on-set coaching for you. I simply must get you on camera, Lillian."

Helen was genuinely flustered. To be in a movie would be one of her greatest dreams come true, but how could she say yes? In this crazy situation, she had no idea what to say to Carlo.

"It's an incredible offer, Carlo, but please let me think about it."

"Of course. Just think it over."

They pulled into a long driveway flanked by palm trees. Helen's eyes widened as the mansion came into view...Carlo's house was *enormous*. She hadn't expected this. It was one of those houses you often looked at and wondered who the hell lived there and how they could possibly afford it—but tonight she knew all the answers to those questions.

* * *

The house was three sweeping levels, the surrounding grounds large and immaculately kept. The limousine stopped outside the grand double front doors. The men led their ladies out of the car, and Carlo swung open the doors to his mansion. He let Helen step in first, and she paused for a moment to take it all in. The ceiling was thirty feet high and the floor was covered in slick, gleaming marble tiles. A huge, intricate wrought-iron staircase wound its way upstairs from the center of the vast living area, with a black grand piano sitting underneath it. Helen thought it was spectacular, and her face must have shown it.

Carlo was smiling with pride, awaiting her approval.

"It's just magnificent, Carlo."

"Thank you. I'm very comfortable here. Let's sit out by the pool."

The pool area was sleek and stylish. Helen sat next to Carlo on one lounge, with Sebastian and Christina opposite them on another. Carlo poured everybody a wine while telling amusing stories about drunken pool parties he had held in the past.

Time flew by and soon Christina and Sebastian were kissing and cuddling in a world of their own. Lillian glanced at Carlo's watch: it was 1:30 a.m. Sebastian stood and took Christina by the hand. "We are going to leave you two now. Your wonderful guest room awaits us, my gracious host," he said, bowing.

"Sleep well, my dear friends," Carlo said.

"We will, eventually," Christina added with a smirk. "Goodnight, Lillian. Pleasure to meet you. You're in marvelous hands."

"The pleasure's been all mine."

Christina blew her a kiss as she headed upstairs with Sebastian.

Carlo leaned in and began kissing Helen's neck, working his way up to her ear, nibbling softly. Helen squirmed in delight. This night was a waking dream. She had no idea how it had happened or how long it would last. She only knew it was the greatest experience of her entire life.

Thank God for the perfume! What a night. To be adored by a man like Carlo, spoiled in a five-star restaurant, treated like a queen. Oh, how easily it had all come to her this glorious night. *Thank you, Lillian Kelly.*

Before she knew it, Carlo had whisked her up the winding staircase and into his colossal master bedroom. The ceiling was cathedral-shaped, and there were huge arched windows carved into the walls, and even a fireplace.

His bedroom is three times the size of my house.

Carlo opened the doors to a balcony and gestured for Helen to step out. She did, slack-jawed at the view before her. She loved her mountain view from her humble little home, but this was indescribable.

The vast twinkling sprawl of LA seemed to stretch out forever. The night was perfect, and stars littered the sky. The balcony also had a distant view of the Hollywood Sign. Helen giggled, giddy on champagne, and waved to it.

"Did you make a wish?" asked Carlo.

"Not just now, no, but the last wish I made has certainly been answered."

CHAPTER 5

PASSION

Carlo took her shoulders firmly and kissed her deeply. Helen *loved* it. She couldn't get enough of this handsome man, his incredible looks, his deep voice. He had wooed her all night and treated her like a lady. *And this house—he must be one of the most eligible men in Los Angeles.*

He led her back inside and kissed her once more, then threw her onto the king-sized bed with playful force. Helen shrieked with laughter. His clothes fell to the floor quickly, as lust burned in his eyes. He stood completely naked before her. His chest was smooth and muscular, with just a small amount of hair. His arms were divine, with rounded shoulders and ropey forearms. Helen realized she had never watched a man undress in front of her before, let alone a man like Carlo, waiting to pounce on her...to *devour* her. She had lost her virginity after her prom, but after that she had made love with a man on very few occasions.

He's gorgeous.

A tinge of panic ran down her spine. She had such limited experience, but Carlo was a grown man who had no doubt bedded dozens of women. What was he going to expect of her?

He dropped onto the bed and began sliding her dress up, rubbing his hand up her legs, kissing from her ankles to her knees. Helen shuddered with pleasure.

He slid off her shoulder straps and gently pulled down her dress, whispering softly in Italian, which drove Helen wild. She could not believe how ready she was for him. Never had she felt so alive. This man was taking her to places she had never even imagined. His mouth smothered hers, and he looked into her eyes.

"You are the most beautiful woman in the world," he whispered.

The words echoed in Helen's mind. She felt like a teenager again, spellbound to him, as fluid as melting candle wax.

Helen almost didn't notice his knee nudge her legs apart. His hardness found her quickly, and before she knew it… gently, perfectly…he entered her. It was breathtaking…She had no idea it could be so magical.

Slowly he thrust, harder and deeper each time. Helen shook uncontrollably, dragging her fingernails down his hard, muscular back. *This…is lovemaking*, Helen thought. *This is how men make love to women they are crazy about.* He kissed her deeply with each thrust of his hips, and Helen ran her hands down his arms, enjoying the physical power of this man.

Strange images flashed into her mind: bodies…naked, numerous people entwined intimately. Helen shook her head, confused. She felt a fire in her belly, and the urge to sink her fingernails into Carlo and take control rocketed through her for a split second. But she resisted it; she was loving the way Carlo was making her feel. Soon it came, the sensation that only a woman saturated with passion can feel. She trembled from head to toe, breathing hard, and Carlo sensed her pending climax.

She opened her eyes to see his, inches from hers, then it happened. Helen let out a cry that she felt could have been heard all over Los Angeles—she had no choice. Her body shuddered in sublime pleasure as she surrendered to it. Carlo climaxed seconds later; his long, deep moan and the stiffening of his powerful body thrilled her. Her female instinct told her this gorgeous man had made certain he pleased her first, but now his full passion was unleashed.

Finally, they both caught their breath and came back to the real world. He gazed at Helen with a question in his eyes.

"That was perfect," she whispered.

Satisfaction flooded his face as he smothered her neck with soft kisses. "Darling, you're incredible."

He lay next to her, running his hands lightly across her breasts and stomach until he fell asleep, his face nuzzled in her hair. The overpowering feeling she'd experienced on the dance floor swept through her again. Helen lost herself for a moment. She slid her finger down her neck and across her breasts where she had applied the perfume, she then stroked her finger gently under Carlo's nose. "*Amour*," she whispered. Helen could not know it was the French word for love, but Lillian certainly did. Instantly, Carlo moaned in his sleep, and his body trembled briefly. He then inhaled deeply and lay perfectly still.

The feeling left Helen then. She shook her head, wondering what had just happened, then lay there and watched him sleep, wanting this never to end. It wasn't just his looks and wealth. He was such a gentleman. And even with her lack of experience, as a woman she knew instinctively he was an amazing lover. A breeze tumbled in from the balcony. She pulled the satin sheets up to her shoulders and watched Carlo breathing until she, too, drifted off to sleep.

CHAPTER 6

RUDE AWAKENING

A sharp pain jolted Helen from her slumber, like jumping into ice-cold water. At first she thought it must have been the champagne, or too much of it. But within seconds she knew it was far more serious. She sat bolt upright, and sweat broke on her forehead as the first rays of dawn began seeping in through the windows. A sliver of sunlight stretched across her thighs and grew uncomfortably hot. Her head throbbed. Searing pain struck again, and her stomach swirled as a tingling sensation spread into her arms and legs. Her stomach heaved.

Helen scurried into Carlo's bathroom, locking the door behind her. Her whole body was tingling ferociously now, and it hurt. Her face was flushed and hot. She looked in the mirror, clutching her stomach. It felt as though her ankles were being crushed, and her body and head were on fire.

The stark reality of the situation then struck her like a blade of ice in her chest…

Oh my God! I'm changing back into myself!

A tide of sickness swirled in her stomach and made its intentions clear. She leaned over the toilet.

Oh no.

Her mouth opened, and a flood of green bile burst out of her, putrid and disgusting, followed by another. She gasped for breath while flushing the toilet, horrified at the sight of it. It was like nothing she had ever seen before. There was a strange luminous glow to it. She knew it was not from the wine or the food. This was the beginning of the transformation back to her real body, and it wasn't over yet. Another jolt of pain rocked her violently, and she bit her hand to avoid screaming.

Not here. I can't let him see who I really am!

She snatched a black bathrobe from a hanger and threw it on quickly, then opened the door and peered out at Carlo on the bed. He was still sound asleep. Helen tiptoed to the bedside and snatched up her dress, shoes, and handbag. With searing pain in her arms and legs, she took a last glance at Carlo and swiftly left the bedroom.

The marble stairs were hard and cold under her bare feet. She had almost reached the bottom floor when a fierce pain shot through her body, sending her to the floor in agony. She got up and raced across the massive room as the sun's rays began to flood in through the windows. She needed to get home fast. Helen had no idea how she was going to get there, but she knew she could not let anybody see this happening— not here, not anywhere. Her stomach swirled. She had almost made it to a glass door leading to the pool area when she dropped to the floor again.

It's happening! I'm turning into myself again. Please, no!

She lay there gasping for breath, grimacing in pain, until she spotted a small brick hut by the pool. She recalled seeing it last night and now realized it was a changing room. Heart pounding, she dragged herself up, slammed her hand on the door handle, and raced across the pool area to the door of the change room, shoving it open. She slammed it shut behind her and crumpled to the floor.

It was happening now.

She looked down at her legs and actually *saw* them swelling. The pain was unbearable. It moved into her arms next. She hunched over, eyes clamped shut as she howled in agony.

She reached up and grabbed the edge of the sink, pulling herself up. She looked into the small basin mirror, heaving for breath, and what she saw terrified her. Her long blonde hair was retracting back into her scalp, replaced by her usual thin mousy-brown hair. Searing pain rocked her face as she saw her true self returning.

Good God!

Another flood of bile shot out of her and filled the tiny basin. Its foulness burned her throat and nostrils. Now on the verge of passing out, she stumbled back against the wall and slid down to her knees, trembling in pain as she transformed into Helen Elliot. Laying there on the cold cement floor, everything went inky and gray.

And then there was darkness.

* * *

For a moment she didn't know where she was, but then the reality came rushing back to her. The silver dress was sprawled on the floor next to her, the stilettos discarded by the door. Helen slowly stood, thankful there was no more pain.

I've got to get out of here…

But she had to look in the mirror, had to face her old self and accept that the spell—the fairy tale—whatever it was, was over now. She looked into the mirror and staring back at her…was her true self, Helen Elliot. Plain, overweight, and clad in a man's bathrobe with dried spittle and bile spattered down the front.

How can this be? How can this happen?

Helen reached up and touched her face. "I don't want to be you…Nobody wants you." Tears welled in her eyes, but this was no time to start crying. *I have to get home.* She cleaned up as best she could, then opened the door slightly.

There was nobody around. She guessed it was around six o'clock, judging by the light. She moved quickly across the sprawling manicured lawns and headed for the road, praying nobody was watching her. Beside the main gates was a small gate, slightly ajar. She stepped through it and out onto the sidewalk, looking up and down the road. She headed quickly down the hill.

What a sight I must look, walking through Beverly Hills at this hour.

She moved clumsily down the sidewalk, squinting in the bright Californian sun. She needed a cab or she had quite a walk ahead of her, but what else could she do? It started to sink in then—it was truly over; she was now just plain Helen Elliot from Beachwood Canyon, who lived with her cat and worked at the store.

She would no longer be a towering beauty, commanding the attention of every man who laid eyes on her, and there would be no more handsome strangers wooing her and buying her dinner and champagne. Here, stumbling along the road barefoot, in a man's robe that barely concealed her girth, she was just Helen.

I'm nobody, she thought.

As she rounded a corner, a patrol car swerved into the curb in front of her.

Oh no. A middle-aged policeman stepped out.

"Everything okay, Miss?"

"Yes, officer. I'm fine, thank you."

"I couldn't help but notice you're wearing a bathrobe and you have no shoes on. This is Beverly Hills, Miss. You kind of stand out, you know?"

"Yes, I understand, officer, but…the thing is…I was at a pajama party and my car broke down. I stayed the night and I have to get home to my cat; he'll be hungry."

"And where is home?"

"Twenty-five Hillwood Drive, Beachwood Canyon."

"Well, how 'bout I give you a ride?"

Helen knew he probably just wanted to see if she was telling the truth or not, that he most likely thought she was some crazy homeless woman roaming around Beverly Hills in a bathrobe, but she was still glad to climb inside the police car.

After dropping her home, the officer drove off with a friendly wave.

She opened her front door and stepped inside. She looked around in surprise. *Wow*, it just seemed so different, so small and stuffy now, after the whole Lillian experience.

"Shadow, come here, baby boy."

Shadow meowed from atop the bookshelf, twitching his tail happily.

"There you are," she cooed. She moved to him, and he slid down into her arms. "Mommy's so sorry she frightened you last night. Come on, let's get you some food." She sat and watched him happily gulp down his meal.

Exhaustion set in. The events of the previous night raced through her mind. The glamor, the excitement…everything now over. Feeling spent, she headed to her bedroom, hung up the dress, placed the shoes by the door, and collapsed onto her bed, hugging her pillow as she cried herself to sleep.

It was dark when she finally woke. She snapped on the lamp and glanced at her clock.

Good heavens, six-thirty! I've been sleeping all day.

Shadow was curled up on the corner of her bed, watching her. She gently scratched his ears. "Mommy was a princess last night, baby. A beautiful princess."

She looked at the silver dress, then at the jewelry box on her dresser. *It was worth it; it was excruciatingly painful, but by God, it was worth it.*

She gazed at the poster of Lillian on the wall. "You—I was you! How wonderful it must have been for you every single day. So beautiful. So desired. Thank you."

She took a long, hot shower, her mind racing with thoughts of Carlo. Did he miss her? Was he looking for her? Was last night special for him too? She truly believed it was. The incredible lovemaking came back to her clearly—his chest, his arms, the smoothness of his back, and his incredible home.

Will I ever see him again?

Helen knew she had to find out more about Lillian Kelly. She searched online more thoroughly and eventually found a short list of movies the actress had starred in. *Lady of the Darkness, Queen of the Zombies, Bride of Doom,* and, of course, *Mistress of Evil.* She was again saddened at how little information she could find about Lillian; no wonder she'd never heard of her. She did a search to see where she could buy the other movies Lillian had starred in, but she came up with nothing. After fixing herself a hamburger, she curled up on her couch with Shadow to watch *Mistress of Evil* again. Helen sighed as Lillian came into view, her long blonde locks flowing in the wind.

"I was you," she whispered. "I really was you."

She fell asleep, dreaming of the dark, smoldering eyes of Carlo, of his silky hands sliding up and down her body—Lillian's body. In her dream she was on top of him, taking him deeply and clutching his chest. He pulled her face down close to his, his adoring eyes looking into hers. Suddenly his eyes began to widen, the lust turned to fear…In the dream, Helen felt the pain set in, her body swelling and changing as she sat atop him.

No…oh no!

She lurched so violently in her sleep that Shadow jumped off her lap. In the dream, she could feel Carlo's hands trying to push her off as she transformed. She screamed aloud as the pain rocked her, staring down into Carlo's eyes.

* * *

She awoke with a jolt. The movie had ended, and Shadow was on top of the bookshelf watching her. Sweat trickled off her brow as she stood slowly. She walked out to the deck in her backyard and looked up at the Hollywood Sign.

"Why couldn't I just stay as Lillian?" she whispered. "You gave me what I asked for, but it came at a price, then it ended. Will it work again? I don't know, but I think I want it to." It was time for bed now, to go to sleep and dream of the incredible night she had with Carlo.

Helen awoke to a lovely peaceful Sunday. She spent most of it dusting her memorabilia collection and watching more old movies. Soon enough she lay down to sleep, knowing she would wake up as Helen Elliot, unnoticed by men, cleaning and mending clothes and costumes and wishing she could be Lillian Kelly the movie star.

CHAPTER 7

BACK TO REALITY

Early next morning, Helen caught a cab to pick up her car and drove to work with the silver dress to give it a clean. She wore a black dress and heels that she hadn't worn in ages. They were only small, but she was enjoying the extra height. She made her way into the shop and had just begun the first orders of the day when Ashley arrived.

"Good morning. Well, look at you with your hair down, and that dress and shoes. Trying to impress anybody?"

Helen laughed and realized she had indeed worn her hair down today. She hadn't really given it any thought.

"Well, I guess I just felt like a change."

"I like it. I can't stay today. I'm going to see my old friend Brenda in hospital; she's had a stroke."

"Oh, that's terrible. Do send my best wishes."

"I will, sweetheart. So how was your weekend?"

"Same old, I guess, but I did pick up some gorgeous items from a yard sale."

"You always do. Thanks for holding the fort, and I'll see you tomorrow morning."

The day felt long and painfully boring; all Helen could think of was the incredible night she had spent as a goddess…a Hollywood queen. All those people watching her with adoring eyes, aware that every move she made displayed every part of her perfect body. How she had loved it; *everyone* wanted to know her when she was Lillian. *Beauty is so powerful. No wonder the media is obsessed with it.* She had merely walked down the street as Lillian Kelly, and her white knight in a chariot had appeared from nowhere and whisked her away to the most perfect night imaginable. Until she changed. Until she transformed back into her true self.

Why did I have to change back? Why did the perfume's magic last only until dawn?

She looked up at the silver dress hanging at the back of the store, deep in thought, when the shop's bell rang. She turned to see Peter Jameson smiling at her.

"Hello. I was wondering if my suit was ready to pick up?"

His voice always melted her. She thought he sounded like one of those smooth late-night DJs who played love songs for lonely people. "Yes, it is, let me just…um…grab it for you." She picked up his suit from the rack. He was dressed more casually today, in a brown suede jacket and black shirt and pants. She handed him the suit.

"Here you are, sir."

"Please, call me Peter."

He paid, and she handed him his change, which he took with a warm smile.

"Thank you. You have a lovely day."

Helen watched him go. Breathing in the delicious scent of his cologne still lingering at the counter.

If only you could see me as Lillian; how would you react to me then?

Soon enough it was nearly five o'clock, and Helen began closing up the store. *Another lonely night with old movies.* It wasn't that she didn't like her life, but now she had experienced Lillian's life, things would never be the same. No matter how hard she tried, she couldn't stop thinking of Carlo.

Daniel stepped into the store, smiling. "Hi, Helen. How was your weekend?"

"Hi, Daniel. It was nice. Just a quiet one."

"Oh, really? Me too." He fidgeted nervously with his hands. "Are you…heading straight home? I'm going to grab a coffee across the road. I was, um, I was wondering…" His cell rang, and he looked at the screen. "Oh, it's head office. I have to take this. I'm really sorry."

"Not a problem, Daniel. Have a nice evening."

Daniel put the phone to his ear and gave Helen a look of regret as he stepped out of the store and took the call.

He does seem a very nice man, and rather cute in his own way, Helen thought as she locked the store and left for home.

* * *

At home, Helen picked up Shadow and cuddled him. "Baby boy, let me get you some din-din." She fed him, then set about making herself some dinner. A nice big bowl of nachos loaded with cheese. She ate out on the deck. The night was lovely, and the sky was clear. She surprised herself by enjoying a glass of wine from a bottle that had been in the pantry for years. It seemed the whole Lillian experience had given her a taste for it. Her mind drifted constantly to the bottle of perfume, and a tug-of-war began to play out in her head. *I can't. The pain when it happened—it just hurt so much.* Transforming back into herself had been more painful than she could have imagined.

Perhaps the second time it won't be quite as bad. At least she knew what to expect—before and after. But what if something went wrong? Or worse…She didn't want to think about it. After washing the dishes and taking a steaming hot shower, she dried herself off and sat on her bed in her bathrobe. She gazed at the silver dress; it was immaculate. The shoes were back in their box, tucked safely in the cupboard. Helen stared at the jewelry box on the dresser.

She tried to resist it, to ignore the urge…but she couldn't help herself. It was as if she was being drawn to it. She needed to touch the bottle, just once. She slid out the drawer and pried open the secret compartment. She lifted the tiny bottle out and marveled once again at the way it felt so cool to the touch, as if it had been kept in the damp depths of the Earth.

She held it up to the lamp and felt a pang of disappointment at the tiny amount of liquid left inside. *Is there even another full spritz left in there?* She looked underneath the bottle at the words engraved on the bottom.

"*Sang de la jeunesse éternelle.*"

I wonder what it means. She fought the urge to sniff the nozzle; if it brought on even a trace of the flashbacks, she did not know if she could stop herself applying the perfume. She sighed and put the bottle back in its hiding place. She curled up in bed with Shadow and went to sleep, dreaming of when she might ever dare to become Lillian Kelly again—and wondering if the perfume would work its magic a second time.

She could only hope.

CHAPTER 8

LOVE-STRUCK

In his monstrous home perched high over Los Angeles, Carlo Genisi paced back and forth across the expanse of his downstairs office. He was in lust…love…something. Never had he been so struck by a woman like Lillian. *Never*. But Lillian who? He didn't even get her full name. *Damn it*. The most sublime, intriguing woman he had ever met, and she had vanished before dawn. He was gutted.

She had left no note, no message in lipstick scrawled across the mirror. Nothing. He had searched his entire mansion in vain, hoping for some clue she had left so he could contact her again, but the only thing he noticed was that he could not find his favorite silk bathrobe.

Since their encounter, he hadn't stopped thinking about her. It was the most incredible luck meeting her that night walking along the sidewalk…like a goddess with that long blonde mane flowing behind her. How he had loved being with her, and then to make love to her like he hadn't made love to a woman in years, only to be left alone in his bed in the morning. It made no sense, and the frustration was tearing him inside out.

Surely, he and Lillian were meant to be. Why else would it have happened that way? He wasn't even planning on going out that night, then there she was, just walking along. He had been spellbound the second he laid eyes on her. And that voice...so deep and rich, velvety, and husky, with the wisdom of a thousand years. And those sky blue eyes. *You could look into them and just lose yourself.* It was as if those eyes had seen everything there was to see, all the pain and agony of the world, all the joy and beauty, and yet they still held the clarity and tenderness of a child's.

Somehow, he knew Lillian was no ordinary woman. It was her; she was the one he wanted. He had thought of her nonstop since she had disappeared. He had been using everything in his power to track her down, but so far *nothing.*

Carlo was a very connected man in Hollywood. He had already made several phone calls to people in LA and New York, thinking somebody in his social circles must know something about the stunning six-foot blonde named Lillian. The dress and the shoes she wore were designer, surely. Ordinary women did not dress like that. Somewhere, somebody must know who she is, or more importantly...where she was.

Carlo gazed out at his vast estate, wondering if he would ever see Lillian again.

In truth, he had long lost count of how many attractive women he had bedded, but he was a thirty-six-year-old man, and an extremely good-looking one at that. Women had always thrown themselves at him. He had made his mark at twenty-seven when a low-budget made-for-TV thriller he directed had turned out a treat. With a budget of only five million it had been modest in Hollywood terms. But he had helped select the cast and he'd put everything he had into making the film a winner, and it was. The ratings skyrocketed, and the public response was huge. Half the cast were unknowns who became stars overnight. Immediately, Carlo Genisi was considered a real director, and money and respect had soon come his way.

And attention, lots of it, from gorgeous young women looking to become the next big thing. He loved women and had slept with many of them in his teens and twenties, but after the success of his first film, it was just all too easy. An endless number of attractive young women vied for his attention everywhere, hoping to snare an eligible young Hollywood director. After a while, only the most astonishingly attractive women caught his eye, but they always seemed so shallow to him, hoping for a part in this or that and lapping up the paparazzi, who sometimes photographed him when he was out. By Hollywood standards he was still only considered an up-and-coming director, but he was making his mark fast. How, he wondered, would he ever know if a woman truly wanted him for who he really was? And not for what he had become—a young, rich film director.

Lillian. When they met, she had no idea who he was, and she truly hadn't cared that he was a director. Hell, she had even practically declined a chance to audition for him. She had wanted him on that magical night for who he was. She had chosen to come home with him and let him have his way with that mind-blowing body of hers.

His cell phone rang, and he snatched it up. "Carlo Genisi."

"Mr. Genisi, it's Dale Sullivan here. I'm sorry, but I haven't found a thing so far."

Carlo's brow creased. "You've got to be kidding me. I was told you could find anybody. I've already paid you three thousand dollars."

"Sir, it's only been a couple of days, and you really didn't give me much. I mean, a first name, description, a story about her father being a soldier...It's just not enough, I need more information and a last name."

"I don't have any more information. Did you try Upstate New York? That's where she came from."

"Yes, of course, but no luck."

"Like I told you, her real father died in Germany, in an army training accident. Surely that must help," Carlo pleaded.

"A lot of people have died that way, sir. And I don't have access to military records; it might be possible, though. If you want me to keep searching, I'll need more information. And it's going to get a lot more costly, I'm afraid. And there'll still be no guarantees."

Carlo sighed. "Okay. I've told you everything I know so far. Just keep looking." Carlo ended the call and gazed out the window.

* * *

The rest of the week went by much faster than Helen expected. It was Friday before she knew it. Her thoughts all week had been with Carlo and the glamorous night she'd had with him, to the point where she had even made a few mistakes with orders in the shop, which was very unlike her. She kept thinking of the offer he had made her.

A part in a movie? Imagine being on set, the cameras, the lights…

She couldn't stop thinking about it. Was Carlo looking for her? Or had she been just another conquest? Was he serious about giving her the part? Would he give the part to somebody else? She knew she would never get an opportunity like that again. But even if she did become Lillian again and got the part, just how would it all work? She hadn't really thought it through—she had been blinded by the excitement of it all. There would be questions, many people to meet, contracts to sign, and so many details, none of which she had answers for. And what about the effects of the perfume? How long would it last? If she sprayed it on heavier, would she stay transformed as Lillian longer, or would she simply change back in the morning again? She had so many questions and nobody to ask.

Ashley had commented on her clothing every day this week, and Helen had realized she had been getting far more adventurous with her wardrobe. She wasn't sure why, as she certainly had not lost any weight. She just felt like a change, and she had been wearing perfume as well, nothing special… just some cheap stuff she had at home.

Lunchtime rolled around. She headed down the escalator and found a seat in the corner of the café. She took her first sip of her coffee when Peter Jameson strolled in.

He was in the black suit today, looking fantastic. She had personally looked after that suit before. He only ever wore the expensive designer brands. He ordered a coffee and Helen watched his natural charisma work on the waitress. Thankfully, he hadn't noticed her.

Helen sighed as she recalled the men like him who had paid her so much attention when she was Lillian. His cell rang and he answered it.

"Hi, Ted. Oh, it's going to be a great night. No, I'm flying solo. Karen's in New York. It's an incredible venue. Yeah, the Fallen Temple, and of course it's VIP invitation only. This is going to be the biggest fashion event of the year. I'm going to turn up early to get a start on things. Okay, see you tonight."

Wow, what a magical night he's going to have. A VIP fashion event at the Fallen Temple, and it sounded like his current flame was out of town. Imagine a man like him alone on a Friday night at a club like that.

She finished her meal and a piece of chocolate cake, then headed back up the escalator to the store. She turned the corner past the tobacco store, which she had never really paid any attention to before, but now she stopped and gazed in the window at the cigars and cigarettes. One brand stood out, and Helen recognized it as the cigar of choice for many actresses back in Hollywood's golden days. It was a sleek, glossy white tin with silver writing across it: "Vanilla Dove, Ultimate, since 1940."

The tin was partially open, displaying some of the thin white cigarillos inside, a silver band wrapped around the head of each one. They were beautifully presented.

Something stirred deep within Helen. It was only a tiny tremor, but it was most certainly there. She began to crave the cigars, imagining she could feel one between her fingers, breathing in the sweet smoldering tobacco.

Almost without hesitation, she headed into the shop and bought a tin. Back in the store, Helen struggled to concentrate on her work with thoughts of Peter Jameson and the big event at the Fallen Temple that night.

CHAPTER 9

TEMPTATION

Helen looked at the clock. Ten minutes to closing time. She switched off the lights and locked the door right on five. Traffic was light, and in no time Helen was cruising up Beachwood Drive, looking forward to a cuddle from Shadow and a glass of wine.

Once home, she felt like some music. Soon some classic Hollywood tunes floated throughout the house from her mother's old record player. Helen sang along, happily tipsy, cooking herself some hot dogs.

She loved this album; it brought back wonderful memories of all those nights when she, her mother, and her aunt would dance and sing along to old records. They would roar with laughter, putting on performances for each other. She missed them dearly, and still whispered goodnight to them every night.

After dinner Helen sat petting Shadow on the couch. Her mind wandered to Peter Jameson in his dashing black suit and, of course, she had been thinking of Carlo nonstop. Was he looking for Lillian? She had even thought of trying to find his mansion, just to drive past to see it with her own eyes.

Surely it wouldn't be that hard to find, even among all the mansions in Beverly Hills. Carlo's was a standout.

Oh, what a night it had been.

As much as she tried to douse the thought of it, to extinguish the very idea of it…she couldn't. How could she? Just the mere *thought* of Peter seeing her as Lillian…

Would it be like it was with Carlo?

And how wonderful it would be to see Carlo again. Would he be happy to see her? Or angry that she had disappeared on him? Would Peter Jameson react the same way, or would he be impervious to Lillian's charm and beauty? Just the thought of him touching her sent a shiver of excitement through her. The wine was kicking in. And somewhere deep inside her was an unremitting urge, like whispers in the very air around her… to flirt with danger and excitement yet again. She stepped out onto her deck. The sun had slithered down behind the hills and the night temperature outside was perfect.

The sky was immaculate, with not a trace of cloud anywhere, just the ever-present stars beckoning her…tempting her. Dare she? She looked back inside her house, quiet and empty except for Shadow. She loved her little home, her shrine to Hollywood's yesteryear, but somehow, it all paled in comparison to the adventure that could await…if she just used the perfume again.

Somehow, standing there looking up at the sky, she knew she would succumb. With one spray of the mysterious scent, she could become gorgeous, perfect, lusted after…But the pain…the agony, the risks, and the aftermath…It didn't matter, the urge was far too powerful.

Inside her the urge became stronger, snippets of Lillian flashing in her mind. A tug-of-war began playing out, common sense against thrills and excitement, safety and normality against passion and luxury. Visions of Carlo popped into her head. Limousines, champagne, dancing, romance—how delicious it had all been. Helen sighed and gave in to the natural human craving in every single person: the need to be loved, accepted, respected, and desired.

She headed to her bedroom and sat on her bed, looking up into those blazing ice-blue eyes on the poster, readying herself for what she knew was to come, if the perfume worked its magic again.

Almost mechanically, she slid open the drawer and lifted the bottle from its secret compartment. A mixture of fear, adrenaline, and passion pulsed through her body. She didn't have a psychic bone in her body...yet something about this bottle had awoken her sixth sense like nothing she could ever have fathomed.

Will it work again? Is there even enough perfume left?

The breeze blew in her bedroom window, as she sat there in her bathrobe with an incredible power in her hands, one she really knew nothing about, but which she simply could not refuse. She knew what it was capable of, and how much she had to have it again, *needed* to have it again. Shadow watched from the doorway, his tail twitching nervously.

Strange how you sense it, darling, that you know something is about to happen. "It's okay, baby boy. If this works, Mommy will be back, I promise. I'm just...not going to be myself for a little while."

She lifted the bottle and took one last look at herself in the dresser mirror. *Tonight I will be you again…and everybody will love me.* She looked up at Lillian's poster.

"Please let everything be okay."

She slid her robe off and stood there naked, like a sacrifice to the gods, but what gods? The craving to become Lillian again was so overwhelming she didn't care. She pointed the silver nozzle at her lower neck. With a deep breath, she squeezed the pump firmly. The liquid bubbled and worked its way up from the base of the bottle, releasing itself in a delicate little cloud from the tiny nozzle.

Helen's heartbeat echoed in her ears as the red mist disappeared into her skin. The power of it unleashed itself quickly. The images started again like a high-speed movie: the bliss, the glamor, Lillian Kelly's life streaming into her mind. The curtains billowed against the ceiling as the wind gushed in.

It was happening again…but then the *pain*. It set in much faster this time.

Helen's screams sent Shadow fleeing in terror. He settled for a hiding place behind the curtains in the spare bedroom. The mournful, gut-wrenching sounds coming from down the hallway did not belong to the warm, lovely woman who fed and held him every night. More chilling screams and moans followed, until there was only quiet…

Nothing…

Just the wind whistling down into Beachwood Canyon, from high above the Hollywood Hills. And once again, the magnificent naked body stood before the full-length mirror. It had been excruciating, but the perfume had worked its magic *again*. Helen Elliot was Lillian Kelly.

She put on the silver dress with a peculiar feeling of control and familiarity. She applied her makeup, finishing with a layer of blood-red lipstick, then slipped on the stilettos. Helen beamed at her reflection: magnificence. She looked up at Lillian's poster.

"Thank you. Thank you so much."

She brushed her hair in the mirror with ultimate satisfaction. Hollywood and the Fallen Temple awaited—and Peter Jameson had better notice her, because if he didn't, she knew plenty of other men would.

She held the perfume bottle up to the light and frowned. There was barely enough liquid left to cover the base of the bottle. A sharp pang of fear struck like an icy tremor inside her, but only for a moment.

Well, I've got tonight at least.

She took her purse and car keys and strode up the hall. "Shadow, come here, baby." But Shadow wouldn't come; he crouched in his hiding place.

"I'm sorry, baby. Mommy will be back soon."

Helen had learned her lesson from last time, so she stuffed a change of clothes and shoes into a small bag. She stepped into the garage and slid into her car, before starting the engine and driving toward the bright lights.

After parking in a backstreet, a short walk from Hollywood Boulevard, she slipped on the stilettos and began walking. The summery night air felt fantastic on her skin, and soon she reached the glitter strip. Helen stepped onto the star-studded sidewalk, where the world's biggest names were immortalized in stars embedded into the ground for generations to admire.

Shen began moving elegantly down the Walk of Fame. She had barely taken ten steps in the neon lights when wolf whistles erupted from passing cars. Men and women stared, their mouths agape at the sight of the towering blonde gliding past them. Helen felt elated. It was electrifying to know that Lillian must have also walked along here, back in the true Golden Era of Tinseltown, decades ago. But here, tonight, Lillian Kelly was alive and well and soaking up her old stomping ground. She reached the place where only Hollywood royalty was allowed to leave its mark, outside the famous theater.

This was the place where the greatest stars had their names preserved in cement for all to see. Every day thousands of tourists placed their own hands in the imprints of their idols and had their photos taken. So many of the greats had left their mark. A couple of tourists began taking pictures of Helen, one even asked if he could have his photograph with her.

She politely declined, then continued down the boulevard with the Fallen Temple club firmly in her sights. This was Hollywood, home to some of the most beautiful women in the world, and tonight Helen knew she was one of them.

She arrived at her destination and looked at the line of limousines pulling up outside the club. The front entry had been sealed off with velvet ropes and cameras flashed among the crowd craning their necks, hoping to spot celebrities.

She stood back and admired the scene for a few moments, when she detected a familiar scent of cologne. She turned around to see none other than Peter Jameson standing right next to her in a charcoal suit. He was holding a cigarette and flashing his dazzling smile.

"Good evening. Wow, what a dress. I'm Peter Jameson, I'm hosting the event here tonight." Helen stared at him, unsure of what to say.

"May I ask your name?"

She snapped out of it.

"I'm Lillian." Her deep seductive tone hit him hard. Lust swirled in his eyes.

"Well, Lillian, it's a pleasure to meet you. And being such a beautiful woman, I can only assume you are a VIP guest here tonight and that you are probably represented by somebody already. May I ask who your agent is?"

"I don't have an agent, and…I'm afraid I'm not invited here tonight. I came into town for dinner with a friend, but she had to cancel. I just came over to see what all the fuss was about. I've never been inside this place. I must say, though, it looks marvelous." Opportunity flashed in his eyes. He ditched his cigarette and took her right hand and kissed it gently.

"Well, in that case, Lillian, would you do me the honor of being my guest for this evening? I will see to it you sit in the front row with an abundance of champagne."

Helen laughed, and Peter melted at the sound of it.

"I would love to be your guest tonight." She extended her hand.

"Wonderful." He led her to the front door as the long line of onlookers stared at them.

The doormen ushered them inside, and Helen entered the venue on the arm of Peter Jameson. It was *magic*. The club was impressive, with a catwalk right down the center. Celebrities and models were everywhere. Peter took two glasses from a passing waiter and turned to Helen. "Champagne?" She took a glass. It was divine. People constantly shook Peter's hand, he in turn introduced them to Helen. Compliments, offers of modeling work, and business cards were flying at her. Peter was fending them off and accepting the cards on her behalf, which she found flattering and amusing. The champagne went quickly to her head. She noticed Peter's arm never left her waist and she loved it. He kept looking at her with admiration in his eyes. An attractive young redhead approached them in a sleek black dress.

"Peter, we're on in ten minutes."

"Oh, Jennifer, this is Lillian."

"Hello, Lillian, what a dress! And those shoes—they're beautiful."

"Oh, thank you," Helen replied.

"I hope you enjoy the show tonight. We're showcasing some great new talent," Jennifer said.

"Lillian will be sitting in the front row. I've taken care of it."

"Wonderful. We'd best get backstage. Lovely meeting you, Lillian." Jennifer darted off.

Peter showed Helen to her front-row seat then bid her goodbye. She was warmly greeted by an older man with black leather gloves and sunglasses, who she guessed must have been a "somebody" in the fashion world. On her left sat a colorfully dressed young man who smiled politely at her. She took another glass of champagne from a waiter as the lights dimmed.

Music started and Helen's eyes widened. She had never attended a fashion show before, and it looked like it was going to be fantastic. Peter and Jennifer stepped out onto the stage both holding microphones. A round of applause greeted them, and Helen was impressed at how comfortable Peter looked on stage. Jennifer looked great as well.

"Good evening, Los Angeles!" Peter boomed. The crowd roared their approval. "Welcome to this year's Hollywood Hot Fashion week for new designers. I'm Peter Jameson, and this is my lovely co-host Jennifer Simons, and tonight we are going to bring you a dazzling array of incredible new creations—made by our very own designers, right here in Los Angeles."

More loud applause.

"I'm very pleased to say that many of the gorgeous models strutting the catwalk here tonight are represented by my very own company, Peter Jameson's Hollywood Talent. But now, let the show begin!"

Music thumped from the speakers. Young men and women came cruising up and down the catwalk one after another. Helen was so close to the action she could see some of them sweating under the powerful lights. The show was superb, and Peter handled his task of hosting brilliantly. The outfits worn by the models were gorgeous. The new designers had come up with some excellent ideas. There was also a strong display of the usual elite names. It was a flawlessly presented show. The designers all lined up after the parade onstage and received a well-deserved round of applause. After the awards were handed out everybody mingled, drinking.

Helen found herself showered with compliments by bold young men. She was thrilled when Peter appeared swiftly by her side and placed his arm around her waist, sending the small crowd of hopefuls away, disappointed. Helen surprised herself by planting a firm kiss on Peter's cheek, which he clearly loved. In no time, she was paraded around the room like royalty, as people congratulated him on the show. Helen had never met so many people or received so many compliments in her life. *This is what it's like when you are beautiful.* The night with Carlo had been an experience from heaven, but this…to be Peter Jameson's date at a Hollywood fashion parade? This was beyond anything Helen had ever even fantasized about. Her cheeks ached from smiling.

Peter whispered in her ear. "Can I sneak you outside with me? I'm dying for a cigarette." Helen took his hand. He led her to the exit, and she noticed she was actually a good two inches taller than him, thanks to the stilettos, which amused her slightly because in her real body she wouldn't have reached his shoulder.

They stepped outside onto the sidewalk and he led her to a small alcove nearby, in front of a closed jewelry store, he pulled her gently in next to him. He placed one hand on the center of her back and with the other he stroked her cheek. She knew what was coming next, she had seen the same look in Carlo's eyes. Peter's lips covered Helen's. It was *perfect.* His hunger surprised her as his kisses went deep. He pulled her in closer to him.

She opened her eyes as he kissed her. His were closed, but she didn't care. She just needed to see it for herself. This was *real*. Peter Jameson, the man she had dreamed of kissing for so long…was kissing her, right here on Hollywood Boulevard.

Dreams really do come true. He finally came up for air. "Now that was a kiss. I couldn't help myself."

Helen could think of nothing to say. She just wanted him to kiss her again. He lit a cigarette and breathed it in, and Helen found herself reaching into her bag and taking out one of the cigars she had bought at the mall. He lit it for her, and the two puffed away looking into each other's eyes.

Jennifer appeared next to Peter. She took the cigarette from his mouth and dragged on it long and deep. Helen was surprised at how casually she did this. She exhaled and placed the cigarette back in his mouth. Helen tapped the ash off the end of her cigar gently, with the ease of a seasoned smoker.

"Did you enjoy the show, Lillian?"

"Very much. You and Peter did a marvelous job."

"Thank you. We must see if Peter can get you to model for us some time. You have an incredible look."

"I'm working on it. I cannot believe I have never seen this gorgeous lady around town before," Peter said, turning to Helen. "But I'm determined to sign you up and get you on our books."

Helen smiled.

"Are you joining us for drinks back at Peter's apartment?"

"Am I invited?" Helen asked, looking at Peter.

"You most certainly are."

"Then I'd love to."

"Wonderful." Peter beamed.

Back inside the club, everybody had drunk their fill of champagne and wine, and eaten their share of caviar and nibbles. The show wound to an end, and Peter and Jennifer saw all the guests off at the door. A black stretch limousine pulled into the curb, and Helen sat next to Peter. She watched, amused, as many of the very attractive young models tumbled into the car, all very excited and clearly affected by the champagne. Peter soon had everybody laughing with his jokes. Corks popped, and Helen sipped another glass of champagne as they headed for Peter's apartment.

As they drove along, Helen looked at the homeless out on the street, huddled in doorways and checking in trash cans for food scraps. This had always amazed her about Hollywood: the contrast of rich and poor, how some lived in cardboard boxes in alleyways, while the ultra-rich and famous were all around them living like royalty. Multimillion-dollar movie deals were made here every day, yet you could hardly walk in many parts of LA without somebody begging you for change.

Helen had always donated to the poor, she knew how hard it was for some. Although her life had been lonely, she had never been hungry or homeless. Her mother and her aunt had seen to that by leaving her the wonderful cottage that had been their home. And now, this magic had entered her life… *Look at me now.* Peter's lips smothered the side of her neck, and she noticed it wasn't so noisy in the back of the car anymore. She turned and was surprised to see that several of the young models were passionately kissing one another. Jennifer seemed to be quite engrossed watching them.

Soon Peter was helping her out of the car and into the entry of his lavish apartment building. Although there was a large party following them and another carload pulling up outside, Peter made Helen feel like it was just the two of them. He kissed her again inside the elevator car, oblivious to the chatter of the others as they ascended to his apartment.

Peter's home was sleek and modern. The carpet was jet black and a huge white leather sofa dominated the room. Dance music was pumping and already a dozen or so people were partying. A pair of young waiters were mixing drinks and making hors d'oeuvres.

"Everyone, make yourselves at home," Peter announced.

People were unwinding and chatting excitedly about the show. Peter led Helen out to his main balcony and produced a cigarette. He offered her one, which she took. He kissed her again and then lit the cigarette. Helen looked out over the city lights. It all looked so different from this angle. Peter lived at the far end of Hollywood Boulevard. Helen had never been up this high before in Hollywood itself, and she was impressed. So this was where he lived, up here in this palace in the clouds, overlooking the town where he helped make stars. *How fitting.* An attractive young blonde who looked barely eighteen approached Peter and placed an arm around him with a seductive grin. Peter stoked her shoulder. "Perhaps later, darling." The girl winked at Peter and left them. Helen was a tad surprised at their interaction.

Judging from his surroundings, he clearly did very well for himself. "It's a marvelous view," Helen remarked.

"It's even better from my bedroom," he added with a suggestive grin. He exhaled a cloud of smoke. She watched it float over the edge of the balcony and disappear. They kissed again and finished their cigarettes, Peter took her hand and led her back across the living area, which had fast become a dance floor. Peter proudly displayed some framed photography on the walls, explaining he had taken the shots himself. The photos were taken in cities all around the world: Paris, Rome, China, and many more. He led her down the hallway, where they intercepted Jennifer heading into a bedroom with a handsome young man and two young girls. Before closing the door behind her, she turned to Peter and Helen with a sly grin. "Have fun you two."

CHAPTER 10

LUST UNLEASHED

Peter's bedroom was large and impressive, Black velvet drapes hung over huge windows, and there was an eclectic mix of modern and antique furniture which somehow seemed to blend effortlessly. The bed was enormous, with black satin sheets and pillows. Peter closed the door and put his arms around her.

"I want you, Lillian."

He led her to the bed and laid her down, kissing her, sliding her dress up higher and higher. Helen reached down to undo the straps on her stilettos. "Leave them on, please," he begged. He kissed her, as Helen lay back and soaked up every second of it. After all, this was something she had dreamed about for years, and now it was happening. Peter Jameson was making love to her.

She felt her lust building fast; she wanted this man badly. She had desired him for years, and now her dream had come true.

Something stirred deep inside her, and it surfaced quickly, a fusion of passion and dominance, it was powerful enough to make her lift his head and pull him up toward her. She flipped him onto his back with surprising strength. He gasped with surprise and lay there looking up at her. She tore open his shirt, popping his buttons off.

He slid his pants off fast and tossed them to the floor. He lay there completely naked. He was *perfect*, just as she had envisioned in her many fantasies about him.

She was more than ready to live out her long-awaited fantasy with this man. A sexual aggression like she had never felt in her life suddenly pulsed through her. His eyes were fixed on her.

Oh, how she loved it: the power she wielded with her beauty, seeing this perfect man craving her. She ran her tongue across her top lip slowly. The feeling struck her again, rocking her body, this time though…she realized it was the same feeling she had experienced on the dance floor with Carlo. Wild, forbidden…like a beast in a cage, waiting to be unleashed.

Peter was breathing like he'd just run a marathon, every pore of his body craving her. But it wasn't Helen…It was *Lillian*. Helen had felt it coming, but still it was both unexpected yet inevitable, like a thunderstorm that came out of nowhere. She felt the transition of power deep inside her body and mind. Almost instantly she felt herself fast fading away from the present, completely lost in decadent lust, sinking down to a place she could not comprehend. Lillian had control now. Helen was still there…but now deep down inside.

Helen felt herself ebbing away, plunging down into a deep swirling pool of darkness, and she was frightened, but there wasn't a thing she could do about it. She felt herself lapsing in and out of consciousness inside Lillian's body. Helen saw fragments, shadows. And then nothing, just darkness.

Lillian mounted Peter, his eyes glazed over with complete and utter ecstasy.

Lillian adored it. Oh, how long she had lay dormant, but now she was *back*. This new modern world was not her time, and much had changed, but she didn't care.

This was what she was used to enjoying back in her first life. The pleasures of the flesh, satisfying her voracious desires with men and women, where and whenever she liked. Her sexual appetite had grown along with her fame in her first life, as she had been introduced to sex parties, often hosted by movie company owners and film directors, and she had truly loved it. But it was the gatherings in Europe with the secret cult that had really unleashed her true sexual demons, the festivals of flesh and lust. This current experience was certainly wonderful but had been mediocre in her other life.

Thank God the mortal found the perfume.

With Peter now enjoying the pleasures of her body, Lillian closed her eyes, lost in sexual ecstasy. They satisfied their lust for hours, until they were both truly spent. Peter was in awe, he had never encountered anything like Lillian. A sleeping sexual giant had been awakened and was for now content.

Helen Elliot had no idea what had transpired. She had long since faded away, deep down inside Lillian.

Lillian Kelly was in complete control of her body and loving every moment of it. Most of the partygoers were falling asleep now; the sex, drugs and alcohol had taken their toll.

CHAPTER 11

BLOOD AND SOULS

It was well into the dark early hours, Peter was sound asleep, but Lillian was wide awake and she felt like a shower. She walked out into the main room, naked except for the stilettos. The lights were dim, but she could see the same kind of sexual escapades had certainly been taking place in the living room, as well. Naked bodies were passed out and lying on the floor and the sofa. A bowl of white powder sat in the middle of the sleek glass coffee table, colorful pills were scattered next to it. Empty wine glasses and beer bottles lay everywhere. Music was still playing, but only softly. Most people had left, and those that were still in the apartment were either asleep or too wasted to even know where they were.

The apartment was much larger than she had first realized. There was another hallway that led to another two bedrooms. She found a bathroom and stepped into the shower, enjoying the warm water on her body. She could see herself clearly in the mirrored wall opposite. She smiled at her perfect figure, but a tremor of cold fear flickered within her. She was back, yes, but for how long? She knew she had been dormant for decades, trapped inside the bottle until the mortal had used the perfume. And she had been present enough during the latest transformation to see through Helen's eyes that there was practically no liquid left in the bottle. *Damn.* She had only just regained control over her body. She would need to let her presence subside just enough to let the mortal lead her back to the bottle, but an empty perfume bottle was of no use to her, no…not at all.

The pathetic mortal within her might have thought a couple of exciting encounters in her body was enough, but Lillian Kelly wanted to be *back*. Back in permanent control of her body, and back in Hollywood for good, and by God she would have her way.

She usually did.

There was one thing she needed now, more than anything else in the world…She needed the deep red, life-giving liquid that flows in the veins of every living being in the world.

Lillian needed blood.

She thought back decades ago to the ceramic canister she carried when she had been on the hunt. It had been perfect, just the right size.

Her mind snapped back to the lovely young bodies strewn about the apartment. She knew exactly what she needed was right here waiting for her. A sinister dark cloud crept through her body and mind as she prepared herself for what she had to do. She dried herself off and slipped on her dress, then headed back up the hallway bare-footed. She noticed a bedroom door partially open. Inside was a figure lying on a bed. She stepped inside, the room was mostly dark, but from the glow of the city lights outside pressing through the curtains, Lillian could see a pretty young girl with delicate features, sound asleep. No doubt she hadn't been alone in the bedroom earlier, but now she was alone.

Her long, dark hair was splayed across the pristine white pillows, like jagged shadows. Her shoes were still on her feet, and her left hand was hanging over the edge of the bed. Cheap silver rings adorned most of her fingers. An empty wine bottle lay on its side by the bed. Lillian stared down at her.

She could be no more than twenty—perfect.

She left the room and headed into the kitchen quietly and soon found a drawer of sharp knives. She selected one, she then continued looking around the kitchen and saw a glass jar up on a shelf. It had a hinged, snap-down lid, she reached up and took it down.

Yes, it will easily hold over two pints.

She headed back to the bedroom, then closed the door and clicked the lock. She opened the curtains a little, letting more light in, then kneeled and took the girl's hand in hers. She turned it over gently, stroking the soft, tender flesh. A silver bracelet hung from the girl's wrist. Lillian slid her forefinger slowly down her own neck and between her breasts, where she knew Helen had applied the perfume. She gently slid her fingertip underneath the girls' nose, and quickly made the sign of the Ancient Ones.

"Sleep," she whispered.

Instantly, the girl's chest rose up high, then lowered as she exhaled. She was out like a tombstone now, her mouth partially open, a fine line of spittle across her lower lip. A pretty young thing who had drunk, and probably snorted, far too much anyway. Lillian's jaw set hard.

It was time now, to take what she needed. She closed her eyes and summoned the power, and it came like ripples across a deep dark river.

She held up the cold steel blade and touched its edge, satisfied at its sharpness, she took the girl's wrist in her left hand turning it palm up, she then pressed the point of the knife into the soft flesh with a practiced hand, perfectly piercing the radial artery, she sliced three inches deeply, up the arm toward the elbow, with just enough pressure to make a perfect, clean incision. Lillian's eyes gleamed as the red liquid flowed. She was very pleased at how well she could still perform this act now, just as she had decades ago.

"*Sang de la jeunesse éternelle*," she whispered. Almost instantly, a small white cloud of vapor materialized and floated out from the incision with the blood. No larger than the size of a human hand, it rose up slightly and hovered before Lillian's face in a perfect little sphere. It then twisted itself into a tiny spiral and floated down into the bottom of the glass jar Lillian had placed under the girl's hand. She watched with wicked glee as the blood still pumped out from the slender body, sliding down in a thick, perfect line under the bracelet and across the fingers, into the jar. The tiny white cloud sank lower and mixed itself with the dark red liquid.

With the jar full, she snapped the lid down firmly and stood. The girl was now ghostly pale. With nothing there to collect it, a pool of blood began soaking the carpet under the girl's wrist. Lillian looked at her face but felt absolutely nothing for her. She had what she needed now, the blood and soul of this young woman, and now she saw her as nothing more than a spent, mindless piece of flesh. Lillian unlocked the door. Spotting the girl's slinky little back coat lying on the floor, she scooped it up and wrapped the jar in it. She held the knife in her right hand and opened the door, checking the hallway. It was deathly quiet. She wiped down the doorknob, walked silently back to the bathroom and set the jar of blood down on the vanity. She washed only the handle of the knife thoroughly. She then wiped it with a hand towel and wrapped the knife handle in another towel. She picked up the jar and headed back out to the living area. A shirtless young man lay passed out on the rug in front of the sofa. Lillian switched off all the lights and knelt beside him. She wiped the bloody tip of the blade on his jeans and fingers, then she carefully unwrapped the knife's handle and placed it in his right hand, curling his fingers around it.

Lillian headed for the door.

She made her way down the corridor to the elevators and hit the ground-floor button. She looked at herself in the mirrored walls, clutching her prize under her arm. What a night this had turned out to be. How she had loved engaging in such long-desired lust, and now she had also obtained the blood she so badly needed. Now, she knew she would have to let the mortal within her regain some control over her body, to find the perfume bottle and perform the ancient ritual.

Lillian exited the elevator on the ground level and moved swiftly down the corridor and past the entrance. She saw what she was looking for: a fire door. Her experience had taught her discretion was crucial for survival in these situations. She opened the door and headed down the stairs into the car park. There was nobody around. She made her way outside, the cool night air pressed against her skin. She paced down the sidewalk, toward the bright lights of Hollywood Boulevard. It was time now to let her control lapse a little. Time to let the mortal guide her back to the bottle. She placed the bloody hand towel in a trash can.

"All right," she whispered. "You may return now, just enough to give me what I want." She made the sign of the Ancient Ones, tapping the points of a triangle on her chin and shoulders. Immediately, somewhere deep down inside Lillian, Helen heard her. She *felt* Lillian talking to her, granting her permission to return to her body. Helen felt as though she had been lost at sea in a dark storm, and now some kind of force was bringing her back in to shore against the tide. Had she drowned? No, there was no water, but she could feel herself being dredged up from the deepest, darkest shadows she had ever known. She felt the presence of Lillian, and somehow Helen understood what was going on. She was not alone in this body, she was *sharing* it with Lillian, and now she could see the light emerging from the darkness.

Where had she been? What had happened? And why did she feel as though she was being carried?

Helen tried hard to recall what had happened, but she simply could not. She could only partially tell her body what to do, what Lillian *wanted* her to do, and what Lillian wanted to do more than anything right now, was to get back to the perfume bottle.

Helen had enough control now to guide herself to the Walk of Fame. With her stilettos dangling from one hand, she padded silently on bare feet down the star-studded sidewalk. Shadowy figures moved and lurked in doorways and alleys as she strode along the boulevard. The homeless who lived here, in the nooks and crannies of Hollywood were getting some sleep in these precious last moments before the dawn. Helen realized what a sight she must be, walking along the most famous sidewalk in the world, a woman like her, bare-footed and carrying her shoes.

This was Hollywood Central at its quietest, well after the witching hour but still shrouded in darkness before the dawn. Soon the sun would rise over the hills and bring everything back to life again. The shadows and darkness would dissipate, and Hollywood and all its glamor would be revealed once again, in the glorious LA sunshine. The car wasn't far away now. She knew the street where she left it, that much she could remember clearly. But what had happened after the fashion show? What happened at Peter Jameson's apartment? She remembered kissing him and falling into bed with him—oh that she recalled, and it had been *wonderful*. A dream come true.

But then something had happened.

Her memories became blurry, snippets and fragments of the events in the bedroom flashed in her mind. Had she drunk too much? Did somebody spike her drink? Why could she recall almost nothing? And what was she carrying under her arm, wrapped in a black coat? She would look at it later. She had to get to her car now. She walked faster, rounding a corner, and made her way quickly down to the backstreet where she had parked. A gust of wind scattered litter across the narrow, deserted street.

Spotting her car, she pulled out her keys and climbed in, then turned the key and sped out onto the boulevard.

She settled back into her seat trying to recall just what the hell she had been doing for the last several hours. But now, she needed to get home, Shadow was waiting for her. But there was another sense of urgency pushing her to go faster, a strong presence *within* her. She knew it was Lillian. An icy cold tremor of pain spread throughout her stomach.

Oh no, the change! It was coming, but would it be as painful as the last time? She drove faster than she had in years toward Beachwood Canyon.

CHAPTER 12

CRUEL INTENTIONS

Helen made her way out of Hollywood Central and soon hit Beachwood Drive. She recalled the first stages of making love with Peter—then nothing. Why? The next thing she knew she was striding down the Walk of Fame, carrying her shoes. *A bolt of pain splintered through her body.*

It was happening, the transformation. Helen braced herself. She hunkered low over the wheel and looked up at the sky. The ominous glow of the looming morning sun was pressing against the dark of the fading night. Panic set in, she could feel it, like a cold mist settling deep in the pit of her stomach. She felt the panic of Lillian, too, surreal and eerie. She planted her foot harder, the first tiny sliver of sunlight sliced down upon the windscreen and fell across her wrist with a prickly, stinging sensation. Helen shrieked and whipped the sun visors down. Almost home, she took the last curve with the tires screeching as she headed up Hillwood Drive.

She skidded into her driveway so fast she almost collided with the garage door then dashed to the front door. The sun's first rays were splintering across the lawn. She had almost made it when the pain struck hard. She shrieked and fell sprawling across the paving stones. Blood seeped from her knees. The object in the black cloth was safe, though, still grasped firmly under her arm; Helen could not seem to let go of it. She got up and unlocked the door then rushed inside, slamming it shut and heaving with relief. Somehow, she knew that shutting out the sun would not stop the transformation. It was coming now—the pain, the vomiting, the agony—but she

knew she had to deal with it. Just as she began bracing herself, she felt Lillian's control kick in. Before she had time to think, Helen felt herself walking mechanically down to her bedroom. She placed the wrapped-up object on her dresser by the jewelry box, then pulled the black material away. To her surprise, she saw a large glass jar filled with a dark red liquid. Sharp pain struck, her stomach swirled, and she raced to the bathroom, making it to the sink just in time for the first gush of dark green bile. Her throat burned as she coughed and spluttered, but she stood strong, gasping for breath and bracing for more. A vicious tingling spread through her ankles.

She heaved, and another load of bile shot out of her and filled the basin. She watched it, spluttering as it slid down the sink hole, knowing this was far from over.

She stared into the bathroom mirror, pale and wide-eyed, with spittle hanging from her chin. "Get out of me," she growled, to the ice-blue eyes looking back at her.

"No!" she heard Lillian spit back from somewhere deep down inside her.

Helen staggered back against the wall in shock. Lillian had *spoken* to her.

She stared at her reflection as the blood-red lips peeled back into a hideous grin. A low, mocking laugh echoed around the bathroom, or was it just in her head? The sound was utterly chilling.

The pain in her ankles spread up to her legs, she felt Lillian taking control again. Helen was aware of her everything around her, but she was not in control of her body. She headed robotically back to her bedroom and stood before the dresser. She stared at the jar, then slid open the bottom drawer of the jewelry box. She lifted the secret panel, as her eyes fell upon the crystal bottle, a warm tingle of glee filled her stomach.

She lifted the bottle out and placed it next to the jar, then unscrewed the tiny silver lid. She felt herself reach out and lift the jar of red liquid.

Oh no…What are you making me do?

The wind forced her bedroom windows open, and Helen knew an unnatural power had entered the room, and it frightened her.

If she thought she had no control before, now…now she was about to become little more than a puppet inside another person's body. Lillian's power swept through her like a wave hitting the shore. The wind powered into the windows, billowing the curtains. Helen felt herself ebbing away quickly again to that dark place, the place where she had no memory or control of anything. And it seemed there was nothing she could do to stop it.

This was Lillian's time now. Time to perform the secret ritual she had been given by the Ancient Ones, decades ago. She closed her eyes and breathed in deeply, as the wind rattled the framed pictures on the walls. Helen was virtually dismissed from this event, only from somewhere deep, deep down inside Lillian's body did she have the faintest trace of awareness. She felt as if she was watching the world outside on a tiny television screen in pitch blackness, from a mile away, and nothing else existed, just dark swirling shadows like heavy velvet blankets around her. She had no idea what was happening, and there was no sound. She only knew that something dark and not of this world was happening in her bedroom, something she had no say in whatsoever. She knew now, that by using the perfume she had danced with the devil, and now she would have to sit in the shadows and watch his hand unfold.

Lillian placed the large glass jar under her nose and inhaled the sweet metallic aroma of the rich dark blood. She let out a long, satisfied hiss as another gust of wind filled the room, fluttering her hair about her shoulders. She stood trancelike now, in perfect control. Holding the jar high above her head, staring into the mirror, she spoke the sacred words.

"Le sang de la jeunesse éternelle. Nourrisez mon âme et remplissez ma chair."

Her deep, strong voice cut across the room. An eerie silence fell throughout the house. Shadow lay under the bed in the spare room, trembling in fear, as Lillian continued the incantation.

"Je succombe à votre puissance, oh les Anciens Grands."

Another blast of wind burst in through the bedroom windows, knocking over two of the display mannequins.

"Avec votre bénédiction je défie le temps. Je me soumets à votre volonté et à votre pouvoir. Je vous en supplie, Ô, Tous-Puissants."

With another deep breath, she spoke aloud the last line of the spell: *"Accordez-moi la jeunesse et la beauté éternelle."*

The wind grew even stronger now, and not just in the bedroom. Outside, all over Beachwood Canyon, an enormous gust blasted its way down from the Hollywood Hills, sweeping up the narrow streets. Tree branches twisted and swayed, as swarms of leaves went tumbling across the lawns, roads, and sidewalks. Dust and dirt spiraled up high into the air as the powerful gust forced its way deep down into the canyon. In Helen's bedroom, however, there was now only a soft breeze ruffling the curtains.

Lillian set the jar down next to the perfume bottle and watched. At first, it was only a tiny wisp of smoke, like the last breath of a dying discarded cigarette, but it soon increased. It spread out from atop the jar of blood and formed an almost transparent white mist that rose higher and higher. Lillian smiled, transfixed. Tiny bubbles formed at the jar's base, then slowly rose up to the top, sending little tremors across the surface.

The cloud of white mist contracted into a long, thin cylindrical shape, reaching almost from the top of the jar to the ceiling. It spiraled around like a delicate little tornado balanced perfectly over the surface of the blood. The bubbles became bigger, popping and sending little spatters onto the mirror. The spiral spun faster, generating a soft humming sound. It slowed and the bubbles subsided. An incredible aroma filled the room, flooding her senses, one she had craved for an eternity, but now…it all came rushing back to her like a dear old friend, filling her with complete ecstasy.

It was an intoxicating scent that almost defied description. Mysterious, seductive, and intimidating, yet somehow also welcoming and intriguing. The scent conjured up all manner of things from deep inside one's forbidden imagination. The exciting blissful moments before losing your virginity, wild exotic flowers sprouting from thick vines tangled around towering trees, deep in hidden jungles. Freshly cut wood from clifftops on the edges of the darkest forests, the smell of secrets and antiquity…of history, and people and places that had flourished centuries ago, combined with the pulsating power and energy of modern-day concrete jungles. It exuded sexuality, fear, and adrenaline, but also promise, strength, and confidence. It was somehow all these things at once, and it stimulated the mind and body so that one felt *invincible*, and completely empowered as it played blissful havoc with one's senses.

Lillian breathed it in deeply.

"How I have missed you."

The white vapor vanished down into the jar, and the blood inside had mostly evaporated, with only a very small amount left in the bottom. Lillian sighed. The spell had worked perfectly, the correct amount had been sacrificed to the Ancient Ones, but this precious tiny amount left was for her. She reached out and lifted the jar. Slowly, she began to pour the red liquid into the tiny perfume bottle.

The wind outside had all but subsided, and many confused residents of Beachwood Canyon were wandering the streets, looking around at the mess, and asking each other what on Earth had happened. It never got this windy at this time of year. But inside Helen's bedroom, all was still and quiet.

Lillian poured the final precious drops of the liquid into the crystal bottle, filling it perfectly to the top.

She screwed the silver lid back on and picked it up.

"Thank you," she whispered.

Standing before the mirror, she slid down her shoulder straps, and brought the perfume bottle up to her breasts, her fingers paused on the pump. She was about to squeeze when a bright sliver of sunlight shot in through the window and struck the dresser mirror. Lillian shrieked in horror as its powerful rays reflected off the glass, blinding her. Searing bolts of pain shot through her body. She stumbled back, dropping the perfume bottle to the floor. It rolled out of sight under the bed. She howled as the biting rays ravaged her skin. She dropped to the floor clutching blindly for the perfume, but it was out of reach.

"*No!*"

More pain struck her from deep within, the agony continued to race throughout her. It was too late now, the sun had risen fully, and a new day had begun before she had applied the fresh perfume. This was her weakest moment. The spell's power from the last application had run its course, and now the transformation back to the mortal was taking place. She had missed her chance.

Lillian had no choice. With a morbid howl, she accepted defeat.

She would have to wait now. Wait until the mortal who had awakened her, gave in to the perfume's power once again, but the pain, ah the pain…at least she did not have to endure that. Now she would gladly give the mortal her body back. She relinquished her stranglehold over Helen, and Lillian Kelly disappeared, plunging deep down inside herself, allowing Helen Elliot to return once again.

Down in the cavernous darkness, Helen felt herself suddenly emerging upwards at a dizzying pace. She rose quickly up and out of the shadows and felt her own presence flooding Lillian's body again. Suddenly, she could see everything, and she realized she was standing in her own bedroom; in a split second she was being *rocked* by the pain.

She knew all too well what was happening; she was turning into herself again, turning back into Helen Elliot.

What the hell was going on?

She remembered coming home, but now this? She screamed as a searing bolt of agony shot across her chest and into her arms.

How can it hurt even more? Please make it stop!

It wouldn't stop, and already she could feel her arms expanding, her face contorting, it was excruciating. She lay on the floor of her bedroom, wondering if she would even stay conscious while it happened.

She did not.

Helen woke in the fetal position on the floor in darkness, the stench of the foul green bile she had thrown up on the rug filled the room. The silver dress lay on the floor next to her. Her ears detected a faint rumbling sound she knew well; she turned her head and looked under her bed. A pair of warm amber eyes peered back at her. Helen's heart glowed. "Baby, come to Mommy," she croaked.

Shadow crept up and rubbed his nose tentatively over her cheek, twitching his tail as Helen stroked him. "It's okay, baby boy. It's me. It's Mommy. Let's get you some din-din."

She dragged herself up, puzzled at the darkness. She switched on the light and saw her wall clock showing almost six at night.

"No, it can't be!" she cried.

She looked out the window. Sure enough, the streetlights were on. And there were leaves and branches scattered all over her front lawn.

Goodness me, what a mess.

She slipped on her gown, scooped up Shadow and looked around at the disarray in her bedroom. Her mannequins and ornaments lay on the floor, some broken, her framed posters hung crooked. She stared at a large glass jar with red smears inside it on her dresser, and on the floor lay a small black coat she did not recognize. It was then that she saw the bottom drawer of the jewelry box open. She reached into the hidden compartment but could feel nothing.

Panicked, she looked around for the bottle but couldn't see it anywhere. She kneeled to look under the bed, and at once she spotted it. She moved the bed aside, then scooped up the bottle, turning it slowly in her hands, checking it for damage.

To her utter amazement…it was *full*.

How? When?

She wiped her eyes. *It can't be*, but it was. The bottle was full to the top with the dark red liquid. She sat on the bed and tried to think, tried to recall, but nothing came to her. All she could remember was the feeling of sadness she had the last time she used the perfume, as she was fully aware the bottle was practically empty. Now, here it was, full again. It made no sense at all, but then again, what really did make sense? It was hardly normal to find a bottle of perfume that transformed you into a dead movie star from the fifties. She had tampered with a force not of this Earth, and many of her questions would quite simply never have answers. Perhaps the forces that granted her wish had somehow magically filled it again for her. Or perhaps she was just going crazy. The fact that she could recall almost nothing from the previous night made her question whether the bottle really had been empty in the first place. She placed it back in its hiding place and closed the drawer. Then she picked up the silver dress, carefully cleaned it in her laundry, and tidied up her bedroom.

Helen fixed Shadow a bowl of cat food, then half-stumbled to the bathroom exhausted. She turned on the taps and stepped inside the shower, sighing as the hot water cascaded down.

She tried to think back but couldn't recall much. One thing she knew for certain was that Peter Jameson had kissed her, and so much more. She remembered sharing a cigarette with him and being in his bed, but then what? She simply could not remember. And what had happened on the way home? Fragments clouded her mind: panic, racing home in her little blue car, but then…nothing.

She dried herself and put on her gown. How had she slept all day? And why was her bedroom such a mess? *Where did the black coat and the glass jar come from?* Inside, she knew something was wrong. *I must have been a fool to think it could have been as perfect the second time around.* But wasn't the pain enough price to pay? Why was her memory being taken from her?

She was starving. She tore open a large packet of chocolate cookies and ate every one of them, then switched on the radio and made herself a pot of peppermint tea as the news reported that a young girl had been found close to death in a Hollywood apartment. Details were sketchy, but it was believed she'd been stabbed and had lost a lot of blood. She was in a coma in hospital, and a twenty-two-year-old man had been detained and was helping police with their inquiries.

Helen shook her head. What was the world coming to? She headed to her bedroom with a mug of tea and looked at the silver dress, then picked it up and sat down in her sewing room. As she stared at her beloved old sewing machine—the one her mother had used to teach her how to sew—she decided to make a new dress, one that would fit Lillian. She laid the silver dress out across her sewing bench and began copying the pattern onto paper. She chose a deep burgundy velvet she'd had for a long time and got started.

The hours flew by as Helen enjoyed herself immensely; never had she made a garment for a woman of Lillian's height and proportions. Her many years of experience meant she was almost finished in six hours. After some final alterations to the hemline, she hung the dress from the display mannequin and stood back to inspect her work. The dress had fine shoulder straps, a sweetheart neckline, and a split from the thigh. Helen was impressed with her new creation and knew it would fit Lillian perfectly. But when would she become Lillian again? Would it even be possible?

She began watching Lillian's movie once again. Soon she was engrossed in a scene where Lillian's character was enslaved by the evil Lord Zhargon. Lillian was clad in a long, fitted black gown with laced sleeves. She was chained to a wall with her arms spread high above her head as Zhargon slowly traced a whip along her thighs, his followers kneeling beside him. Wow, *no wonder magic happens when I become you. Just look at you, you're so beautiful.* The movie ended, Helen went to her bedroom and fell asleep.

CHAPTER 13

THE HUNTED

Many a hard man had carried the badge of LA Police detective over the years, but the solidly built man with thick charcoal hair, clad in a jet-black suit and standing in the doorway of the crime scene, was one of the hardest of them all. His penetrating green eyes sat riveted in a chiseled face that was almost too hard to be handsome. Detective James Karson had arrived at Peter Jameson's apartment fast after getting the call. At forty-four years of age, he had become one of Los Angeles' most respected detectives, known for his efficiency and tough no-nonsense attitude. Karson lived and breathed police work, and he generally liked to work alone. He had known instantly that the girl in the bed was dangerously close to death, and he held little hope for her as he watched the EMTs haul her away. He had set up a makeshift interview room right there in Jameson's apartment, personally interviewing and taking statements from each and every groggy partygoer who was still present. He had soon established one thing: almost everybody at the party had mentioned seeing a woman, one that nobody seemed to really know much about at all. Her name was

Lillian, and by the numerous descriptions, she was tall, easily six feet. She had long blonde hair and was very beautiful. Almost every person in the apartment had given close to the same description of her, yet nobody knew anything else about her. Even the apartment's owner, Peter Jameson, could not give them a last name. And his story about meeting her by chance on Hollywood Boulevard didn't hold much water with Karson.

He had made Peter very uneasy with his piercing green eyes…his deep voice and unnerving stare. Karson had wanted details from Peter, but he got very few. "Beautiful," a deep "breathy" voice, but not even a last name. Peter had known instinctively that Karson was a man not to be trifled with. He told Karson about meeting Lillian and inviting her into the fashion show, taking her home in the limousine with all the young models. He even talked about the sex. He told him everything, besides, the cops had been all through the apartment before he'd had time to clean things up anyway. They bagged and took numerous items, glasses, bottles, and tiny bags of pills and cocaine. Karson didn't flinch. He just took notes and recorded the entire interview. Peter could only tell him the truth about Lillian: she had simply vanished in the night.

Karson had already viewed the in-house security footage from the cameras inside the apartment building, but the one he needed the most, the one that covered the corridor to the elevators, had malfunctioned a week before and was still not fixed. He would certainly be looking at footage from the Fallen Temple club and other cameras along Hollywood Boulevard, but this was Los Angeles. Tall, beautiful blondes were plentiful around these parts. But there was something about this mysterious blonde that had his curiosity aroused. His gut instinct told him that something very strange had happened in this apartment, and he wanted answers. Karson was thorough—very thorough. And even though it looked like an open-and-shut case, complete with a suspect and even a weapon with prints on it, he wasn't satisfied. To tie up all the loose ends and cover all bases he needed to talk to everyone who had been at Peter's party, and that included the mystery blonde. He would find her; that was what he did.

* * *

Ash tumbled down from the cigarette between Peter Jameson's trembling fingers and settled on his fine black pants, as he sat on his balcony in the bright morning sun. Even two hours after being grilled in his living room by Karson, he still hadn't managed to calm himself completely. He had woken that morning in his apartment, at around six-thirty, to the sounds of a young girl screaming. He had leaped from his bed and run down the hallway to see Siobhan, one of his most popular models, slumped against the hallway wall, staring into a bedroom with tears rolling down her cheeks, her eyes filled with shock.

"It's Angie. I think she's dead."

He had stepped into the room and switched on the light. The girl had been almost as white as the satin sheets on which she had lain. Her right arm was dangling over the edge of the bed. A thick streak of congealed blood ran from her wrist to the tips of her fingers, and there was a large dark pool of it on the floor. His first thought was suicide, until another scream erupted from the living room.

Matt, a young male model, had just woken up with a bloodstained knife in his hand, and blood on his fingers and jeans. He was standing with utter confusion in his eyes, as he held the knife blade up, staring at it in horror.

Peter glared at him, "What the fuck did you do?"

"I...I didn't do *anything*...I swear!" He dropped the knife and fled the apartment.

Peter had called 911 at once, and ten minutes later an ambulance and three police cars had gathered outside his apartment building. Some media were there, too, taking photos and asking all manner of questions.

Karson had interviewed thirteen people in all. Mostly young models and aspiring actors aged eighteen to twenty-three, though one of the girls turned out to be only seventeen. Word had already gotten out that a young model had almost died in Peter Jameson's apartment, and being one of Hollywood's top talent agents, the story had the potential to become very juicy tabloid material.

As soon as the police had been informed about Matt with the bloodstained knife in his hand, they had issued a warrant for him. He was picked up very quickly at LAX airport trying to board a plane bound for New York. His prints had matched the ones on the knife and he was being held by police. Forensics had carefully gone over everything in Peter's apartment, and one by one, all the hungover and shaken young models and actors were eventually allowed to leave. Peter knew the cops had found drugs, and he also knew they were now aware that underage people had been drinking in his apartment. He shuddered to think what may be on the horizon if some of his other young models spilled their stories about what had really been going that night. He lit another cigarette with shaking hands, then called his lawyer.

* * *

On location at Rodeo Drive, Carlo Genisi was filming his upcoming movie. He was planning to shoot three scenes today. The cast and crew were taking a well-earned break, as Carlo sat in his director's chair, sipping a cappuccino and talking on his cell.

"You still haven't found her? You're fucking kidding me. Seven grand and still nothing?" he hissed at the private detective.

"Look, Mr. Genisi, again you only gave me a description and a first name. I've managed to access military records but I'm still coming up with nothing. I'm sorry."

Carlo shook his head in disgust. This so-called "best" private investigator in LA, was getting nowhere.

"Fine, just forget about it then," Carlo muttered.

"Look sir, I've put a lot of hours into this. I've exhausted every option and contact I've got to find this woman. I've searched everywhere that her background and the life story she gave you corresponds with, but there's just nothing."

Carlo was feeling defeated. He was starting to give up all hope of ever finding Lillian again.

The investigator continued. "The only thing that got my attention was something I found from the war archives which I managed to access."

"Go on."

"Well, there was an American soldier from New York who married a German war widow, and she had a daughter named Lillian, and they did move to New York, but it's of no use to us anyway, as you say this woman could only be in her late twenties?"

"Yes," said Carlo, "at most."

"Well that's the thing, this was World War Two; this Lillian would have to be over eighty years old by now, going by the records I discovered, so clearly not her. It's an odd coincidence—there is the small possibility of identity theft. I know it sounds odd, but it does happen. I'm sorry, but apart from that, I've got nothing. I'm assuming you don't want me to search for her any longer?"

"No, just let it go for now." He ended the call and sighed. *How hard can it be to find a woman like Lillian?* Sebastian approached him tapping his watch.

Carlo nodded, "Yes, get everyone back on deck. We've got a movie to make."

And I thought it was something special. His heart ached. He had fallen hard for Lillian and he knew it, but where the hell was she?

CHAPTER 14

THE INEVITABLE

After sleeping in late, Helen woke and cleaned up around the house, then raked up all the leaves and branches in the front and back yards, wondering how such a mess had occurred. After looking at her neighbors' yards she could see that she wasn't the only one who had suffered the effects of the freak winds.

She spent the rest of the day dusting and rearranging her memorabilia collection, then working on new dresses while listening to old records. She made herself a cup of peppermint tea and nibbled chocolate biscuits while watching the news. The young woman who was attacked in a Hollywood apartment had died. The case was now being treated as a murder. Helen sipped her tea, shaking her head.

"Another quiet night at home, baby boy. You want to watch a movie with Mommy?" Shadow purred lovingly, as he always did when Helen spoke to him. She felt like a glass of wine. After the way she felt when she woke up, she was amazed she'd even thought about drinking. She caught a faint whiff of tobacco and guessed it came from the artist who lived in the big house next door. With the size of his estate and the thick trees and shrubbery surrounding it, she seldom saw him, though she had spotted him occasionally puffing on a pipe. The scent was rich and enticing, and Helen found herself craving a cigar. It amused her. She had never smoked in her life. Well, not until she had become Lillian.

She found her handbag and took out the sleek tin and was soon enjoying a glass of wine and a smoke out on her deck. After she finished, she went inside and browsed her movie collection, but she was compelled to watch *Mistress of Evil*, yet again.

She had already watched the movie four times, but that was nothing for a diehard film fan like Helen. She had never really been a fan of horror, but she simply *loved* this movie.

She poured another glass of wine and sat down on the sofa.

Halfway through the film, Helen had finished her third glass. Once again, she stared mesmerized at the screen as she watched Lillian scaling down the castle wall on a rope. Then her white knight came storming in with his small army to rescue her. Lillian dropped the last eight feet into his strong arms, before they galloped off into the forest.

Helen sighed, what *a movie—true love at first sight*. Something stirred, it was very deep down, but it was there, and she knew what it was…somehow, she sensed that a part of Lillian had never quite left her. She had tried so hard to remember what had happened after Peter's party, but only fragments had come back to her, and nothing about them made sense.

The stirring became stronger. Helen knew she was tipsy, but it felt good.

By the time the film ended the wine had gone to her head.

She laid back on the sofa, a familiar feeling began to creep throughout her body. It was nothing like the feeling when she used the perfume. This was different, a strong, calm, deep sensation.

She lay there almost trancelike and breathed in deeply. The sensation had her well in its grip now. It was as if she could see into her own soul, her own being…and what she saw amazed her.

She saw Lillian Kelly's *face*, it was merging in and out of shadows, but there was no mistaking it. And she was making her presence known, Helen could feel Lillian reaching out to her.

Helen spoke aloud, "Hello, are you there? What's happening to me?" She heard nothing in response, but she could sure as hell *feel* Lillian.

A warm, comforting sensation flooded Helen's body. It felt wonderful, she knew the feeling was Lillian, she felt close to her, cloaked in her impeccable beauty, her warmth and charisma. She felt Lillian imploring her to accept her friendship. At first she had been frightened, but now…she knew this was a wonderful thing. Unlike everybody else in her life, Lillian was *accepting* her. Inviting her to become part of her.

Lillian's face faded away, and the perfume bottle filled her mind. She entered her bedroom and stood before the jewelry box. She felt Lillian urging her to take out the perfume—and she did.

Lillian's glee surged all over her body, and the message was clear.

Use the perfume; everything you want is waiting for you.

Although she had little memory of what had happened the last time, and no idea how the perfume bottle had become full again, she knew she wanted this to happen, *needed* it to happen. Why should she just be Helen Elliot all the time when she didn't have to be? All the glamor, romance, and excitement in the world was waiting for her, if she just applied the perfume. She lifted the bottle to the base of her neck, shrugged off her gown, and let it fall to the floor.

She sprayed a small cloud of the fresh red mist onto her neckline and bust. It vanished into her skin, buzzing and tingling as if hungry for her flesh. Helen had gotten used to the initial sensation, but now she braced herself for what was coming next—pain. And it came like a blade of ice that struck right through her core.

She shuddered, clutching the dresser for support.

The splintering, searing shards spread out like tentacles into her limbs. She moaned, then slumped to her knees and waited for the inevitable.

Nothing is free; everything comes at a price.

The agony set in. Shadow cowered low behind the record player, terrified once again at the guttural chilling screams coming from Helen's bedroom, as the perfume performed its task.

The clock in the living room chimed nine. A half-moon hung high in the night sky over Los Angeles, as the wind that had torn through Beachwood Canyon moments ago now settled. Helen Elliot was standing once again in front of the full-length mirror in her bedroom, but in *Lillian Kelly's body.*

Thrilled with the utter physical perfection she had become once again.

"Why couldn't I have been born this way?"

She did her hair and makeup and then nervously slid on the new dress she had made, but she needn't have doubted her skill—the fit was perfection. She put on the stilettos. It was time to go out now, and let the night unfold.

When you look like this, anything is possible. That, I know.

As she stood there admiring her reflection, a chill spread through her body. It was unpleasant, but not painful. Something was wrong. It became stronger. Instinctively she looked up at the blazing blue eyes on the poster, and she knew it was Lillian. She had played with fire again, she had succumbed to temptation and danced with the devil one more time, and now she knew she would have to submit to his bidding.

She had been tipsy when she decided to apply the perfume, she knew, but she also knew wine or not, she would have used it again anyway. How could she not? After a lifetime of struggling with her weight, being laughed and sniggered at, ridiculed, lonely, and starved of romance…how could she not want to use the perfume again? It made all her dreams come true. Beauty, Carlo, Peter, the high life, oh how glorious it had been when she was *Lillian*.

The feeling dug its claws in deeply now. Helen tried to stay aware of what was happening, but it was becoming harder by the second. Deep inside her, Lillian's presence ebbed out from the shadows, from the place of darkness, of mystery and spells…black magic and voodoo. Lillian would have what she wanted, and what she wanted now was control of her own body again. She had been furious when she was denied her chance to apply the fresh perfume. But now, all she had to do was keep the bottle filled with the fresh blood and soul of a young woman, and Lillian Kelly would live again, forever.

She had been living a perfect life many years ago; she had been well on her way to the top of Tinseltown—until that fateful night she had tried to make too much of the precious liquid, tried to mix in far more than she knew she should have. Six pints of blood and the souls of three young girls, all who died at her murderous hands in one fell swoop. Her plan had been to make much more of the blood in a much larger bottle in the hope it would last longer, requiring less killing and hiding in the shadows, making her life much easier.

But the act had infuriated the Ancient Ones. They had thrust their anger down on her and banished her soul into the perfume bottle, sealing her mortal fate by destroying her in a fire. The flames and smoke had engulfed the mansion around her that terrible night. She had thrust the perfume bottle back inside the jewelry box and fled downstairs to the basement to escape through a back door. To her horror, she could not open it. Screaming in terror, she had made a dash back up the stairs, but not before placing the jewelry box up on a ledge, in between the large cement pillars supporting the lower levels of the house. She had then made her way back to the front doors to escape, but the Ancient Ones had seen to that too. She had screamed and pulled with all her might, but the doors may as well have been welded shut. She had perished there on the floor of the great mansion, surrounded by the roaring flames.

Lillian seethed at the memory of it. She banished it from her mind; she had to focus on the task at hand now, taking complete control of her own body again, *permanently.*

Helen tried to stay present but could not. The sensation had taken over completely now, somehow…she knew Lillian was claiming her body, and there was nothing she could do about it. She felt as though she was standing on the edge of a deep, dark ravine, the ground crumbling beneath her. In her mind she could see Lillian, rising to the surface.

Helen felt herself sinking down, lower and lower, into the inky-dark shadows of nothingness, where she knew she had been before, a place where she became merely a distant bystander, a helpless captive observer, peering out into the world through eyes that were clouded and foggy, like melting frost on a pane of glass. She was trapped once again, probably for quite some time.

Wind gusted into the bedroom, knocking figurines to the floor as Lillian's hair billowed around her face like a ghostly mane of woven gold. A pack of coyotes howled and yipped mournfully, high on the mountain behind the little cottage. With Helen now banished again, Lillian laughed aloud with satisfaction. She didn't know how or where Helen had found the perfume bottle, and in truth, she didn't care. She was now truly back—that was all that mattered.

Back in complete control of her body; and with her sublime beauty and her powers at full force, she could have anything she wanted. And oh, how she wanted to be a movie star again. To be in front of the cameras once more and claim her place as the rightful Queen of Hollywood. She had been cheated in her previous life. In her first life she had been as good as any of those stars who made it to the top back in the fifties and sixties. She had stood by and watched them rise to the top, while she had been used, lied to, deceived, and cast aside. But now she would show them. Oh, how the world would see her now.

CHAPTER 15

BLOOD TRAIL

The cup of black coffee sitting on the desk was two hours cold, and the lamp next to it barely illuminated Karson's office. That was how he liked it. Karson had never liked working under glaring lights at night. He was searching through all the closed-circuit camera footage from the fashion show. For the most part, there was nothing of use. The footage from inside the club was grainy and dark—as it often was with in-house security cameras. The show had been thick with beautiful women, dressed in all manner of dazzling outfits, but so far nobody matched the description of the mystery blonde who had vanished from Peter Jameson's apartment. Things were looking grim. There was five minutes of footage left to watch, and he didn't have his hopes up. The lights had been low for most of the show.

It had seemed an open-and-shut case at first. Your typical drug-fueled party, complete with models, drugs, and loads of sex and alcohol. But this was no ordinary party: a young woman dead from a knife wound to her wrist, and a young man found with the murder weapon in his hand, with the victim's blood on it. Just too easy.

As soon as he had arrived at the crime scene, the hairs on Karson's neck had bristled. Something unusual had happened in that apartment; he could sense it. Twenty-two years on the job and a razor-sharp instinct told him something was up. They didn't call him "the human lie detector" for nothing. The extra training with the FBI had helped, but his was a genuine gift, an instinct, and in his whole life he had rarely been wrong about anything. After two-and-a-half hours of grilling the young man who was found with the knife, Karson still hadn't been satisfied. The kid's name was Matt Jacobs, an up-and-coming young actor who had appeared in some TV ads for jeans and swimwear. He had worked as an extra on a couple of teen soaps, too, but not much else. He had sat wide-eyed and petrified as Karson interrogated him with those hard green eyes. The kid had wept openly and readily admitted to snorting cocaine, but he'd sworn repeatedly on his life he had not touched the girl...Hadn't even tried to sleep with her, and he most certainly did not pick up a knife at any time that night. He had wept and trembled as he told Karson every detail about his entire life and the night of the party. *He's just another small-town kid with big dreams, fresh off the bus from Philadelphia eight months ago and looking to make his way in showbiz.*

Karson had checked him out, of course, and found nothing, not even a traffic violation. The kid was from a devout Catholic family, and from what Karson could see, he had never put a foot out of line in his life. Peter Jameson, his agent, had given him a glowing report, saying that he was one the sweetest and most honest kids he had ever represented. But at the end of it all there was a dead girl, and this was now a murder investigation, and it was Karson's job to find the killer.

They were not able to find any prints or DNA from the girl's body or the room in which she was found. The other thing that puzzled Karson was the blood. There was a large pool of it under her hand on the carpet, but the coroner was sure there should still have been more. A lot of her blood was…*missing*. It just didn't add up. And his prime suspect, this twenty-two-year-old choir boy, had broken down in tears and looked him straight in the eye and sworn on his life he was innocent.

And Karson believed him.

He had let the boy go home to his tiny apartment on the Sunset Strip, and Karson thought he had never seen a person more relieved to walk out of a police station in his life.

He stared at the screen, watching almost all the guests exit the club, when something made him lean forward sharply. It was the side of a woman's head, a woman with thick, long blonde hair. He wound the footage back and then moved it forward frame by frame. The woman looked to be taller than most of the other people around her. And she appeared to be exiting the club with Peter Jameson and the last of the partygoers, who obscured most of her face and body. There was a brief glimpse of a shoulder strap peering out from beneath the woman's hair, and a partial shot of the side of her face in shadowy lighting, and that was it; the club was empty, and the staff began locking the doors and cleaning up. A large, heavy fist pounded down, sending droplets of cold coffee spattering across the desk.

"Goddamn it!" Karson scoured the entire footage again, but there was nothing else. There was a hint of satisfaction, though. At least he had caught a possible glimpse of this mystery blonde. It wasn't much, but it was something.

* * *

Carlo Genisi sipped his gin and tonic in the bar of a Hollywood hotel. It had been a long day's filming, with technical difficulties that had held him up and wasted valuable time on set. On top of that, it looked like one of the main actors was getting the flu. *Perfect.* Sebastian sipped a beer next to him.

"Don't let it get you down, Carlo. It's just one of those things; everything's been great so far, until today. Technically, we're still ahead of schedule."

"I know, but I like to keep way ahead, and I just cannot believe how many things went wrong today."

Sebastian knew there was something else bugging Carlo. He had overheard Carlo talking on his cell to a private investigator about a woman he had met one night in Hollywood, a woman who had vanished after staying the night at his house. There were rumors about it on the set, and he knew the woman was Lillian. Although they were good friends, Sebastian knew to keep well out of it unless Carlo brought it up.

She sure must have been something in the sack. He knew Carlo had the pick of the bunch. He'd lost count of how many times gorgeous young actresses, and even just women standing around watching them film on location, had given him their business cards and cell numbers to pass on to Carlo. Carlo was young, handsome, rich, and extremely eligible, but right now he was depressed, staring down into his drink.

Carlo's world had been turned upside down the night he had met Lillian. Never had he been so spellbound by any woman in his life. Her voice, her hair, her sheer elegance… her *everything*.

She had given him the most incredible, passionate night of his life, then just disappeared. He had practically given up and come to terms with the fact that it had meant nothing to her to sleep with a man like him.

She could have any man she wants, he thought glumly.

But he had been so sure there was something special between them besides the mind-blowing sex. It was the way she had looked at him with those enchanting eyes, the way she had touched his arm and held his hand. Carlo was not an insecure man, nor was he a man who needed to be touched and reassured all the time. But with Lillian, he swore he'd felt electricity every time she stroked his wrist or placed her arm around him.

He drained his glass and signaled to the bartender to pour him another. *The only woman I've ever really wanted, and she flits on me in the night.*

A noisy crowd of attractive young twenty-something girls strutted into the bar, all dressed to kill and ready to let their hair down for a night's drinking and dancing. Sebastian nudged Carlo, tossing his head in their direction.

Carlo glanced at them. They were certainly lovely, he thought, but still just your typical young gorgeous wannabes with stars in their eyes and heads full of dreams. *This town is crawling with them.* Two of them had already recognized him and began playing the usual eye contact games and tossing their hair about in his direction. Carlo couldn't have cared less; he wasn't looking for sex, just a couple of drinks, a meal, and a quiet night at home checking over the script changes and call sheets for the next day's filming. And of course, he would be brooding over Lillian.

CHAPTER 16

THE SECOND COMING

Lillian stood in the living room of the little cottage, searching through Helen's handbag. Inside it was Helen's wallet, tissues, a lighter, some spare change, a candy bar, deodorant, a pen and notepad, and a small black device with numbered buttons and a tiny screen. (She had no idea it was a cell phone.) She also noticed a tin of mini cigars and smiled as she recognized the brand, Vanilla Dove. One of her favorite brands she had enjoyed in her first life. Lillian placed the perfume bottle inside the bag, which she had wrapped carefully in a dish towel. She did not want it out of her sight. It was the most precious thing in the world to her—literally her lifeblood—and she would always keep it close.

She looked around the little house with distaste at the many posters of movie stars covering the walls, the ones who had beaten her to the prize. *Lucky breaks, all of them*, she thought bitterly. She had met most of them and hadn't cared much for any of them, but in truth it was just petty jealousy.

She moved into the kitchen and saw a calendar. She stood there stunned as she tried to wrap her mind around the year.

Unbelievable. She knew a long time had passed, but it still just did not seem possible. She had seen some astonishing things in this new age, but it still shocked her how many years had passed while she had lain dormant.

She stepped outside onto the back deck and looked down at the distant lights of LA. It had changed, that was for certain. It was so much larger now. The sprawl of city lights seemed to go on forever. She turned to her right and looked up toward the hills, and her breath caught in her throat as her gaze fell on the Hollywood Sign. Her face lit up. She had forgotten how truly majestic it was, standing up there on the mountain. A monument, a beacon of hope and promise for the thousands of dreamers who arrived in this town every year, just as she had, as a young unknown actress all those years ago.

"We meet again, old friend." She blew a kiss to it and went back inside.

Lillian opened the door to Helen's garage and looked at the little car. She had enjoyed driving in her first life and had even owned a sports car. But that was a long time ago; it had startled her how much traffic there was on the roads in Los Angeles now. Even if she'd allowed Helen's presence to guide her, she was not prepared to try driving yet. That could wait. She closed the door. She knew she would have to learn a lot of new things. She would use Helen when she needed her, but only to a point. She had been warned by the master sorcerer long ago not to give the mortal's presence too much rope. There was the tiniest possibility of resistance... of the mortal soul within her earthly vessel fighting against her to reclaim the body. But Helen was weak, and Lillian was strong. She would keep Helen in her place, far, far down in the shadowy depths, using and extracting what knowledge she needed when it suited her. Tonight, she had Hollywood to get reacquainted with, and the night was still young.

She opened Helen's wallet and was pleased to see nearly three hundred dollars. Currency hadn't really changed all that much, she noticed as she looked at the bills. She also saw what appeared to be an assortment of business cards, but these were not paper; curiously, they seemed to be made of plastic. She picked up the strange black device with numbered buttons. It was like nothing she had ever seen. It appeared space-age, with a small screen that glowed when she touched it. She dropped it back in the bag and closed it. Then she looked around the living room at the big-screen TV and the sleek DVD and VCR players underneath it. Numbers and words were illuminated on them. She spotted the old record player and recalled having something similar herself, so many years ago.

Lillian looked at more framed posters covering the walls in the living room and even the kitchen; again, most were people she had known on the Hollywood scene when her star had first started to rise, when she began receiving invitations to some of the A-list events. That was a very long time ago, she knew, but here they were, people she had known in her first life all over of the walls of this house, as if they were still young and famous. It puzzled her.

Many appliances in the kitchen were foreign to her, but she knew in time she would become accustomed to the modern world. One thing she saw on the wall that hadn't changed much was Helen's telephone. It was like the ones they used to have in all the best hotels, back when she was a star. Little did Lillian know it was a modern recreation of a vintage telephone, one of Helen's favorite collectibles. It was wired up and it worked perfectly. What Lillian needed now was a taxi. She picked up the handpiece and held it to her ear, but something wasn't right; no operator came on the line to ask her who she wanted.

"Hello? Hello?" Nothing. She clicked the receiver down and lifted it again, hearing only a buzzing sound, but still no operator. She slammed the phone back in its cradle. "Stupid, wretched thing," she muttered. She would have to walk. This was still Los Angeles, and surely she would be able to flag down a cab in no time.

A framed picture sitting on a small table caught her eye. It was a photo taken when Helen was only sixteen. She was flanked by her mother and her aunt, her arms over their shoulders; all three of them were smiling. Lillian knew it was Helen. She frowned and shook her head at Helen's size, even at such a tender age. "No wonder you loved being in my body," she jeered.

She pulled the door shut behind her and stepped out into a perfect night. The moon was only a sliver, but the stars were twinkling brightly, as they always did over Beachwood Canyon. Lillian soon made her way down onto Beachwood Drive. Passersby stared at the astoundingly attractive blonde striding along the sidewalk. She paid little attention to them. Up ahead, outside a small cluster of stores, she saw exactly what she wanted: a line of cabs, four of them ready to go. Lillian took the first one, much to the pleasure of the middle-aged driver, whose eyes bulged with delight as she swung the door open and got in the car. He stared slack-jawed at Lillian, who smiled back at him.

"Take me to Hollywood Boulevard please, handsome."

He lit up like a school boy.

"Yes, ma'am." He pulled out from the curb and headed toward the bright lights.

Lillian gazed out the window. It had changed so much, but here and there she still recognized something: a building, a store, even some of the old mansions dotted up in the hills.

A chill ran through her as she recognized a steep winding road; she knew it was Cielo Drive, the street where she had died in the flames—well, when her *mortal* body had died. She recalled the night clearly but immediately put it out of her mind. That was not something she ever wanted to think about.

She looked down the road ahead of her. It was all here before her: the new Los Angeles and the new Hollywood. She wanted to think of the future, not the past. She had a lot to learn with modern technology, she knew, but she wasn't too bothered. In time, she would learn all she had to and fit in perfectly. The thought of being recognized had occurred to her, but nobody would ever assume she was the real Lillian Kelly. Nonetheless, to be extra safe, she had been thinking of dyeing her hair…black perhaps, or maybe a dark brown. The thought appealed to her of sitting in a salon, being pampered and fussed over like in the old days.

A man was imperative, she knew, a wealthy one, of course, one who was respected but who would bend to her will.

One who could provide the luxurious lifestyle she needed and to which she was accustomed. *That will be the easy part.* Hollywood was full of men with loads of money, and they all loved being seen with beautiful young women on their arms.

A small illuminated screen perched on the dashboard of the cab seemed to be speaking to the driver and giving him directions. *Unbelievable.* She had been very surprised to see how cars had changed over the decades. Gone were the large sedans, heavily laden with gleaming chrome. Now everything looked much lighter, sleek and rounded. Most of the interior of the cab looked and felt like plastic. It was glorious to see everything with her own eyes now. Helen was there, of course, deep down inside, peeping out at snippets and fragments, but Lillian was in power now, and loving it.

The cab hit Hollywood Boulevard and Lillian was happy. To her surprise, it didn't seem to have changed as much as she'd predicted. She noticed the sidewalk was covered in stars. *They kept up the tradition, and look how many stars there are now.*

The cab cruised past the world-famous theater, and Lillian was thrilled to see it again. Like every actor, back in her first life she had craved the honor of laying her hands in the wet cement, her name immortalized for future generations.

"Stop here, please." The driver pulled in to the curb, and Lillian turned to him.

"How much do I owe you?"

He smiled sheepishly. "Ma'am, for you, it's on the house. You are the most beautiful lady I've ever seen."

"Thank you, darling." Lillian kissed her forefinger and touched the tip of his nose. He giggled like a child.

She stepped out of the cab, walked over to the famous handprints and signatures in the cement, and sighed. *I never even came close.* Things had gone so wrong for her: the wrong parts, the wrong agents. It just hadn't worked out like it should have. She remembered many of the slimy, lying film directors and casting agents she had slept with so long ago, and submitting to their depraved sexual fantasies. So many who had promised to make her a big star. In her depression and desperation, Lillian had believed every word they said… had let them pass her around like a worthless toy. All of them wanted to enjoy her incredible body, but none of them wanted to take her seriously as an actress, just a scream queen. One had convinced her to pose naked for erotic photos—a very risky thing to do back in those early days of Hollywood. He sold the photos to a nude magazine behind her back for a tidy sum, of which she never received a dime, and word had spread all over Hollywood like wildfire. The tabloids tore Lillian's reputation apart. It had been pretty much ended her declining acting career. She lost faith in people, life, and humanity. She became hard and jaded, with hatred in her heart. But that was then and this was now. Things could change, and change they would.

It was time to find a man with money, and plenty of it. She headed down the Walk of Fame, amazed at the number of stars now studded into the pavement. Many were names she did not know, of course. She looked around. It was different but familiar. The thing that took her by surprise was the lights. *So many of them, and so bright*—glowing, flickering lights were everywhere. She was also surprised at the number of tourists out at this time of night, their cameras hanging around their necks, and it seemed nearly everyone was talking on miniature devices held to their ears. She realized they must have been telephones! Now she understood what the strange device was in Helen's bag. She was truly amazed.

Dozens of men stared at Lillian as she headed down the boulevard. More memories came flooding back to her: the clubs, the bars, all the places she used to frequent. But many were long gone. Everything was sleek and flat now. Opulent old-style charm seemed to have given way to wide, open areas and rectangular buildings.

A group of motorcycles cruised past her, and Lillian marveled at the sleek machines. *They are like something from outer space.* She moved further down the street and noticed a brightly lit club. There were marble-like columns out the front of it, and grand arches flanked the huge entry. Feeling it resembled the clubs from her time, she stepped up to the entry to look. The doorman's jaw dropped, and he ushered her in at once.

"Welcome."

"Thank you, darling."

She stepped inside and looked around, astonished. The bar was very long. The walls were silver, and colorful lights seemed to come from everywhere at once, flickering on and off, making everybody appear to be moving in slow motion.

A large crowd of people were dancing without even touching each other. She observed their clothing and was surprised that people dressed like that were allowed into a club like this. Nobody at all had a suit jacket or tie on, and many of the young women wore tiny skirts well up above the knee, and almost nothing to cover their torso and cleavage;

she was taken aback at the amount of flesh on display. She sat at the bar, perching herself gracefully on a stool and crossing her legs seductively.

Almost instantly a good-looking young man appeared by her side, muscles bulging through his tight shirt and faded blue jeans. He had a head of thick brown hair and a warm demeanor. He was the type of specimen she usually liked to devour in the bedroom when she was in the mood. But she was looking for a man tonight, not a boy. A mature gentleman with wealth and experience, class and taste.

"Wow, you're like…totally beautiful!"

Lillian smiled at him, knowing he could only be in his early twenties. "Well, thank you for the compliment; you have a lovely night, sweetheart."

His face dropped. He had been shot down…elegantly, but still shot down. He slinked away to the dance floor and was soon caught up with a small crowd, all dancing to the strange music, which sounded bizarre to Lillian. It was very fast, with a constant heavy drumbeat that never seemed to change, and strangely there were hardly any lyrics, almost just an endless sound without words, yet many people were dancing to it happily.

The bartender approached her. "Can I get you a drink, Miss?"

"I'll have a Manhattan, please."

"Coming right up." He got busy making the drink. Lillian hoped the recipe had not changed over the years. The Manhattan had been her drink of choice since she was eighteen years old. The first film director she had ever slept with had bought her one in a cocktail bar. It had struck her as a little strong at first, but then there had been no other drink she desired more. She loved good champagne and fine wine, but the bittersweet aftertaste and gentle burn of the rye whiskey in a Manhattan had hooked her on the first sip.

She casually glanced over to her right and saw at least a dozen young men staring at her, eyes ablaze with hope. The bartender set the drink down before her on a coaster. He had added a small umbrella and straw, and even the trademark cherry sitting at the bottom of the glass.

Lillian picked up the glass, her perfect long nails glistening under the flashing dance-floor lights. She took a small sip. Memories flooded back as the sweet liquid swirled across her tongue. She remembered the old days, when she was a sweet young girl with hope in her heart and stars in her eyes. She recalled her old group of friends: names, faces, and all the parties and the fun they'd had—and all the gorgeous men and women she had bedded.

Here's to my new life, to the new Lillian Kelly. She drained the glass.

She set it down on the bar and opened her eyes, with the bartender watching her.

"How was it, Miss?"

"Perfect."

He grinned. Another young man appeared abruptly by her side, this one short and stocky; clad in black leather, tattoos covered most of his arms. Lillian stared bemused at a row of silver studs across his bottom lip. He had multiple rings through his nose and even tattoos on his neck. "Can I buy you another one?" He asked.

"I haven't paid for the first one yet."

"It's on the house, Miss," the bartender said.

"Thank you, sweetheart."

The pierced young man piped up again, "So, how 'bout it, gorgeous?" His voice and manner irritated Lillian.

"I'm fine. Thank you for offering."

"Oh, come on, don't be like that. A smoking hot lady like you walks into a club like this, and you're trying to tell me you're not after some action?" He leaned in close to Lillian's face and placed a hand on her back. The seed of anger fired in her belly. This intrusive boy had not taken her hint, and he was now invading her personal space, even touching her.

In her first life, Lillian had learned how to deal with unwanted attention efficiently, and many an overly confident and brazen young man had been quickly sent scurrying away red-faced after a vicious tongue-lashing from her. Lillian had been a movie star once, albeit not a very big one, but nonetheless she had been famous at a time when there was strong respect and admiration for screen sirens, and she was not amused by this intrusion now.

"Remove your hand from me right now." Her tone was pure ice.

"Oh, come on, babe. Let's cut the bullshit, huh? I got an apartment two blocks from here. How 'bout we take the party back to my place? I'll give you the fuck of your lifetime..." He leaned in to kiss her neck.

Anger flooded Lillian's veins. Her ice-blue eyes glazed over as her right hand flew up in a blindingly fast motion.

Her palm slammed hard against his right cheek with a crack like a starter's pistol, and the force of it sent him two steps sideways. He stood there holding his face, staring stunned at Lillian, who sat coolly on her chair, glaring straight back at him. And something told him not to bother this woman any further.

"Fuck you, skank!" he hissed with a filthy look, and stormed out of the club.

Lillian looked at the bartender, who smiled back at her in respect.

"He's a jerk, that guy. He's always hassling girls in this place. Good work, Miss. That was really something."

Lillian laughed. "Perhaps he will think twice before he puts his hands on a lady without asking her permission again."

"I dare say he will," the bartender agreed. "Miss, if you don't mind me asking, why did you come here tonight? I mean, don't get me wrong, beautiful women are always welcome here. It's just…you're really quite breathtaking, and the way you're dressed—we just don't usually get ladies like you in this place, that's all."

"Well thank you for the compliment. I am new to town. Exactly which clubs would you expect a lady like me to go to around here?"

"Well, straight up, I'd have to say the Star Tower Hotel. It's not far away from here. It's a really classy place. Lots of rich and famous people go there, you know. I just thought it's the kind of place that would really suit a lady like you, that's all."

Lillian gave him a genuine smile; it was good to know there were still gentleman around.

He went on. "And you've also got the Cracked Chandelier just a few doors down. That place is really nice, way posh, you know."

Actually, Lillian *didn't* know, but she found the way he spoke amusing. "And then there's the Ming Vase too. It's very nice. Again, classy people, big-dollar crowd. I'm gonna hate seeing you leave, but I really think those places are much more your style, Miss."

"Well, you really are quite the gentleman. And thank you for the drink."

"My pleasure."

Lillian stood and made her way past the doorman.

"Have a good evening, Miss."

She headed to the sidewalk. Dozens of cabs were cruising up and down the boulevard. She had barely raised her hand when one pulled in to the curb before her. She climbed inside.

"The Ming Vase, please."

The crowds were growing thicker on the sidewalks, and limousines were cruising up and down as the cab made its way along the street.

CHAPTER 17

NEEDLE IN A HAYSTACK

Back at the hotel, Carlo and Sebastian were finishing their drinks. Two young girls had recognized Carlo and were doing their utmost to gain his attention. One had even scrawled her number on a napkin in lipstick. Carlo was not interested; he wanted to go home.

He slipped on his black leather jacket, bid the disappointed ladies goodnight, and left with Sebastian in tow.

"You seriously didn't want to take any of them home?"

Carlo shook his head. "Not tonight, my friend."

"Okay, I just thought it might take your mind off things."

Carlo chuckled.

"You want a ride home in the limo?"

"Sure, boss."

They climbed into the car and headed down the boulevard as Carlo stared disinterestedly at the crowds on the sidewalk. Traffic in the oncoming lane was moving quickly. He turned to his right and gazed into a cab as it passed them, catching a glimpse of long blonde hair and the side of a woman's face.

It hit him like a thunderbolt. His eyes widened, pumped with adrenaline.

"*Lillian!*" he yelled, startling everybody in the car.

"Jesus!" Sebastian exclaimed. "You scared the shit out of me."

"Stop the car now!"

"Sir, I'm in the middle of the road. I can't…" the driver stammered, slowing the vehicle's speed.

Carlo didn't wait for the rest of the sentence. He exited the car, slamming the door behind him while it was still moving, catching his footing on the road.

Sebastian watched him, dumbfounded. Then he, too, leaped out of the car. Carlo was weaving through the traffic like a madman.

"Carlo!" he cried. Carlo didn't even slow down.

Sebastian ran after him, dodging pedestrians and trying to spot Carlo through the crowd. And then there he was, standing perfectly still, staring down the road.

"Carlo!" Sebastian yelled as he approached him. He placed a hand on Carlo's shoulder. Carlo turned to him, his eyes wide.

"It was her…it was Lillian."

"Really? Where?"

"In a cab, I lost sight of the damned thing."

"Are you sure it was her?"

"I know it was. She must be going to one of the clubs or restaurants along the boulevard. I've got to find her."

"She could be in any of these places, Carlo."

Carlo turned to him, eyes burning with adrenaline and determination.

"Then I best get started right away. You go home. I'm fine."

Sebastian knew how hard Carlo had fallen for this woman. He slapped a hand on his shoulder.

"Teamwork my friend, teamwork. Let's get looking."

The two men began searching every club, bar, and restaurant along Hollywood Boulevard.

* * *

Lillian's cab swung into the curb outside the club. She opened her purse to take out some cash, but the driver waved his hand and shook his head. "No charge, Miss."

"Thank you, sweetheart." She stepped out and looked up at the building, feeling perhaps she recognized it from long ago. She made her way to the entrance and stepped through as the glass doors slid open. A doorman in uniform greeted her.

He led Lillian down a wide, lavishly decorated corridor. Muffled music thumped through the walls. Smoked glass doors slid open to reveal an impressive outdoor area with plenty of people mingling and drinking. The crowd was aged from their late twenties to forties and over, and the people were considerably better dressed than in the last club she had visited. She made her way to a leather sofa and sat down. A quick glance around the room assured her she had already gained the attention of several men. This was far more her style. Well-dressed men in expensive suits sipping wine and champagne. Yes, this was a place where she should be able to find exactly what she needed. She ordered a Manhattan from a waiter and settled into her seat.

* * *

Carlo and Sebastian had been in and out of a dozen clubs and bars. They had also been staring into restaurant windows, scouring the diners, with no luck. Carlo leaned against a wall, his brow creased with helpless frustration. He looked across the road at the Ming Vase, then shot a glance at Sebastian.

"Why not? Lucky last."

They entered the club. It was crowded, and Carlo's blazing dark eyes swept the area carefully. Sebastian followed him, moving like a stalking assassin through the crowd, around the dance floor and out into the open seating areas with the black leather sofas. Carlo scanned the area, eyes dimming with defeat, until he turned to his right and froze, his gaze fixed across the floor. There she was: Lillian. It struck him again just how gorgeous the woman was. An energy buzzed around her like a golden aura. She was a goddess.

She was wearing a long sleek burgundy dress and looked incredible in it. Four well-dressed men were seated around her. Carlo could see she had the full attention of each of them as she spoke. He broke into movement and ambled forward until he stood right before Lillian. He said nothing; he just smiled down at her incredulously.

Lillian had been in the middle of telling her life story when she looked up and saw the intensely attractive tall man looking down at her. He was dressed completely in black, and everything about him oozed class. Immediately, she sensed a distant rumble from inside her. His presence had stirred the mortal hidden deep within her. Lillian's eyes locked with

Carlo's, and it was as if nothing else existed for a moment. The hopeful contenders seated around her exchanged puzzled looks. Two simply got up and left to pursue other quarry, while the remaining two became more aware by the second they had been outclassed by the impressive dark-haired man who clearly had the stunning blonde momentarily spellbound.

The rumbling inside her grew, stretching out like fine inky tentacles. There was something about this man she recognized instantly.

Fragments flicked through her mind, like thousands of dots that needed connecting, and seconds later she knew that the mortal had met and made love to this man in the first transformation. There was solid recognition in his eyes. *Yes, you know this man. You shared my body with him, didn't you?* And she could tell by the look in Carlo's eyes it had made quite an impact on him. Carlo stepped in close to her and extended his hand. Lillian took it and stood, her face inches from his. She was impressed. Something about this man had affected the mortal deeply. *You chose well*, she thought with an approving smile.

"Lillian." Carlo kissed her hand. "I thought I'd never see you again. May I sit with you?"

"Of course." The remaining two men exchanged a look of amused defeat. They got up and left Lillian and Carlo to whatever strange energy was crackling between them. Sebastian watched, amused at how happy Carlo looked to be reunited with Lillian.

Carlo gazed into her eyes. "When you vanished, I was hoping you'd call me or…something. I woke up and you were just gone. I felt such a fool, I never got your number after we met…Lillian, I asked around town. I'm very well-known and connected, but nobody seemed to have a clue who you are."

Lillian felt this coming. She was a master of lies and excuses, and she had already realized she would need to tap into the consciousness of the mortal within, the pathetic creature who could only have *dreamed* of receiving attention from a man like this in her real body. Already she had begun to allow Helen to peer out from the depths, to tap into her thoughts; she needed to extract Helen's memories of this man, and already it was working. From far down inside her, Lillian sensed Helen's excitement and passion for this man, but she would not be enjoying him again—not ever.

She sensed Helen had learned about her past. Not much, but enough to tell others her background. She was correct, and with a few more lies of her own and some seductive persuasion, she would have this man eating out of her hand.

"Oh, darling," she purred. "I'm sorry about that, really. I'm so very happy to see you again."

Carlo lit up. "Really? Oh, that's wonderful. I thought…I mean…after that night we had. I thought it was special. I just felt it was right somehow."

"It *was* right, but I am not long out of a horrible relationship with my last partner, so I guess I just fled in fear of the commitment. I am so sorry, but it was a very special night for me too. I really missed you."

Her words were like music to Carlo's ears.

"He treated you badly, didn't he, Lillian?" Carlo's eyes were filled with genuine concern. Lillian knew in a heartbeat he was in love with her, or at least very close to it.

"Yes, he did. He was possessive and cruel. He is a rich and intimidating man, and that is why I had to leave New York. It is the reason I have decided not to tell people my last name. He is very jealous, and I just know he would have people searching for me."

Carlo was horrified at the thought of losing Lillian. At that moment, he wanted nothing but to look after her, to protect her. He stroked his hand gently down her cheek.

Sebastian cleared his throat.

"Oh, forgive me, you've met Sebastian," Carlo said.

"Wonderful to see you again, Lillian," Sebastian said, kissing her hand.

"You too, darling." There was something distantly familiar about him.

"Should I get some drinks, Carlo?" Sebastian asked.

"That'd be great. A bottle of their best champagne. Put it on my tab."

So that is his name: Carlo. It suited him perfectly, and he had just ordered some very expensive champagne. Lillian was liking this man, and fast. She looked him up and down again. The clothes were definitely expensive, most likely tailor-made. Italian shoes, upmarket cologne, superb grooming, and to top it off, a diamond-studded watch. Yes, she was liking Carlo very much indeed.

A young man in a suit approached them. He abruptly extended his hand to Carlo, who looked slightly annoyed. "Mr. Genisi, I'm really sorry to disturb you. I'm an actor, and I just wanted to quickly introduce myself to you and say that you are a fantastic filmmaker, and it would be an honor to audition for…"

Carlo cut him off quickly with a brief handshake and a firm glance. "Thank you. If you go to the Vonhampton website you'll see where to submit your details and photos to the casting team, okay?"

The young man nodded. "Yes, sir, thank you. Have a lovely evening."

It was another young unknown actor vying for his attention. Carlo didn't begrudge them for being assertive, but at times it got to be too much, and this was not a good time. His prayers had been answered; he had found Lillian, and she was impressed. Carlo was clearly a somebody in this town, but how wealthy was he? She needed a place to live, and not just any place, a place like she had been used to back in her Hollywood days. She couldn't possibly live in the stuffy little cottage the mortal dwelled in. She would see what Carlo was worth and take it from there.

Sebastian returned with a waiter carrying a silver bucket of champagne and another gentleman beside him. Sebastian smirked and raised his eyebrows. The other man looked at Carlo and Lillian. "Mr. Genisi, a pleasure to have you in the club, sir. Please enjoy this. It's our finest champagne, and it's on the house. I'm looking forward to seeing your new movie when it's released."

Carlo smiled. "Thank you. This is a beautiful club, and I'll certainly be considering it for the wrap party after the film's finished."

The manager beamed at his response.

"I'm pleased to hear that, sir. Enjoy the rest of your night." He turned and left, and the waiter poured everybody a glass.

Lillian was again impressed.

Sebastian gulped down a glass but could see he would be a third wheel tonight. "I best head off too. Christina will be wondering where I am. She'll be very pleased to catch up with you again, Lillian."

"I look forward to it."

They said their goodbyes, and Carlo and Lillian were left alone on the sofa, sipping champagne, and there was nowhere in the world Carlo would rather have been. Like so many other men before him, he was mesmerized by Lillian. At her prompting, he soon told her everything about himself: his family, his school days, growing up in America, his dream to be a filmmaker since he was a boy, everything. He wanted her to know who he really was as a person. Over the next two hours, Carlo and Lillian had exchanged their dreams, hopes, ambitions, and even their funniest stories.

Lillian had told Carlo she had only some recollection of their night together, as she had been taking strong medication to help her sleep, and she found it was affecting her memory. She explained that her relationship with her ex in New York had made her fret terribly. But she made it clear to him that she remembered the fantastic lovemaking—that much she had recollected from Helen's memories.

Carlo swelled with pride. She went on to tell him that she had even almost taken a cab to try find his home, to see him again, but she had been worried he might have been angry with her for disappearing on him. She told Carlo she hadn't realized he was such a well-known director, or she would have been able to find him easily. She felt a fool now, she told him.

Carlo had heard everything he wanted to hear. Everything Lillian said made sense. All that mattered to him was that she'd wanted to find him. He was thrilled.

She explained that he couldn't find her because since she had fled New York she had been using an alias for a surname. Lillian carefully used fragments and snippets from Helen's recollections to pick and piece her way through the entire conversation. She had used her skill as an actress to play Carlo like a violin, and it worked.

"I would love you to come stay the night at my place, Lillian. You could have your own room, if you wish. However you prefer it. My home is your home. You are welcome to stay as long as you like. Or I could just have my driver take you to your place. Are you happy where you are staying now? Is it a hotel?"

Lillian's mind flashed back to Helen's little cottage. She turned her nose up in disgust at the thought of spending a night there. "I would love to come see your house again. I am not very happy where I am. It is really not suitable for me."

Carlo was extremely pleased. He could think of nothing better than Lillian staying at his house, but he would not rush her. He would be very careful and take his time, but surely once she got there, he would have a very good chance of talking her into staying.

"So you'll come?"

"I would love to."

Carlo kissed her cheek in satisfaction. "But please, before anything else, you must give me your cell phone number." He laughed. "I couldn't bear to lose you again."

Lillian felt a tiny tremor of panic, but it all made sense now. *Cell phone. So that's what they called them.* She had seen people using them everywhere, but she had no idea how to use one. "Of course. It's just that…it's a brand-new number; I just can't think of it right now." The harsh reality of her situation hit her again; she had much catching up to do with modern technology. She was also aware of the fact that eventually questions would be asked, and she had no proof of her existence at all. No identity, nothing. But Lillian knew these were just technicalities. Her first life had taught her money bought anything, legal or illegal, and quite often sex did too, so soon enough she would completely reinvent herself and learn all she needed to.

"Never mind, I'll get it off you later, but until I do, I'm not letting you out of my sight," said Carlo, warning her playfully. He escorted her out of the club to his limo. They were soon on their way to his mansion. He played tour guide for Lillian on the drive home, pointing out landmarks and briefing her on the history of Hollywood and LA. Lillian couldn't help but feel amused.

If only he knew. She had been here, back in the early days of this town, so many years before he had even been born. She had made a mark here and carved her own path. And now that she was back, she planned on staying.

CHAPTER 18

HOME SWEET HOME

As the car wound its way up high into the hills, Lillian recognized more along the way: a street here, a mansion there, from so long ago. Soon they pulled into Carlo's estate. The long palm tree–lined driveway was breathtaking, and Lillian stared as the mansion came into view. It was impressive—very—even in Beverly Hills.

They pulled up to the entrance, and Carlo helped her out, then bid his driver goodnight. He took Lillian's hand and led her up the stairs to the gleaming double front doors. "I almost forgot how magnificent your home is, Carlo."

"Thank you." He opened the doors and led her inside. Lillian's eyes gleamed. This house was incredible. Deep inside her, Helen stirred with recognition.

Yes, you were here with him, I know, but it's my turn now.

She extinguished Helen's presence and walked with Carlo across the marble tiles, through the huge living area and into another enormous room, with a large pool table and antique furniture. Carlo stepped behind a wood-paneled bar in the corner of the room and selected a bottle of wine. May I pour you a drink?"

"Oh, Carlo. Really, it's not necessary."

"I insist. I'm so happy to have you back here in my home."

"Well, then how could I refuse?"

He opened the bottle with an experienced hand. He poured two small glasses, handed one to her, and they clinked them.

"To finding each other," Carlo said.

"Indeed."

They sipped their drinks, and Carlo placed an arm around her. "Please let me show you the entire house this time, Lillian."

Together they strolled through all three levels of Carlo's mansion. Lillian could not have been more pleased. It was opulent luxury, situated high above Los Angeles and nestled among the most elite real estate and the power players of Hollywood, the wealthy and the famous. It was exactly what she wanted, and she knew she had Carlo wrapped around her little finger.

She was surprised the mortal had managed to snare such a big fish in just the first transformation. Men like Carlo usually took a bit of looking for. The mortal had just gotten lucky, that was all, and now Lillian would enjoy the spoils.

It was the early hours now, and the two of them were snuggled on a lounge on the top-level balcony, gazing down at the view.

Carlo kissed her neck softly, "How about I carry you to my bedroom?"

Lillian knew very well not to give in too fast with men like Carlo. Oh yes, he was a gentleman, that she knew, but she also knew you had to keep them begging, or they soon owned you with their wealth and status. A smart woman made them wait. She wanted to live in this house, that was for certain, but she would have it her way.

"It is a lovely offer, Carlo, and I know we have been together before, but that was very out of the ordinary for me, that night. You see, I really have not been with many men in my life. I am very fond of you, though." She looked down, away from his gaze, with perfect feigned innocence. "If you want us to see each other, well, maybe we should just take it a little slowly this time. I am really an old-fashioned kind of girl."

Carlo was disappointed but happy at the same time; he believed every word that came out of Lillian's mouth.

And he now felt a solid respect for her. He wanted her even more. He had known since the second he saw her she was nothing but pure elegance…beauty and class. Looking deeply into those blue eyes, he knew he was in love.

"Of course. I understand."

"Oh, Carlo. That is so wonderful. I need to take things slow as I have just come out of that horrid relationship; I need to have trust in a man again." She stroked his cheek. "Will you give me that trust, Carlo? Will you?"

Carlo melted. She had touched his soul. He decided he would mend this fallen angel. He would gently sew her silver wings back on and fill the cracks in her heart with pure love and affection, and anything she wanted, *anything*—he would give her.

"I swear you can trust me, Lillian. I promise you." He kissed her hand and hugged her. "I will look after you. Why don't you stay the night in one of the guest rooms? It will have everything you need."

She kissed him gently on his lips. "Thank you. Now I think I need some sleep."

"Of course. I'll show you to your room."

Carlo led her to a grand bedroom and opened the door for her. "I'm so happy I found you again."

"As am I, darling," she whispered back.

He kissed her goodnight. "See you in the morning." He closed the door.

Lillian looked around at the large, luxurious room. She slipped off her heels and dress, then stood before a large full-length mirror and admired herself. She opened Helen's handbag and unwrapped her perfume bottle. She sprayed a heavy dose of it across her neckline, breathing it in. She glowed with satisfaction, feeling it once again renewing her beauty. Youth—there was nothing in the world like pure, genuine youth. In these modern times, skilled surgeons could achieve some amazing results with their scalpels and high-tech procedures, "turning back the clock," as they say, but nothing compared with genuine pristine youth. It was a magical thing granted to every human being only for a limited period in their lifetime, and once gone, it could never be retrieved. But as long as she kept sacrificing innocents and applying her perfume, eternal youth was hers forever; it was the ultimate gift. She stepped out onto the balcony, naked. She looked down at the vast, twinkling lights of Los Angeles, and to her left, high on the mountain in the distance, was the Hollywood Sign. With a tone of pure satisfaction, Lillian spoke to it.

"Hello, Hollywood. I'm back."

* * *

Tension etched its way into Karson's face as he furrowed his brow behind his desk. The mayor had been leaning on the chief of police for results on the murder of the young model in Peter Jameson's apartment. The media had nearly hyped it up into a high-profile case. So far, he had little to show, only a grainy bit of footage from a nightclub.

The police chief had snorted at him in disgust. "That's it? This is all you've got? A first name and a shitty picture of some blonde? You can't even see her face properly. There's a million of them in this town. Find me *something*."

Karson was irritated; he wasn't used to taking abuse from anybody, especially about his work. And he had always kept a good relationship with his superiors. He always got results, and fast. He needed a new plan of attack to track down this mystery blonde; he'd interviewed everybody else at the party that night, but nobody had stirred his gut instinct.

Nobody, that was, except the elusive blonde named Lillian.

CHAPTER 19

HOOK, LINE, AND SINKER

Fine silk sheets lay delicately over the naked body lying on the bed. Lillian opened her eyes and looked around the room, again impressed. Above her was a carved wood-paneled ceiling from which hung two large, sparkling chandeliers. On the opposite side of the room was an antique dresser adorned with a large mirror and matching chair, and on the dresser sat an old-style ornate grooming set with a silver hairbrush and matching handheld mirror.

A chilling twinge of sudden panic struck her as she quickly slid her hand under her pillow. The panic was replaced with a warm glow as her fingers touched the perfume bottle, still laying where she had placed it. Yawning, she sat up and rose off the bed, slowly unraveling to her full height, like a statue of perfection coming to life. A clock on the wall showed half past eight. She stepped before the mirror, admiring herself as the morning sunlight glowed through the flowing white drapes. This body that men the world over lusted after was hers again, and for good this time. Carlo, she knew, was completely smitten.

After a hot shower she pulled a bathrobe from the wardrobe and slipped it on. She then brushed her long, thick golden locks.

There was a gentle knock at the door. She opened it to reveal Carlo, dressed in a pair of jeans and a sporty white jacket.

"Good morning. Did you sleep well?"

"I did." She put her arms around him and kissed him. Carlo beamed at her.

"I have never seen anybody make a simple robe look so spectacular."

"Oh, you're too kind, my dear man. I have nothing to wear but my dress from last night anyway."

"We'll soon take care of that. But first, please join me for breakfast."

Carlo led her downstairs to the kitchen, where a petite woman in a spotless white dress and apron was cooking. The aroma of freshly toasted bread wafted in the air.

"Lillian, this is Paulina, my housekeeper. Paulina, meet Lillian." Lillian sensed immediately Carlo was very fond of this little woman. She turned and bowed her head politely, the morning sunlight highlighting the fine whispers of silver laced through her dark hair, which was pulled up tight into a bun. A silver crucifix dangled at the base of her neck.

"Hello, Miss Lillian." She spoke in a strong Hispanic accent.

"Hello," Lillian replied.

"Pleasure to meet you, ma'am," Paulina added, gesturing to the balcony. "Mr. Carlo, breakfast is ready."

Outside on a perfectly set table was an assortment of fruit on a heavy silver tray. A large coffee pot sat next to a platter of bacon and scrambled eggs, flanked by solid silver cutlery. Paulina pulled a chair out for Lillian, who thanked her and sat down, marveling at the splendid sight on the table. Carlo sat down opposite her.

"Juice or coffee, Miss Lillian?"

"Coffee, please." Paulina poured her a mug of rich, freshly ground coffee. She could see Carlo lived like a king, and why shouldn't he? He obviously had the money to do so, and he clearly loved indulging in the finer things.

Carlo helped himself to a good portion of bacon and eggs and chatted with Lillian about the film he was making. He was passionate about his work. He told Lillian he wanted to become one of the biggest directors in America; clearly, he was very proud of what he did. Lillian was impressed at his determination, and it appeared he was well on his way to achieving his goals.

"I've got to leave now to go on set—we start shooting some action scenes today. I'd still love you to appear in the film, or perhaps even in my next project. I wondered if you would like to play an extra. There are some scenes coming up in the next few days with no dialog; you'd simply be a beautiful woman from Beverly Hills, shopping on Rodeo Drive. What do you think? I'd so love to get you on camera, darling. I'm sure you'd have a great time."

An extra. Lillian felt a tinge of disgust at the word. Well, she may have been a professional actress in her first life, but now she was nobody. She would have to start somewhere.

"Well, I did do some parts in high-school plays and enjoyed the experience. But I must say, I'm worried about my ex-partner seeing the movie, or even hearing about it. I'm fearful of him tracking me down."

Her fear of this man truly bothered Carlo. He leaned over to her. "Lillian, I know we don't know each other very well, but I don't care. I want you to stay here in my home with me. You could come and go as you please; I just I don't want you to disappear on me again. And this ex-partner of yours—I don't care who he is or how much money he has. Believe me, I'm well connected. If he rears his head and gives you even an ounce of trouble, he will be dealt with. Nobody harasses friends of mine, I promise you that. So if that's what's making you reluctant about appearing in my film, forget it; you don't need to live in hiding anymore. Why not just appear in the film? It will be like starting your new life. I'll see to it that you are treated like a star."

Lillian glowed at the word "star." She had been used to star treatment at the peak of her fame decades ago, when her horror films filled the cinemas. She still felt repulsion at the word "extra," though, knowing it was the word used for unknown, and usually untrained, actors. Clearly, the word had not changed over the decades. She knew an extra was just background fill-in, cannon fodder on a film set. But she was smart enough to know that times had changed and technology had advanced greatly. It would be a no-pressure way to learn her way around a modern-day film set and adjust to the way things were done nowadays.

"Well, I must say, my current lodgings are certainly not ideal. Compared to your home, Carlo, it's like a cabin in the woods. It's a very nice offer, and yes, I will stay here, and I do want to keep seeing you. I really feel something very special for you."

Carlo stroked her arm.

She continued. "But I just couldn't intrude. I can't even pay my way. My ex-partner has frozen all my accounts. All I have to my name is only have a few hundred dollars and a small suitcase with some clothes. He frightens me, Carlo. I left so quickly…I have practically nothing."

Carlo was touched, deeply. He simply couldn't fathom how any man could have treated a woman like Lillian so terribly. He took both of her hands.

"Lillian, I want you here. You will not need money; you won't need anything at all. You'll be very well looked after. It will be an honor to have you." He kissed her. "So it's settled, you're staying."

"Yes, I am."

"Fantastic. We're going to have a marvelous time." His cell phone rang, "Excuse me, darling." He stepped away from the table and began speaking to somebody about filming.

Lillian beamed with satisfaction. *Oh, how I am going to enjoy living in this house.* Carlo finished his call.

"I'm so sorry; something has come up and I need to leave fast. I'll send an assistant for you to get your things from where you're staying. Today I insist you go shopping and buy anything you need—*anything*. Buy yourself a whole new wardrobe, shoes, clothes, whatever you like. It'll all be taken care of."

Lillian stood and hugged him. "How can you be so generous to me?"

"Think nothing of it, and forget all about that man in New York. You have me now." He kissed her, then grabbed his car keys and left.

Lillian sat down to continue her breakfast. Moments later she heard a deep rumbling and looked down to see Carlo's gleaming red, high-powered sports car prowling slowly out from the garage under the house and down the long driveway to the street. She turned to see Paulina smiling at her.

"Mr. Carlo likes you very much. I can tell."

Lillian looked away. Mingling with the hired help had never really been her thing.

After breakfast, Lillian freshened up, then slipped on her dress and stilettos. She took the perfume bottle from the drawer, pointed it at her lower neck, and squeezed a layer of the cool red liquid across her skin. Then she went downstairs and waited. The limousine soon arrived and out stepped Morgan, a pretty young brunette who introduced herself politely. Morgan seemed very nice and organized, and she assured Lillian she would cater to her every need, and that they were going to have a fabulous day. She even handed Lillian an envelope from Carlo with two thousand dollars inside it, explaining Carlo wanted her to carry some cash for emergencies.

In a short time they arrived at Helen's home. Lillian opened the front door, sneering in disgust. How glad she would be to never see this pokey little dump again. She walked to Helen's bedroom and applied some makeup. She then took the only thing she really wanted…the silver dress. She had always been fond of it. It was the only thing she really cared about from her first life, apart from the perfume bottle, of course. She had no interest in taking the jewelry box and was happy to leave it there. She headed to the living room and was about to leave when a movement caught her eye. It was Shadow, perched high atop the bookshelf, meekly peering down at her. He had run out of food and his water was almost gone. He was too frightened to meow at the stranger. She snorted at him; she'd never liked animals, and at least now she wouldn't have to see the wretched little creature again. She pulled the door shut behind her and climbed back into the limousine, eager to spend plenty of Carlo's money.

* * *

On location at Rodeo Drive, Carlo was preparing to begin filming a foot-chase scene along the sidewalk. The lead actress, Chasey Wells, was to be pursued by a deranged killer who was stalking her from a dark sedan. She was to run along the strip of boutique stores and seek refuge inside one of them. It was a big scene to shoot, and lots of excited tourists and paparazzi crowded along the barriers, hoping to get a look at the stars. Carlo was in a great mood, no longer moping around like a lost puppy. He thought he had lost Lillian forever, but good fortune had come his way, and he had *found* her. And she was moving in with him! *Things just couldn't get any better.* Sebastian noticed how happy he seemed.

"Somebody looks like he's won the lottery."

"That'll be enough from you." Carlo laughed.

"Seriously, it's great to see that smile back on your dial again. How's Lillian?"

"I've got Morgan looking after her; they're going out shopping today."

Carlo said, "I have a feeling you're going to be seeing a lot more of her."

"Well, for the moment it looks like she's going to be staying with me. I'm very happy about it; I feel like I've known her for a long time. I know it sounds crazy, but I just do."

"Go with that feeling then. Life's short; just let it roll."

Carlo chuckled. "Yes, I will let it roll indeed. I've even asked Lillian to be an extra in the shop scene, and she's agreed."

"Great idea. She sure is a drop-dead gorgeous lady."

"Yes, that she is. Okay, let's get this movie made."

CHAPTER 20

RODEO DRIVE

The limousine dropped them off in the heart of the exclusive Golden Triangle in Beverly Hills. Soon Lillian was having a wonderful time browsing and trying on designer clothes at the high-end stores on Rodeo Drive. Morgan was proving very useful. Although Lillian had been paying close attention to what other women were wearing, Morgan was a godsend, having worked extensively in clothing and costume design for movies. At first, Lillian was shocked at the prices; it amazed her what people paid for clothes. Morgan had mistaken her reaction as concern about spending too much and assured her Carlo wanted her to spare no expense—and that Carlo's credit card was gold platinum. Lillian wasn't sure, but assumed this meant the owner was worth a lot of money. She could recall some people using these new "credit cards" back in the late fifties, but the world had mostly operated on cash then.

As Lillian stepped out of the changing room in a sleek, red strapless dress, Morgan and two sales assistants gasped.

"Oh, Lillian, that fits you like a glove," Morgan remarked.

"Yes, it really does look marvelous on you," the senior assistant agreed.

Lillian was having a ball. Already, she had bought four pairs of shoes, a black leather coat, and a brown suede one, two hats, a handbag, and six dresses. And the day was still young. She had even bought herself a wallet to carry the cash Carlo had given her.

"I love it too, so I suppose I'll have to take it."

"Carlo's orders," Morgan giggled.

At many stores Lillian tried on dozens more dresses of all types, from formal gowns to casual and evening wear. By the time she and Morgan decided to take a break, the chauffeur had almost filled the large trunk with dozens of designer-label bags.

They took a break at a coffee shop; it had been a fantastic day, and it wasn't over yet.

"Wow, you've done so well, Lillian. You have impeccable taste in clothing."

"Oh, thank you, dear. I will certainly be telling Carlo how helpful you were today."

Morgan blushed.

Lillian could see that, like most people, Morgan was affected by her beauty and charisma, and the young woman had been seeking her approval.

"Thank you. You're so lucky. Carlo is such a lovely man. You're the envy of every woman in LA."

"Yes, he's quite wonderful," Lillian agreed.

A suave-looking man in a sharp suit approached their table and placed a business card in front of Lillian.

"I'm sorry to intrude, but I noticed you don't have a ring on the finger that counts, and I'd kick myself forever if I didn't at least come up and tell you how incredibly beautiful you are."

Lillian looked him up and down and liked what she saw.

"Thank you for the compliment, but I'm afraid I'm spoken for."

His face dropped in disappointment. "Well, whoever the lucky guy is, he best get a ring on your finger fast. Perhaps you could keep my card in case things don't work out," he added with a cheeky smile.

"I guess it never hurts to make a new friend, does it?"

"Very true," said the man. "It's been a pleasure to meet you."

"Likewise," Lillian purred. The man left.

Morgan was quietly surprised at Lillian's flirtatious response to the man and that she had accepted his card.

"You really do attract attention," she commented.

Lillian took a last sip of her coffee. Her handbag began vibrating. She stared at it, puzzled.

"I think someone's trying to call you," Morgan said.

"Oh, of course." Lillian had known the cell phone device was in the bag, but the thing had never made any real noise, just a few odd beeps, until now. She fished it out and laid it on the table, where she could clearly see the name Ashley flashing on the little screen. Lillian watched it until it stopped.

"Not someone you want to talk to?" Morgan asked.

"Oh, well, the truth is I've never really used the thing. I've just come out of an awful relationship with a man from New York, and he gave me that phone. It's only got people from his circles on it. I'm afraid I just don't want to hear from him or his associates ever again. I just want to make a new life here. It's…the first phone like that I've ever had, and I don't really know how to use it. He insisted I carried it so he could keep track of me."

"Lillian, that must have been dreadful, being in a situation like that."

"Yes, it was most unpleasant. I couldn't have any friends, and I couldn't go anywhere I wanted to go on my own. He was possessive and controlling. I was frightened of him. I always felt I was being watched. I knew I had to leave and just get away from him, so when he went on his last business trip to Europe, I fled here to LA."

"You're so brave to just leave like that. I'm so happy you did, and now you've met Carlo. I have a feeling you two are going to be great for each other."

"Thank you, darling."

Morgan pointed at the phone's screen. "You're almost out of battery too. Hey, I know, let's get you a new cell phone. You'll have a new number, and the only thing you're going to put in it is new friends. How 'bout it?"

"I think it's a good idea, but you know I'm just terrible with phones. I'm not technical, so I really struggle to use them."

"Oh, there's nothing to it. We'll get you a nice basic one and I'll show you how to use it. You'll be back on the air in no time."

Lillian nodded. "Okay, I think it's a good idea."

"Great, next stop: phone shop."

An attractive woman walked into the café. Her jet-black hair reached almost to her waist.

Morgan noticed Lillian watching the woman intently. "Okay, what's got your attention?"

"Oh, I was just thinking, I've been feeling like a change; perhaps after the phone store we might visit a hair salon?"

"Sure thing. In fact, I know just the place."

After buying a new phone, Morgan briefed Lillian on how to use it. Lillian was surprised at how quickly she learned, much faster than she'd expected. It amazed her how you could use these little things to call someone from practically anywhere. What a change from those big old heavy phones connected to the wall. She was also astonished at how people could simply extract cash from machines that seemed to be everywhere, without even having to walk into a bank. Oh, how things had changed. And it seemed *everything* was done on computers now—devices that had usually been reserved for science fiction films back in her first life.

Morgan made a call to Sacha's, which was close by and pretty much the most exclusive hair salon in LA. Its clientele included a dazzling array of movie stars and the super wealthy. Appointments were strictly by approval only. You usually had to book weeks in advance, or you had to be a "somebody"— or at least be very well connected to a somebody—to have your hair done here. Morgan had gotten lucky; there had been a cancelation earlier that day, and she had mentioned that a very close friend of the film director Carlo Genisi was hoping to have her hair done at the salon. Very soon after, Lillian and Morgan were greeted by Sacha himself, a celebrity in his own right. He had come to America from his native Paris as a young man, and over the years he had become *the* hair stylist to the stars. In a charming French accent, he graciously welcomed Lillian and Morgan into the lavish salon.

It was everything one would hope for from a salon that had a reputation for charging seven hundred dollars for a haircut. Lillian was at once seated in a plush leather chair and pampered with French coffee and imported Belgian chocolates on a silver tray. Morgan sat comfortably across from her, indulging in an ice-cold fruit juice served in a heavy crystal glass. Lillian looked around at the sleek salon. Even blow-dryers in this time looked like something from the future. *Well, this* is *the future.*

"And what can I do for you today, Lillian?" Sacha asked, as he ran his fingers gently through Lillian's locks.

"Well, I was thinking I would like to go darker. Much darker."

"Do you mean dark brown, or are we talking stronger?"

"I'd like you to make my hair black. Jet black."

Morgan's jaw dropped.

"Really, Lillian? Wow, to go from such beautiful blonde hair to…jet black? Gosh, are you sure?"

"Yes, I'm sure."

"Your wish is my command," Sacha promised. He set about his task as Lillian and Morgan browsed fashion magazines and chatted.

Lillian's new cell rang with a classical piano tune Morgan had programmed into it. She looked at it, surprised, as Morgan laughed.

"Go ahead, answer it," Morgan said. Lillian picked it up and could see Carlo's name flashing.

"Press the green button," Morgan reminded her.

Lillian pressed it. "Hello?"

"Hello darling, Morgan texted me your new number. I just wanted to be the first person to call you on your new cell. How is your day going so far?"

"It's been marvelous, Carlo, and Morgan has been the perfect hostess."

"I'm pleased to hear that."

"I'm now having my hair done by a wonderful gentleman named Sacha."

Sacha bowed at the compliment.

"Great, I was calling to see if you'd like to have dinner tonight downtown. There's a restaurant I like very much, and Sebastian and Christina want to catch up with you again. Would you like to go?"

"I'd love to."

"Excellent. I'll book a table. I look forward to seeing you very soon—I'm having Morgan drop you off here at the set later this afternoon."

"I can't wait to see you, Carlo."

"Me too."

Two hours later, Sacha bid a fond farewell to Lillian. She shook her hair out as she stepped onto the sidewalk. Morgan had been waiting for her outside while she changed into a new dress and shoes, and she gasped at Lillian's now gleaming black hair; the change was *devastating*. She looked completely different. Her blue eyes now stood out even more against the sleek black mane that cascaded down her back and around her shoulders. Lillian was very pleased. She had only dyed her hair black once before, for a horror film back in 1958. The movie hadn't done particularly well at the box office, but Lillian had loved her look and was loving it all over again. She was at once far less fearful of being recognized, but she knew that was a long shot anyway in this time.

"Carlo is going to get the surprise of his life," Morgan commented.

"Well, I hope he likes it."

"I'm sure he will. How 'bout we go pay him a visit on set?"

"I think that'd be nice."

* * *

Ashley sat in her apartment, slightly worried. She had left two messages for Helen about a dinner party she had invited her to that night. The venue had been changed, and she needed to make sure Helen was still okay to come, but Helen had not gotten back to her—not on Saturday and not on Sunday either. It was odd; Helen was the most reliable person she knew, which was why she basically let Helen run the shop on her own. Ashley planned to call her once more, around six. The dinner wasn't until seven-thirty, so Helen would still have plenty of time to respond before it started.

But the tiny seed of worry had been planted.

* * *

On Hollywood Boulevard, Detective Karson had just been up and down the Walk of Fame, armed with a grainy black-

and-white picture of the side of Lillian's face, mostly covered by hair. He knew it wasn't much to go on, but he was under heavy pressure to get some results. He had visited all the major clubs and bars, elite clothing stores, shoe shops—everywhere he could think of that a beautiful, classy lady with expensive tastes might frequent, but so far nobody had heard of an apparently stunning six-foot blonde named Lillian. Not even with an accurate description of the silver dress and stilettos. He had also put the word out to a few local street hoods, small-time thieves and informants, the kind who always had their ear to the ground to have some information up their sleeves to offer to the cops, hoping to bargain for leniency during their inevitable next arrest. But so far, no luck.

At first, he had considered Lillian simply a loose end, but the fact that he couldn't find her was starting to bug him. He couldn't fathom how a woman supposedly this tall and striking, who was seen by so many people at a fashion show and then at Peter Jameson's party, could simply vanish. And why had nobody ever heard of her or seen her around Hollywood before? It was as if she had simply materialized out of nowhere. His gut told him something wasn't right. He detoured off the main walk to the backstreets. He knew the homeless lived here, the ones everyone liked to call the crazies, the unfortunate and downtrodden.

Karson had always felt empathy for these souls. He knew a lot of them had come to LA hoping for fame and riches, but sadly many them only found a very tough life and a harsh dose of reality. During his years in LA, he had seen it all: murder, suicides, sex scandals. You name it, Karson had dealt with it. He had heard every story there was, especially from all the dreamers with high hopes, the ones who had stepped off the buses and planes by the hundreds every year with stars in their eyes. Mostly just regular kids from small towns, with their whole lives wrapped in a suitcase and dreaming of the big time. But the big time didn't always come; it seemed only to come to the chosen few, that tiny blessed percentage who somehow filtered through the massive machine that was Los Angeles.

Often Karson had found that with a little respect—and some cash in their hands and food in their bellies—he could extract some very useful information from the homeless. He knew they were the eyes and ears of the street, and they had provided him with many useful leads over the years.

Broken glass and old newspapers crunched under his shoes, and the stench of filth and poverty filled his nostrils, as he headed up a network of alleyways he had visited many times before. It never ceased to amaze him how many homeless people lived here, all tucked up in their cardboard boxes with raggedy old blankets and their shopping carts parked beside them filled with their meager possessions. It was a terrible way for a human being to live. And though over the years Karson himself had become as hard as the very streets he protected, he still felt for these souls.

This place was nothing like Skid Row, the notorious crime-riddled area where up to five thousand homeless were crammed at any given time; this was a far lesser-known and far less violent place, where perhaps only a few hundred older homeless folk lived, hiding in the backstreets and shadows of Hollywood. He rounded a corner, stepping around trash and bottles. Nervous eyes glanced up at him from shadowy nooks, and with good reason. Everything about Karson oozed cop; a blind man could have seen it. But he wasn't here to bust anybody.

He spied a particular shopping cart he knew well; a glittery old curtain dangled over it, and an old radio strapped to its side softly played music. An elderly woman leaned against the wall beside it, like a discarded raggedy doll in her dirty multi-colored overcoat.

Old Ethel had been living on the streets of LA for far too long. Years of sadness and hardship were etched into the deep lines on her face. Many local restaurant owners knew her by name and gave her leftovers. Nearly everyone on the street knew Ethel; she always seemed to know what was going on, and everybody talked to her. Her eyes were closed as she tapped her fingers to the music from the radio. Karson knelt next to her.

"Hello, Ethel."

The creased old eyelids fluttered open. Her soft dark-brown eyes smiled back at him in surprise. "Well hey, Mr. K. What brings you to this glamorous part of town?"

"I'm looking for a woman."

"Well it's about time; shoulda been married long time ago, handsome man like you."

Karson chuckled. "Yeah, well, married to the job, you know how it is. How've you been keeping?"

"Same old thing: finding junk here and there to trade, getting a meal for odd jobs, the usual. But you didn't come down here to ask me that, did you?"

Karson held out a photo of Lillian. "I'm looking for this woman. This picture is all I've got. It's not much, I know. Her name is Lillian, but that's all anyone seems to know about her. She's about six feet, and they say she's very beautiful and has long blonde hair down to her waist. I believe she likes to spend time here in Hollywood. I don't know if she's a high-class hooker—or anything, really—but I'm told she wears designer clothes and she likes to party…if you know what if I mean."

Ethel chuckled and raised her eyebrows. "So, what'd she do?"

"I'm not sure she's done anything yet, but I really want to talk to her. So if you see her or you hear anything, you know where to reach me. I'll make sure whoever finds me something useful is looked after, so spread the word around, would you?" Karson slipped a fifty-dollar bill into her hand.

"You know I will, Mr. K. Bless your soul."

Karson headed back to Hollywood Boulevard.

* * *

The limousine pulled up to the curb on Rodeo Drive. Carlo was about to shoot a scene as Lillian and Morgan stepped out of the car and walked to the barricades erected to keep the gawking public away from the film set. Lillian looked around. Oh, how she remembered this life. The memories came rushing back: the lighting, the cameras, the sound equipment, and the trailers. It was all here, and she couldn't wait to be a part of it again.

Carlo called for quiet on set. "Action!"

Chasey Wells scurried out of a restaurant with her cell phone to her ear, begging the police for help. Her stalker had been watching through one of the restaurant's windows and emerged from around the corner to pursue her down the street as she fled to her sports car. It was the eighth take of the scene, and Carlo was pleased with this one.

"Cut! That's a take," he yelled. "Okay, everyone, break time."

The actors and crew headed off for food and coffee. Sebastian tapped Carlo on the shoulder and pointed to Lillian and Morgan. Carlo looked over to see Morgan and a dark-haired woman standing next to her, who he suddenly realized was Lillian. He stared for a moment…and then his face broke into a huge smile as he approached her. He pushed the barricade aside and kissed her.

"Lillian, your hair…I nearly didn't recognize you."

"I was worried you wouldn't like it."

"Are you kidding? It's beautiful. You look so different. But I love it—really." Lillian leaned in and kissed him. "Thank you for today, Morgan."

"A pleasure," she replied.

"Please come with me, Lillian," said Carlo.

Lillian followed him into his set trailer. Inside, the trailer was impressive. It was air-conditioned and had everything he needed, including a fully equipped office. They sat down on a small leather lounge. Carlo stroked her hair.

"Are you sure you like it, Carlo?"

"I would like it even if you dyed it pink and blue."

Lillian giggled. "Well, I'm not about to do that."

"May I ask why you changed the color?"

"I just needed to change, reinvent myself. I want to be a new person here. And if my ex has anybody looking for me, which I truly think he does—well, I thought dark hair might help make it harder for them to spot me."

"I understand—and forget about him." He leaned over and kissed her. He was besotted by this woman. He wanted nothing but to make her happy. "How was your day? Did you get everything you need?"

"I most certainly did, thank you. I'm looking forward to showing you all the new clothes I bought…with your generosity, I might add."

He placed a hand gently on her chin and turned her face to his. "Lillian, I'm not trying to buy your affection. I just want you to be happy and be with me. It's that simple."

"I've already made my choice, Carlo, and I'm not going anywhere."

It was all he wanted to hear. *I've found her. I have found my woman, finally…and she is perfect.*

"Maybe you could wear one of your new outfits to dinner tonight?"

"That would be wonderful," she replied.

"Excellent. We're going to have a great time."

"You are so good to me, Carlo. I feel safe, and I haven't felt that way in a long time." She kissed him deeply.

"I think I can get used to this," he said.

"Perhaps you better. There's a lot more where that came from."

She knew she had this man exactly where she wanted him; he would do anything for her.

"I should let you get back to your work," she said.

"Don't forget, I want you on set tomorrow. It's your big debut."

"I'm nervous, Carlo. You'll have to tell me exactly what to do."

"There's nothing to be nervous about. Besides, you've done a little acting before, you said, in high school? So you'll be fine, darling."

"What shall I wear?"

"Wardrobe has your costume all sorted out. You just need to turn up at eleven o'clock. I'll need an early start tomorrow, but you can sleep in a little. Morgan will collect you in the limo."

"Okay. I'd like to go home now and put my new clothes away, and perhaps have a nap before dinner tonight."

"Of course. I'll have the driver take you home."

Lillian kissed Carlo again and they stepped outside.

CHAPTER 21

PLEASURES OF THE FLESH

At Carlo's mansion, the chauffeur and Paulina had already carried most of Lillian's new items into her huge bedroom. She began trying on some outfits and was soon parading in front of the mirror in a pair of black jeans so tight they looked like they had been spray-painted onto her legs. She pulled on a new pair of knee-high black leather boots and added a tight-laced black satin sleeveless top. She caught the scent of tobacco and sauntered onto the balcony, which overlooked Carlo's swimming pool. A shirtless, well-muscled young man in a pair of torn jeans and leather work boots was cutting branches that were overhanging the pool. A cigarette was clamped between his teeth. His long, dark ponytail shook wildly as he worked, and his muscles flexed as trickles of sweat ran down his back. He was no more than twenty-four, she thought. The sun was starting to set.

She felt it then, only the slightest tingle—*it's time*. She took out the perfume and sprayed a layer of it across her neck and chest, sighing with pleasure as it sank into her skin, feeling the genuine essence of her youth once again flow to her core.

She looked down at the bottle and frowned. Already, it was at the halfway mark. It held so little yet the ritual required so much blood.

This was the thing that was so difficult about it all, her cross to bear. It wasn't hard to obtain blood, but she needed a living *soul* as well.

Never mind; in time, I will simply do what needs to be done.

* * *

Carlo had just wrapped for the day, and the crew were packing up the lights and equipment. Shooting for the movie was nearing completion, and he was pleased. He was looking forward to getting home to Lillian.

Sebastian appeared beside him. "Got some great scenes today."

"Yes, it was a good day's filming."

"How 'bout a drink? There's a great little bar just up the road."

"No thanks, got to get home. But I'll have a couple with you at dinner tonight."

"You bet," Carlo laughed. "I'll see you later."

* * *

Lillian had been trying on more clothes when she stepped onto the balcony again and saw the young man who had been trimming the trees earlier, packing up his gardening equipment and puffing a cigarette. Lillian took a deep breath and slid her forefinger down her neck and between her breasts. She placed her fingertip in front of her lips and blew in his direction gently. She made the sign of the Ancient Ones and stared down at the young man. "Succumb," she whispered. Seconds later, he looked up at her and held her gaze with no fear at all, cigarette smoke billowing seductively from his nostrils. She guessed with his good looks he'd had his fair share of women and wasn't intimidated by her beauty. Lillian gestured to him with her forefinger, mimicking a cigarette to her lips. He strode across the lawn, then nimbly began climbing up a wooden trellis under the balcony. Within seconds, he was over the ledge and standing before her. He took a cigarette from the packet and handed it to her. She placed it between her lips. He stepped in close, matching her height. He leaned in further and placed the tip of his cigarette against hers and puffed hard, igniting it while she dragged on it deeply, thoroughly enjoying the electricity of this gorgeous young man's face inches from hers. She exhaled a cloud of smoke.

"Thank you," she said.

"You welcome." His accent was deep and thick.

"Where are you from?" she asked.

"Spain," he answered, holding her gaze. "I leave my country to come here, to the great America…and now I am a gardener." He laughed and so did Lillian.

His eyes were swirling pools of black. He placed his arm against the flat of her back, pulling her tight against him. Lillian gasped at the bulging muscles of his arm against her. He kissed her and tossed his cigarette on the ground. Lillian dropped hers too. He spoke no words as he led her inside by the arm and took her over to the dresser. He bent her over against it and pulled down her jeans. Within seconds she was filled with his hardness. He pulled her hair into a ponytail and yanked hard on it with each powerful thrust.

"This you like, eh?"

"Yes…yes, I like it…" Lillian grunted back. The dresser shook and banged against the wall. Lillian stared at her reflection in the mirror and that of the young man behind her, his face contorted with furious desire as sweat trickled down his muscular chest. The door swung open and Paulina walked into the room. She took two steps and froze in her tracks. Lillian glared at her with ice in her eyes. The young man hadn't noticed and continued his powerful thrusting as Paulina spun around and darted out of the room, closing the door behind her. Soon after climaxing, he sat on the bed catching his breath. Lillian pulled up her jeans and sat coolly on the stool by the dresser and began brushing her hair.

He turned to her. "Cigarette?"

"No, you can go now, the way you came," she ordered, pointing her finger at the balcony dismissively. He chuckled, then walked out to the balcony and climbed back down to the ground.

Lillian showered, slipped on a bathrobe, and went downstairs to the kitchen. Paulina was standing at the bench with her back to her, preparing food. Lillian moved silently up behind her, then spun the tiny woman around firmly by her shoulders. Paulina gasped, then stared nervously at her feet as Lillian towered over her.

"You will be far more respectful of my privacy in future," she growled. "You will never enter my bedroom again without knocking. Do I make myself clear?"

Paulina nodded quickly. "Yes, I so sorry, Miss Lillian."

Lillian quickly dragged her finger across her own neck and then lifted the little woman's chin with the same finger. Paulina stared directly up into those fierce blue eyes.

"You will not say one word to *anybody* about this. Do you understand me?"

"Yes, Miss Lillian, I sorry...I..."

"Shut up...just make sure you keep your mouth closed. You do *not* want to interfere with me. If you do, I promise you shall deeply regret it. Understood?"

Paulina nodded, terrified.

Lillian turned on her heel and headed back upstairs. The little maid stood there shaking like a leaf, almost too frightened to move, tears welling in her eyes as she made the sign of the cross. She placed her trembling fingers over the silver crucifix dangling around her neck, trying to calm herself. Almost from the moment she'd met her employer's new girlfriend, she'd had a very uncomfortable feeling about her. For some reason, this woman, Lillian...gave her the creeps.

Lillian stopped at the top of the stairs and looked down at Paulina. The tiny maid had her back to her in the far corner of the kitchen. Lillian focused her thoughts on her completely, then made the sign. "Forget," she whispered, then quickly headed back to her bedroom.

Paulina was busying herself putting dishes away, still trying to calm herself after Lillian's tongue-lashing, when a peculiar feeling struck her. It felt like a distant memory, somehow intertwined with a present thought. The sensation clouded her mind and surrounded her…like a smoky whisper from the very air itself…as light as dust on a summer breeze. It crept into her thoughts and lingered there a moment, as if conspiring with her mind against her will. For a moment, she couldn't think, couldn't focus. She shook her head and took a deep breath. She splashed chilly water onto her face and looked around the kitchen as if checking her senses were still intact. The bizarre sensation then left her. *Nerves; it was just the run-in with Lillian,* which she had not forgotten.

A little later, Carlo arrived home very happy. He'd gotten more filming done than he expected, and the most beautiful woman in the world was waiting here for him. He felt he was in for a wonderful night. He had bought a bunch of red roses for Lillian on the way home. He was greeted at the door by Paulina.

"Mr. Carlo, such lovely roses."

"Hello, Paulina. Where's Lillian?"

"Miss Lillian is upstairs, sir. Coffee, Mr. Carlo?"

"Thank you."

Carlo headed up the staircase to Lillian's room. He knocked on the door, it opened, and there stood Lillian in a figure-hugging white dress and matching stilettos. He was speechless. He held out the flowers.

"Oh, Carlo." Lillian took the roses and put her arm around him. "Roses after what you treated me to today?"

"If you are going to live with me, you best get used to it."

"Carlo, really, it's more than enough that you let me live in this beautiful house."

"Nonsense. I'll spoil you as much as I like. We'll leave for dinner at seven-thirty. Is that okay? I have some calls and emails to tend to just now."

"Sounds perfect."

He kissed her and then cocked an eyebrow. "Have you been smoking?"

"Oh, yes. A bad habit, I know. It's just a little indulgence I crave at times."

Carlo shrugged. "Okay, I'm off to take a shower. See you soon." He left and closed the door behind him.

* * *

Ashley was worried. After leaving messages on Helen's landline and cell, she still hadn't heard back from her, which was highly unusual. Darkness was falling, and she was contemplating going to Helen's house to check on her. Dinner was only two hours away, so she picked up her car keys and headed for Beachwood Canyon. The situation was niggling at her, and she knew she wouldn't have peace until she saw Helen for herself.

Ten minutes later she parked in Helen's driveway. The house was in total darkness. She knocked on the front door but got no response. Leaves and small branches were strewn across the front yard. She walked around to the side of the house and tried peering in the windows, but it was too dark to see anything through the small gaps in the drawn curtains. One of the curtains ruffled.

"Oh!" She stepped back quickly. Shadow was looking at her through the glass. "Hello, Shadow, darling."

He meowed back loudly. Ashley felt uncomfortable with this whole situation. She headed around to the backyard but saw nobody. She walked up the flight of stairs to the back deck. An empty wine glass on the outdoor table puzzled her, as Helen rarely drank or had visitors.

Looking in through the glass door she saw nothing. Shadow appeared again and began scratching at the glass. Ashley tapped on the back door, but she knew nobody was home. *This is just all very odd.* She tried the sliding door and was surprised to find it unlocked. Slowly, she stepped inside and flicked on the light.

"Hello? Helen?" Dead silence answered her.

Everything in the house felt wrong. She turned on the living room light and looked around. The quiet unnerved her. She gazed around at Helen's movie memorabilia, and though she'd seen it before, the range of it always amazed her. She didn't bother yelling out again; she knew Helen wasn't home, and the creeping tentacles of worry spread.

Shadow stood by his food bowl and meowed loudly. It was empty and his water was low.

"Oh, sweetheart, we'll fix that right away." Ashley rinsed his bowls and soon had him topped up with food and fresh water. He munched away happily as she emptied and refilled his litter tray.

She looked inside the garage, and to her surprise Helen's car was parked inside. *I don't like this at all.* In the living room, she spied a video cover of *Mistress of Evil* on Helen's coffee table.

Nothing unusual. Helen was always watching old movies. DVDs, video cassettes—you name it, Helen had the machinery to play it. Ashley headed down the hall, trying to ignore the feeling that she was intruding. But she was a longtime friend of Helen's, and she was genuinely worried about her. She almost didn't want to look in Helen's bedroom. *What if she's had a heart attack and died in bed?* She shook the thought from her mind and peered into Helen's bedroom. The bed was empty. She stepped into the bedroom relieved.

Her gaze fell on the large *Mistress of Evil* poster over Helen's bed. She recognized it from the video cover she had just seen in the living room but thought nothing more of it. She noticed a few figurines laying scattered on the floor, though, which she thought a little odd. She picked them up and placed them on the bed. She looked inside Helen's sewing room and saw the dresses Helen had been working on; they were very impressive, as usual, and were well underway. Ashley had mentioned to Helen several times over the years that she should try selling some of her dresses in the shop, but Helen had always refused. Ashley knew it was just a lack of confidence. She headed back to the living room and found Helen's notepad and pen on a table by the phone. She wrote a quick message:

Helen,

Have left messages for you on both your phones. Worried. Just fed Shadow. Please call me ASAP, honey.

Ashley x

P.S. You left the back slider open.

She left the note in the middle of the kitchen table with a salt shaker on it. Then she leaned down and stroked Shadow.

"Goodbye, lovely. Don't worry. I know your mommy isn't too far away."

He meowed softly as Ashley turned off all the lights but one, then closed the back door, trying to disregard the gnawing ache of worry in her gut.

CHAPTER 22

HOLLYWOOD NIGHTS

Lillian felt like a million dollars in the back of the limousine with Carlo. They were heading to a restaurant in downtown LA, known for its opulence and fine food. It also boasted its fair share of celebrity clientele. Carlo was in the mood for a nice meal and a relaxing drink. He had his arm around Lillian, and the two were kissing like teenagers. Carlo could not get enough of her.

As they approached downtown, Lillian looked out at the towering buildings. Oh, how long it had been since she had driven along this stretch of road at night. How she had missed the lights and excitement of LA. But she was back now, and she was here in style, too, riding in a limousine next to a rich, handsome man. Things were just the way they should be.

"Tomorrow is your debut, darling. It's only a small part, but I'll make sure you get your beautiful face on the big screen when this film comes out."

"I'll do my best."

"We'll run you through the scene a few times to get everything sorted and make sure you're comfortable."

Lillian smirked to herself. *I'll get by just fine.*

"Christina is dying to see you again," Carlo said.

The car pulled up, and they stepped out and entered the exclusive restaurant.

Lillian was impressed. The outside was lovely, but the inside was extraordinary. Eight huge crystal chandeliers hung low from the ornate plastered ceilings. Rich purple velvet lined the walls around the dark lacquered oak panels. Paintings hung in specially carved recesses with soft, tiny lights shining down on them. The floor was polished marble, and the furniture was divine. Heavy wooden antique tables were surrounded by plush black velvet chairs, and the tables were draped with pristine white tablecloths and adorned with large silver candleholders and vases with lush red roses sitting inside them. It reminded Lillian of the old days, when one expected this of a top-class establishment.

Carlo had already noticed with satisfaction most of the male diners were stealing glances at Lillian. A waiter led them to their table, where Sebastian and Christina waited for them. Sebastian stood as they approached the table. The two men shook hands, and Sebastian kissed Lillian's hand. Christina stepped over to Lillian and gave her a gentle hug.

"Lillian, I'm so happy to see you again. Oh my, look at your hair, and what a dress."

"Thank you. Carlo bought it for me."

"I'd buy you the moon if I could," Carlo said.

"Smooth talker," said Christina with a giggle. Lillian sensed that she had met Christina before, obviously when the mortal had control of her body.

They ordered their meals, and Carlo ordered two bottles of the most expensive champagne on the menu. Soon the table was covered in trays and dishes laden with exquisite food: lobster, steak, caviar—a genuine feast. The evening was going splendidly; Carlo and Sebastian were telling more of their hilarious stories, making the women laugh. Christina chattered away, complimenting Lillian's new hair color and clothes.

"You have such good taste, Lillian. Did you buy anything else?"

"Oh yes, lots of things. Shoes, dresses, coats. It was wonderful of Carlo to treat me to such a shopping spree like that. I even had a helper, a lovely girl, Morgan. She proved to be very useful, showing me around all the stores."

"Oh, Morgan, yes. Pretty little thing? Very young?"

"Yes, do you know her?"

"Oh, we met a couple of times. Carlo had a little fling with her a few months back, nothing serious. I'm sure she was shattered when he ended it, though. Carlo's a dream catch. You really are lucky, Lillian. You've found yourself a wonderful man, and he's crazy about you, I can tell."

Lillian smiled politely, but inside she stirred. She had no idea Carlo and Morgan had dated. Neither of them had mentioned anything about it. She knew it would have been easy for Carlo to date women as young as Morgan. That didn't bother her, but she was slightly irritated he had chosen to send one of his very young, and rather recent, conquests to assist her with her shopping trip. In her experience, having somebody like Morgan around was not good at all, and almost an insult.

Morgan would still see Carlo as a hope, a possibility for a life of luxury and opportunity…and Lillian knew, if given half a chance, she would sleep with him again in a heartbeat. That's just how it was with men like Carlo. He was every girl's dream. Morgan was now a nuisance and a threat, only a small one, but a threat nonetheless. She decided not to let it bother her for now.

After her third glass of champagne Lillian was feeling happy and aroused, and Carlo stroked her thigh beneath the table as the chat continued. Lillian had struck up a conversation with Sebastian about how filming was going on Carlo's latest project; she could tell that he, too, was passionate about filmmaking. She noticed Carlo and Christina were deep in discussion about the movie as well. It appeared she had underestimated Christina's position in her role of marketing and promotions at Vonhampton Films, as Carlo was paying serious attention to what she had to say. And she seemed to know what she was talking about.

Soon everybody at the table was enjoying delicious desserts and coffee as the conversation continued about Carlo's new movie.

"You must be excited about your part tomorrow, Lillian," Sebastian said.

"Oh, yes, it's exciting. If it weren't for Carlo directing, I would be far too nervous to even think about it."

"You'll be fine; being an extra is a piece of cake. I even did it myself a few years back, just for the experience. Remember, Carlo?"

"I do indeed."

Carlo turned to Lillian. "It'll be great to have you on set, dear. I can't wait."

Lillian smiled back at him. They finished up and headed outside to the waiting limousine.

* * *

Ashley was frantic. Helen had not turned up to the dinner, and she still had not responded to any of her messages. It was now nine-thirty. She decided to go back to Helen's house again and planned to call Helen's friend Tisha to see if she had heard anything. Maybe Helen had gone to visit her. But that didn't make sense; even when Helen did go away for a couple of nights, which was rare, she had always asked Ashley to check in on Shadow.

Ashley hadn't enjoyed the dinner at all; all she had thought about was Helen's dark, empty house, and Shadow with no food. She pulled into Helen's driveway, dismayed to see the house still in darkness. She knocked on the front door loudly, but again no response. She tried the front door and was surprised to discover it was unlocked. *This is just getting stranger by the minute.* She stepped inside and hit the entry light switch. Shadow appeared before her.

"Hello, lovely. I'm very worried about your mommy. I wish you could talk, dear." He rubbed affectionately against her legs. Ashley petted him for a few moments, and then looked around the house. Nothing had changed, and the note she had left appeared untouched. She headed out the door with a cold lump of worry in the pit of her stomach.

* * *

After seeing Sebastian and Christina off after dinner, Lillian had cuddled and kissed Carlo in the back of the limousine all the way home. She was satisfied and content after such a wonderful meal. The mortal within had managed to send out a few harmless grumblings from within her, but another good dose of perfume tomorrow morning would fix that.

The perfume, always on her mind. Such a tiny amount it held, that precious little bottle…and how quickly it was spent with every use. The Ancient Ones had granted her the greatest gift in the world, eternal youth and beauty, only to curse her at the same time with the dark and bloody task of refilling the bottle regularly.

At least Los Angeles had no shortage of suitable victims for the upkeep of her macabre self-preservation. This time around, though, she knew well to adhere to the sacred commandments, the words and rules of the Ancient Ones. She had tried to cheat so many years ago, had tried to concoct a much larger amount of perfume to fill a much larger bottle, but she had infuriated the dark forces that had granted her this unholy gift of an ageless life. They had punished her, and she had perished in the flames, a faded B-grade Hollywood star who had never really made it.

But now she was *back*, in all her glory, and here she intended to remain and make her mark in spectacular fashion. And she intended to make her presence known on set tomorrow, any way she could.

At home, Lillian and Carlo stepped inside, and Paulina appeared.

"Mr. Carlo, Miss Lillian. May I prepare anything?"

"No, thank you, Paulina. You may retire for the evening," Carlo said.

"Thank you. Goodnight."

Lillian headed to her room with Carlo.

"Darling," Carlo said, before they reached her door. "Would you sit with me?"

"Of course."

They sat down on the black leather sofa in the main upstairs room. Lillian cuddled up to Carlo.

"Did you enjoy tonight?" he asked.

"It was wonderful. You are too good to me."

Carlo reached into his jacket pocket. He pulled out a small black box and opened it. Lillian stared with genuine surprise at a large diamond pendant on a sleek white-gold chain.

"Carlo, really, you shouldn't have."

"But I wanted to. So, you like it?"

"It's gorgeous."

They kissed, and Carlo removed the necklace from the box. He held it by the chain and let the large, oval-shaped diamond dangle.

"Let me put it on for you."

Lillian scooped up her hair and held it over her shoulder while Carlo draped the necklace over her chest and fastened the clasp. It looked incredible; the diamond sat perfectly just above her cleavage and seemed to glow against her skin.

"Carlo, I'm overwhelmed."

Carlo leaned in close. "I care about you very much. I want you to stay here with me, for good."

"I'm not going anywhere, Carlo. I only want to be with you."

He stood and led her to his bedroom. In moments, Lillian was sprawled across his bed, with Carlo smothering her in kisses. Soon Carlo's lust was fully unleashed. They made passionate love until he collapsed next to her. He soon caught his breath and lay there looking at her like she was the only woman on the planet.

"God, you're amazing."

"I'm all yours, my love," she purred back.

Carlo looked into those eyes, the eyes of a mysterious stranger he'd had the incredible luck of meeting on the roadside one night. He could have no idea there was another, secret lifetime hidden within them. *A man can certainly be lucky sometimes.*

Moments later, he made love to her once more with everything he had, until he was completely spent. As he drifted off to sleep, he thought how much he wanted it to be like this every night, lying next to this perfect woman he truly believed loved him.

Lillian lay awake, turning the diamond around in her fingers. It was beautiful, and she knew there would be plenty more. Men like Carlo could afford to keep women like her; they had the wealth to do so, and when they found what they wanted, they came at it full force. She was very much looking forward to being back in front of the cameras, back in the movies, where she belonged. Her career had gone so wrong in her previous life, but she would not let that happen this time. *Besides, I am the director's girlfriend.*

* * *

Ashley had been pacing up and down the mall outside the store since 6 a.m. Helen had not arrived, and her cell just kept going to voicemail. Nothing made sense. She opened the shop, switched on the machines and started some of the orders. A hem on a dress, changing the buttons on a shirt, the usual things—but it was no use: she simply couldn't concentrate. An hour later she was in tears. Helen was never late, let alone this late. Something was terribly wrong, and she knew what she had to do. With trembling fingers and a heavy heart, she called the police.

CHAPTER 23

LIGHTS, CAMERA, ACTION

Lillian had been up since 6:30 a.m. She had smoked a cigar on the balcony, watching the sun rise. The view from Carlo's mansion was commanding, and Lillian felt like a queen in her castle, perched on the hill looking down on everyone and everything. She wore a dark navy dress with three-inch heels, but it didn't matter: the costume department would soon be showing her what she was to wear on set. She stepped before the mirror in her bedroom and picked up the large diamond Carlo had given her, admiring it as it glistened on its chain in the morning sunlight.

"Men need women…and women need diamonds," she whispered to herself with a satisfied smirk.

After applying some makeup, she headed downstairs to the kitchen for some breakfast. As she reached the bottom of the stairs, Carlo appeared.

"Good morning, beautiful."

"Good morning, handsome."

He was wearing his white silk robe. He put his arms around her. He loved having this incredible woman in his home, and now she would be with him at his work today as well. He was as happy as a man could be.

"I love waking up with you."

"I feel the same way," she purred back.

Paulina appeared. "Breakfast is ready."

Lillian enjoyed a fruit salad and fresh orange juice while Carlo tucked into an omelet. He took calls during breakfast, organizing the day's shoot. Soon they were in the limo and off to the film set at one of the most exclusive clothing stores in Beverly Hills, Stelano's. It was a large, lavish store, and very famous. Vonhampton Films had paid a huge amount of money to book it for the shoot. In the scene, the main actress, Chasey Wells, would be trying on clothes when she discovers that her deranged stalker is hiding in the changing room next to her. A chase ensues, and she flees the store. She then makes her escape out into the street, eluding his clutches once again.

As they arrived on set Sebastian rushed up to greet them. "Good morning, you two. Lillian, welcome to the set."

"Thank you."

"Good morning. Is everything ready?" asked Carlo.

"All set to go, boss. The actors are going through their lines."

"Excellent, the weather is looking great, and I'm in the mood to make a movie. Find Morgan for me, please. I want her to look after Lillian today. Morgan can brief her."

"Right away," Sebastian replied.

Carlo turned to Lillian. "Okay, darling. I must go now. Morgan will take you to costume and makeup; just relax and everything will be fine. We'll start doing some rehearsals shortly, once the lighting is all set. Okay?"

"Yes, I'm looking forward to it."

Carlo gave her a kiss and headed off.

Morgan appeared by Lillian's side. "Hi, Lillian."

"Hello, Morgan."

"Nice to see you again. Let's get your hair and makeup sorted out, and then we'll find you an outfit."

Lillian held out her black handbag, the perfume bottle still inside it.

"Morgan, I'd like you to look after this. It has my personal belongings in it, and they are very dear to me. I'd rather you did not let the bag out of your sight."

"No problem. It'll be perfectly safe with me."

"Thank you."

Lillian was soon being given the five-star treatment; the word had been out for days that Carlo's new girlfriend was an extra in the film, so everybody knew that Lillian was to be treated like a star. It was only common sense to treat the director's girlfriend very well. Lillian was loving it. It was just like the old days: people fussing over her hair, her nails, and her makeup. Everybody was on her at once. Things had changed a lot with technology and time, but it was still a lot like her first life. Susan, the head of wardrobe, decided on a gorgeous white dress for Lillian's scene. It was knee-length with a white leather belt. Lillian loved it. The stylists pulled her hair into a ponytail with a low-slung band. Susan had put her in a pair of white leather boots with a very small heel, so Lillian wouldn't tower over the other actors.

Lillian was admiring herself in a full-length mirror when Chasey Wells entered the wardrobe trailer and stopped in surprise.

"Hello," Lillian said.

"Hi," Chasey replied. Chasey knew full well who Lillian was; she had been informed by her personal assistant. And now here she was, standing in front of her in the wardrobe trailer that was usually strictly reserved for the lead actors.

Lillian held out her hand. "I am Lillian."

Chasey took her hand. "Chasey Wells. Welcome to the set, Lillian."

"Thank you, it's very exciting. Everyone has been so nice to me."

"That's wonderful. What part are you playing?"

"I'm one of the customers looking at dresses when your stalker enters."

"Oh, wonderful, it's going to be a great scene. I'm looking forward to running from the store shrieking in terror," Chasey said.

Lillian laughed.

Morgan popped her head inside the tent. "Excuse me, Lillian, the director wants to see you. It's rehearsal time."

"Okay, thank you. Lovely to meet you, Chasey."

"Likewise."

Lillian was ushered inside the dress shop and loved what she saw: row upon row of designer dresses. Morgan explained that she hadn't taken her here for her shopping spree because the shop was being fitted out for the scene they were filming today. Crew members were everywhere, setting up lights and checking camera angles, and Carlo was in the center of it all, giving commands. Morgan ushered Lillian over to four attractive, well-dressed women standing in a corner—the other extras. Morgan introduced them all to Lillian.

Sebastian came over and briefed Lillian and the other ladies on what they were to do. It sounded simple enough: just be engrossed in looking at dresses and idle chitchat, and then give a strange look to the creepy man who walks in and heads to the changing rooms. Lillian took this all in and noticed Chasey had also entered the store and was quietly rehearsing her lines in a corner; she was using her personal assistant to rehearse the part with her, because the woman who was to play the shop attendant had suffered an allergy attack that morning, and Carlo had sent a crew member to a drugstore for medication.

It was only a small holdup but an inconvenience nonetheless. Chasey's assistant was hopeless at reading the lines, and even with a script in her hand she could barely get them right.

"I'm sorry, you know I just can't do this acting stuff."

"It's okay, don't worry about it," Chasey said.

"I'll find someone else, just give me a minute," she said, darting off.

Lillian was standing only a few steps away, and she had overheard their conversation and saw the script on the counter. She picked it up and began reading it, and everything came rushing back to her. There were a few technical changes here and there compared to how scripts were written back in her first life, but she could see a script was pretty much still a script. As Chasey stood in the corner mumbling her lines to herself, Lillian read the scene she had just been rehearsing. It was basic dialog. Back in her acting days, Lillian had become quickly known for her fast and precise memory. Memorizing lines was easy for her; she would often even get bored and memorize the other actors' lines, and she would prompt them on set when they forgot them.

There wasn't much to the part, and Lillian had the words down pat in seconds. She laid the script back on the counter, stepped over to Chasey, and began the dialog.

"Good afternoon, Miss. Welcome to Stelano's." Lillian's rich, husky voice cut through the room. Nearly everybody turned to look.

Chasey turned in surprise to see Lillian standing there in character awaiting her response. She smiled and laid her script down on the counter. "Why, thank you. It's such a beautiful store. I heard so much about it in New York, I just had to come see it for myself. I must say, it's everything they say it is."

"Oh, you're too kind. Were you looking for anything in particular today?"

Carlo watched this exchange with genuine surprise, impressed at how natural Lillian looked beside one of Hollywood's leading ladies. Everyone was watching now. Moments later, Chasey and Lillian finished the scene perfectly. Carlo playfully yelled "Cut!" and they even drew a small round of applause.

Carlo was amazed at how well Lillian had just performed a speaking part opposite Chasey Wells, with no training and no preparation. As a director, he knew she was a natural. He moved over to Lillian.

"Lillian, that was, it was…"

"It was very good," Chasey chimed in, with genuine respect.

"Oh, thank you. I always wanted to read lines with a real movie star. I couldn't resist the opportunity."

"You're a natural," said Carlo.

"Yes, you must be. You've never acted before?" Chasey asked.

"Oh, many years ago in some high-school plays."

"I'm impressed," Carlo remarked.

"So am I," Sebastian added. "That was great, Lillian. How did you learn the lines so fast?"

"I've always been lucky to have a good memory, that's all."

"Well, I'll have to consider you for something more than just an extra part in the future, after what I just saw," Carlo decided.

Sebastian told Carlo the woman playing the shop attendant had taken her allergy spray and was ready. Filming began, and everything went beautifully. Lillian was pleased with herself; she had taken the initiative to show her skills, and it had worked like a charm. All her old acting instincts were still there and as strong as ever, and most importantly, Carlo had noticed—everyone had noticed. And already Carlo had hinted he would consider her for future speaking parts, and not just this silly extra business. Now she had her sights set firmly on becoming a star again, and this time she would not be just some B-grade scream queen. No, this time she wanted to sit on the throne, to be the biggest in Hollywood, and anybody who tried to step in her way would soon feel her wrath.

* * *

Ashley was a mess. The police had just left her store after asking her all manner of questions, which had only upset her more. Was Helen a heavy drinker? Did she take drugs? Did she have a boyfriend in another city? Did she have mental health problems? Did she often go missing? On and on, the questions went. Ashley had felt like they were making her beloved friend out to be a criminal. And they were not even going to consider Helen a missing person for another forty-eight hours, though she explained to them how long it had been since she had heard from Helen. They wouldn't even go around to Helen's house to look inside, given Ashley had told them she had been there twice and noticed nothing suspicious. They promised to do a drive-by the next day; better than nothing, she thought. They took her details and a photo of Helen, and left. They just didn't seem very interested. Ashley knew she wouldn't be able to sleep until she heard from Helen. She decided she would go to the house again later that night to check on Shadow. She was about to close up and go home when Daniel walked in.

"Hello, Ashley. I don't mean to pry, but I noticed the police were here. Is everything okay?"

Ashley looked at him and burst into tears.

"Oh dear, what's wrong?" he asked, putting his hands on her shoulders.

"It's Helen—she's disappeared. I've got no idea where she is. First she missed dinner, and now she hasn't come to work, and her cell…it just keeps ringing out."

Daniel led her to a bench outside the store. "Sit down, sweetheart."

Ashley sat next to Daniel and explained the entire situation.

"I'm sorry, Ashley. I had no idea."

"I didn't want everyone to know until I was sure she was missing."

"I understand, I really do. You said you plan on going back to her place tonight?"

"Yes, I have to check on her cat, and you never know, she might turn up," Ashley said, with hope in her eyes. Daniel stroked her back gently.

"Of course she might. And I'm coming with you. We'll look for Helen together."

"Thank you, Daniel."

CHAPTER 24

CATCH A THIEF

Lillian had enjoyed her day immensely. After finishing her scene, she had gone to a nearby restaurant with Morgan and Chasey. Carlo had to continue filming, but the three women were free for the rest of the day. Chasey had been telling the story of how she had worked her way up in LA. She explained that, ultimately, fame wasn't all she had hoped it was. She claimed she had no real friends, her family were always trying to bleed her for money and that she often felt lonely, with no privacy at all. Lillian pretended to be sympathetic, but she didn't care. She thought Chasey was ungrateful for the success that life had rewarded her. The women finished their meals, and Lillian scooped up her handbag then headed to freshen up. Earlier in the day she had felt the faintest rumblings inside her, and it was time now for some perfume.

Lillian entered the ladies' room and reached into her bag for the perfume bottle. She found her cigars, lighter, lipstick, and cell phone, but not the perfume. She felt around the bottom of the bag and then looked inside.

She realized there were two things she could not see: her wallet and the perfume bottle. A cold bolt of fear seized her as she frantically turned the bag upside down onto the counter. She stared in shock and disbelief…the perfume bottle was *gone*. Her mind raced in ten different directions at once…She checked the bag again and opened the side pocket: nothing. The perfume and wallet were definitely gone. She couldn't have cared less about the wallet, but the perfume bottle meant everything to her. Anger and confusion swept through her.

Lillian shoved the items back into her bag and stepped out of the ladies' room. From the doorway she glared at Morgan, who immediately knew something was wrong. She quickly approached Lillian, who closed the door after her as she stepped into the ladies' room. Lillian stood just inches from her, fury in her eyes. Morgan stepped back, her stomach already churning.

"I want to know where my perfume bottle is," Lillian growled.

"What do you mean, Lillian?"

Lillian pointed to her bag sitting on the bench. "I mean, I want to know where my perfume is. My wallet is also missing, but I don't care about that. I want my perfume bottle. I gave you my bag to look after and now my bottle is missing. Where is it?"

Morgan stared, dumbfounded. "I…I have no idea. I had it with me all the time, Lillian. If it was in your bag, it should still be there."

Lillian's eyes flashed. "It is not, and if you had it with you all the time, then you would know where my perfume is, wouldn't you?"

Morgan flinched at the icy response. "I did leave it, only very briefly. I left it on the table with the other actors' things. Lillian, I don't think anyone took anything from your bag. Really."

"I am telling you my perfume bottle is *missing*. I want it, do you hear me? I want that perfume bottle *back*."

"Okay…I'll try to find it. I'm sorry, it's just, we have security on set, you know, and…it's just very strange, that's all."

Lillian seized Morgan's wrist.

Morgan winced at the pressure on her arm. "Lillian, please, that hurts."

"You get back to that set now and find that bottle. Understood?"

"Okay. Please let go of me."

Lillian released her grip, and Morgan stepped back away from her.

"Call Carlo right now and tell him what's happened," Lillian commanded.

Morgan began dialing on her cell.

"Hello, Carlo? Oh, thank goodness. Lillian is missing some things from her bag, her wallet and…a bottle of perfume. She's really upset, so if somebody could take a look around the table where…Oh no, really? Yes, I'll tell her. She's right here." Morgan looked up at Lillian with wide, frightened eyes. "I'm sorry Lillian, but it appears you're not the only one with things missing. Carlo has had lots of complaints today from other actors saying they've had stuff stolen from their bags too."

Lillian snatched the phone out of Morgan's hand. "Carlo, darling. I don't care about the wallet. It's the perfume bottle; it's very special to me. It's an heirloom. It was my grandmother's. I must get it back, Carlo."

Morgan listened as Lillian finished her call with Carlo.

"Yes, I'm okay. I just really need that bottle back, sweetheart…Yes, I know you will. Okay, goodbye darling."

"Lillian, I'm so sorry, I really am."

Lillian glared back at her. "I trusted you."

* * *

Back on set, Carlo was standing where the thefts had taken place. The first he had known about it was a complaint from one of the extras whose purse was missing. More complaints soon followed: a watch, a cell phone, Lillian's perfume. Clearly, there had been a thief on set, and in all, seven actors' bags had been rifled through and robbed. This was a rare occurrence on a film set, let alone one he was directing. Carlo was furious. He had immediately, and at the top of his lungs, berated the two set security guards, who'd feebly admitted they were not paying enough attention. Carlo had them down on their hands and knees looking for Lillian's perfume bottle. He had been extremely upset at the tone of her voice; he could hear the panic and sadness in it, and he was angry anybody dared steal on his set, let alone from the woman he loved.

He also had crew members searching everywhere when the police arrived. He was speaking with two officers when Sebastian appeared with an anxious look.

"What's wrong?" Carlo asked.

Next to Sebastian was a teenage girl, one of the extras.

"This girl just told me she saw the kid who played the boy waiting for the bus going through people's bags while we were filming the store scene."

"Is that true?" the senior officer asked.

"Yes, sir," the girl replied.

The cop turned to Carlo. "I'm gonna need his name and a description of him, and any information you have about him, as well as a list of everything that's been stolen."

"I'll do better than that." Carlo turned to Sebastian. "Go print out that kid's photo off the website. Call his agent right away. Get his phone number, address, everything. Let's help these officers any way we can."

"Right away," Sebastian darted off.

Carlo turned to the cop and handed him his business card. "Officer, my girlfriend's handbag had items stolen from it. She's very upset about an antique perfume bottle that was taken; it was her grandmother's. If you find it, could you please contact me directly, and I will send somebody to collect it at once. I can assure you I do not forget a favor." Carlo extended his hand, and the senior cop shook it.

"I'll do everything I can, Mr. Genisi. I'm a fan of your work. Hopefully, we'll get everybody's things back."

* * *

Lillian and Morgan were heading back to the set in the limo. Lillian was in turmoil. *How could I have gotten so relaxed about the perfume?* It was literally her lifeblood, her everything. She was just as angry at herself as she was at Morgan. Already, she had felt the mortal within beginning to stir, and now… no perfume. She had to find the bottle fast. She knew she had two days at most before the transformation occurred, and then it was unstoppable. The perfume had to be applied regularly to preserve her youth and beauty.

Lillian and Morgan arrived on set and Carlo rushed over to Lillian. His frown told her he had bad news.

"Darling, I'm so sorry. No sign of it. But we do know who the thief was, and the police are looking for him as we speak."

Lillian took his hand and led him away from everybody else. "I know you're doing all you can, but I need you to understand that perfume bottle is really all I have left to me from my family. It means everything to me. I will be destroyed if I can't get it back. I know it must sound silly to you, but…"

"It doesn't sound silly at all. It only makes me love you more that you care for an object so deeply, that its sentimental value is everything to you. I'll do everything humanly possible to get it back for you, Lillian."

"Thank you, Carlo. I'm worried it will be thrown away or sold or something like that, and I shall never see it again. Is there anyone besides the police we can get looking for this thief?" Lillian begged.

Carlo thought a moment. "Well, there is a guy I know who…finds and persuades people, people who owe money. He's very good at what he does. I could call him."

"Oh, please do. Please do it now. I was so stupid to carry it in my handbag. I should have left it at home."

"Don't blame yourself. People steal things. It wasn't your fault."

"I just want it back."

"Just try and relax. I'll take you home now."

"I don't want to go home. I feel like I should be looking for this horrible thief and trying to find my bottle."

"The police will probably find him, but I'll call my friend; we'll do everything we can."

Carlo led her to the limousine and they headed home. Morgan sat on a chair away from everybody, close to tears.

Lillian was frantic all the way home. Reality was sinking in: the perfume was out of her grasp, and it could not be replaced. The bottle was unique; it had been handmade by the master sorcerer himself, back in the castle in Europe so many years ago. It had been blessed by him with the power of the Ancient Ones, and the dark mysterious forces unknown to the modern, civilized world. Lillian was powerless without it, and she knew it. She was furious—she had trusted Morgan, and Morgan had failed her. But now was not the time for revenge or punishment. She needed that bottle back, and fast. The faintest stirrings of Helen rumbled deep inside her again. Had the mortal already sensed her distress and panic? She knew she still had some time up her sleeve, and even if she had to transform back into the pathetic creature that had rebirthed her, she would still look for the bottle. But as she knew so well, *everything* was easier when she was Lillian.

Back at the mansion, Lillian had Carlo call his friend to start searching for the thief. Carlo brought up a picture of him on his agent's website. His name was Phillipe and he was nineteen, with short, spiky black hair and dark eyes. Lillian etched his face into her brain.

I will find you, you thieving little germ, and you will pay.

She showered quickly and slipped on a pair of snug black jeans, a black sweater, and black leather boots, then tied her hair back into a ponytail before heading into Carlo's office. He was getting off the phone when she walked in.

"Darling, I just spoke to my friend, Shark. He is going to start looking for this kid right now. He's very good at finding people, so try to relax."

"Shark?"

"Yes, well, he's an interesting character. He used to be a loan shark, the kind you don't want looking for you, but now he mainly tracks people down. He's good at what he does. Trust me, sweetheart."

"I do trust you, but perhaps you could give me his cell number so I can get word from him right away if something happens?"

"Yes, of course." He punched the number into Lillian's cell phone and handed it back to her.

Carlo's cell rang. He answered it and then became irritated. "How did it happen? This is unprofessional. I'm not happy. Yes, I'm heading over now." He ended the call and turned to Lillian. "Lillian, I'm so sorry, there's some dramas at the studio, I have to get over there now. I'm sorry, darling."

"It's okay, I'll be fine." She kissed him, and he left in a rush. She whipped out her cell and at once dialed Shark's number. A deep, gruff voice answered.

"Hello, Shark? This is Lillian, Carlo Genisi's girlfriend. I understand you are looking for the kid who stole my perfume bottle."

"I'm already onto it, Miss."

"Well, that bottle is very, very dear to me, and I'd like to come along with you to perhaps help convince the thief or anybody else involved to do the right thing and give it back to me. I'd like you to come pick me up at Carlo's house right now."

"Look, Miss, no offense, but I don't usually take the customer along for the ride. My line of work is…well, sometimes it's not that pretty, you know? Why don't you just leave it to me and I'll call you the second I know something."

Lillian was not about to take no for an answer. "Listen, Shark, this bottle means everything to me and I want it back *fast*, and I don't care what you have to do to get it back for me. I will personally see to it that Carlo pays you very handsomely indeed."

"He's already promised me four thousand dollars, Miss. That's plenty for this gig."

"You'll get more than that if you find it for me, I promise you, but I want to be there with you. Come and collect me from Carlo's house right now, okay?"

"Okay. Be there soon," he grunted.

Lillian ended the call.

CHAPTER 25

DESPERATION

Lillian paced up and down in front of the stairs at the mansion's entrance as she waited. She had smoked two cigars in twenty minutes, and her stomach was in knots. She turned at the sound of a loud rumbling; like distant thunder, it crept closer as a large black old-style sedan cruised down the drive toward her. Heavy chrome gleamed in the sunlight, and dark windows added to its menacing appearance. As it pulled up, the passenger window slid down to reveal an enormous man who looked as though he could barely fit behind the steering wheel. Mirrored sunglasses covered his eyes, and he was completely bald.

Muscular, tattooed forearms gripped the steering wheel. Large, heavy silver rings adorned his thick fingers, and he seemed to have almost no neck at all. *Good Lord, no wonder he was a loan shark.* She opened the car door and stepped in. The interior reeked of cigarette smoke. As she sat down, he removed his sunglasses. A pair of hard brown eyes squinted at her, set in a rugged, fearless face dotted with scars and lines. A small tattoo of a pistol crept onto his cheek. He was dressed completely in black. His head almost hit the roof lining of the car.

"I'm Shark."

"Hello, Shark. What's your plan?"

"I was about to go to the kid's house when you called, so let's go now, huh?"

"Yes, let's go. I want to find this thieving little shit," Lillian spat.

Shark chuckled in surprise at Lillian's venom. He accelerated down the drive.

They approached downtown as the last light of the day illuminated the LA skyline with a majestic amber glow. Downtown LA, a fantastic place loaded with shops, markets, restaurants, and bars. But at night, when darkness fell and the shadows crept out from the alleys, many parts of the city became pure gangland. LA's gangs were feared and notorious, and there were many of them, all protecting their territory, their "turf," dealing drugs, weapons, death…anything they could to get by. Guns and knives rule the streets at night; this was when Los Angeles became dangerous. Yet Lillian sensed she was safe with Shark.

"This kid lives in the project area, Hazna Park," Shark explained. "It's gangland, if you know what I mean."

Lillian nodded. In truth, though, she didn't know. Back in her first life, the city was young, clean, and fresh. There was always a criminal element wherever you went, she knew, but what she had heard and read about contemporary street gangs had surprised her. The world seemed a far more violent place now. They drove on a few more minutes until Shark slowed the car down.

"It's that block of apartments up there." He pointed in their direction.

It was a run-down old apartment building. There were lots of youths sitting around, many covered in tattoos.

"I'm gonna park on a side street and see if there's a back way into the building. You'll be okay. Just keep the doors locked. If you need me, sound the horn."

Shark pulled over into a backstreet, under a large overhanging tree, and got out. Lillian noticed a bulge under his shirt at the base of his spine before he put his jacket on, and knew it was a gun. She watched him lumber across the road and up the stairs into the building; *God, he is enormous.*

She turned her nose up at the filthy, messy neighborhood around her. She lived in splendor, high above the city in a castle with a rich man who adored her and a maid at her disposal. But here…these people barely survived. A chill spread in her stomach, and the seriousness of her predicament struck her hard. The mortal within was stirring again, and she knew it wouldn't be long before she badly needed the perfume. She unclenched her hands and tried to calm herself. *Would she find the bottle?*

She could only hope. Carlo would spend whatever it took to get it back for her, that she knew, and he would stop at nothing to make her happy. That gave her some peace, at least. Moments later, Shark stomped back to the car and climbed in.

"He's not home. A kid from next door took a twenty off me and gave me this address; says it's his girlfriend's place and he's always there. It's not far. He said the cops have been here today, too, but nobody told them anything."

Lillian's hopes soared; perhaps the thief still had the bottle with him. Or maybe with a cash incentive and some persuasion from Shark he would tell them where the bottle was. Time was of the essence.

They cruised along the main boulevard in the trash-strewn neighborhood in Shark's big car, getting all kinds of looks from all kinds of people. Hookers were plying their trade on street corners, and drug dealers were selling openly. These people feared little; they were all about survival. The only thing they would run from was a fully marked police car or a loaded gun.

"Should be just up here," Shark muttered.

Lillian looked to her right and saw a row of badly neglected little houses. Graffiti gang markings covered the walls, and most of the windows were boarded up. Shark cruised along until the very last house, from which rap music blared. Darkness was falling fast. Shark parked behind the house.

"I'll go check it out." He got out of the car.

Lillian watched as he walked straight in the back door of the house without knocking. She chuckled as she imagined the reaction of the people in there.

Another rumbling struck from deep within, and Lillian frowned. The mortal was getting restless again. *She can sense my worry.* She had never been in this situation in her previous life, had never been so careless as to lose the bottle. Suddenly, a young man dashed from the side of the house. Lillian sat bolt upright. The *thief*! She recognized him immediately. He had a black sports bag over his shoulder, and he was moving fast. Lillian leaped out of the car and took off after him as Shark ran down the stairs.

"No, stay in the car!"

Lillian ignored him, and within seconds she built up a furious pace, even in the high-heeled boots.

The kid ducked down an alley, but Lillian was closing in on him fast. He took a right and began climbing a high wooden fence. He reached the top and was about to throw his legs over when Lillian leaped up high and slapped both hands firmly around his ankle, digging her nails in deep. The teenager screamed as she used all her strength and weight to try drag him back down into the alley, but his grip on the fence was firm, and he pulled hard away from her.

"Lemme go!" he screamed.

Shark came lumbering down the alley, puffing heavily.

"Here. I've got him!" she screeched.

Shark wrapped one huge bear-sized hand around the kid's lower leg and gave an almighty tug. He fell in a heap, crashing to the ground so hard it knocked the wind out of him.

Lillian was on the bag in a heartbeat. She unzipped it and shook out its contents as the teen stared up at Shark towering over him.

Philippe figured this must have something to do with the items he had stolen today, but he really didn't think he'd taken anything important enough to have people like *this* chasing him. Even in his blind panic as he ran from her, he could not help but notice the woman with the long black hair pursuing him was astonishingly beautiful, like a movie star. But the big man…He had known in a second he was serious. He had seen men like this before. His drug-dealing uncles had associated with men like this over the years, men called enforcers… large, tough men with battle scars on their faces and knuckles, and cold hard cruelty set in their eyes. He knew he was in a bad situation, though he was still high from the grass he had just smoked, and he could not comprehend how things had happened so fast. One minute he was lying on a couch getting high while his girlfriend took a shower, and the next, a huge man with a gun had walked into the living room. He tried to catch his breath and make sense of things.

Lillian riffled through the contents of the bag, now scattered before her on the ground. Her heart raced as she spotted her wallet; she tossed it aside and kept searching. There were cell phones, sunglasses, jewelry, watches, but *no perfume bottle*. She checked again, but it simply was not there. Seething with anger, she stared at Philippe, still sitting dazed on the ground.

"Is it there?" Shark asked.

"No, it isn't." She stood over Philippe and glared at him. "Where is it? Where is the bottle of perfume?" she demanded.

Philippe stared back at her. "What?" he mumbled.

"I asked you a question, you little shit." She kicked him hard in the stomach. Shark chuckled. Philippe curled up in pain, wincing and coughing.

"Check his pockets," she ordered. Shark picked Philippe up with one hand and slammed him against the fence. He pulled off the kid's jacket and began searching it. He found a pack of cigarettes, a lighter, a small plastic bag with some white powder, and a tiny pipe that smelled like it had been used recently. There was a pen and a pocket knife, but no perfume.

Lillian stepped close to Philippe. "You stole something from my bag today on the set of that movie. A little glass bottle. Where is it?"

Philippe stared up into those furious ice-blue eyes that seemed to have no end to their depth. He was fearing for his life now, in this alley with a gigantic man and a woman he could only have fantasized about in his dreams.

"Answer the lady," Shark snarled, twisting Philippe's right ear so he winced.

"I…I don't know. I'm not sure."

Lillian glowered down at him. "Well, you better think fast, or I promise you, you will be very sorry. Do I make myself clear, you little piece of trash?" She threw a look at Shark for him to endorse her threat, and he responded by slapping the kid upside the head, hard. The teen grunted in pain.

"I sold half the stuff already. I swapped it for some meth and weed. Honest, I don't even know where it is now."

Shark grabbed him by his throat and raised him until he was on tiptoe. Philippe trembled.

Shark leaned his huge head in close to Philippe's face. "You see this nice lady? Well, I work for her, and when I work for people I *always* make them happy, and to make this lady happy, I need you to think very hard about where that bottle of perfume is. It can't have gone far; you didn't steal it all that long ago. I can see by your eyes you're wasted, but you understand me, don't you?"

Philippe nodded.

"Now, I will do *anything* to get that bottle back for this lady, and if that means hurting you until you tell me the truth, kid, believe me I'll fucking hurt you. So this is your only chance to tell me the truth, right now. Where is that bottle?"

"I…it's…I remember it! It was small and shiny. It had… red stuff in it."

Lillian's heart raced. "Yes. Where is it?" she hissed.

"I swapped it for the weed."

"Swapped it with who?" Shark demanded.

"Please, you can't say I told you. He's a bad guy. I'm scared of him."

Shark applied crushing pressure to the kid's forearm, and Phillippe slumped to his knees, howling in agony.

"Never mind being scared of *him*. Worry about me. Now give me a name and an address or I'll break both your arms."

Philippe nodded, and Shark released the pressure.

"They call him Pannato. He's in the big house on the corner of Sacamane and Wesley."

"And why would a guy like Pannato want a bottle of perfume?"

"His girlfriend was there when I was showing him all the stuff in the bag to swap. She saw the bottle and she liked it, so he took it as part of the deal."

Shark looked at Lillian. "I've heard of this guy. He's a major dealer, and a scumbag in general. This could get ugly; this guy's got a large gang." Shark turned to the kid again. "Listen, punk, you better be telling the truth about this, because if you're not, I'll come find you again. I know where you live, and I know where your mother lives. You can't hide from me, and the cops can't protect you from people like me. You understand?"

Philippe nodded, terrified.

"Let's get moving," Lillian urged.

"Wait, this guy's no pushover. He'll have lookouts watching his place. I'm not sure how to play this," Shark warned.

"I don't care. I want that bottle. Get me to this place now."

Shark pointed at the kid's face. "You're coming with us."

Minutes later, they were parked down the street from Pannato's house, a big two-story building with a large, high fence around it. The second they had entered the street Lillian knew the bottle was close; she could sense its presence, and she was excited. "It's here," she whispered.

Shark looked at her. "What?"

"Never mind."

A dog began barking, and Lillian spotted a lookout watching them from an attic window.

Shark saw him too. "He won't be the only one watching. We go near that place and we'll have half a dozen gang members with guns coming at us," Shark warned.

Lillian turned to Philippe. "You go in there and tell him you made a mistake and that you need that perfume bottle back. Do you understand?"

"Yes, but…he won't like it," Phillipe stuttered. "His girlfriend, she liked the bottle a lot. And what if he wants money? I have none."

Shark gave him a chilling stare. "If he does want money, we'll give him money, but you better not try and scam this nice lady. You hear me?"

Philippe nodded. "Yes, sir."

Shark handed him a wad of cash. "That's five hundred dollars. Should be plenty. If you can get it for less, do it."

"Give him a thousand," Lillian said.

Shark stared at her, astonished. "What?"

"Just do it. I don't care what it costs. Carlo will pay you back. Give him a thousand. I want that bottle."

Shark handed another roll of cash to Philippe. "Move it!"

Philippe walked quickly toward the house, and the guard dog began barking like mad. In a matter of seconds, two muscular men materialized from the shadows and blocked his path. The man in the attic window waved down and they let Philippe go to the front door. It opened and he entered.

Lillian sat nervously and fidgeted. Deep inside her the rumblings were getting stronger; Helen wanted out, and she was making her intentions known. Waiting in the car, the passing minutes seemed like hours. The door opened, and Philippe scurried back toward the car holding something in his hand. Lillian stared. Shark drove slowly toward the kid, who climbed in the back of the car. He held out his hand to Lillian and opened it to reveal her precious perfume bottle.

"Give to me." She snatched it from him but immediately frowned. The bottle was filled with a clear liquid. "No!" she yelled. She turned to Philippe. "What is this? Where is the red perfume that was in it?"

"I saw that too. Pannato's girlfriend said she tipped it out to put her own perfume in. Sorry, Miss." Lillian put her face in her hands in silence.

Philippe handed Shark back one of the rolls of cash. "Sir, he only charged me five hundred."

"Miss, I got the bottle back. I'm sorry I stole from you. Can I go now?"

Lillian flicked her hand dismissively.

"Get lost, kid," Shark ordered. Philippe opened the door and scurried into the night.

"Take me home," Lillian whispered.

She sat silently on the way home. It certainly felt good to have the bottle back in her hands, but it was empty now. And the mortal was stirring; she knew time was running out fast. She sighed as she looked out the window. *The curse*, the only thing that plagued her. She needed the blood and soul of a young girl, and she needed it very soon. Already her mind was racing with solutions. They were cruising along Sunset Boulevard now, and Lillian gazed at the many hotels dotted along it. She recognized the famous Sun Mirage hotel, sitting high and proud, and her thoughts drifted back to the many sex parties and secret trysts she'd had there, often with wealthy married men and film directors. Most of them had promised her the world but had just ended up using her. *It hasn't changed much*, she thought.

She had calmed down considerably since she had gotten the bottle back, but Helen's resistance was getting stronger, unpleasantly so.

From her prison of shadows, deep inside the depths of Lillian, Helen had sensed something was wrong. Tiny splinters of blurred light had appeared to her as she felt Lillian's panic and fear swirling throughout her body. She sensed it would still be some time before she could try to exert enough power to free herself, but nevertheless it was a chance, and God, how she wanted out of this eerie wasteland of darkness and muffled echoes.

As Lillian looked out at the dozens of cheap motels they were passing, she began hatching her plan. She felt like strangling Pannato's girlfriend for replacing her precious scent with some cheap garbage. But done was done.

CHAPTER 26

SEDUCTION OF THE INNOCENT

"Drop me off up here," Lillian commanded, pointing to the roadside.

"Here?"

"Yes, I've got some things to do. I'll get a cab home. Carlo will pay you the money you're owed. And I shall see to it he doubles it. And, Shark…if anybody asks, now or ever, you and I got the bottle back and then we got some takeaway food and drove around sightseeing for a couple of hours, okay?"

"You got it."

"And I do appreciate your help tonight, Shark, thank you."

"Anytime."

Lillian got out and headed to the nearest phone box and dialed Morgan's number. She then switched off her cell.

"Hello?"

"Hello, dear," Lillian purred.

"Oh, Lillian, I'm so sorry. I can't apologize enough. You trusted me, and I screwed up. I'm a screw-up."

"Listen, dear, never mind. It wasn't your fault. These things happen. Don't worry yourself about it. Besides, I got the bottle back. I feel terrible about how I spoke to you, darling. I insist you have dinner with me and Carlo tonight so I can apologize in person."

"You got it back? Oh God, I'm so pleased you found it! And thank you, I'd love to have dinner with you."

"Wonderful, I shall call you back shortly with the details. And don't call my cell; the battery is flat, sweetheart." Lillian lied as she ended the call. She didn't want calls from Morgan's cell to hers, especially tonight. She wanted to cover all bases. She headed along the Sunset Strip. The night was young and most of the stores were still open. She lit a cigar and relaxed a little. The rumbling struck deep within her again, "Stop it, you pathetic wretch. Shut up and be still." She was worried; the withdrawal was beginning faster than she expected. She could feel it.

She stepped into a souvenir and gift store and browsed a row of sweaters. She chose a black one with a hood, then headed over to a glass display case filled with pocketknives. Her eyes fixed on a neat little folding number with a black handle and a gleaming silver blade. She spied some glass vases too—*perfect; exactly what I need.* They were long and made of thick glass. Moments later, Lillian was heading down the Sunset Strip in her new sweater, with the hood pulled up over her head, and her new items in a carry bag. She found a drug store and bought two boxes of the strongest sleeping pills available over the counter.

Further down the strip she found a cheap motel, arranged a room for the night, paying in cash, then called Morgan again from a phone booth in a backstreet and invited her to a pre-dinner drink. Morgan was delighted. Lillian gave her the address of the motel and her room number. She then found a liquor store and bought a bottle of wine. She headed back to the tacky little motel, the kind mostly frequented by cash-strapped tourists or hookers and their clients. When she booked, she'd been careful to tuck her long hair under the sweater, and the hood was pulled up over her head, hiding most of her face. She also put on her large dark sunglasses. The old man at the counter had barely glanced at her anyway, especially after she'd handed him four hundred-dollar bills and told him to keep the change. She guessed that he was used to being tipped for discretion, and she was right. The little spell she had cast on him should blur his memory a little, too, even though her power had been at its lowest without fresh perfume.

Lillian turned the key and stepped into the room. Faded wallpaper from decades ago lined the walls, a stale stench hung in the air that no amount of deodorizing would ever erase, and the carpet was worn down to threads in places. There was a tiny sink and benchtop and a single chair. A beat-up old double bed took up most of the floor space. She opened the wine she had bought and filled two glasses she'd found under the sink. She then tipped a dozen of the tiny sleeping pills into one of the glasses and stirred it. The pills dissolved and disappeared quickly. She opened the ratty old balcony doors and stepped into the night air, catching the typical touristy scent of fast food and coffee on the breeze, mixed with the ever-present traffic fumes.

She lit a cigar and tried to clear her head, but Helen was still making her presence known. Lillian tried to ignore the cold, dull ache looming in her gut, but she couldn't.

And deep within her, Helen felt her chance inching closer; she knew she'd been hopelessly confined in the perpetual darkness of Lillian for some time, and she was not going to let this glimmer of hope pass by easily. She focused hard on the snippets of the outside world.

Lillian clenched her fists.

"Just deal with it, you hopeless creature. You will never surface again. You had your fun with my body, and now it belongs to me, for good."

As if in response, Helen sent another cold chill throughout her, which unsettled her even more. Perhaps the mortal was stronger than she had first thought. The perfume's power was waning fast. Lillian calmed herself with deep breaths. It would all be okay soon. *Morgan will be here, and everything will be fine.*

She focused on the task at hand. She had done it many times before, and she knew she would do it many times again. It was her absolute right. She had missed her chance in her first life. She had been screwed over in her youth, lied to, used, discarded and abused until she had lost trust in practically everybody. She had become hard and jaded by men, women, the acting industry, and life in general. People far less worthy than her had succeeded greatly. She'd had to endure seeing their faces on billboards and the silver screen, while she had faded into nothing, and her career had wasted away. She had gone back to Europe then, to escape her depression, searching for something…anything. A new life.

The move had proven to be her rebirth it was there she had found the cult who took her in and embraced her, her brothers and sisters of the dark arts. Over time, she had won most of them over with her beauty and charm, eventually seducing even the grand master himself. They had let her join in their macabre ways, and she'd personally witnessed some of the astonishing feats of which they were capable.

They were known, nearly always in whispered tones as, "*Les Gens du Sang*," or more commonly TBP, the "Blood People." Their true origins were shrouded in mystery, but reached back as far as the sixteenth century, when they had numbered in the tens of thousands and had amassed great wealth and influence. A highly secretive cult that worshiped human blood as a sacred life force…they practiced rituals similar to those of the ancient Aztecs, a once-vast culture with a fascination for blood and human sacrifice. It had been said the Blood People also practiced elements of primeval African voodoo.

After being all but wiped out by order of the king of France himself, who was displeased at their growing stature, wealth, and rumors of their dark practices—the remaining members, dwindling in number, had fled underground, only to grow steadily in power and wealth again over the centuries, sometimes hiding in plain sight. Stories of their murderous bloodlust, powerful curses, and perverse sins of the flesh had spread to the far corners of the world, leaving most too frightened to even utter their name aloud. Their victims' bodies were rarely found but were said to number in the thousands. It had even been whispered they could raise the dead. They had been branded vampires and worshippers of evil. And now, in modern times, it was rumored they had infiltrated Europe's corridors of power. Most religions, sects, and churches preferred to completely deny their existence, daring only to whisper their name.

Lillian puffed her cigar and thought back to when the grand master himself had created the perfume bottle especially for her, a reward for being used pretty much as a sex slave by men she would rather never have touched her. And one of her final tasks, her initiation into this seemingly perfect life of never-ending youth and beauty, was to prove her worth by bringing the grand master the blood and soul of a young girl. The requirements were clear: the victim had to be female and beautiful, a girl who had passed through puberty but was no older than twenty-five.

She thought back to her first kill, so many years ago. Nervous and strolling the dark, filthy backstreets of Paris with a razor-sharp knife and a cold, hard will to murder. She knew it was a test to determine if she was truly deserving and trustworthy.

She had not disappointed him. She had soon found the perfect victim, a young blonde, cold, hungry, and tired, sitting alone under a streetlamp in the red-light district. This was where so many homeless young girls ran, to escape troubled homes and lives, only to sell themselves openly to men who would ravage them and treat them in ways they could never treat their wives. Lillian had approached the girl and told her everything was going to be fine, that she would work for her in her home as a servant, where she would be well looked after.

The girl's prayers had been answered. Lillian had taken her to an isolated château owned by the cult and fed her wonderful warm food, which the girl had wolfed down. In the light, Lillian could see she had chosen well; the girl was very pretty, with sandy blonde hair and a slender, willowy body. She had told Lillian she was eighteen, which was music to her ears.

After plying the girl with three glasses of wine and winning her trust, Lillian had struck from behind. The chloroform-soaked rag had landed perfectly over the girl's face, and Lillian had applied enough pressure to break her nose. The girl had screamed and struggled briefly but fell to the floor in seconds. Lillian had then taken the knife and placed it against her throat. She'd hesitated a moment then, when it truly hit home that she was about to take the life of another human being, to crush any of the hopes, dreams, and happiness this girl would have experienced in her future.

But that did not stop her. And with a deep breath and an iron will, she dragged the blade across the girl's throat, slicing open the jugular vein. She felt shocked at first, at how quickly the blood had gushed out. She had thrust the canister under the wound and watched as it rapidly filled to the top. After speaking the first line of the incantation aloud, she had watched as the misty white vapor that was the girl's soul materialized from the wound and settled into the canister with the blood. Afterward, she had wrapped the girl's body in an old carpet with heavy stones and dragged it to the nearby River Seine, in the dark early hours. She then stood and watched her first victim sink slowly into the filthy depths. She knew there were many more victims to come. She decided there and then that to get what she wanted she would become as hard and ruthless as anybody.

A knock at the door snapped her back to reality. She tossed the cigar into a garden below and stepped back inside. She opened the door; Morgan stood there in a white coat, blue jeans, and sneakers. She gave Lillian a feeble smile.

"Lillian. I'm so sorry about today. It was all my fault."

"Oh, darling, never mind. Everything is okay now. I'm sorry about how I spoke to you. Please come in."

They hugged briefly, Morgan entered, and Lillian helped her remove her coat, noting the confusion on the young girl's face as she looked about the seedy motel room.

"I know, it's a dump. Carlo just hired it for some crew members to stay here for a few days, and I had to drop in to sign some contracts for the film," Lillian lied. "I was so pleased when you said you'd join us for dinner."

Morgan smiled. "That's so sweet of you. I was so happy when you said you'd found the perfume bottle. I'm so sorry. I should have watched your bag more carefully."

"Not another word. I was wrong to have blamed you like that. You must understand—that bottle, it's an heirloom and very dear to me. That's why I got so upset, that's all."

"I know, and I'm so glad you got it back."

Lillian took the two glasses of wine and handed Morgan the one laced with the pills. She raised her own glass.

"To finding lost belongings, and friendship."

Morgan beamed. They clinked glasses and Morgan took a long sip of wine.

Lillian's eyes gleamed. "Tell me more about yourself, Morgan. We haven't really gotten to know each other properly. Do you have any family here? A boyfriend?"

"No, I only have my dad. He's in Nevada. I had a boyfriend here, but he was cheating on me with everybody, so I moved out of his apartment. That's how I wound up in the awful little place I'm in now." Morgan took another sip from the glass.

"Well, I'm sure things will improve for you very soon. I told Carlo how wonderful you were to me when we went shopping, and he was very pleased."

"Oh, thank you. Carlo is great. He's always treated me very well, and he's so good at what he does."

"Yes, he is," Lillian replied, noticing Morgan had nearly drained her glass. Her speech was already slurring, and her eyelids were getting heavy. Lillian topped up the glass for her, almost spilling it as she gasped softly and touched her stomach. Helen was stirring again.

"Are you okay, Lillian?"

"Yes, it's just the wine on my empty stomach, dear."

Deep inside Lillian, Helen had sensed the murderous intent spreading and the presence of the young innocent. She had gathered enough strength now to begin to cause Lillian troublesome physical pain. Lillian felt panic set in; she had to act fast. She checked the door was locked and felt the knife inside her sweater pocket. She sat next to Morgan, who was halfway through her second glass of wine. Her head drooped as Lillian stroked her long sandy hair.

"You're tired, aren't you, darling? Why don't you lie down and have a nap? I'll wake you when Carlo gets here, and we shall go for a lovely meal."

"I...I am tired." Morgan mumbled. As Lillian stroked her head, she lay down on the bed and quickly fell asleep. The pills had worked perfectly. A train wreck wouldn't have woken Morgan now.

Lillian's heart rate increased rapidly. She had come to know this feeling well over the years, the feeling before the kill. The adrenaline was kicking in, but it was different this time. Helen was at play now, meddling with her thoughts. Lillian took a deep breath and tried to clear the mortal from her mind. Nothing would stop her now, she was too close to her prize.

She looked down at the sleeping Morgan, who, even at twenty-three, looked childlike in her slumber. Lillian made the sign of the Ancient Ones, then placed her hand on Morgan's heart. "Sleep," she whispered. The young girl's chest rose and sank, as she descended into deep unconsciousness. Lillian took the knife from her pocket and unfolded the blade, and the second she did…Helen struck out so hard that she dropped the knife onto the bed next to Morgan's face. Lillian grunted at the pain. She gritted her teeth and turned to the mirror.

"Stop it, you miserable wretch," she hissed. Helen responded by sending a sharp, chilling spasm throughout her. As she stared at her reflection, Lillian thought she caught a flash of Helen's eyes. She turned away and stepped to the bedside. The mortal was gathering strength fast; she needed to fill the bottle, and quickly. Lillian picked up the knife and placed the glass vase on the floor. She took Morgan's wrist, and she was about to slice open the tender flesh when Helen struck again, protesting hard against the slaughter of this innocent young girl for the sake of Lillian's insatiable vanity.

Ice-cold jolts shot through Lillian's veins, and she doubled over in pain, but it was no use. Helen was still far too bound by the spell to overpower her.

Lillian caught her breath and knelt down on the carpet. Her murderous instincts had come flooding back again and would serve her well. She was hell-bent on taking Morgan's blood and soul, and she would do it. She looked down at the soft young flesh, and against Helen's will, and against any laws of human kindness or common decency, Lillian sliced into Morgan's wrist. Instantly, she felt the disgust and sorrow from Helen within her, as Morgan's blood flowed out. Thick and dark, it gushed down in a stream across Morgan's fingers and into the vase.

Lillian's eyes sparkled. This was what she needed, the key to her preservation, her eternal life. As the jar filled rapidly, Lillian closed her eyes and spoke aloud the ancient words. "*Le sang de la jeunesse éternelle.*"

The words barely left her lips when a tiny, silvery, smoky spiral of white gently wound its way from the gash in Morgan's wrist and hovered delicately over the vase. Morgan's soul spiraled around slowly for a moment, and then vanished down into the dark red liquid. Her body was just an empty vessel now, a blank, dying piece of flesh. With the vase now full, Lillian carried it to the scuffed old benchtop and placed it in the center. She then took out the little crystal bottle, unscrewed the lid, and placed it next to the vase. She stood with reverence before the mirror, her arms folded across her chest.

It was time now.

She inhaled deeply, and a breeze flooded into the room, billowing the curtains over the balcony door. Morgan's face was now an eerie white; the blood flowing from her wrist had slowed a little now, but a large pool of it had gathered on the floor under her limp, dangling hand.

Lillian recited the rest of the spell; her words rang out loud and strong, the power of the dark forces flooding her body, as wind gushed into the room, knocking the rickety old framed pictures off the walls. Outside on Sunset Boulevard, a huge gust of wind suddenly swept down over the streets and sidewalks, startling the drivers and pedestrians.

Back in the room, Morgan's blood bubbled and hissed in the vase as Lillian stood over it with blissful satisfaction. Minutes later, she lifted the precious liquid and began to carefully fill the tiny crystal bottle. As she did, a delicate white vapor rose gently over the perfume bottle. The dark forces had once again distilled the blood to a tiny amount; the power and accuracy of the spell never ceased to amaze Lillian. She watched in ecstasy as the deep red liquid filled the perfume bottle to the top. Behind her, Morgan lay dying on the bed. A cold, damp feeling of defeat and sorrow ached inside Lillian. It was Helen, of course; she had sensed the death of the innocent.

"And there you will stay," she snickered. She pulled off her sweater and top and held the bottle over her naked breasts. She squeezed the pump, then reveled in the sensation of the red mist settling over her skin, tingling and penetrating its way deep inside her. A warm blanket of calmness swept over her. It was *done*.

She was safe now, or at least until the next kill was needed. The bottle was full again, and she had crushed any hope of Helen had of resurfacing.

Lillian was revitalized, back to full strength. And she had learned a valuable lesson. Never again would she let the bottle out of her sight—*never*. She looked down at Morgan with a mocking grin. *You should be more careful when somebody asks you to mind their belongings.* She took the knife into the bathroom and carefully washed the handle under the running water. She dried it with a hand towel before carefully placing it in Morgan's hand, wrapping her fingers around it. Next, she wiped down the wine bottle, the glasses, and the vase. She pressed Morgan's fingertips on the wine bottle and on one of the glasses, before placing the bottle and one wine glass next to the bed. She took the vase and the empty sleeping-pill boxes and placed them inside a pillowcase, along with Morgan's wallet and cell phone, knowing it would buy her some time before they identified her. She placed the perfume bottle in her handbag. She had carefully wiped down anything else she had touched in the room, including the doorknob, and now, satisfied, she put her sweater back on and pulled the hood up over her head. She headed to the door, pausing to turn and look at Morgan's body. *You certainly will not be sleeping with Carlo again; that's for certain.* It had bothered her ever since Christina had told her that Carlo and Morgan had dated briefly, but now she had taken care of that niggling little problem. She slipped on her sunglasses and headed out into the hallway.

She took the fire escape stairs to the lower parking lot, quickly exited, and headed back out onto the sidewalk. Much farther up the Sunset Strip, she headed into a dark alley where she took out Morgan's cell and stomped on it. She put it back in the pillowcase with the other items and tossed everything into a dumpster, feeling very pleased with herself—Morgan's death was the last thing on her mind. As she strode along the sidewalk, she thanked the Ancient Ones by whispering the words of the spell:

Blood of eternal youth,
Nourish my soul and fill my flesh,
With your blessing I defy all time,
I submit to your might and power,
I beg of you, Great Ones…
Grant me eternal youth and beauty,
Always and forever.

* * *

Ashley had returned to Helen's house with Daniel. It looked the same. When her knock went unanswered, she headed to the back deck and entered through the sliding doors. Daniel followed her in. Shadow appeared instantly.

"Hello, Shadow," she said, scooping him up. He purred lovingly. "Is this Helen's cat?"

"Yes, and she adores him."

Daniel stroked Shadow's dainty little head. "He's lovely."

"He sure is."

"Let's get you some fresh food and water. Won't that be nice?" Daniel stood in the living room, staring at Helen's vast collection of movie memorabilia.

"Amazing, isn't it? And it's all through the rest of the house too." Ashley said.

Daniel shook his head softly. "It's incredible. Look at this stuff; it must be worth a small fortune."

"I wouldn't doubt it at all. Helen's mother and aunty both lived here from the seventies and started the collection. They've both passed away now. Helen still collects, so it keeps growing. Collecting this stuff, watching old movies, and making beautiful dresses—that's what she does."

"I collect too." Daniel said, still looking around. "But nothing like this. Wow."

Ashley looked through Helen's fridge, shaking her head at all the food going bad. Her gut wrenched with worry as she wandered around Helen's empty house yet again with Daniel in tow. She knew nobody had been home. She looked in the garage; Helen's car was still there. She checked the answering machine, but there was nothing on it. "Nothing's changed, it's exactly the same." Ashley whispered.

Daniel looked in every room of the little cottage. Last, he stepped into Helen's bedroom and spotted the poster of Lillian over the bed. He looked over the outfits Helen had created; his gaze fell on the jewelry box on the dresser. He stood before it. *What a beautiful piece.* He slid a finger gently down the side of it and smelled a trace of something so vague and delicate it was barely perceivable. It was there and gone in a flash, so extraordinary that somehow it clouded his mind's eye, but just for a second. He pulled his hand back and shook his head slightly. He headed back to the living room.

He searched the garage and even the front and back yards, but nothing looked unusual. He headed back inside, where Ashley sat on the sofa with Shadow. "I've had a good look around, but I agree there's nothing that looks too strange." He sat next to Ashley, then pointed to a photo of Helen on the wall. "She sure does have a great smile."

"Yes, she does." Ashley turned to him. "You like her, don't you?"

Daniel grinned. "Yeah, I do, a lot. I've barely spoken to her, but…there's just something about her. She seems such a gentle person."

"She's one of the sweetest people I've ever known. Tell me about yourself, Daniel."

"Not a lot to tell. Born and raised in San Francisco, worked there in maintenance all my life. Came out of an awful divorce last year, no kids, and now I'm following a dream by moving out here to Hollywood for a fresh start. I just love movies. I'm renting a little place in Laurel Canyon, and I'm even taking some acting lessons in my spare time, you know, as you do when you're a forty-five-year-old divorcé." He chuckled.

Ashley laughed too. "You do whatever makes you happy, Daniel. That's what's important in life."

"You're right, and it took me a long time to realize that, and right now I'm happy. I love living here. Ashley, try to take it easy. I'm going to help you find Helen any way I can. You're not alone in this."

Ashley touched his hand. "Thank you."

Ashley called Helen's friend Tisha, but she hadn't heard from Helen either. And the police were still not all that interested; she knew that hundreds of people went missing in LA every year. Some turned up and some didn't. Ashley didn't want to think the worst, but how could she not? She tried to retrace Helen's last movements, but it appeared she had simply closed up the store, left the mall, and vanished. One of the girls who worked in the cafeteria recalled seeing her headed toward the car park, and that was it. There was nothing else to go on at all.

She sat on the couch with Daniel, silently praying that Helen would turn up. She looked up at Helen's picture on the wall, smiling with her mother and aunt. "Where are you, my dear friend? Please come home."

Shadow purred softly on her lap.

CHAPTER 27

DEATH PAYS ALL DEBTS

Lillian walked for over twenty minutes and got a good distance from the hotel. She remembered to cover her tracks and was sure to keep the hood pulled low over her face. Although times had changed, she still knew the basic principles of being careful. She waved down a cab and climbed inside, relieved, then listened to a message on her cell from Carlo, saying he was looking forward to seeing her at home later in the night.

The cab stopped at a set of lights, and Lillian noticed a sleek sports car idling next to them. She was impressed. A pretty young blonde behind the wheel was checking her hair in the rearview mirror. *My own car would be very useful.* Many bodies would have to be disposed of over time, a task she knew she would have to handle personally. Leaving her victims strewn all over Hollywood would not be prudent in this new life. Discretion would be vital if she was to survive. She loathed the idea…but she knew eventually she'd probably have to drive herself around in this new and incredibly busy town. She had the cab driver let her out a short distance away from Carlo's mansion, and she walked the rest of the way, just to be safe. Paulina let her in.

"Miss Lillian, can I fix you something?"

"No, I'm going for a shower."

"Okay, I'll a have wonderful dinner ready for you and Mr. Carlo tonight."

Upstairs, Lillian stripped off her clothes and placed them in a corner of the bathroom, intending to put them in a plastic bag and dispose of them the next day. Careful and safe, that was how she did things.

She then showered, enjoying the steaming hot water on her skin as her mind flashed back to the motel room. Morgan, the knife…Lillian put it out of her mind, with not a shred of sympathy or regret for the life she had just taken, nor for any she had taken in her past. Murder was a necessity.

Soon after, she was wrapped in a bathrobe and enjoying a cigar on the balcony as she waited for Carlo. A delicious aroma wafted up from the kitchen, and her stomach growled. Lillian felt complete, happy, and safe. Now that she had the bottle back and it was full, she could focus on her acting career again. She had impressed Carlo with a mere taste of what she was capable of. Soon he would give her major speaking parts in his upcoming projects, though…she knew Carlo was still considered small-time compared with the truly great directors, those men who directed the superstars of Hollywood. They had budgets sometimes in the hundreds of millions. Lillian's mind boggled at the thought of so much money being spent to make a film. In her first life, two million dollars was a respectable budget for an entire movie. Now it would barely secure you a half-decent actor.

A set of headlights illuminated the driveway. Carlo was home. She headed downstairs to see him, and his face lit up when he saw her.

"Darling, I'm sorry I took so long. I couldn't believe it when you called and said Shark got you the bottle back. I'm so happy, sweetheart."

"I know, Shark was wonderful. And it's all thanks to you." She put her arms around him and kissed him.

"What else did you do to pass the time, my lovely?"

"I had Shark drive me around a little and then drop me downtown. I went and did a bit of shopping to release the tension, I had a coffee and a small bite to unwind, and then I came home."

"I'm just so happy you found the bottle. You know I would have paid any amount to get it back for you, don't you?"

"Yes, I do," Lillian said, stroking his cheek.

After dinner, Lillian treated Carlo to a night of incredible sex. She then slept soundly without a hint of guilt.

The next morning at breakfast, Carlo's cell rang. He answered it and frowned. "She hasn't called anybody? And she's not there?"

Lillian stared down at her food.

"Okay, if she doesn't call in or turn up in the next hour, have someone fill in for her." He ended the call.

"Something wrong?"

"Oh, just Morgan. She was supposed to have emailed some stuff to my producer last night, but it didn't happen, and now she's not on set and won't answer her phone. She's usually quite reliable."

"I'm sure she'll call."

"What are you doing today, my dear? Would you like to come to the set? We're shooting on Hollywood Boulevard today. Cliff Summers is going to drop by to say hello and take a look around. He's pretty much the biggest director in the country. I'm very pleased he's stopping by. They say he usually only does that when he's thinking about working with another director."

Lillian's ears pricked up at once. She had read about this man in the newspapers. She knew he was on top of his game. He commanded some of the world's largest film budgets, and though in his late fifties, he was very well known for dating beautiful, and much younger, women. "That's wonderful, darling. I'd love to drop by today and take a look. I'll stay out of the way, though."

"Nonsense. If I can, I'll introduce you to him. And I've got some great news: I've received the green light for my next project, and I'm going to audition you for a speaking part. Just a few lines, but it'll be a great start."

Lillian stood up and hugged Carlo.

"Thank you for doing that for me."

"Darling, after seeing you read those lines to Chasey, I could see you were a natural actor. I know you can handle a small part."

Lillian kissed him.

"I'll send the car for you later, after we've filled most of the morning scenes. Cliff should be arriving just before midday, so maybe we could have lunch with him?"

"Sounds wonderful."

Morgan's body at the hotel niggled at her mind, but what was she to do? Time had been of the essence. As much as she would have liked to, she just didn't have the time or the means to dispose of the body properly. The suicide scene she had arranged would work fine, she reassured herself. She knew that in the future, though, she would have to be more careful. Many more young women were going to die at her hands; that was certain. From reading and watching modern television, she was fully aware that police forensic technology had improved vastly over the decades. But she did not fear it. She would simply educate herself to compete with it. Now that she was finally back and on her way to her long-deserved stardom, nothing would stop Lillian Kelly conquering Hollywood.

Nothing.

* * *

Ashley cut a lonely figure as she wandered along Hollywood Boulevard with dozens of leaflets in her hand. They were printed with color pictures of Helen's face, with the words "MISSING! REWARD FOR INFORMATION" across the top in large letters. Sadly, even though she had taped up over forty of these leaflets around Beachwood Canyon over the last couple of days, nobody had called. Not *one* person. Daniel had helped her post some around the Hollywood Highlight shopping center, and he had posted some at Laurel Canyon too.

Ashley had been calling the police for updates, but they insisted there was nothing they could do yet. Helen was just another missing person in LA, and they just didn't seem that interested in finding her. She fought back tears as she taped another leaflet to a phone pole outside a café. People stared, but she didn't care. Helen was her friend, and she would do whatever it took to find her. Soon she would bring Shadow to her house to live with her. At least then he wouldn't be so lonely. And somehow, with Shadow at Helen's house, it gave her hope that Helen would return soon.

All the other shop workers back at the shopping center were very sad to hear that Helen had disappeared. They had been coming to the store daily to see Ashley for updates about Helen; some brought flowers to cheer her up, which was sweet, but she still feared the worst. Clearly, she had to confront the big question: was Helen dead? Had she been murdered? Ashley's head told her yes, but her gut and her heart told her… maybe not. There was something very peculiar going on; she could feel it every time she entered Helen's house. And for some reason, inside her was a tiny flicker of hope that she might one day see her friend again.

CHAPTER 28

MONEY TALKS

Lillian stepped out of the limousine at Carlo's film set on Hollywood Boulevard. The barricades were up, and part of the street was sealed off with security guards keeping the crowds away. Lillian was turning heads the second she got out of the car; she was hard to miss in her sleek black dress with her jet-black hair shimmering down her back.

She moved through the crowd and approached a security guard she had met before, who let her in at once. Some of the ever-present paparazzi took a few snaps of her, surely thinking she must be one of the stars. She spotted Carlo talking to an assistant and made her way toward him. He kissed her on the cheek.

"Hello, darling. We've got a few more scenes to shoot, and then we'll wrap for lunch."

"Sounds wonderful. I'll just sit by and watch, if that's okay."

"Of course. Take a seat and have some cold water."

Moments later, Lillian was sitting under a large umbrella with a glass of water and watching Chasey and another actor run through their lines.

Lillian watched them closely. Chasey was good, but the other woman was only average. Her responses were slow, and she simply wasn't convincing. She read her lines robotically and with no conviction. Lillian remembered the words of her first acting teacher from so many years ago: if you don't believe your own dialog, don't expect the audience to believe you either. Lillian had taken that advice to heart: she made herself truly believe what the script said. In her first life, she would take on the persona of her characters and become them, sometimes for days at a time, until the script was second nature.

There was a slight commotion on set, and the crew began whispering excitedly. Lillian turned to see what the fuss was about and spotted Cliff Summers, the man himself. He was dressed in a long-sleeved black shirt and khaki pants with black leather shoes. Silver collar-length hair was swept back elegantly over his head, and a matching goatee frosted his chin. Black aviator sunglasses shielded his eyes, and a gold watch sparkled on his wrist. *Impressive. Very.* Cliff moved like he was the biggest director in the world, probably because he was. There was a youthful energy around him that was far from extinguished, and the man looked exceedingly rich just standing still. Lillian had read that his personal fortune was estimated at over a billion dollars, and his last two films had broken almost every box office record. He was trailed by a petite and attractive woman with long ginger hair. Her demeanor and attaché case clearly signaled she was an assistant. Carlo approached Cliff and shook his hand, smiling. He had earlier told Lillian he aspired to be as successful as Cliff.

Some of the crew took photos of the two men together. Chasey also came over to say hello to Cliff. Lillian was impressed she made the move. She knew Chasey had never appeared in a Cliff Summers movie, but it appeared she was making an impression on him fast.

Carlo arranged seats for Cliff and his assistant in chairs next to Lillian. That was when Lillian made her move. As Cliff turned in her direction, Lillian stood slowly, removed her sunglasses, and looked directly at him. The effect was instant. Cliff stared, mesmerized at the towering dark-haired beauty before him. He, too, removed his sunglasses and stared into those hypnotizing blue eyes. He looked Lillian up and down, taking in her physical perfection.

Carlo stepped between them. "Cliff, I'd like to introduce my partner, Lillian."

At first Cliff didn't react; he just stared. He had been with hundreds of stunning women in his time. He had been a heavyweight in the global film industry for over two decades and had satisfied his every sexual whim, desire, and fantasy with scores of breathtakingly attractive women. But this woman…was truly *something else.*

He snapped out of his trance and realized he had just been introduced to this specimen of female perfection.

"I'm…I'm sorry?"

"This is my partner, Lillian," Carlo repeated.

"A name so fitting for such an exquisite lady," Cliff complimented.

Lillian was pleased her looks had struck him hard. She had thought, given who he was, that she may have been just another beautiful woman to him. But no, again Lillian Kelly had stopped another powerful, wealthy man dead in his tracks.

"How do you do, Mr. Summers?" Lillian asked.

"Please, call me Cliff."

"Thank you, Cliff. Carlo and I are big fans of your work."

"Well, I've been very impressed with Carlo's work too, especially the last film you did," Cliff said, smiling at Carlo.

"Thank you," Carlo replied.

Sebastian appeared by his side. "Almost ready to start, Carlo."

Carlo nodded to him.

"Looks like you've got some filming to do," Cliff remarked.

Carlo laughed. "Perhaps you can give me some pointers?"

"I think you're doing just fine. I've already watched you do a few scenes from behind the barricades. But I'll watch a few more, if you don't mind?"

"Be my guest. My crew will get you anything you need." A crew member fetched another umbrella, and soon Cliff and his assistant were sitting next to Lillian.

Cliff turned to Lillian. "Lillian, this is my personal assistant, Bronwyn."

"Hello, Lillian. I must say, you're very striking."

"Oh, thank you."

Carlo called action, and filming was underway. Chasey Wells stepped on set and approached the other actress, who had just stepped out of a sleek sports car. Chasey began asking the other woman about where she had bought her car. In the script, the car had belonged to Chasey's character; the stalker had stolen it and sold it to the unsuspecting buyer. After two takes the other actress began dropping her lines and stammering.

Carlo called cut. "Everybody, take five," he yelled.

He approached the actress and spoke quietly to her for a few moments. She nodded and went to sit down.

Carlo then approached Chasey, who was talking to Lillian and Cliff. "I'm sorry, Chasey. She told me she's nervous Cliff Summers is on set. After a short break I think she'll be fine."

"Okay, but she needs to be more professional. We never really got through the scene properly once. I'll go run through it in my trailer," Chasey said.

"I'm sorry, Carlo. It happens," Cliff apologized.

"No, really, I'm honored to have you on set."

"Could I be of any help with your lines?" Lillian asked Chasey.

"Well, yes, if you wouldn't mind. Perhaps we could run through the scene together?"

"I'd love to."

"Do you act, Lillian?" Cliff asked.

"She's done some acting in the past, and she's a natural," Carlo said. "I'm planning to give Lillian a little part in my next film."

"I can only imagine how incredible you'd look on camera," Cliff added, smiling at Lillian.

Carlo beamed at the compliment about his girlfriend.

"Perhaps I could watch the ladies in action, if that's okay with Lillian and Chasey," Cliff asked.

Lillian could tell Chasey was thrilled at the chance to perform in private for Cliff Summers.

"Absolutely fine with me," Chasey said.

"I'd love to," Lillian agreed.

"Marvelous," Cliff said.

"I've got a few things to take care of for the next scenes. I'll join you as soon as I can," Carlo said.

Chasey led everyone to her trailer. It was air-conditioned and as luxurious as one would expect of a leading Hollywood star. Cliff and Bronwyn took a seat on a plush sofa as Lillian went to work memorizing the lines in moments. Her razor-sharp memory never failed her.

"I'm ready if you are."

Chasey stared, surprised. "Already?"

Lillian nodded.

"Okay, let's do it." Chasey began her lines. "Excuse me, but where did you get that car?"

"Why do you ask?"

"Well, it belongs to me. It was stolen a week ago."

"I'm afraid you're mistaken. I purchased it from a dealer downtown, and it's my car."

Cliff watched, focusing on Lillian in particular. She looked unbelievable, and she had a voice to match. Her presence was off the chart, though he knew she had only studied the dialog for a few moments. And here she was performing it flawlessly and convincingly.

Cliff knew the traits of a great actor: a fast, precise memory and the ability to convince the audience. These, topped with Lillian's mind-blowing looks, left him impressed.

Chasey and Lillian continued with the scene.

"I can assure you it is not your car," Lillian insisted.

"It *is* my car. Somebody has changed the license plates, but that is *my* car and I'm calling the police."

"Then call them. I have a receipt for it in the glove box. I paid cash for it and it belongs to me, and I'm afraid that's all there is to it."

The women finished the scene, and Cliff and Bronwyn applauded them.

"Lillian, that was great," Cliff said. "I can't believe you only learned the lines a few minutes ago. Thank you, Chasey. Well done, ladies! Great work."

Both Chasey and Lillian thanked him.

There was a knock at the door and Carlo entered. "Have I missed the show?"

"You missed a great performance," Cliff said. "And you really need to get this beautiful lady in front of the cameras," he added, nodding at Lillian.

"Don't I know it. So, shall we go to lunch?"

Twenty minutes later they were sipping wine at a popular restaurant just off Hollywood Boulevard. While they waited for their meals, Cliff told stories about his life; he was quite the personality and had a very smooth way about him. Lillian warmed to him quickly. They had finished their meals and ordered coffee when Carlo's cell rang. He excused himself and stepped outside to take the call. Cliff leaned in close to Lillian.

"Lillian, you must audition for me, perhaps at my home; it's not far away. I'm sure I could give you a part in something I have coming up very soon."

The look in his eyes reminded her of all those film directors and wealthy men so long ago. They would promise her anything to sleep with her, to have their way with her… but she had gotten nothing in return. But that was before, in her first life. Now she was wiser…*reborn*…and she knew from the look in his eyes alone that one sexual encounter would not be enough for Cliff. She would get a part in his films. That she was already sure of.

"I'd love to audition for you, Cliff."

"Perhaps today?"

Lillian nodded, while Bronwyn looked at her with a gleam in her eye.

"Sounds wonderful." Lillian said.

Carlo stepped back inside. "There's a problem with our next location. It's a department store we booked, but there are some issues. I need to get down there and sort it out. Cliff, I'm so sorry."

"It's fine Carlo. These things happen. Do what you have to do."

"Darling, is it all right if I spend the afternoon with Cliff and Bronwyn? I could drop back on set later?" Lillian asked.

"Yes, of course it is." He kissed Lillian goodbye and shook hands with Cliff and Bronwyn. "Cliff, thank you so much for stopping by today. I appreciate it."

"You're welcome, Carlo. You were doing a great job. Let's talk soon."

Carlo glowed at the compliment.

In no time, Lillian was sitting comfortably next to Cliff in the passenger seat of his luxurious sedan, with Bronwyn in the back. She loved the way he told stories. He had a charismatic confidence with a dash of humor that women the world over loved, and he knew how to use it. They cruised into Bel-Air. The houses were every bit as palatial as Carlo's, and most were complete with huge sprawling grounds. Cliff turned into a paved drive, and Lillian stared up at an enormous set of golden gates, each adorned with a huge lion crest. Commanding and elegant, they stood around twenty-feet high and would have been more at home in front of a castle in Europe. Cliff pressed a button on a remote control and the gates swung open to reveal a long, pristine drive flanked by palm trees and exotic shrubbery. As they drove, Lillian realized this wasn't a driveway; it was a private road—Cliff owned the *entire street.* The estate around her seemed to stretch forever. She was stunned.

"Cliff, this is incredible."

"Thank you, Lillian. I really like it here."

Lillian looked ahead and tried to comprehend what she was seeing. Carlo's house was magnificent, yes, but the one in front of her now just defied words…Cliff's house was *enormous.* There appeared to be a main building in the center flanked by another two extending out from either side of it. Lillian stared in awe. She saw a huge garage with men in white overalls polishing vintage cars and limousines. A dozen gardeners were tending to the lawns and the immaculately shaped hedges. It was almost unbelievable to think that one man could afford all this.

Cliff parked outside the mansion's entrance, and two attractive young maids came rushing out and stood obediently by the door, as if awaiting a command from their master. As they stepped inside Cliff's house, Lillian struggled to take it all in. Carlo's mansion could fit inside this one four times over.

Cliff led the women inside, and Lillian gazed around at the wealth surrounding her. *The life of a billionaire.* They headed into a large room with scripts lying on a table. There were cameras on tripods, white screens on the walls, and tape marks on the floor—all the usual audition equipment.

"Would you like a drink, Lillian? I'm going to have a scotch, and Bronwyn usually likes a wine about this time of afternoon."

"Wine would be lovely, Cliff."

Cliff nodded at one of the young maids standing by the door, who left to fetch their drinks. Cliff picked up a script and handed it to Lillian.

"This is a movie I'm going to start casting in a couple of months. I think you'd be perfect for the part of the main character's wife. It's going to be a huge production. I'm sure you know I don't do anything by halves."

"I'm well aware you don't."

"Have a browse at it and then run through the scene for me."

Lillian knew he was testing her memory under pressure, and her ability as an actor, and she was more than up for the challenge.

She glanced through the part. It was only a few pages. Her character was an attractive woman who seduces her husband's friend and his wife. The scene was full of nudity and sex, and Lillian knew if Cliff Summers was directing, it would be a blockbuster. She studied the lines for a few moments as Cliff sat next to Bronwyn, chatting quietly. Lillian noticed the body language between the two; clearly, their relationship went beyond professional.

The maid arrived with a tray of drinks as Lillian put down the script.

"I'm ready when you are."

"Okay, let's roll," Cliff said, switching on a camera.

Cliff and Bronwyn read the lines of the other characters. The scene was written as a prelude to a ménage à trois. The male character offers Lillian a huge amount of money to have sex with him and his wife. Lillian worked the part perfectly, improvising with highly sexual movements and standing very close to Cliff, and even running a finger down Bronwyn's cheek. In a few minutes they had run through the entire scene and Cliff was very impressed. His eyes craved her.

"Well done, Lillian. You truly do have an incredible memory, don't you?"

"I'm lucky."

"You act very well. Let's watch the playback."

Cliff played back the scene on a big screen. Lillian was very happy with her performance. She *loved* the way she looked on camera, especially with her black hair.

An hour later, the three of them had consumed several drinks. Cliff amazed Lillian with stories of his world travels making his hugely popular films. Lillian was enthralled. His knowledge of Europe was extensive, and he had a wisdom about him that genuinely impressed her.

"Well, Lillian, I'd like to formally offer you a chance to audition for the part. I am impressed; you are exactly what

I'm looking for. I was determined to find an unknown for this part. And I think that just may be you."

Lillian glowed inside. Everything was going so perfectly in this new life. This was how things should have gone, so many years ago, but hadn't.

And now she would make up for it unforgivingly.

Here she sat, in the home of pretty much the biggest film director in the world, and he had just formally offered her an audition for his next mega-budget movie.

"Thank you, Cliff."

Cliff raised his glass. "To new friendships."

The three of them clinked glasses and drank. Cliff ran his hand up Bronwyn's back, and she responded by stroking his leg. They enjoyed a passionate kiss as Lillian watched. The wine had kicked in, and she was feeling very nicely lubricated indeed. Bronwyn stared seductively at her.

"Forgive us, Lillian. The drink brings out the worst in us, I'm afraid," Cliff said.

"Oh, don't apologize. I was rather enjoying the show."

"In that case, feel free to sit a little closer," Cliff offered.

Lillian moved over next to Cliff. His eyes sparkled with delight. Lillian knew this was exactly what he'd been hoping for.

He kissed her deeply, desire burning inside him. Bronwyn slid her dress off. Cliff smothered her chest in kisses. Lillian slid down her own dress, and Cliff stared lustfully at what was probably the most perfect bust in Los Angeles. He was on Lillian like a wolf. Hollywood's most powerful film director was clearly in awe of her; it was a power trip beyond *belief.* She knew there and then she would get exactly what she wanted. Carlo had been useful so far, but Cliff could offer her the world, and she had known since the second he'd laid eyes on her he wanted to possess her. As she lay back with Cliff and Bronwyn unleashing their hunger on her, Lillian saw it all before her, living in his mansion…being cast as the leading lady in his movies; it was all right here waiting for her. The three of them indulged in each other until the sun went down.

Three hours later, Cliff and Bronwyn waved Lillian off as she left for home in one of his limousines. She checked her phone and saw Carlo had called a few times.

She lit a cigar and called him back. "Hello, darling."

"Lillian, I've left messages. Is everything okay?"

"Perfect, sweetheart. Cliff and Bronwyn and I went for coffee and then drove around a little and looked at the sights, and then we went to Cliff's house. Oh, Carlo it's incredible. He had me audition there; he's offered me a part in his upcoming film—isn't that marvelous?"

"Uh, yes, it is. Well done, darling."

Lillian detected an odd note in his voice. "Where are you now?" she asked.

"I'm on the way home, not far away."

"I'm looking forward to seeing you."

"Me too, darling."

CHAPTER 29

SECOND BLOOD

Detective Karson stood in the middle of the seedy hotel room, surrounded by the familiar scene of death. On his hands were standard police-issue latex gloves. Forensics had just finished taking photos and video.

The familiarity of the scene had struck him instantly. The knife clasped in the dead girl's hand did nothing to dissuade him that this was the second murder by the same person. The phony suicide attempt hadn't fooled him for a second. In his eyes, everything about it resembled the murder scene in Peter Jameson's apartment. He knelt beside the girl's outstretched hand dangling inches above the floor, staring down at the large dark bloodstain on the carpet under it. The incision in her wrist was identical to the one on the other victim. Clearly, the same person did it, and they knew exactly what they were doing. Once again, there were no signs of a struggle. But why would somebody choose to kill by cutting the artery like this and letting the victim bleed out? The hairs on Karson's neck bristled.

The head forensics officer began packing his equipment into a bag. He looked at Karson. "What a shame. Just a kid."

Karson nodded. "I guess."

"Why would a pretty young thing like this kill herself? I just don't understand. There must have been someone she could have talked to."

Karson shot him a firm glance. "Sometimes bad things just happen."

The media were already gathered outside, chomping at the bit for whatever information they could get. Karson had given strict orders nobody was to mention the similarities to the crime scene in Jameson's apartment. The last thing he needed was a serial killer media frenzy. For now, he wanted things quiet.

He searched through the small room. There was nothing else to indicate anybody else had been there besides the victim. He ordered a young cop to search Morgan's pockets, then headed down to speak to the hotel manager.

"Describe to me exactly this woman who rented the room."

"Well, like I told the uniform cops, she was pretty, I mean, more like, well…I don't know, attractive, great body, but she had that hood and big sunglasses on."

"And there's nothing else that stood out at all?"

"Well, no, just…she was tall, and she had those black boots and jeans."

Karson sighed. "Tattoos, scars, piercings, jewelry… anything?"

"I don't remember. She paid with cash and tipped me too. I'm sorry, but that's all I remember about her."

Karson stared at him. "Describe her voice."

The manager's eyes trailed back. "Her voice, yeah. Actually, I do recall she spoke very classy…kind of a…sexy kind of voice, I guess. Husky. I can't remember much else."

"And you didn't see the other young woman enter the building?"

"No, but I'm not always at the desk. She must have slipped by me when I was out the back."

Karson held out his card. "You think of anything else at all, and I mean anything, you call this number. Got it?"

"Yes, sir."

The young cop came down the stairs and stepped over to Karson. "Sir, I found this in an inside pocket in her coat," he said clasping a piece of paper.

"Nothing else? No ID? No cell?"

"Nothing, sir, just this."

Karson took the piece of paper, a folded-up set list. At the top was a letterhead for Vonhampton Films. He knew it was one of the larger film companies in LA.

The front door of the hotel burst open, and a uniformed officer rushed to Karson with a small plastic evidence bag.

"Detective, I found this in the garden. There were lots of cigarette butts, but this one's different; it was right under the balcony of the room where we found the body, and it looks really fresh. There's no others like it, just this one."

Karson's eyes narrowed as he took the bag off the young cop and studied the white cigar closely. He looked carefully at the elegant silver band and the fine writing just above it: "Vanilla Dove."

* * *

Carlo was waiting on his front stairs as the limousine pulled up. He opened the door for Lillian, and she stepped out and kissed him. He closed the door and waved the driver off.

"Hello, beautiful. So, you auditioned for Cliff Summers?"

"Oh, Carlo, it was a great experience. We went over some scripts, but I couldn't wait to get home to you."

"And I couldn't wait to see you, my love. Cliff will have to wait in line; I want you in one of my movies first."

Lillian laughed. "Of course, sweetheart. I'd love nothing more than to star in one of your films."

Carlo turned sharply. "Uh…star?"

"Well, yes, Cliff did say he would give me a lead part, not just a few lines. Surely you think I'm good enough to be a lead actor in one of your films too?"

"Well, yes…of course you are; you're a natural. I'll do everything possible to secure you a lead role in my next project."

She kissed him again.

He took her hand. "Now, let's eat. I'm starved."

After dinner and wine, they sat on Carlo's bedroom balcony under the stars. Lillian sensed he had some questions. "So, you saw inside Cliff's house?"

"Yes, I did. It's very large, rather too large. Not really to my taste. I much prefer your home."

"And he auditioned you for quite some time I take it?"

"Yes, he certainly put me through my paces. We must have gone through about twelve different scenes. It took hours and was quite exhausting, and he really is no-nonsense; he's just all business. I was rather relieved to finally take a break from it. I felt a little overwhelmed and unprepared."

Carlo relaxed and believed every word.

"Darling, when I was downtown recently, I saw the most beautiful little sports car parked outside a café. I had a similar one years ago back in New York. I loved the feeling of independence it gave me."

"What happened to it?" Carlo asked.

"Well, my ex-partner actually owned it. It was supposed to be a gift to me, but he bought it in his name. He took it from me after an argument and sold it. I realized today after the whole missing perfume bottle ordeal how much I missed that feeling of driving myself around. I felt so helpless. Thank goodness for Shark. Perhaps in time, if I get some work, you might help me find a cheap little vehicle, just something basic maybe?"

"Of course, sweetheart. Whatever you like. But in the meantime, you know you can have the limo when you need it, and taxis too, whenever you like."

"Yes, I know. Thank you."

They made wild love on Carlo's bedroom balcony under the night sky. It was Lillian's second romp that day, but her appetite for sex was voracious and getting stronger by the day. After some incredible climaxes, Carlo headed inside and fell asleep. Lillian stood on the balcony and lit up a cigar. She'd had Morgan pick up a few tins of them for her, before her untimely demise. She looked out over the city lights.

Her cell beeped with a text. It was Cliff, thanking her for a wonderful afternoon and telling her how much he was looking forward to seeing her again. She smiled; already she had him around her finger, and now she'd put Carlo in a position where he simply had to give her a major part in his next film. But what if Cliff came up with a part for her first? There would be no contest. She would follow the fastest path to the top. She looked inside at the sleeping Carlo. *Such a sweet man, but he simply isn't one of the major players.* Until Cliff delivered what he'd promised, Carlo would do just fine.

* * *

Ashley had just left the police station, but there was no news at all. The cop at the front desk had even told her that calling them three times a day wouldn't make them find Helen any faster. She knew they had made some inquiries around the mall, but they just weren't taking Helen's disappearance seriously enough at all for Ashley's liking.

She made her way back to the shop with a heavy heart. Soon she would take Shadow and his basket and toys to her place. She wondered whether she would ever see Helen again. She sat down on a bench on the sidewalk and stared at the ground as a tear rolled down her cheek. How could this happen? How could Helen just vanish? How?

Helen was one of the most reliable and habitual people Ashley had ever known, and now she was just gone, her car in the garage, her front door unlocked, and her cat wandering around her empty little house. Nothing made sense. Even with all the flyers she'd put up with Helen's picture on them and a generous reward for information, she'd only received a few prank calls from some kids and crazies. Ashley would never give up looking for her friend. Never.

CHAPTER 30

THE WHEELS OF JUSTICE

Karson watched through the glass window. The terrified middle-aged man stared as the coroner lifted the sheet from the pale, lifeless body. The man's eyes widened, and his head nodded as he broke down in tears.

It was confirmed. Morgan's father had positively identified her. Now that Karson knew exactly who she was, he could go about his investigation full speed. He now had his sights set firmly on Vonhampton Films. He had already found out the deceased had been employed there for over two years, working in many different departments. She had also more recently worked as personal assistant to one Carlo Genisi. Karson knew who he was, and he had even seen a few of his movies. Half an hour later, he was on his way to Carlo's film set.

Karson parked his car and hung his police badge on his suit pocket as he walked toward the crowd gathered around the barricades. He chuckled; it always amused him how normal people had the same fascination with fame…a mere illusion created by magazines and television, and a whole lot of hype. Nevertheless, people loved it, seemed to need it, staring at their idols as if they were not human, but rather gods from another planet.

He moved through the crowd, the gold badge commanding people to quickly step out of his way. A burly security guard blocked his path at the final barricade, until he, too, spotted the badge and moved aside. Karson walked onto the set and at once spotted Carlo. He was briefing the actors; Karson recognized the movie star Chasey Wells, an actress whose work he had admired in the past. He approached them, then stood by and waited for Carlo to finish speaking to them.

Sebastian noticed him and came over.

"Hi, I'm Sebastian. May I help you?"

"I'm Detective James Karson. I'd like to speak with Mr. Genisi. It's of an urgent but private nature."

"Certainly, one moment." Sebastian headed over to Carlo and tapped his shoulder. He spoke quietly in Carlo's ear a moment, then gestured to Karson.

Carlo excused himself from the actors and approached Karson. "Hello, Detective. How can I help you?"

The two men shook hands.

"Is there somewhere more private we can talk?" Karson asked.

"Yes, please follow me." Carlo led the detective to his on-set trailer and closed the door behind them. "Please, take a seat. How can I help you?"

"Mr. Genisi, two days ago there was a report to the police regarding the disappearance of a young woman named Morgan James."

Carlo frowned. "Yes…has she turned up?"

Karson took a deep breath. "Sir, I'm sorry to inform you that Miss James has been found dead in a hotel room. I believe she was murdered." Karson stared directly into Carlo's eyes, watching every move the man made, his pupil dilation, his breathing, body movements, everything. This was what he was trained for. This was the moment every detective closely scrutinized the person they were speaking to, watching carefully for that first reaction to the news that somebody they knew had been found dead…murdered. Over the years he'd seen so many guilty people, trying to fake grief and shock only to be ultimately found out as the perpetrator themselves.

The law stated that someone was innocent until proven guilty, all right, but so many times Karson had known by his gut instinct within seconds, that the person he was breaking the news to *was* in fact the guilty party. So far, though, Carlo displayed no guilt whatsoever. He appeared genuinely shocked and upset; he stared down at the floor with that horrible stunned look Karson had seen so many times in his career.

"How…how did she…"

"At this stage we're not releasing any details, except that the young lady has been positively identified. I understand you knew her reasonably well, and that she worked directly for you."

"Yes," Carlo mumbled, dazed.

"When was the last time you saw her?"

"It was after we finished filming on Tuesday. There were some items stolen on set. We called the police and they came out to investigate."

"Sir, is there anything at all you can tell me about Miss James? Anything out of the ordinary? Did she use drugs? Did she have any enemies? Anything at all."

"Oh God, no, not Morgan. She was a very fit and healthy person. She didn't drink much, never smoked, and she was careful with what she ate. And enemies? No, Morgan was a sweet girl. I can't imagine anybody being her enemy."

"Okay. Do you know of any women associated with Morgan by the name of Lillian?"

Carlo looked up sharply.

"Well, yes. My girlfriend's name is Lillian."

Karson's eyes narrowed. "Your girlfriend?"

"Yes, she and Morgan were friends. Well, I mean, Morgan sometimes worked for me as my personal assistant, but recently I had her helping Lillian with shopping trips and the like."

"What's Lillian's last name?"

Carlo stared at him with an empty look. "I, well...I actually don't know."

Karson cocked his head slightly. "Excuse me?"

"I just...I really don't know. We...haven't known each other all that long, you see."

"Okay. Where can I find Lillian?"

"I think she's at home today, or she could be out shopping."

"Would you please call her on her cell for me right now and let her know I'd like to speak with her immediately in person, Mr. Genisi?"

A shiver crept down Carlo's spine. "May I ask why you want to talk to Lillian?"

"Oh, her name just came up during our investigation, that's all. It's just standard procedure to interview everybody in recent contact with the deceased. When you said home, did you mean that you and Lillian live together?"

"Yes, she moved in with me not long ago. Things have moved rather quickly between us."

"So how long have you known Lillian?"

"Oh…a few weeks."

"And where did you meet her?"

Carlo wriggled uncomfortably. Not only did he dislike the questions, but it occurred to him that he knew very little about the woman he loved so much. "I…well, we met in Hollywood one night."

"Any particular place? A club?"

Carlo dreaded what he was about say, but his gut told him not to bend the truth with this man. "The thing is, I met Lillian on the street one night and I gave her a lift into Hollywood. We had dinner, and then we just fell in love."

"Where did Lillian live before she moved in with you?"

Again, Carlo was embarrassed. He shrugged. "I never went to where she was staying, so I'm really not sure."

"Okay. If you wouldn't mind calling her now?"

"Yes, certainly." Carlo dialed Lillian's cell. She answered quickly.

"Hello, darling."

"Hi, sweetheart. I have a police officer here with me. He'd like to come to the house and talk to you." Carlo truly did not know what else to say. He told Lillian not to worry and just to speak with the police officer. He was still in shock himself.

He decided to let Karson go and break the bad news about Morgan to her. He had some very serious scenes to film today, and he really did not want to hear his beloved Lillian breaking down on the phone. "It's just to help him with his inquiries." Carlo looked at Karson, who gave him a stern nod.

"Okay, sweetheart, I'll see you tonight." Carlo ended the call and took out one of his business cards. He wrote on the back. "That's my home address. I'd come along, but I have some major scenes to shoot today."

"That's fine, Mr. Genisi. You've been very helpful. Thank you, and good luck with the film."

After Karson left, Carlo sat anxiously in his trailer. He contemplated calling his lawyer to see if he could be present while Karson spoke to Lillian, but why did he feel like that? He truly didn't know. He only knew that he didn't like the idea of Karson breaking the awful news to Lillian without him there to comfort her. He suspected she'd get no compassion from Karson; the man appeared to be as tough as they came, and Carlo had felt quite uneasy every time he looked into those hard green eyes. But right now, he had two of Hollywood's biggest actors on set, and an army of extras; each hour was costing hundreds of thousands of dollars. Still, out of respect for Morgan, he called the people in charge at Vonhampton Films and informed them of Morgan's death. He was hoping he could call off shooting for the day, which would also enable him to rush home to comfort Lillian while she spoke with Karson. The answer was a flat no. Carlo was disappointed with the response. The Vonhampton people knew that each day was costing them a fortune, and they wanted things finished on time. *Always about the money.* He truly could not leave the set until the scenes were shot.

Why would Karson want to talk to Lillian? She had gone shopping with Morgan and had spent a little time with her on set, but why did he need to speak with her? An uneasy twinge shadowed his soul. He had to admit to himself there was something very dark and unusual about Lillian, something deep below the surface he had never quite managed to figure out. But he loved her; she could do no wrong in his eyes, and he did not want her upset. She would be shattered enough knowing Morgan had been murdered. It was tearing him up…but he simply couldn't leave the film set.

* * *

Karson was glad to be out of Carlo's trailer. He had seen that look dozens of times over the last two decades, the pale, incredulous face of a human being who had just been told that somebody they knew had died. He saw that face in his sleep, and he never liked to hang around to see people wallowing in shock. He'd done that far too many times before. Besides, his gut told him he had found the mysterious Lillian. He got in his car and headed straight for Carlo's home.

* * *

Karson drove down the palm-studded driveway, shaking his head at the gargantuan mansion before him. *Wealth.* This town was just saturated with money. He parked out front, and Paulina opened the front door and greeted him.

"Hello, sir. Mr. Carlo says you're coming. Miss Lillian is waiting for you. Please, this way."

"Thank you," Karson replied. He followed Paulina through the main living area, taking in the opulent interior. Paulina opened the double doors and gestured Karson through, closing the door behind him.

Karson stepped inside and looked around. He felt his breath catch in his throat, for there, on the far side of the room, standing with her back to him, was a woman in a perfectly figure-hugging black dress with long black hair flowing to her waist. She stood perfectly still in front of the huge windows that overlooked the incredible view. Karson took a moment to take her in. She was absolutely mind-blowing. As a man who had spent over two decades in Hollywood, he had seen some stunning women in his time, but this woman's body…was *unbelievable*. Although momentarily stunned by her looks, he registered at once that she was not blonde.

He cleared his throat. "Lillian?"

She turned and looked at him; Karson was caught off guard. Even standing twenty-five feet away from her, he could see she was an extraordinarily beautiful lady.

"Yes, hello."

She made her way toward him, and Karson thought he had never seen a woman move more gracefully in his life. Her movements seemed effortless, and suddenly she stood right before him, almost matching his height. Now up close, she hit him even harder: the flawless skin, the full, luscious lips…but what really got his attention was her eyes. They were large and blue, *very* blue, and they immediately threw him. His specialty was reading people, and he knew that the eyes really were the windows to the soul. He had always seen exactly what he was looking for in people's eyes, and his gift never failed him. Lies, truth, jealousy, secrets—everything was right there in people's eyes, if you just knew how to look for it. But this woman's eyes were different, and though amazing, there just seemed to be nothing behind them at all.

Lillian extended her hand. "How do you do?"

Karson shook her hand gently, marveling at the softness of her skin. "I'm Detective James Karson. I'm very well, thank you."

"Carlo said you would like to speak to me about Morgan. I hope everything is okay?"

"Would you mind if we sat down?" Karson gestured to the plush leather sofa in the middle of the room.

"Of course, forgive me. Please sit."

Karson followed her to the sofa, his eyes transfixed on her seductively long legs and perfectly round behind. Lillian sat next to him and crossed her legs. Karson had already switched on the miniature digital recorder in his pocket, but he still took out his notebook and pen. "Thank you for speaking with me today, Miss…?"

Ah…clever. Even if he had asked Carlo what my last name was, he wouldn't have known it. She'd predicted this and had already invented a new name for herself. "Raines," she replied coolly, even spelling it out for him. She had invented the name for herself only a few days ago and rather liked it. She had already decided this would be her new real last name when she reestablished her identity, and she was planning to tell Carlo this. Karson jotted down the name, and now he understood why everybody at Peter Jameson's party had commented on this woman's looks. There was no doubt this was the Lillian he had been looking for. He could tell her dark hair was not natural, she had simply dyed it. He usually had no problem concentrating on his job under any circumstances, but this woman was certainly affecting him. He could not recall the last time a woman had made him feel nervous.

"Miss Raines, I'm afraid I have very sad news. I regret to inform you Morgan James has been found dead."

He watched Lillian's immaculate face closely. He stared straight into those large blue eyes as her pupils darted about and her breathing quickened…She looked down at the floor in disbelief, then leaned forward, her hair shrouding her face like a mourner's veil. Karson watched as her shoulders began to heave softly, and then she looked up at him…the exquisite face had cracked, and her eyes were filled with tears. She placed a hand over her mouth and looked up at Karson. "Morgan's dead?"

"I'm afraid so."

"But…how did she die?"

"I believe Miss James was murdered."

"Murdered! Why on Earth would anyone harm that sweet child?"

"That's what I intend to find out, Miss Raines."

Lillian sobbed and shook. "I…just can't believe it!" She put her head in her hands and sobbed—a convincing performance, very worthy of the professional actress she was.

Karson took the bait. He felt bad about breaking the awful news to this gorgeous woman. Clearly, she was in shock and terribly upset, but he still had some hard questions for her.

He sat closer to her and offered her his handkerchief. She took it and wiped her eyes.

"Thank you, Detective. May I call you James?"

"Uh, yeah. Call me…Jimmy."

Lillian leaned in closer to Karson. She looked into his eyes and placed one hand on his. Ripples shot up his arm; it was a little inappropriate to make physical contact like this under the circumstances, but it wasn't just that. Her presence rattled him, and her very touch had given him butterflies, but her emotional state made him reluctant to remove his hand.

Lillian erupted into tears again. "I'm sorry. I'm just in shock. Morgan and I spent time together; we became friends."

"When was the last time you saw her?"

"Well, I guess it was on set. Tuesday, yes." Lillian dabbed at her eyes.

Karson looked down at her trembling hand still on top of his. Her skin was like silk, and her nails were coated with a thick, gleaming coat of red.

"How did she seem? Did anything out of the ordinary happen?"

"Well, I was playing a small part in the film, you see, and Morgan was assisting me. There was a robbery on set and my bag was stolen. A lot of things were stolen." Lillian trembled. "Oh, that poor child! God rest her soul."

Karson hated himself more than he had in a long time for being the bearer of bad news. "I'm sorry, Miss Raines, really. I know you're upset. But I need to ask you some questions. They're very important."

Lillian wiped her eyes and regained her composure. "Forgive me, Jimmy. Yes, please go ahead. Ask me anything you wish."

"What can you tell me about a party you attended in an apartment owned by a man named Peter Jameson?" Lillian was quietly surprised. *So he has traced me back that far; no matter.* She had anticipated this possibility.

"Oh, yes, he's…the talent agent? I met him in Hollywood one night and he invited me to a fashion show he was hosting."

"And what happened after that?"

"I ended up accepting his invitation to a party at his home. There were many people there. The thing is, Jimmy, I really do not recall much. I'm…very embarrassed to admit this, but…I drank far too much, and I did something I do not usually do. I ended up…sleeping with him, and that's nearly all I remember. I remember suddenly feeling very ill, and I only barely recall leaving as other people in the apartment began to behave, well…intimately. Not my kind of thing. Looking back, I'm convinced somebody spiked my drink. I even threw up. I remember going outside feeling unwell, and the next day I was ill and incoherent for hours. It was a most unpleasant experience, and I truly recall very little of the whole event."

"Okay, what time did you leave the apartment?"

"I really cannot be sure. As I mentioned, I do believe my drink was spiked, and I could not think clearly. It was all I could do to get a cab. However, I do believe it was still rather early."

"Before or after midnight, would you say?"

"Oh, I believe it was well before midnight, Jimmy. But I honestly cannot recall clearly."

"Are you aware there was an incident at the apartment that night, Miss Raines? A young woman died—murdered. It's been all over the news."

Lillian looked into Karson's eyes, shocked. "Oh, my goodness! That was the night it happened? I mean, I heard something on the radio, but I didn't realize…oh no, that poor girl." Lillian sobbed. "I'm sorry, Jimmy, really."

"It's okay, Miss Raines. Take your time."

Lillian composed herself.

"You said you caught a cab after you left the apartment?"

"Yes, that's right."

"And where to?"

"It was a little hotel, somewhere in one of the backstreets off Hollywood Boulevard. I stayed there a few days. I don't recall the name right now, but I could find it for you if you wish."

"Thank you, I'll get that off you later. How long have you been in LA, Miss Raines?"

"Oh, a month or so, I guess."

"And where did you live before that?"

"New York. I've just come out of a very unpleasant relationship, and I needed to get away. I've been staying in some small motels around the area looking for work, but not having much luck. Well, not until I met Carlo, that is. We hit it off very fast."

"Do you smoke, Miss Raines?" Karson had noticed a silver ashtray on a small table when he had entered the room. Although it was empty and spotless.

"No, well…I should say hardly ever."

"Any particular brand?"

"No, any really, just the odd cigarette every now and then."

"Can I ask how long your hair's been colored black?"

"Just a few days. I had it done for my little part in Carlo's movie."

Karson nodded.

Lillian discreetly made the sign with her right hand out of Karson's view and then slid her finger down her neckline, where she had applied fresh perfume that morning. She took both of Karson's hands in hers and leaned in close to him.

"Jimmy, I can sense you're a very decent man. Please tell me you'll find the person who killed that sweet child. Please." Lillian slid her finger down his cheek while looking into his eyes. "She was just so…*innocent.*" Something happened to Karson, unlike anything he had experienced before. It was faster than lightning…it swept through his mind, as gentle as a teardrop falling. Karson gazed into Lillian's eyes, bewildered. He then broke away and looked around the room, trying to focus and collect his thoughts. Lillian sobbed and put her head on his shoulder.

Karson placed his hand on her back, wanting very much to comfort this gorgeous grieving woman. He tried to ignore the arousal of her touch but couldn't. He didn't know why, but for now, somehow…he felt she had nothing to do with the murder. There was a strange connection on some level, but for reasons he wasn't sure of, for now…he decided she was not the killer he was looking for. He had already begun thinking of re-interviewing everybody else at the party when he bid Lillian goodbye and apologized for breaking the bad news about Morgan to her. As he drove away, he could still smell her incredible scent. It lingered in his mind.

CHAPTER 31

THE HIGH LIFE

Two weeks had passed since her lust-filled afternoon with Cliff, and Lillian had since met up with him on three more occasions, two at lavish hotels downtown and once more at his home. Each time she knew Cliff only wanted her more, but so far she had refused to grant his more perverse sexual fantasies. She would, however, happily indulge him when she had solid confirmation of the leading part she so much wanted from him, and no sooner. She would not make the same mistakes she had in her first life. On one occasion in his mansion, she had even watched him walking two of his maids on their hands and knees on leashes attached to diamond-studded collars around their necks, obeying his every command. But she would not give in to Cliff's dark power-trip fantasies until she had a script from him with her name on it.

Carlo had been busy finishing his film and consoling his crew over Morgan's death. And he was usually dead tired. Between seeing Cliff, shopping sprees, and beauty salon visits, time had simply flown by. Despite Christina's attempts to meet with her for coffee, her bubbly and inquisitive personality had Lillian making excuses to avoid her. In truth, Lillian didn't care for her very much, or for any of her friends. *Such boring, kept little housewives.*

But Lillian didn't know that Christina had been having coffee with a friend in a hotel one afternoon when Lillian had walked past through the foyer with Cliff. She'd rushed out to say hello to them and almost caught up with them at the front doors when she had stopped and watched in surprise as Cliff's hand slid down onto Lillian's buttocks as he hugged and kissed her goodbye before sending her off in a limousine. Christina moved away quickly. That night, she told Sebastian what she had seen. Sebastian had warned her not to mention it to another living soul and tried to pass it off as just two friends catching up and Cliff being his usual flirtatious self. Christina was not convinced, but she agreed that she would need to be absolutely certain about her suspicions before she could even contemplate speaking to Carlo about the matter.

He was the biggest director Vonhampton Films had, and he wasn't just a dear friend; he was also one of their bosses.

There wasn't a day that went by that Carlo didn't call and text Lillian. He often sent her flowers; the man was completely in love with her, and Lillian knew it. He had comforted her about Morgan the day she had spoken to Karson. Lillian had played the shocked and grieving friend part to the hilt, breaking down, crying and sobbing, and clutching him for support. Carlo had held her and told her terrible things sometimes happen to good people for no reason. He'd been touched at her deep grief over Morgan.

Everything had gone according to plan, and nobody suspected a thing, Lillian thought smugly. She had pulled off the perfect crime yet again. She had evaded capture decades before, and she would evade it now. She was living the life all right, and it was wonderful.

But it wasn't enough. In her heart, she believed she had been granted this second chance to conquer this town, to become the Queen of Hollywood, and to make her mark at the top of the movie-star ladder. Carlo had nagged her a little about her drinking and smoking, both of which had steadily increased, but she assured him she would cut back.

At dinner one night with Christina and Sebastian, Carlo had surprised Lillian with a brilliant diamond bracelet and a movie script. He took great delight in pointing out a name highlighted on the cast list: Lillian Raines. She squealed in delight and hugged and kissed him while Christina and Sebastian clapped.

Lillian was thrilled; her dreams in this new life were made a reality when Carlo presented her with a script with her name on the cast list as a main actress. He had the clout to make this happen, and he'd done exactly what he'd promised. She knew he'd sped things up to beat Cliff to the punch, but she didn't care. This was it, a major part in a big-budget movie in modern-day Hollywood. She had done it. Everything was going perfectly to plan, and she couldn't wait to get started reading the script and rehearsing her lines. The mortal within had been relatively silent, suppressed with fresh applications of the perfume every morning and night.

The only thing weighing on Lillian's mind was that the perfume was already getting low again. It was still good for a little while, which gave her some peace. She had been thinking of new ways to lure her future victims and dispose of their remains. Dumping bodies in lakes and rivers after weighing them down with large stones had worked well numerous times in her first life. And she had even dug a few shallow graves back in Europe. But she couldn't continue to leave her victims strewn all over Hollywood like she had done decades before. Murder was an inconvenience, but one she had to deal with, and deal with it she would.

* * *

Ashley arrived at Helen's house again, as she'd done every afternoon since she'd vanished. She took the key from under the mat and opened the door. Shadow greeted her.

"Hello sweetheart." He meowed, and Ashley fed him fresh tuna. She wandered through Helen's house checking everything, as she did each time she came over. But nothing had changed. Everything was always as she had left it: the car in the garage and all the curtains drawn.

Ashley had knocked on every door along the entire street and told them of Helen's disappearance, but nobody had seen or heard anything. The police had eventually arrived and looked around briefly but told her that there were no signs of a struggle or forced entry, so there wasn't much they could do.

Tears welled in her eyes as she looked at the pictures of Helen on the walls, placed lovingly between all the movie-star posters.

"Where are you, my friend?...Are you okay? Please come back."

She thought of Helen's house sitting here forever empty. Did Helen have a will? And even if she did, who would she leave everything to? She imagined in the years to come Helen's house still sitting here with nobody in it and this shrine to Hollywood's yesteryear covered in layers of dust. Her heart ached just thinking about it.

Shadow finished his food and rubbed against her legs. She scooped him up and sat on Helen's sofa, petting him.

"It's all right, Shadow, soon you can stay at my place, and you'll have my cat, Sugar, to keep you company. Won't that be lovely?"

Tears rolled down her cheeks.

CHAPTER 32

BORN AGAIN

Shark had just left Carlo's mansion with a thick envelope full of cash. Lillian was pleased, as was Carlo: Shark had just dropped off Lillian's new identification, which included a driver's license, a birth certificate, and everything else she needed to formally exist under her new name.

Lillian Kelly was now officially Lillian Raines.

Many palms had been greased with copious amounts of money, and plenty of strings had been pulled. Carlo and Shark had worked hand in hand using every contact they had to pull it off. Obtaining a completely new identity like this was no easy feat, but this was LA, and big money talked.

Lillian had told Carlo she wanted the new name to escape her past and her ex in New York, but in truth she *needed* a new identity. She had nothing at all to show she had ever existed. But now she was Lillian Raines, an up-and-coming Hollywood actress soon to make her big debut. She hugged Carlo.

"Thank you, sweetheart, for all you've done for me. I don't deserve it."

"You do deserve it, and at least now I know your last name." He laughed and so did Lillian.

"Yes, I'm sorry I never told you my full name."

"I don't care you never told me, and it doesn't matter now; you've got a new one. I've got good news. I negotiated a very good deal for your part with the studio. They are going to pay you two-hundred thousand dollars."

The figure startled Lillian. She had been so happy about getting a real part she had practically forgotten about negotiating a salary. She hadn't seen this coming. The amount sank in, and a feeling of independence enveloped her. She was going to be paid a large amount of money—her *own* money— to star in a movie.

"Trust me, it's a very good figure for an unknown actor. Congratulations."

"Carlo, I don't know what to say."

"Then say nothing." He took her hand. "Come, I have another surprise for you." He led Lillian down the stairs into the underground garage where he kept his four cars.

"Cover your eyes." She did, and he led her across the garage. She knew what was coming.

"Okay, you can look now."

Lillian took her hand away from her eyes and saw a sleek black sports coupe, complete with a huge red bow and a bunch of red roses sitting atop the hood.

"It's yours, Lillian."

She threw her arms around Carlo. "Oh, it's so beautiful!" she cried, feigning perfect surprise.

"So, you like it then?"

"I love it. I can't believe you bought it for me."

"Well, I have, and it's in your name. I've also booked you lessons with the best driving school in town. I know you're worried about the heavy traffic we have here, but don't be; you'll be zooming around LA in no time."

He had taken Lillian's hint about her having her own car. And she was truly impressed; she stroked her finger along the car's silky jet-black paintwork. It was a lovely vehicle. Carlo swung open the driver's door, and out wafted the delicious untouched smell only a brand-new car can possess. She sat in the driver's seat and looked over all the instruments and gauges, and a wave of anxiousness washed over her. She had driven in her first life, but that was a very different time. Cars were much simpler then, and the roads were nowhere near as chaotic, and these new cars seemed to have so many buttons and switches.

Carlo knelt beside her and took her hand.

"Don't be frightened; it's just a car. I'll take you out in it soon, and we'll drive around the hills, where it's quiet, so you can get used to it."

She stepped out of the car and hugged him.

"You are so good to me."

He kissed her and looked into those eyes that always made his heart skip a beat. "Well, you're my woman."

For a fleeting moment, Lillian felt genuine empathy for this man. She knew he had fallen hard for her, and she knew she hadn't treated him well behind his back, but her intention was not just to marry some wealthy man and sit around in his castle doing her nails until he came home every day.

She wanted her *own* castle. She wanted to carve her own path and have the masses know her face and scream her name, like they had for so many big stars all those years ago. She had never reached that status, and it had frustrated and tormented her into deep depression in her first life. Countless days of drinking and smoking had passed by in a blur. She had been on her way to the top once, but everything had gone wrong. Now, though…now she had been given a second chance to get it right. This time, she was older and wiser.

And if people like Carlo had to get hurt and discarded along the way, then so be it.

CHAPTER 33

HISTORY REPEATS

Karson sat back in his office chair. The moon was high outside and he was tired. He had spent the day visiting and calling tobacco stores. He'd discovered there were seventeen stores in LA that sold Vanilla Dove cigars. They were a very old brand, high quality and expensive. He was surprised at how many of these cigars were sold.

He knew it was a long shot, but it was still a chance, and Karson was thorough. He had left his card with every shopkeeper he visited and asked them to contact him if they recalled anything unusual about customers who purchased these cigars, but so far nothing.

He had also visited the Hollywood tobacco store where Helen had purchased her tin of cigars. This store had his interest, as he knew it was very close to where Lillian had attended a fashion show with Peter Jameson. But again, no luck. The shopkeeper didn't recall anyone like Lillian. Karson gave him his card and asked the shopkeeper to contact him if he recalled anything out of the ordinary; the man assured him he would. While he was there, though, Karson noticed flyers stuck up around the shopping center, offering a reward for a missing person: one Helen Elliot. He had also noticed some of these flyers along Hollywood Boulevard. Hordes of people went missing in LA each year, but missing persons was not his area. He was a homicide cop, and a damn good one at that.

Karson massaged his temples. He hadn't felt the same since his encounter with the woman who called herself Lillian Raines. She had been clouding his thoughts, and he had even found himself dreaming of her: her captivating eyes, her seductive voice, her voluptuous body. After one of these dreams, he had woken in the early hours and found himself more aroused than he had been in years. In it, Lillian had been standing before him in a large empty room with pristine white walls. Slowly, she removed her dress, sliding it down as she stared into his eyes with a wicked grin across those full, blood-red lips. She spoke to him.

"I am real, not myth. I am that very woman that every man dreams of and desires."

Karson had woken sweating and confused.

He had been spoken to firmly by his boss yet again for having no results, and he was getting frustrated. Why didn't he have an arrest yet? Why hadn't he made much progress?

He had no answers. He had spoken to several people from the movie set that Morgan had been working on, but he was no closer to discovering what had happened to her that night. It appeared she had gone home after the robbery on set, eaten a small meal alone, and then just vanished. A neighbor vaguely recalled seeing her getting into a cab, but he wasn't sure. Karson had gone over everything, but still nothing made sense. Like the first victim, Morgan's body also seemed to have a large amount of blood missing, according to the coroner. The pool of blood on the floor simply wasn't enough to account for the amount of blood missing from her body.

What kind of macabre situation was he dealing with here? Some deranged killer obsessed with vampires or drinking blood? *God only knows.* He had seen everything in his time; nothing much could faze him. He never minded putting in the long hours, and his success rate over the years was extremely high. Failure was not an option to him, but he was getting frustrated. A dozen photographs of the first victim and Morgan were spread out across his desk, several of them close-ups of the slashed wrists. He stared down at them, searching for the answer.

Footsteps sounded from the corridor. It was almost midnight, so he was surprised anybody had bothered to come back any further than the front desk. His office door creaked opened gently. Karson looked up and smiled; it was Lesley Simmons. He was long retired now, but he had been a legendary detective in his time. He had started his career in New York but had taken a transfer to LA in his thirties and had stayed there. Even in retirement he had broken many a cold case and was often in the newspapers for doing so. These days he was a part-time private investigator and a longtime personal friend of the chief, which pretty much gave him the run of the precinct.

"Working overtime again, Jimmy?" Les crackled in his rusty voice.

"No rest for the wicked," Karson replied.

"I guess." Les stepped into the office. With his long gray coat, thick black glasses, and brown leather shoes, he always reminded Karson of one of those cliché detectives from old movies.

"What can I do for you, Les?"

"Aw, nothing, I just saw your light on. Reeves said he left some papers on his desk for me to take a look at. A missing child case from back in the nineties. I think I may have found a lead in Mexico."

"I hope it pans out for you."

"How 'bout you? What's got you burning the midnight oil, young man?"

Karson gestured at the photographs. Les stepped in and leaned down to look closely at them. He stared at them a long time with a grave expression, and Karson sensed his curiosity was aroused.

"I've been on vacation. When did these happen?" Les asked.

"Only very recently. Why?"

Les stared at the photographs. "How many victims?"

"Two—well, that we know of. What is it, Les?"

"You need to take a look at an old case from back in my day. The press went crazy for it, and so did the public. The media dubbed it the Hollywood Slit Wrist Murders. It wasn't my case; I came to work in LA just as everything was dying down. I saw all the photographs, though, and some lab reports. I think there were twelve or more bodies in total. But you'd have to check on that."

Karson was typing into his computer's search engine as Les spoke, and instantly…up it came, a newspaper headline from 1961: "Hollywood Slit Wrist Murderer Strikes Again!"

Karson read the article, dumbfounded. Les watched silently as Karson checked the crime database records. The case was considered ancient by today's standards, but with a little more searching Karson managed to find two old black-and-white forensics photos of murdered women lying on beds with their right hands dangling inches above the floor, both slit at the wrist. Karson stood slowly, stunned. It was so similar, no… it was *exactly* the same scenario as the two murders he was investigating. The position of the bodies, the hands dangling down over the floor with a pool of blood underneath. The resemblance was uncanny.

"Holy shit."

"You read my mind. The second I saw your photographs I got chills down my spine. It's just too similar. I daresay you have a copycat on your hands, young man."

"I'd say you're right," Karson shot back.

"To my recollection, they never caught anybody; there were a few suspects but never an arrest."

Karson stared at the photographs. "Well, I sure am glad you dropped by tonight, Les. I just don't believe it."

"From what I remember, one of the victims was a celebrity, a young actress. I don't recall her name, but she had some parts in a couple of movies that made it big. I guess she was on her way until they found her dead in a hotel room. I remember there was also a triple homicide, three young girls found dead in the same room. I think after that the murders just stopped."

Karson turned to him. "A triple murder?"

Les nodded. "It was as gruesome as it gets."

Karson's mind was in overdrive. The first recent victim was a model, and the second was working for a film company. A coincidence?

"I probably can't tell you any more than what you'll find in those old tabloids and reports, but if you need to call and ask me anything at all, you're most welcome."

"Thanks, Les. Really, thanks a bunch."

Les nodded and headed off down the hall. Karson's eyes were wide open, adrenalized. He was now more determined than ever to find out who the hell was killing and taking blood from young women in Hollywood. He started searching for every single shred of information he could find on the Hollywood Slit Wrist Murders.

* * *

Lillian had read the script through over a dozen times in the last week. She loved it; it was well-written, and the characters were diverse and interesting. Her character was a wealthy, dominating woman who owned a chain of exclusive clothing stores. Lillian loved her character, who had inherited the stores from her much older fashion designer husband, who'd passed away, forcing her to fend off his greedy stepchildren, who wanted nothing more than to get their hands on his empire. The script involved plenty of sex, action, and even a murder. Lillian couldn't help but feel amused at how closely it resembled her own life. She had plenty of experience to bring to the part. She had been going over her lines daily, sometimes with other unknown actors Carlo had hired to help her prepare for the part.

Carlo had sat and watched Lillian perform her lines more than once, often shaking his head in quiet amazement. It truly boggled his mind how she had become so adept at acting in such a short time. She was practically ready to start her scenes already. But filming was still months away. News of the film had been leaked and was all over the tabloids. To star in the film, Vonhampton had secured Chelsea Aims, a well-known TV actor who had pulled off a couple of good films recently, and Josh Jaxon, a young heartthrob with masses of female fans. With Chelsea and Josh attached to the film, it was off to a flying start. Carlo had been very effective at convincing Vonhampton Films to grant Lillian her part. They'd had many questions. Who was she? What films had she done? Why should they risk an unknown in a big-budget feature?

Carlo had been smooth and tactful in his response. It was time to bring in a newcomer, he'd told them, and her looks and acting ability were superb. And though nobody had seen her before, he told them he knew for a fact that Cliff Summers had auditioned her and was considering her for one of his upcoming films. That had been the clincher, and after seeing the audition footage of Lillian, they had to agree she was perfect for the part. Within a couple of hours Carlo had won them over, and Lillian had her part in the movie.

* * *

Karson had been at his desk all night. He had dozed off and woken at around four in the morning, then got straight back to work. He had already discovered plenty about the

Hollywood Slit Wrist Murders. The first victim was a young actress named Liza Venner, who had only performed minor parts in a few television shows. Her body was found in a hotel on the outskirts of town. Karson had studied the crime scene photographs, again noting the similarities to the two murders he was investigating. He discovered there had been a total of ten bodies found in the original series of murders. Seven of the victims had had their wrists sliced in almost identical fashion, targeting the radial artery, and the other three had their throats slit open, the killer targeting the jugular vein each time.

The entire case disgusted him. Each murder was eerily similar and brutal, but the one that had made him sick to his stomach…made him gasp at the cruel theft of human life, was the triple murder of three young women in a small hotel in downtown. He could only find three black-and-white pictures of the crime scene, and he stared at them for over an hour, trying to get his head around the fact that the murderer had somehow managed to kill all three victims in the same room at pretty much the same time. All three had their wrists sliced open and were left lying next to each other on a double bed, like sacrificial lambs, their wrists dangling inches above the floor with a sizable pool of blood underneath. *My God, three young women in one hit!*

The scene was surreal, like something out of a movie. He couldn't find the coroner's reports on all the murders, but of the seven he did find, he saw that in each case the victims had almost been bled out, and there had been evidence of the use of chloroform on at least four of them. All but two of the victims had been associated with the film industry. Most were extras or actors, and a couple were film set assistants. There it was again, staring him in the face, the film connection…but what was it? And now, decades later, a copycat killer. Why? He didn't know, but by God he would find out. The general lack of information about the whole case surprised him; it was as if Hollywood itself had tried to ignore this terrible, dark chapter in its history, had tried to sweep it under the rug. It had clearly been a time when fear ruled the streets, and young women were afraid to leave their homes at night for fear of the Slit Wrist Murderer.

Karson had checked out everything he could about Morgan's past and, like the first victim, the girl was a saint—not even a parking ticket. Yet both of them had wound up dead.

His stomach growled. He pulled on his jacket and headed outside to a twenty-four-hour café and bought some half-stale donuts and black coffee. He sat on a chair outside, watching as the first strains of sunlight began pressing their way down from the sky onto Hollywood Boulevard. And he knew that somewhere out there in Los Angeles was the person he was looking for.

* * *

Lillian had accompanied Carlo to the studios to watch him begin the long, tedious task of post-production for the film he had just shot. She quickly became bored with the process. After lunch, her cell rang; it was Cliff's assistant Bronwyn, asking if she and Carlo would like to meet for dinner. Carlo declined, as he would be working late. Lillian had immediately asked him if he was okay with her going on her own. Although surprised and disappointed, what could he do but agree? He was very tired, he also had a mountain of paperwork and emails to tend to, and he needed his rest for the next day.

Lillian noticed his silence in the limo on the way home. "Is everything all right, dear?" she asked.

"Well yes, but…I must say I was a little surprised when you agreed to go to dinner with Cliff, when you knew I'd turned him down."

She took his chin and turned his face toward hers. He looked into those eyes and was once again spellbound by them.

"If you want me to call him and cancel, say the word. The last thing in the world I want is to upset the man I love."

Carlo's face lit up. He was elated to hear her say that she loved him with such conviction. His suspicions melted away. "No, I'm being silly. Go and have a wonderful time. You get to sleep in tomorrow. I have to get up early, but you go out and have fun."

Lillian kissed him, and he smiled all the way home.

CHAPTER 34

CHEMICAL DEMISE

Cliff had booked one of the most exclusive restaurants in town, the Candle. Lillian stepped out of the limo he'd sent to Carlo's house to get her. Heads turned as she stepped onto the sidewalk and entered the restaurant.

She was wearing the silver dress, the one that had survived all these decades. She had always liked it, and tonight she felt it was symbolic, given that she had now officially begun her climb to the top again. She was on her way to true fame and triumph, she could feel it. Her large diamond pendant sat perfectly over her breasts, sparkling, complemented by the sleek diamond bracelet around her wrist. She had also chosen to wear the diamond-studded stilettos, and in this sublime outfit she was impossible to miss.

Cliff was sitting at the table with Bronwyn and two other very attractive young women, both of who looked to be in their twenties. A plump, broad-shouldered man also sat at the table. Thin strands of dark hair strategically crisscrossed his large, balding head. He wore a snow-white jacket and a ridiculously thick gold chain around his neck. Numerous diamond rings covered his fingers. His dark, beady eyes lit up like glowing coal as Lillian approached the table.

Cliff stood and looked her up and down. "Lillian, how lovely to see you again. You look incredible, as usual."

The other women at the table nodded their approval.

"Thank you, Cliff," Lillian replied.

The other man also stood. "Yes, what a beautiful woman."

His loud voice, piercing gaze, and cocky attitude made Lillian instantly uncomfortable. She nodded at him politely.

Cliff gestured toward him. "Lillian, let me introduce my dear friend and financier of many of my films. Larry Sinders, meet Lillian."

Larry stepped around the table toward Lillian. He was very short but powerfully built, with a large stomach and thick, bandy legs. In his glowing white tuxedo-style jacket and matching white pants and shoes, Lillian thought he looked silly. He looked to be in his sixties. He reached out, took Lillian's hand in a firm grip and kissed it, a little further up the wrist than she would have liked. He looked up at her, the top of his head barely reaching her shoulders.

"Such a pleasure to meet you, Lillian. I've heard plenty about you, but a mere description does not do you justice." He kissed her wrist again.

Lillian forced a smile and tugged her arm away from him. "Thank you," she replied coolly.

Larry sensed she was not very taken with him, but he had received this type of response before from beautiful women. Already he wanted Lillian badly, and if she thought she was going to star in a Cliff Summers film that he was putting forty million dollars into, he would have her. Cliff had described her incredible body in explicit detail, and now Larry wanted to experience it for himself. The two men had shared countless women over the years, usually naïve young actresses and high-class big-dollar escorts. Cliff had told him how incredible Lillian was in bed, and Larry wanted to see for himself—and he was used to getting his way.

Cliff introduced Lillian to the women: Veronica, a pretty twenty-four-year-old redhead, and Freya, a petite twenty-two-year-old blonde. Both were actors, of course; Cliff was known for being seen around town with many a stunning young wannabe on his arm, and as the biggest film director in America he had his choice of an endless supply of attractive starlets. He indulged his every sexual whim often. But it was Lillian who had gotten his complete attention; he hadn't desired a woman this much in years.

Sexually, he could not get enough of her, but it had become more than that. He had never met a woman who listened to him so intently, and he loved her incredible eyes. He had never encountered a woman with her style and mystique. Topped off by that breathy, seductive voice, she was simply a mind-blowing woman to be around. She seemed to possess a knowledge far beyond her years, like a much older person who had traveled the world and seen all there is to see, someone who'd had their heart broken many times but had broken a thousand more in return. There was a wisdom about her unlike any other woman he had ever encountered. Even the smell of her got his heart racing. She always smelled incredible.

Lillian's beauty had worked its magic on thousands of men all over the world in her past life, and now in this new life. And she knew it had struck Larry too…like a bombshell. He couldn't take his eyes off her.

Cliff gestured to Lillian to sit next to him, clearly showing his preference for her over the other women at the table. Larry looked on eagerly, barely noticing the other women. Champagne arrived, and Cliff began talking about his upcoming movie. After a few drinks, Larry had taken over the conversation at the table. He was very full of himself and acted like he owned the world. But for whatever reason, Cliff seemed to like him, and their stories made it clear they had spent some time together over the years. Larry mentioned the many companies he owned all over the world, and of course he babbled on about how rich he undoubtedly was. He was trying to impress Lillian, and he constantly reminded everybody at the table how much money he had personally invested in countless films over the years, including Cliff's.

The two younger women at the table were certainly impressed, but Lillian had already grown tired of him. She averted her gaze around the room, noticing all the men in the restaurant staring at her as men always did. Cliff ran his hand suggestively up her thigh under the table, which only pleased her. She didn't mind; after all, he was still dangling the carrot about the big part in his upcoming film. Lillian knew Cliff was slightly peeved Carlo had beaten him to the punch by casting her as a lead already, but she also knew he wanted a lot more of her, and she was certain she'd get her part in his film too.

He had that same look in his eyes as all the other men who'd enjoyed the pleasure of her body: the look of complete and utter desire, and not just for a few lust-filled occasions. No…Cliff wanted her for *keeps*, she could tell. And if she had to go home again with him tonight and engage in more wild sexual festivities with him and his female companions, she really didn't mind at all. But her mind was already made up that Larry would not be laying a finger on her, despite his obvious burning intentions.

With a gentle stroke along Cliff's leg, she excused herself and left the table with her handbag. She stepped out onto the smoking balcony of the restaurant and gazed out at the distant hills fading into the night's darkness. She lit a cigar, and footsteps made her turn her head. Larry also stepped out onto the balcony. He approached her and whipped out a huge, thick cigar and lit it, as if waiting for her to be impressed.

She was not.

"Mind if I join you, Lillian?"

"Why not," she answered flatly, staring out at the view.

"Cliff tells me you are a favorite for a lead role in his next film. I will be one of the major investors. I get a large say in the casting of the movies I back, and I am always very active in that area."

Lillian knew choosing actors was not his decision at all. In her first life she had fallen for lies like this, lies from men like just like Larry, and she had strongly disliked his sexually aggressive staring across the table at her and her breasts all evening. She had known he was bad news the second she'd laid eyes on him, and she could sense the sexually violent intent within him. He awoke bad memories for her. It was men like him who made her ultimately flee the cult in Europe who she had once thought genuinely cared for her. In truth, she had been groomed by them and the high priest purely for her beauty, to be used as a sexual toy for rich, powerful men, men with political influence. Many of them had even beaten her, tying her up and inflicting unspeakable acts upon her. Then she would be sent home to the castle to heal, only for the same vicious cycle to repeat all over again. It continued for years. After realizing she would never truly ascend their ranks, she had fled with her precious perfume bottle and some cash and jewels she'd managed to squirrel away. She had hidden out in Italy, before zigzagging her way across Europe with the Blood People hot in pursuit, but she had evaded them and made her way safely back to America. The few magic spells they'd taught her had come in very handy. Fleeing had not been an easy decision, as deserting the cult brought a death penalty. Despite the dark times and the brutal ways she had been treated, the whole experience had somehow left her with a taste for sex and bondage that she couldn't shake, but at her own desire, of course. Back then she'd had enough of being used and harmed for wealthy men, and now…here she was again in a similar situation. She would have none of it.

Larry rambled on about his importance and his wealth, which did not impress her as she knew Cliff was far wealthier. He reached out and almost touched the large diamond hanging from her neck. "That is very nice, but my last girlfriend, who was twenty-two and not nearly as lovely as you, I bought her a much larger diamond, lots of them, and a car, lots of things.

I love to spoil beautiful women, you see, Lillian. I like to spoil them very much indeed, and Lillian, you are the most beautiful woman I think I have ever met."

His voice irritated Lillian. And his small, dark eyes slid all over her at once. He stared unashamedly at her breasts, as if prompting her to say something about it.

She gave him a weak smile and turned away from him. She puffed on her cigar and looked out across the hills. She could sense his frustration, but she truly did not care at all. Suddenly, his hand gripped her waist with force. He tossed his cigar over the balcony and spun her around quickly, so she was facing him. He was going for broke now; she could see it in his eyes. He had failed to impress her with his big talk and now he was getting physical. The move caught Lillian by surprise.

"I'm happy to make sure you get the part in the movie, Lillian. And I'd like to spend some time with you tonight, alone."

He slapped one pudgy little hand firmly on her breast and squeezed. Anger flooded Lillian like lightning. She slapped his arm away with such ferocious speed and force it shocked him. He gasped and stumbled three steps backward, his eyes like burning embers.

"What's your fucking problem, lady? Don't you understand who I am? Women *line up* to fucking sleep with me."

Lillian glared down at him with those ice-glazed eyes. "That would probably depend on how much you are willing to pay them, I suppose. I don't care who you are. You are not the director, and you are not the head of the movie company. You are just another financier. You sell fast food and lightbulbs, and you do not impress me at all. Do not put your disgusting hands on me ever again. I hope I've made myself clear."

Her tone was lethal, and Larry found it quite unnerving. It had been a very long time since *anybody*, let alone a woman, had spoken to him that way. As he stood there thinking up a vicious response, Lillian flicked her cigar over the balcony and headed back inside the restaurant, leaving him with his fists clenched tight and the bristles on his neck standing up.

Larry Sinders was not a man used to taking no for an answer, not from anybody.

The tension back at the table was so thick Lillian felt she could have dragged a knife through it, but it didn't bother her. She found Larry offensive and unattractive on almost every level, and she would make it clear to Cliff that he would not be involved in any sexual activities with her at any time. Cliff was having a great time and was completely unaware of the run-in between Lillian and Larry, though he did notice Larry looked displeased on returning to the table. Cliff ordered more champagne as Larry drained a glass, excused himself, and headed to the men's room. Lillian relaxed in his absence. She joined in the conversation with Cliff and the other women. After leaving the men's room, Larry intercepted the waiter heading toward Cliff's table with a tray of fresh glasses and another bottle of French champagne.

"Just set that down here, thank you," he commanded, pointing to a nearby table. "I am going to pour them myself as a surprise toast for my friends."

The young waiter looked confused. "But, sir...I'm not supposed to..." he stammered.

"I insist; put it down now." Larry's tone was strong and authoritative. The young waiter put the tray down immediately. Larry whipped out three hundred-dollar bills and slipped them into the young man's coat pocket.

The waiter's eyes lit up. "Thank you, sir."

Larry touched his lips in the "don't talk" gesture. "Come back in two minutes and bring the tray over to me at the table."

"Yes, sir." The waiter headed back to the kitchen.

Larry reached into his inside coat pocket and took out a small plastic bag, inside which were small white pills. He took out three of them and popped them into one of the glasses, then filled all the glasses with the champagne. He set the laced glass further back away from the others, watching as the pills dissolved. The waiter reappeared almost on cue and waited until Larry sat back down at the table, then carried the tray over and laid it on the table.

Larry stood. "This bottle is on me. I would like to propose a toast to delicious food, excellent champagne, and superb company."

Everybody at the table gave him a small round of applause except Lillian, who forced a sickly grin. Larry handed out the glasses, making sure Lillian received the one he had dropped the pills into. He raised his glass, and everybody toasted and smiled, except Lillian. As he took his seat again, he watched on smugly as Lillian quickly drained the contents of her glass, knowing full well the mind-numbing effect just one of those pills had, let alone three. They had served him well in the past with reluctant women, and soon enough he knew Lillian would be in dire need of assistance. He would gladly help her out, too, preferably alone at the nearest hotel. But even if he didn't get his opportunity to ravage her incredible body, he would still at least very much enjoy watching this arrogant smart-mouthed bitch of an actress reduced to a muttering incoherent mess. Nobody insulted Larry Sinders and got away with it. Nobody.

* * *

Carlo was at home going over some paperwork. He tried not to think about Lillian being out with Cliff. He loved Lillian, and love was all about trust. He had a huge surprise planned for the coming Friday evening. In his scarce spare time he had been looking at rings—engagement rings. He had even had some of LA's finest jewelers come privately on set to show him some in his trailer. He had finally made his purchase of a brilliantly cut five-carat diamond ring set in platinum. It was breathtaking. It had been designed by one of Europe's leading jewelers, and it had cost Carlo $220,000, which he paid in a heartbeat.

He had also booked an entire restaurant on Rodeo Drive, one of the most exclusive in town, complete with a string quartet, just for the two of them. This is where he would get down on one knee and propose to his beloved Lillian.

Carlo had told Sebastian and Christina his plan in the strictest confidence, and he'd been a little miffed that Christina hadn't responded like her usual bubbly self, other than to say that she thought it was a very romantic idea. He had made his mind up; no other woman had ever made him feel this way before, not *ever*. Therefore, he reasoned, it must be true love. He had never really thought true love existed until the night he had met Lillian. He had been spellbound from the second he saw her.

No other woman had ever given him butterflies simply by touching his arm or calling him darling. His heart raced every time she called him just to see how his day was going. He could think of nothing he wanted more than to be with her every day and night, and to have his children with her, and travel the world with her in the comfort and style he could so easily afford. He was certain she would say yes.

Why would she not? She loved him back just as much. He busied himself and went about his preparations for the next day's filming.

CHAPTER 35

THY KINGDOM CRUMBLE

Peter Jameson sat alone in the darkness on his white leather sofa. It was one of the few items left in his huge but now nearly empty apartment, and that was only because it was pretty much the only thing he had paid for in cash. Nearly everything else was on hire and had been repossessed, along with his beloved sports car.

Thoughts drifted through his mind of his first encounter with the incredible woman named Lillian. Her face had haunted him ever since that night. After word had gotten out about the young girl who had been murdered in his apartment, he had been through sheer hell. His private life had been revealed, and the media had run countless stories on him and his many sex parties with dozens of his young models, who had since come forward to the press, for very attractive sums of money. They had also spoken to the police.

Now it seemed everybody knew that for years he had been supplying his actors and models with drugs and alcohol, and having sex with them. Reporters had followed him relentlessly; some even camped outside his office, waiting to pounce on him for a comment at any opportunity. He had been subjected to the anger of abusive parents, who had stormed into his office and threatened him with lawsuits, and even physical abuse, for taking advantage of their innocent young daughters.

Nearly all his best models had left him within a week of the incident, and after that, all of his major clients had promptly dropped him like an old newspaper. His cash flow had dried up in no time, and the creditors were soon demanding payments. His office had been shuttered, and he owed thousands in back rent. Now his landlord had given him two weeks to vacate his apartment.

Already the police had interviewed him about numerous allegations of supplying narcotics and alcohol to minors. He had used up the last of his credit to pay a lawyer who was to defend him at his upcoming trial. The police had even discovered disturbing photographs of young models on his personal computer. The lawyer had been frank and told Peter things didn't look good at all, and there were still many more charges to be brought forward against him. In all, over a dozen young models had admitted to being supplied with drugs and alcohol by Peter Jameson at his apartment. The lawyer had warned him jail time was inevitable.

He had even been abused in the street by people who had recognized him from the newspapers. *Oh, how the mighty have fallen.* His friends had not returned any of his calls; even his family didn't want to have anything to do with him. No longer could he walk down Hollywood Boulevard in his three-thousand-dollar suits like a celebrity or zoom around LA in his pristine sports car. No, those days were over. His world had collapsed. He sat alone in the dark in his apartment, naked but for his red silk bathrobe, deep in the unforgiving shadows of depression and with a coarse coat of stubble on his once immaculate face. He was now completely alone.

He had been drinking almost constantly for three days and couldn't remember the last time he had eaten. He had lived the high life for years now, hiding behind a façade of wealth, relying on constant high turnover from big-name clients. He had squandered his money on living big and keeping up appearances, and now, with less than two thousand dollars in cash to his name, and three maxed-out credit cards, he couldn't even afford to leave town. In his heart he knew he could never start over, not after the high-profile mauling the press had given him. Hollywood didn't forget things like this…not for a very long time.

He drained the contents of a bottle of wine, his second for the evening, and stumbled out onto the balcony. He stood there in the crisp night air, staring at the lights of Los Angeles. He had come here all those years ago, a young man on a mission to carve out a name for himself in this town, and he had done so. Once respected and admired, practically a Hollywood A-lister and lusted after by women, now he was just broke and broken. He burst into tears of self-pity for a few moments, then composed himself. He looked to his right, and there in the distance—high among the dark, looming hills, looking back at him in its imperial white glow—was the Hollywood Sign.

He wrapped both hands firmly around the cold, hard steel of his twenty-third-story balcony railing, tears still rolling down his cheeks as he glared defiantly back at the sign.

"Fuck you," he whispered to it, climbing over the rail.

He hit the sidewalk with a sickening thud seconds later. Just another dead body in the wake of Lillian Kelly.

CHAPTER 36

BLOOD OF YESTERYEAR

Karson had dug up every shred of information he could find on the Slit Wrist Murders. The number of victims truly sickened him. They were all young, attractive women between sixteen and twenty-five and mostly somehow connected to the film or modeling industries.

It was staring him in the face, the movie connection. But what about now? Was the copycat killer also involved in the film industry? Something told him he was getting closer to the answer. He didn't know what it was, but it was in his gut and in his bones, and he was rarely wrong. Unbeknown to him, the spell Lillian had cast on him had almost worn off. And he was starting to see things clearly again. Lillian knew it would be temporary, and though her power increased with each application of the perfume, it would be quite some time before she would be back to full strength, and the lasting power of her magic also depended on the mental strength of the people she had placed it on. The strong-minded and strong-willed generally shook it off relatively quickly. Often it had very little power with those who held strong religious beliefs. The fog was clearing in Karson's mind, and Lillian was back on his radar now, more with each passing day. Karson's net was closing in.

* * *

Ashley lay in her hospital bed talking to Daniel. She had been at work one afternoon when she collapsed with chest pains. The next thing she had known, she had awoken in hospital with a doctor and a nurse looking down at her. The doctor informed her she had suffered a mild heart attack, most likely due to stress, and for now she needed to relax and remain at the hospital. Ashley wasn't surprised; the strain of not knowing what happened to Helen had taken a heavy toll on her, and she knew something had to give. Sadly, it seemed it was her heart.

She and Daniel had been having a teary discussion about Helen.

"The police already seem to have lost interest." Ashley said. "I just don't know what to do, except not give up hope. I was going to go over there tonight and collect Shadow and take him to my place, but now I can't until I get out of here."

"I'll go over and check on him tonight if it's okay with you, and if I notice anything different in the house I'll let you know straight away."

"Thank you, Daniel. Please do that."

"You just relax, take it easy." Ashley told him about the good times she'd shared with Helen over the years, until visiting hours were over. Daniel then headed straight to

Helen's house to check on Shadow—nothing had changed. He fed Shadow, petted him, and decided to leave Helen a note in case she turned up.

* * *

Lillian had been ignoring Larry childishly focusing all his attention on the other women at the table after his rejection. Cliff's hand slid up her thigh again, and she responded by placing her hand over his and sliding it up even further, firmly between her legs. Cliff grinned like a schoolboy and leaned over to her ear.

"I was hoping you would join me and the ladies at my house this evening for some more drinks."

"I'd love to, but I must tell you, Cliff, only if Larry is not present."

Cliff chuckled softly. "I had noticed you weren't exactly taken with him. He really is okay. Why don't you give him a chance? After all, we're all here to have some fun, aren't we? And he does put a lot of money into movies, you know, and not just mine. He's a good person to get along with, if you get my meaning."

Lillian was instantly irritated; she knew now that Cliff expected her to entertain Larry. She was annoyed, and he picked up on it immediately.

"Perhaps I could send him off with Freya. I'm sure they'll be happy on their own. Then you, me, and Veronica can have some fun together."

Lillian stroked his crotch. "I much prefer the sound of that."

Cliff smiled.

Lillian excused herself and headed to the ladies' room to freshen up. She noticed immediately that her balance was off. She patted some tap water on her face and caught her breath. She looked at herself in the mirror; her vision was fuzzy. She shook her head and closed her eyes, but it made no difference.

She leaned against the wall for support. Her body felt uncomfortably hot. Clutching her stomach, she tried to focus…to concentrate, but she couldn't. She felt suffocated, she needed air. *Yes, fresh air. I've simply had too much champagne, that's all.* But she knew there was more to it. She headed back into the restaurant on shaky legs and noticed a corridor that led to the street without going through the main room. She headed for the door, longing to fill her lungs with the cool night air. She stepped through the automatic glass doors wobbling on her stilettos and stumbled out onto the sidewalk. She leaned against a signpost to catch her breath.

Everything seemed wrong now. The lights up and down the street seemed to blur and warp. For a moment she forgot where she was; she simply could not think straight. She stumbled to a nearby bus stop and sat on the bench seat. With her head in her hands, she tried to think, but a sudden heavy swirl in her stomach startled her tremendously. She knew it was the mortal within her.

"Oh," she gasped.

What is happening? She had applied a good strong dose of the perfume just this morning—what the hell was going on? Panic spread through her like a chill. She quickly unzipped her purse and took out the perfume bottle. She pointed the nozzle at her chest and squeezed hard. The perfume tingled and buzzed on her skin, but it did nothing to change the situation. She felt worse by the second.

Peculiar thoughts raced through her head. The first was of the tiny little house where the mortal had lived, then the black cat, and then more and more images of the mortal's life flooded her thoughts.

"Oh, damn it, stop!" she cried, but the whir of images wouldn't cease. It sped up, and the realization of what was happening to her hit her like frozen ice in her veins. The mortal was *returning*. She could feel it; her thoughts were being taken over by Helen's. Her stomach heaved and her fingers trembled.

How could this be happening?

Lillian knew she needed to get the hell out of there. She decided to get a cab home to Carlo's house. Everything she looked at was blurry, and she couldn't think straight …she could feel Helen getting stronger rapidly. Panic flooded every pore of her body.

She stumbled to a cab rank close by. Her stomach heaved so badly she barely kept herself from throwing up.

What the hell is causing this?

Helen struck out again hard from within, with cold, stabbing jolts of pain.

"Stop it you bitch! You will not return."

Deep down inside Lillian, in the twisted, murky shadows of her dark and evil interior, a flicker of light had been exposed to Helen. It looked like only a tiny matchstick burning in a huge, dark cave at midnight, but it was there.

It was hope.

Helen felt as though she was on the bottom of the ocean looking up to the sun high in the sky, shimmering over the waves. But how could she get to the surface? It was the only sliver of hope she had seen in the longest time. She knew where she had been, all right, banished deep down inside Lillian, the evil one, the one who had tricked and seduced her into using her body and then took control of her will. She had been trapped down here, lying dormant in the foul depths of this murderous, depraved creature, but now she sensed something had gone wrong for Lillian. *Very* wrong.

Helen could feel Lillian's panic and confusion. It had given her the tiniest chance of return to herself. She didn't know why, and she didn't care. She only knew that she would give everything she had to get her life back, to escape this evil entity that had seduced her into the darkness. She focused hard and visualized herself floating up toward the light, and in response Lillian doubled over on the street, moaning in pain.

Lillian felt Helen's thoughts beginning to overpower her mind. Confused and disoriented, Lillian had no idea where to go, but Helen knew exactly where *she* wanted to go—home… home to her cozy little house, where her beloved Shadow was waiting for her. Home, where she had grown up surrounded by the love of her mother and aunt. Oh, how she wanted nothing more than to just go home and be Helen Elliot again.

Lillian made it to a cab and flung open the back door. She threw herself down on the seat, her head spinning.

The driver turned to her. "Where to, Miss?"

Lillian stared at him blankly. She tried to speak but couldn't. Instead, she found herself trying to suppress Helen from speaking for her. Helen was giving her utmost to force her thoughts into Lillian's mind. The cab driver stared back at her as Lillian stammered and stuttered. She knew she was in serious trouble, but where could she go in this state? To Carlo's? What if the mortal overpowered her and she transformed? Even in her complete confusion, Lillian shuddered at the thought. Suddenly, Helen spoke for her.

"Twenty-five Hillwood Drive, Beachwood Canyon."

The driver headed for Helen's home as Lillian tried to steady herself in the back seat. Her heart was pounding and her head was aching; she was confused, frightened, and angry. The perfume had never betrayed her before. She could not fathom what was going on.

Deep inside Lillian, Helen felt herself slowly emerging from the depths. She had a long way to go but it was happening, and it felt *amazing*. Freedom was now within her grasp. She knew the power containing her had begun breaking down, and she was seizing the opportunity to return to the living, to reclaim her life. She fought and focused on the light, concentrating on overpowering Lillian's mind with everything she had.

"No, stop it!" Lillian screeched.

The driver spun his head around in surprise. "What's wrong, Miss? You want me to stop?"

Lillian stared at him, mouth agape, until Helen spoke for her again. "No, keep going. I'm just not feeling well. Please hurry."

Lillian seethed with anger; the mortal was getting stronger. She knew how to fix this situation, though. She remembered long ago the high sorcerer himself had warned her that sometimes…very rarely, the mortal who dwelled within could find a way to take over and defeat the spell, and the only way to stop them was to send their very soul into the perfume bottle and chant the ancient words. Lillian knew she would have to bottle her own blood and then extract Helen's soul into the perfume bottle. It was dangerous, she had been warned, but she had no other choice. A vicious battle was raging inside her, and she was not about to lose. She was finally getting everything she had longed for in her life, and she would be damned to hell if this pathetic bitch inside her would stop her now.

CHAPTER 37

BACK FROM THE DEAD

Karson sat at his desk trawling through more old reports of the Hollywood Slit Wrist Murders. Instinct told him something eerie was going on that defied human explanation. But what? Karson was not a superstitious man—far from it. He was a man of facts, things he could see and reach out and touch. In the world of police work, evidence ruled supreme. But he just didn't have much of it. Almost every night he was dreaming of Lillian Raines. Why did he keep thinking about her? His head told him the woman was innocent, so why did his gut tell him something else? *Nothing makes sense when it comes to that woman.*

He scrolled through some old black-and-white forensics photographs, shaking his head at the familiarity of the murder scenes. A lukewarm coffee and some cold pizza sitting on his desk would have to suffice as dinner tonight. He flicked through more of the old police records. One victim he discovered was Taylor Brannigan, a young actress on her way to becoming a big star until her premature death. Karson did a thorough search on her and came across an old magazine article. He saw that she had starred in three major films, the last a big-budget feature that was never finished due to the bad publicity from her murder.

He read on and learned that she had been twenty-three years old when she was found dead, her wrist slit open and dangling from the bed, just like the other victims. There was a list of films she had appeared in attached to the article, and Karson went through each of them. He was studying the last movie she had ever worked on, *Flying in Love*. And he saw a list of the cast members' names, followed by a series of photographs of all the actors. Karson clicked through them, a typical assortment of handsome young men and women from that era of Hollywood. He sipped his coffee and took a bite of pizza as he continued to scroll through more of the old photos. One was a shot of all the female actors lined up in front of a gleaming white jet.

One actress was standing behind all the other women, clearly taller than all of them. Long blonde hair flowed down over her shoulders and chest, and the bells of familiarity chimed in Karson's mind. He zoomed in on the woman's face and then enlarged it so it took up most of the screen…and almost choked on the food in his mouth.

There, looking right back at him, was the face of Lillian Raines! He coughed pizza into his hand, staring in shock at the computer screen as his blood ran cold and his mind raced in a million directions at once. He tried to comprehend, tried to understand, how…*just how the hell* this could be possible.

But it was. There, without a doubt, was Lillian Raines, the woman he had spoken to in Carlo Genisi's mansion…the woman he had been dreaming of and thinking about for days, staring right back at him in a photograph from 1962.

He clicked back to the page with the cast list and began to scroll down the names. His heartbeat thumped in his ears as adrenaline swirled throughout his body. And then he saw it; the name stood out immediately. *Lillian Kelly.*

With lightning speed he slammed her name into the search engine and soon found an entire list of movies starring Lillian Kelly herself. Karson could not get his head around it. He enlarged a cover shot of one movie that stood out more than the rest, *Mistress of Evil.* He stared dumbfounded at the striking woman on the cover, the large bust, and those crystal-blue eyes—there was absolutely no doubt in his mind it was the same woman.

But how? *How could it be?* A relative? A granddaughter? What freak of genetics could create such a likeness? Yet there she was, Lillian Raines, or rather…Lillian Kelly, it now seemed.

After more searching, he learned that Lillian Kelly had died long ago in a house fire in the Hollywood Hills. The article described her as nothing more than a B-movie horror queen who had been attempting to make a comeback after a long absence from Hollywood. Karson couldn't make sense of it. How could he? Yet all along, he had known something very unusual was going on. And the woman who had called herself Lillian Raines somehow didn't seem real. She was perfect, far too perfect, and she had been haunting his thoughts for many days and nights now, for reasons he could not fathom.

He gulped down the rest of his coffee. The only thing he knew for sure at this moment was that he had to find Lillian.

He called her cell but she didn't answer. He then called Carlo Genisi's cell and was told Lillian was having dinner in the company of film director Cliff Summers, at the Candle on Hollywood Boulevard. It was only down the street from the precinct. He thanked Carlo but hung up the second he had found out what he wanted to know. Karson pulled on his jacket, then ran down the corridor and out into the night.

* * *

Carlo had been in his home office, busy going over paperwork and contracts, when his cell rang. Detective Karson had immediately wanted to know Lillian's whereabouts. Carlo questioned why, and Karson told him he just needed to ask her a few more routine questions. After telling him Lillian was at the Candle restaurant with Cliff, Karson had thanked him and hung up immediately, leaving Carlo worried and puzzled. He had dialed Lillian's cell twice but got no answer and was about to try again when Paulina knocked at the door.

He was surprised to have an unannounced visit from Christina and Sebastian. Christina was visibly upset. He ushered them into his office and closed the door. Minutes later, through misty eyes, Christina told him everything about what she had seen with Cliff and Lillian at the hotel. She also told Carlo that rumors were circulating around Hollywood, in particular at Vonhampton Films, that Lillian and Cliff had been meeting up for sexual trysts for weeks now. One of the young actresses had confessed she'd had sex with Cliff and Lillian at the hotel where Christina spotted them, after

Christina firmly confronted her about the matter. Clearly, the rumors were true.

Sebastian stood by Christina's side quietly as she informed Carlo of Lillian's deceit. When she had finished, Sebastian told Carlo that even though they knew how he felt about Lillian, as his longtime friends they felt obligated to tell him what had been going on behind his back.

Carlo stared at the floor the entire time. There was no shouting, no displays of outrage, just quiet, stunned disbelief. Deep inside, in some bizarre way, he had always known something was not right with this woman, this being of sublime beauty. From the second he had laid eyes on her she'd hit him like a thunderbolt. At times he had to question whether it really was love or just mind-blowing lust that had drawn him to Lillian. But either way, all along he had known in his heart there was something strangely dark and unusual about her. He thanked Sebastian and Christina for their honesty, then asked them to leave.

He switched off the main light and stood alone in his office with only the desk lamp on. Moments later, he looked up and was surprised to see Paulina standing in the doorway, clearly distressed. He gestured her in.

"Mr. Carlo, I'm so sorry, sir. You so good to me, you treat me like family. I heard what your friends tell you. I'm sorry I listened, but I must tell you some things…please?"

Carlo nodded. He turned his back to her and padded over to the huge windows, where he looked out at the distant glittering lights of Hollywood.

"Go on, Paulina," he said softly.

With tear-filled eyes, Paulina told him all about the tryst with the young gardener she had interrupted in the bedroom, and how Lillian had threatened her to keep quiet. She finished speaking and stood quietly, watching Carlo stand unmoving in the shadows, still gazing through the windows.

"Mr. Carlo…do I still work for you, sir?"

Carlo turned to her, his face half-hidden in shadow.

"Yes, of course you still work for me, Paulina. You may retire for the evening, thank you."

Paulina left the room with tears on her cheeks.

Carlo looked out at the night sky; he was shaken. He tried to recall the last time he had felt like this, but he never had. It felt like his heart had been torn out of his chest, like his whole world had collapsed around him. His hands trembled, and his stomach felt like a cold, empty pit as he thought of the pain that he knew would inevitably come: the cold, searing agony that can only be felt by a person who has offered everything… *everything* they had, to someone they loved with all their heart, someone they adored and trusted and wanted to share their life with, only to be scorned and deceived in return.

Carlo began to cry for the first time in many years. He felt himself starting to give, to crumble. A dagger had been thrust deep into his heart and the blade twisted and turned, and it was Lillian's fingers grasped around the handle. He knew the pending agony was unavoidable. Leaning against the glass, he felt like slumping to the floor, a heart-broken, shattered mess.

But Carlo Genisi was made of very tough stuff. With a few deep breaths, he recomposed himself and took control.

He would not slump to the floor like a spineless quitter. No, Carlo Genisi was far better than that.

He focused his thoughts while staring out at those distant Hollywood lights, where he knew Lillian was with Cliff. The seed of anger glowed in his belly, and it began to grow *very quickly*. He thought of Cliff Summers, once his idol. He had stood by like a complete fool and let this man flaunt his beloved Lillian all over Hollywood. He thought of the two of them together, probably laughing about what an idiot he was as they betrayed him in hotel rooms all over town. And Lillian had even cheated on him with a fucking gardener, in his own home. He knew he would be a mockery all over Los Angeles. Christ, he probably already was.

How could he have been so *stupid*? Two people he had truly trusted and admired had destroyed his entire world, *and* probably his reputation. His hands trembled again, but this time with ferocious anger. With clenched fists, he marched quickly to his desk and tore open the bottom drawer. He reached inside and pulled out a small black pistol he kept for personal security. He checked the barrel. It was fully loaded. He then pulled open the top drawer and took out a small, elegant black box. He opened it and stared down at the large sparkling diamond engagement ring inside. Carlo spat on it and threw it into the trash can next to his desk.

Moments later, Carlo Genisi was behind the wheel of his high-powered sports car, with a loaded gun and a gutful of fury, and he was headed straight to Hollywood Boulevard at more than twice the speed limit.

* * *

Karson was puffing as he reached the doors of the restaurant. He flashed his badge, and the doorman stepped aside. Karson entered and moved quickly across the floor, his eyes scanning the room for Lillian Kelly…Raines…*whoever the hell she was*. He quickly spotted Cliff Summers seated at a table with guests. He approached him and discreetly showed his police badge.

"Mr. Summers, I'm sorry to interrupt. I'm Detective James Karson, and I'm looking for Miss Lillian…Raines?"

Cliff stood respectfully on seeing the badge. "I'm afraid I'm not sure where she is. She certainly was here, but she vanished twenty minutes or so ago. I've been calling her cell, but there's no answer. Is something wrong?"

"Where did you last see her?" Karson asked.

"I believe she was headed to the ladies' room."

Karson moved swiftly in that direction, and the second he did, Larry, unnerved at seeing the police badge, made a hasty exit onto the street. He wasn't sure why the hell a cop was looking for a woman he had just drugged, and he certainly wasn't going to wait around to find out.

Karson burst into the ladies' room, much to the astonishment of the well-dressed occupants. Confirming Lillian was not there, he stepped back into the corridor and tried calling her cell again.

* * *

Carlo screeched to a halt in front of the restaurant, striking the curb with his tires. He leaped out of his car, and with the engine still running he stormed toward the front doors of the restaurant. Carlo was a shattered man, a broken, defeated shell. He felt sick to his stomach…numb and gutted to the core, but he was also furious beyond belief. Molten red anger seeped through his veins as he stormed across the street. The second the doorman spotted the gun in his hand, he scurried away from the crazed-looking man in the blue jeans and black sports jacket. He watched from across the street in disbelief as Carlo kicked open the heavy glass doors and barged into the restaurant.

* * *

Karson was trying Lillian's cell again, when he heard screams of panic from the main dining room. He rushed out to see Carlo pointing a gun at a terrified Cliff Summers, cowering against a wall with his hands over his head. People were fleeing through the front doors.

Karson stared at Carlo's face. He had seen that expression before. It was the look of murder, the face of a human being who was resigned to the fact that all was lost, that their life was now meaningless, and their only mission now was to destroy somebody. And that somebody was clearly Cliff Summers.

As Karson reached for his holstered gun, Carlo roared at Cliff, "You fucking son of a bitch!"

Karson drew and raised his pistol. "Drop the gun, Genisi!" he boomed.

If Carlo knew Karson was there, he didn't show it. With a deafening crack, he fired a shot at Cliff, hitting him square in the stomach. Cliff dropped like a stone, and a split second later Karson fired off two shots, one hitting Carlo's right shoulder and the second striking him in the back as he spun around from the force of the first. He fell, crashing against a large table, dragging the white cloth with him, plates and wine glasses shattering around him.

He lay almost motionless on the cold marble floor. "Lillian," he whispered, blood seeping from his wounds.

Cliff Summers also lay on the floor, moaning loudly, watching his blood gush out of his body.

Detective James Karson stood with gun still in hand, staring in shock and utter disbelief as two well-known Hollywood film directors lay dying on the floor in front of him.

Lillian Kelly's body count was rising.

CHAPTER 38

UNLEASHING HELL

The cab swung onto Hillwood Drive and began the climb toward Helen's house. The driver couldn't wait to get the attractive but very strange woman out of his cab. She had been moaning, shaking her head, and muttering to herself all the way from Hollywood Boulevard. He spotted number twenty-five and pulled the cab to the curb.

"No charge, lady. Just go home and call a doctor. All right?" Lillian stumbled out of the cab and he sped off.

Lillian was hanging onto her last threads of control. She could feel Helen crushing her will from within, but she was fighting back hard. Another violent cramp seized her stomach; she doubled over, then raced toward the house and tried to open the front door, which was locked. She howled in frustration.

Deep inside, Helen could feel Lillian's fury. She urged Lillian to pick up the hidden spare key by the front door. As she opened the door, another jolt of pain from Helen forced her to her knees. She crawled inside the house on all fours and collapsed on her stomach, as her whole body shook in agony.

Helen sensed she was inside her beloved home again, and she was *thrilled*. She had regained enough control that she could see! Although everything was still blurry. Helen didn't know what was happening, or why, but she knew something was affecting Lillian badly. It was wreaking havoc with her mind, and it had broken down her defenses. Helen had smelled the prize, and now nothing would stop her from fighting to return to her life.

As Lillian had come tumbling and crashing through the front door, Shadow dashed off in terror into the bedroom and hid under Helen's bed. Her stomach churned violently as spasms of pain raced through her. She rushed to the bathroom and heaved a thick stream of green bile into the sink, her mind clouded with confusion. She stared into the bathroom mirror as she felt Helen inside her, twisting and turning as if clawing at her insides.

"No!" Lillian screamed. "Never, you bitch."

But Helen had other ideas. She wanted out.

Lillian tried to think, tried to concentrate on her situation. Something was terribly wrong, that much she knew. But how to deal with it? She focused her thoughts. Ah, yes, it came back to her now…She knew what she had to do. She had to use all of her power to kill the mortal within her, to destroy her. And to do so, she knew she would have to bleed herself and extract Helen's soul from deep within her. It was risky…but it could be done, that she knew. *Oh, how did it come to this?*

She entered Helen's bedroom and leaned against the dresser, heaving for breath. She tore her handbag open and took out the perfume bottle. She sprayed more of the precious liquid on herself, but again it did nothing to help. She unscrewed the lid and set the bottle and lid down on the dresser, her anger raging. How dare the mortal do this! How dare she resist the power of the Ancient Ones and seek to destroy this perfect new life. She was about to give Helen the fight of her lifetime.

The wind was building fast outside, and all over Beachwood Canyon, leaves began to swirl and scatter across the sidewalks and streets. The trees began rustling, as if whispering rumors of the deadly battle that was about to unfold in the humble little cottage with the white picket fence. A full moon was peeking down through long, silvery clouds, turning the night sky into a glowing blanket of dark gray. A pack of coyotes unleashed bloodcurdling howls, high in the hills, sensing the pending showdown of good versus evil. The wind became even stronger—it seemed to be coming from everywhere at once. The trees in Helen's front yard were soon bending at breaking point, leaning and straining violently toward the house. Owls took flight into the night sky, escaping the unnaturally powerful gusts, which now blasted open Helen's bedroom windows. The curtains billowed hard against the ceiling, and her framed posters and pictures rattled on the walls. The wind streamed up the hallway, knocking figurines and photographs off shelves. Shadow crouched in terror under the bed, hissing loudly at the supernatural forces taking hold around him.

Helen sent another powerful jolt through Lillian, who shrieked and hurled a thick stream of green bile that splattered against the bedroom wall. She reached out and yanked on the bottom drawer of the jewelry box, when Helen's resistance hit her so hard that she dropped to the floor. The impact knocked the breath out of her. She felt as though an ice-cold vapor was trying to evaporate from her body. Her train of thought was almost derailed. She screamed and howled, but to no avail; she knew what had happened. For the moment at least, she had been overpowered, and like a battered phoenix rising from the ashes, Helen Elliot had returned.

She was *back*.

It felt bizarre to be among the living again. The first thing that struck Helen was the smell—the smell of *everything*. After being suppressed deep inside Lillian for so long, Helen had forgotten all of her senses. Sight, sound, everything. Now, though, it was all rushing back. She was *alive* again. Her eyes adjusted. Things were still a little blurry, but she could *see* again. Oh, how she had missed her little home.

But this was no time to reminisce. She had felt her takeover of Lillian's body like a high-voltage switch flipping inside her. One minute she had been locked away in eternal darkness, praying for the light to become stronger, and the next she was back in control, as if she had been catapulted through the center of a tornado. In her heart, though, she knew that holding onto control would not be easy. She had tampered with the dark side, and she sensed there would be a price to pay.

She was right. The first wave of pain hit her like an electric shock. It seemed to come from just under her chest, and then it spread throughout her entire body, forcing her to her knees. Her stomach heaved. She clutched at the large brass handles on her dresser drawers and hauled herself up to full height. She stared into the mirror, and for the first time in months she looked through her own eyes. But physically they still weren't her eyes; they were *Lillian's*. The mane of black hair was billowing around the stunning face staring back at her. Oh, how she had been seduced by this beauty, but now it was deplorable. It revolted her that she had so strongly desired to become this shallow, murderous creature.

Because of this demonic woman, she'd had to watch innocents die to maintain Lillian's charade. Oh God, how she wanted to rid herself of this evil being completely and just be Helen Elliot again. She knew she had to wait for the full transformation to take place, and she knew the agony of becoming herself again was inevitable. But this time she welcomed it.

Lillian struck out hard for control, but Helen fought back. She tore off Lillian's dress and flung it to the floor as huge jolts of pain ripped through her. She screamed in agony. She stood there helplessly, like a hunched-over puppet with broken strings, and waited for it—waited for the evil to leave her and let her become herself again. But it didn't. Like a thick, icy fog, Helen felt Lillian's anger emanating from within.

"God *damn* you!" Helen shrieked. Although she had regained control, Lillian was still clearly nowhere near surrender. Helen's thoughts were then flooded with death and blood. In her mind's eye, she saw herself cutting her own wrist and bleeding herself into the perfume bottle. She looked into the mirror, into those evil blue eyes, and gasped.

Lillian's deep, raspy voice suddenly filled the room. It echoed off the walls and surrounded her. "Do it. Give yourself to me *now*."

"No!" screamed Helen. The next wave of pain was unbearable, and she silently screamed, crumpling to the floor against the dresser. She dragged herself up again and stared into the mirror, only to see the cruel, mocking eyes of Lillian burning back at her. But she noticed something else—the face was aging; she could see the decades setting in. *The true Lillian is trapped in the mirror, trapped inside me…*She felt the dark power then; Lillian was forcing her to move toward the bathroom. Helen fought back ferociously. Her body jolted violently as she got to her feet, trying her utmost to resist. She glared at the poster of Lillian on the wall.

"Mistress of Evil, and by *God*, you are!" she screamed.

Lillian was now getting stronger by the second. Helen reached up and tore down the poster, and Lillian responded with staggering pain. Helen felt herself being forced to the hallway against her will, jolting and jerking with resistance, writhing in agony.

What are you doing to me? Lillian forced her into the bathroom, and she found herself reaching inside the vanity cabinet. Helen trembled with frustration. *How could she still have this much control over me?* The realization of what she was doing flashed into her mind.

"No!" screamed Helen. Overpowered by Lillian, she picked up a razor blade.

"You evil bitch. Leave me be!" Helen screamed. "You won't do it. I won't kill myself for you!"

Lillian's deep, scornful laugh thundered throughout the house. "You will, you pathetic creature."

Shadow hunkered down low and tight under the bed, terrified.

Helen fought for her life against Lillian; she felt as if she was being torn in two. Through the vicious, overpowering evil of Lillian crushing her more and more by the second, Helen suddenly realized what Lillian was trying to do…

Unable to make herself drop the razor, Helen staggered back to her bedroom, struggling with all her might against Lillian's grip. She had seen Lillian's thoughts and she knew Lillian needed to kill her, needed to destroy her and claim her soul.

If she kills me and takes my soul before I transform, she will reclaim her own body. She will be back, alive again, and I will be gone forever. And God only knows how many more innocents she will murder to cling to her eternal youth.

Helen staggered to her dresser as Lillian taunted her.

"Nobody knows you are *alive* unless you are me. Give yourself to me so that I may truly live again."

"No! I won't!" Helen screamed.

But Lillian's power was astonishing. She forced Helen's arm to yank open the bottom drawer of the jewelry box and fling it to the ground. The false bottom tumbled out. Helen saw the tiny folded-up piece of paper that had been hidden in there when she'd first found the bottle. Under Lillian's control, Helen kneeled down and picked it up. The wind intensified the second she touched it.

Assuming the paper was evil, Helen tried to rip it in half, but Lillian struck again. Helen found the razor moving toward her own *throat*.

Helen fought back with everything she had, but she was shocked and terrified at Lillian's renewed strength. She stared into the mirror and screamed at what she saw. Lillian's face was withered and decaying. She grinned maniacally back at Helen, who was struggling to keep the razor blade from her own throat.

But this time, Helen saw something in Lillian's eyes. She saw *fear*.

Lillian was desperate now, fighting with everything she had. She needed Helen's blood *and* her soul inside the bottle. She needed Helen to read the spell; she needed her dead.

Lillian's piercing blue eyes were now faded and bloodshot. "Give me your soul!" she cried.

"I will not!" Helen screamed back. She threw a candleholder at Lillian's reflection, cracking the glass, which startled Lillian for a second. Helen felt a tiny slip of Lillian's grip on her, but then Lillian struck back again even harder. Helen dropped to the floor in searing pain. "Get out of me, you cursed thing!" she screamed, slowly rising to her feet again.

"I own you!" Lillian screeched.

A blast of wind struck Helen's bedroom like lightning, almost knocking her over. Posters and pictures flew around the room, a supernatural tornado of Lillian's furious wrath, but in creating such havoc, Helen felt just enough give in Lillian's grip on her to break free for a moment.

Helen picked up the jewelry box, took a step back…then flung it into the mirror. Most of the glass shattered into long, thin cracks. A mournful howl erupted through the room. Helen stood, terrified, waiting for what would come next…

And then she realized it was already happening. She felt herself standing still, frozen, almost unable to move. The evil had taken hold of her again completely. Mechanically, she managed to unfold the note that was still clamped between her thumb and forefinger.

"Yes!" Lillian's raspy voice hissed.

The note. She wants me to read the note. Try as she did, Helen could not stop herself looking at the yellowed old piece of paper. She unfolded it and stared at the writing. She could feel Lillian urging her to read it aloud. She stared at the perfume bottle.

The evil inside her spread rapidly. Helen felt it envelop her; she had no idea she was dragging the razor blade across her own wrist until she looked down and saw her blood seeping into the perfume bottle. She stared in shock. Lillian's grip on her felt invincible. She looked into the shattered mirror at Lillian's reflection, or what was left of it, staring back at her.

Murderous, fierce determination blazed in those aging, bloodshot eyes. The wind died down a little, but Lillian was gaining the upper hand. Helen watched her blood flowing into the bottle, staring in disbelief at what Lillian was *forcing* her to do. The tiny bottle was now filling rapidly. She felt Lillian force her attention to the note, and to Helen's surprise, she realized she could understand every word of it…and completely against her will, she read the words aloud.

"Le sang de la jeunesse éternelle…"

The wind whipped around the bedroom as Helen continued to watch her own blood filling the tiny bottle.

God help me. Let go of me!

She took a deep breath and heard herself read aloud the next line on the paper.

"Prendre cette âme prete…"

Lillian hissed in ecstasy as Helen spoke the ancient words. Helen felt as if she was in a trance. A gray mist began creeping out from the mirror and formed a tiny cloud, then a small white cloudy mist rose from the wound in her wrist. The two little clouds entwined into one. Helen watched helpless as the cloud slowly floated down and hovered over the now full perfume bottle. Her blood inside began to bubble softly. Lillian forced her to read the second-to-last line of the ancient words aloud.

"Notre pour l'éternité…"

Helen felt her soul leaving her, her memories, her strength, her everything…she had no choice. She was powerless, completely compelled by Lillian's will as she watched the mist swirling its way down into the bottle. A dark, horrible realization suddenly struck her.

I'm going to die…Right here in my own bedroom, I am going to die.

She tried to reach deep down inside herself and tear away from Lillian's grip, but she only sensed her own demise. She grew weaker and looked at a photo of her mother and her aunt still barely hanging on the wall above the dresser. They were smiling with their arms around each other. It was Helen's favorite photo; she had taken it on the back deck on her eighteenth birthday. She remembered their warmth, their caring words, and the pure, unconditional love that they had all shared. She had always felt safe and protected around them. Her mother and her aunt had taught her to stand up for herself, and Helen always had.

As she looked at the photograph, a warm white light glowed from deep within her. She focused on it. She could still feel Lillian's evil, willing her on to read the last line of the spell, but Helen gave her all to resist. A pure, brilliant light now began to form in Helen's mind.

It was awesome, and she could feel it weakening Lillian's grip. It flooded her senses, and she focused on it as hard as she could. Shapes began to form across it. At first they were silhouettes—dark figures standing against blinding white moonlight, but then…everything became clear. Helen's spirit soared as she recognized the figures. They were her mother and her aunt, standing next to each other, looking right back at her. They simply stood there smiling at her, and that was all it took.

"Oh!" Helen cried. How she had missed them. And now their love completely overwhelmed her…She felt it growing stronger deep inside her, felt their strength flowing through her entire body. It empowered her, adrenalized her, and their message to her was clear: "*Now is not your time…You must fight.*"

And fight she would. Helen would not sit helplessly and watch her soul vanish into the bottle. She would not be just another victim of Lillian Kelly. No, she would fight back, fight for her life.

Helen looked at the note. There was only one more line of the spell to read, and she knew then that it would all be over; her soul would be gone, mixed in with her blood in the perfume bottle and lost with the last words of the incantation. If she read the ancient words aloud, she knew Lillian would win. She knew Lillian would be back inside her own body forever, and Helen Elliot would no longer exist. Her courage had been bolstered by her mother and aunt, and she now began to resist, but she could still feel Lillian's murderous rage.

The spell began to work its magic, and the blood bubbled inside the tiny crystal bottle. Helen felt Lillian's anger as the small cloud rose back up and hovered above the surface of the bottle, stuck in a bizarre spiritual limbo between good and evil. Helen knew it was the strength from her mother and aunt that had stopped her soul from being sucked into the bottle and dissolving with the blood, and Lillian was *furious*.

CHAPTER 39

UNTIL DEATH DO US PART

Helen braced herself, clutching the old dresser. She stared deep into Lillian's foul, rotting, bloodshot eyes and prepared herself for the battle of her life. From deep inside, with the natural instinct every human being possesses to survive, Helen began to scream. It was a guttural sound that came from the very bottom of her lungs, and it was both deafening and bloodcurdling, a sound she had never thought herself capable of. Such was its force and volume that it terrified her. She felt Lillian's shock at this sudden rebellion, felt her absolute wrath and fury, as Helen gave her all to reject her and crush her and this black magic, this evil that had infected her. She felt Lillian's power crack just a fraction, but it was all she needed to regain more control and lash out and tip the perfume bottle over, spilling most of her own blood across the dresser.

Helen snatched up the lid, and despite Lillian's fierce resistance, she managed to screw it back on, hoping to stop her soul being sucked into the bottle. And it worked. Lillian screeched in rage. The two entwined souls hovered and contracted into a tight ball in front of the mirror, which began morphing into two distinct colors, one pure white and the other a dark gray. Helen picked up the perfume bottle and hurled it against the wall, but it merely bounced off with a loud clack.

Lillian struck back hard. Helen found herself jerking and jolting as if she were being electrocuted. Lillian forced her to snatch up the razor blade and attempt to slash her own throat. Helen fought back equally hard, but she felt the razor nick her throat at least twice. Her blood spattered over the old piece of paper still clasped in her left hand. The wind intensified, and the doors throughout the house slammed violently; debris and figurines were sent scattered around the room. Helen knew she was about to face the full fury of Lillian, but she was prepared to fight. She knew it would not be easy, but she was not afraid anymore. She could feel her mother and her aunt guiding her. She knew they were here with her, and they seemed to be urging her to turn over the piece of paper. She did, then realized *it was a reverse to the spell!*

Fighting blinding pain and using all her strength to keep the razor pinned to the dresser and away from herself, Helen knew she had to read the words aloud. She tried to focus, but fear began to set in again fast.

Helen heard something. It was whisper-quiet but it was there, and it soon became louder despite the screaming winds rampaging through the house. Helen focused on it. Tears filled her eyes…it was her mother's voice, urging her to read the words aloud.

Empowered with an incredible new strength, Helen shouted the first line of words in English: *"Blood of eternal youth…"*

A howl erupted from Lillian in the shattered mirror, and the wind intensified, sending objects hurtling across the room at her. But Helen continued: "*Release me from your power…*"

At this second line, Lillian let loose a scream that pierced the air like a thousand wolves howling in unison. The lights dimmed on and off, and a tremor ran through the house. Another blast of wind screamed around her bedroom, wreaking havoc and tearing a huge hole in her bedroom ceiling. Her framed posters were flung from the walls, all of them smashed to pieces. Her dolls and figurines were hurtling around and bouncing off the walls. Lillian was pure destruction now, but Helen knew she was also very frightened. Helen took another deep breath and began the next line from the paper. She could barely hear herself over Lillian's screaming and the howling wind: "*Allow me…*"

A four-inch shard of glass flew from the mirror and stuck in her left shoulder. Helen moaned in agony. Another mournful screech from Lillian echoed around the room. A large porcelain vase missed Helen's head by inches and exploded against the wall above the mirror.

This really is to reverse the spell. She's terrified…This is an escape from the spell for Lillian, in case something went wrong or if she ever wanted out…Out of the life of eternal beauty, the murder and depravity.

Helen ignored the pain in her shoulder and continued to read the words, shouting over the now gale-force winds. "*Allow me to submit to nature!*"

Another gut-wrenching howl from Lillian chilled her to the bone. Lillian was sensing defeat, and another jolt of agony rocked through Helen. She could barely control her hand holding the razor. She thrust it inside a dresser drawer and used her body to force it closed, but she could feel Lillian willing the razor to her throat again. Lillian was not going down easily. Helen looked down at the note again. Blood wept from her shoulder, spattering across the walls by the wind. Lillian's screams echoed in her ears. Helen's old pink cassette player flew from a shelf and struck the back of her head hard, stunning her. She stumbled a step but stood firm. Tiny glass fragments peppered her face and body, but she stood strong.

This was it now, the last line of the spell. Whatever was going to happen would happen after she spoke these words... if only she *lived* long enough. Helen knew Lillian meant to kill her before she could utter them, and she refused to look into the mirror.

The long, heavy brass curtain rod that hung over her bedroom window flew toward her at incredible speed, shedding the curtains as it came. Helen saw it coming and ducked as its point slammed deep into the wall like a spear above the dresser.

Lillian howled at the failed attempt but unleashed more of her deadly fury. The bedroom windows exploded out, sending thousands of glass fragments blasting across the lawn, and the cupboard doors were torn completely off their hinges. The entire house trembled. Objects large and small slammed against Helen's body, and the wind screamed up the hallway, sending furniture and pictures crashing.

With every ounce of remaining strength, Helen stood fast against Lillian's last desperate attempts to destroy her.

But she was tiring rapidly; she felt the life draining from her as she stood clinging to her old wooden dresser. The wind was deafening, but the tiny piece of paper was still clamped between her thumb and forefinger.

Weak, terrified, and exhausted, Helen's knees buckled. She knew she needed to get the last line of the spell out fast or she was finished. She now wondered if she could do it. With her last shred of energy, Helen closed her eyes and focused on her mother and aunt.

Strength exploded inside Helen, flooding every part of her being and dousing Lillian's evil. It was wonderful; Helen laughed aloud in the face of death then, in the face of *Lillian!*

The storm of destruction continued around her, but she was no longer frightened, no longer weak. Helen heard Shadow meowing loudly with fright, and she knew he was calling to her. This heartwarming act of devotion from her darling cat, combined with the presence of her mother and aunt, eliminated any remaining shred of fear in her.

Now…Helen was *unstoppable.* She opened her eyes and stared defiantly at the hideous, foul creature in the shattered glass snarling back at her. She drew a deep breath and screamed aloud with all her might the last words on the paper: *"Power of the Ancient Ones, I renounce you…Now…and forever!"*

The earth beneath her shook.

Lillian's rage was utterly *incomprehensible.* The bedroom ceiling exploded upwards with such force that dozens of the heavy slate roof tiles lifted off and shattered on the front lawn. The wind was so powerful she could barely stand. She couldn't see…couldn't hear…

Lillian's ear-shattering screams were deafening, and debris was tearing across the bedroom and slamming into Helen as she clung to the dresser. Helen's right hand came out of the drawer, and the razor was cutting and slicing her legs as Lillian gave her utmost to kill her. But it was too late; Helen had fully recited the spell, and now the ball of mist that contained the two souls had completely split in two, one white and one gray.

She shut out the deadly chaos around her, and slowly, gradually, she felt Lillian's power fading. Helen sensed her demise. It was done. *The bitch is beaten!*

The wind was dying fast, and she could feel the calm setting in again. Helen's eyes fluttered open, and she looked up just in time to see the foul, dark-gray mist that was Lillian's evil soul hovering over the perfume bottle laying on the floor. Helen knelt and quickly unscrewed the lid. As she suspected, Lillian's evil soul quickly vanished back inside the tiny bottle, and Helen immediately screwed the lid on tight again. She looked into the shattered mirror and saw Lillian's horrible, decaying face still glaring back at her.

It was nothing but a grotesque mask now, the rotting face was the epitome of evil. Helen stared speechless as Lillian opened her mouth wide and screamed in silent agony. And then, to her horror, Lillian's face leaned forward and out from the broken glass. She glared at Helen through bloodshot eyes and released a long, mournful hiss, like the breath of hell itself. Helen stood her ground—she had beaten this vile, murderous creature. Lillian was defeated. Good had triumphed over evil, and Helen Elliot remained, the true surviving star of her own horror film.

Shadow leaped up onto the dresser and hissed at Lillian's face. Helen watched, stunned, as he raised an outstretched paw toward her with his sharp little claws out. Lillian's head retracted back into the broken glass, still a tiny gleam in those horrible eyes. Her mouth opened and her yellowing, rotted teeth were clear to see, and Helen truly thought she was about to speak, to utter her final words. But there was only a soft gasp as Lillian crumbled away and disappeared. Shadow leaped off the dresser and disappeared under the bed.

Helen stood, weak, bleeding, and dumbfounded as the pure white ball of vapor that she knew was her own soul floated down from in front of the mirror. It became thinner and thinner, until it was only a tiny spiral. She watched as it quickly vanished into the slit in her wrist that was still bleeding.

She picked up a T-shirt that had blown onto the floor and wrapped it around her hand, then carefully picked up the perfume bottle so that the evil thing did not touch her skin. A sudden burning and tingling in her arms and legs sent her to the floor. *It's happening; this is the price. I've beaten her, but I still have to become myself again.*

The pain intensified, and Helen curled up into the fetal position and readied herself for the oncoming agony of the physical transformation. Lying there on the carpet, she remembered her mother, her aunt...

And then there was just darkness.

CHAPTER 40

ASHES TO ASHES

The small fire crackled softly in Helen's leafy backyard, lighting up the grassed area under her deck with a soft amber glow. Her shoulder throbbed with pain, but the aspirin was starting to kick in. She would see the doctor tomorrow, she decided.

She had cleaned and bandaged her shoulder, her wrist, and the other small cuts to her body well enough for the night, she thought. They ached, but they were nothing much to worry about. She recalled the pain of the transformation, the burning, agonizing sensation of Lillian's body transforming back into her own. But then she had just blacked out.

She had awoken cold and naked on her bedroom floor. She had no idea how long she had laid there, but she knew it was finally over now. The first thing she had seen was Shadow peeking out at her from under her bed.

"Baby," she'd whispered to him, and instantly he had crept out and nuzzled against her neck, purring. To Helen it was the most wonderful feeling in the world. She lay there with him a little while before dragging herself up and tending to her wounds. Exhausted, she sat on a stool in her shower for a long while. The hot water felt wonderful as she regained her strength. She looked down at her body, her *real* body, and for the first time in many years, she smiled at the sight of herself and loved who she truly was. She was Helen Elliot, dry cleaner and dressmaker, old Hollywood collector, and that was perfectly fine with her.

After her shower, she read all the notes Ashley had left, and she knew she had looked after her darling cat and had been searching for her, and for that Helen would be eternally grateful. She also found a note left by Daniel, explaining that Ashley had been admitted to hospital. She was touched that Daniel had been here too. She suspected there was a mutual spark between them, but she thought it was so sweet of him to be looking for her as well. Helen called the hospital immediately and was thrilled to hear that Ashley's condition was stable and she was sleeping. Helen had no *idea* how to explain where she had been, but somehow she knew Ashley just might be the only person in the world who would believe the story she had to tell.

Helen stood over the fire, satisfied it was now hot enough. She opened the plastic garbage bag in her hands and lifted out the magnificent silver dress; the fabric shimmered in the glow of the flames. Helen gazed at it a moment, then tossed it onto the fire. The flames engulfed it quickly, and she watched as the last remaining piece, a silver shoulder strap, quickly turned into fine black ash.

The shoes were next. She picked them up and stared at them a moment, then dropped them into the flames, one at a time, followed by the box they'd come in. The fake glass diamonds glistened as the flames hungrily licked at the leather. The heels and the soles buckled and melted, until soon all Helen could see was a bubbling little pool of silvery white, disappearing in the bottom of the fire.

Next came the jewelry box. Even out here lying on the grass, it was magnificent. The gleaming lacquered panels reflected the golden orange flames that would soon seal its fate. Helen picked it up and held it out low over the fire, then let it go. It fell perfectly into the center of the flames with a soft thud, sending up a small cloud of smoke and ash. She knew the box would take some time to burn, but she was in no rush. She sat back in her little outdoor chair, petting Shadow and sipping her wine. As she watched the jewelry box burn, she wondered if anything so beautiful had ever been deliberately set alight before. The flames quickly burned the polished surface away from the handcrafted panels, and the exquisite scent of burning antique wood drifted up into the night sky. *Whatever the flames don't destroy, I'll collect and dump somewhere on a walk tomorrow evening, perhaps in Lake Hollywood.*

There was one more item remaining on the grass, a small silk cloth wrapped firmly around a tiny object—the perfume bottle. Although she knew glass did not burn or melt unless in extreme heat, Helen felt she *needed* to see it in the fire. She had seen what was left of Lillian vanish into that bottle, her putrid, dark soul trapped in there with the tiny amount of Helen's own blood that had remained inside it. Helen hoped the heat would make it evaporate.

She had figured it all out now, how Lillian lived, and how she died—burned to death in the huge fire so long ago. She had been killing young women for their blood and their souls; the early murders so long ago and the more recent killings—it had all flashed into her mind during the battle that nearly took her life. She saw Lillian alone in the great mansion all those years ago, chanting the sacred words before a large mirror. She had even seen glimpses of the young girls Lillian had killed, so many innocent souls who had met their gruesome end for the voracious vanity of one woman. Helen saw there were dozens of candles around Lillian, and a breeze was filling the room as the flames flickered.

In the vision, Helen saw Lillian had the blood and souls of three young victims who had died at her evil hands. But the spell did not work for Lillian that time; she had tried to tamper with the dark powers, tried to make too much perfume too fast, and in doing so she had angered the Ancient Ones immensely. And this witchcraft, this black magic, had *rejected* her.

The power had turned on her, banishing her soul into the perfume bottle, twisting and contorting her body and snapping her bones as she screamed in unimaginable agony. In her mind, Helen saw the candles fall to the floor, setting the rugs and drapes alight as Lillian howled. She had tried in vain to flee, before succumbing to the smoke and flames.

"What price for eternal beauty," Helen whispered. Shadow pressed his nose against her hand, and she scratched his ears as he purred. She stood and picked up the bottle, then she reached out and let it fall into the middle of the half-burned jewelry box.

"Burn, you evil, murderous bitch. Just burn."

When Helen had woken after her transformation, she had discovered she was wearing a diamond pendant necklace and also a diamond bracelet. Immediately, she had taken them off and put them into a bag. She had placed them in a cabinet in her spare bedroom, planning to donate them to charity anonymously; wherever they came from, she wanted nothing to do with them. She was deeply troubled over the young girls who had died while she was trapped inside Lillian, but she knew there was nothing she could have done.

She sat back in her chair in front of the fire, watching the flames. *It's over now; you cannot take my soul. It cannot be bought, bargained for, or stolen…it is for loving unconditionally only.*

The fire crackled quietly as Helen looked up at the sky. There was a half-moon tonight. She looked at the Hollywood Sign on the mountain, to which she had made that fateful wish.

"Thank you for listening, but no thank you. Never again. I just want to be me."

She sat and watched until the flames died down to smoldering coals. She went to bed then, and slept as soundly as she ever had, with a photo of her mother and aunt on her pillow, and Shadow curled up against her, purring.

CHAPTER 41

BACK IN THE LAND OF THE LIVING

Helen woke early to a perfect morning, and after a trip to the doctor, and some stitches and fresh bandages, she felt remarkably better. She'd called a local handyman to mend the shattered roof tiles and windows. He'd said he'd also be happy to handle the repairs inside the house over the next week as well. She looked around at the many pieces of her movie collection, still scattered about the house. Sadly, she knew some were beyond repair, but many were still salvageable.

She needed to get to the hospital to see Ashley. After the whole experience, she also felt like going shopping later in the day, for whatever took her fancy. She put on a blue dress that she hadn't worn in years and completed the outfit with a pair of snappy heels. She wore her hair down and applied a deep shade of lipstick. A layer of foundation covered the nicks and cuts on her face nicely. She kissed Shadow goodbye and headed off to the hospital.

She couldn't believe how much better she felt after her ordeal the night before. She knew she had been "gone" for some time, and there were going to be many questions to answer, but for now she was just happy to be alive—and *very happy* to be Helen Elliot.

The nurse led her into the small room where Ashley lay sleeping. Helen choked with emotion at the diminutive figure under the white sheets. Ashley looked old and frail; her skin was pale and her cheeks were sunken. The nurse left, and a tear slid down Helen's cheek as she gently stroked her friend's hand.

Ashley stirred. Her eyes opened slightly. They were dim at first, but then they opened wide and twinkled. Ashley's face broke into the most heartwarming smile Helen had ever seen, and tears flooded her eyes. Ashley squeezed Helen's hand, as Helen leaned down close to her.

"Tell me I'm not dreaming," Ashley whispered. "Please tell me you're really here, Helen."

"Yes, I'm really here, and I'm so sorry I disappeared. I really am, and…I'm really not sure how to explain things to you."

Tears rolled down over Ashley's lips. "I don't care where you've been. I'm just so glad you're back. You're the daughter I never had, you know."

"Yes, and you are a mother to me more than you could ever know," Helen whispered back to her. She lay her head on Ashley's shoulder and the two shed quiet tears of joy together. Moments later, Daniel appeared at the doorway; he stared in utter astonishment. "Helen?"

"It's really her," Ashley croaked.

"You remember Daniel from work? He's been helping me search for you and checking up on me in here. He's such a sweetheart."

"I…came in to see how Ashley was doing today. But I must say, Helen, thank God you're here—it's wonderful to see you. Are you…okay?" Helen stood, and Daniel stepped over to her and hugged her. The move surprised Helen a little, but it felt wonderful.

"I'm going to be fine, and thank you for helping Ashley; that's very kind of you."

"Not a problem at all. I'm just so glad you're back. I'll give you ladies some privacy." Daniel headed back out into the hallway. He looked so different and relaxed out of his work uniform, Helen thought, in his blue jeans and sneakers.

"He's quite fond of you, darling, he really is. I knew it from the start," Ashley whispered.

Helen blushed. "I rather like him too."

Ashley stroked her hand. "Helen, I saw those gorgeous new dresses you're working on at your house. I've made a decision on something I've been thinking about for quite some time. You've made so many beautiful garments over the years. I've had clarity lying here in hospital: I'm going to open another shop…a dress shop, and I want to sell your dresses in there too. You're so talented, darling, and we need to get your designs out there. What do you think?"

Helen was deeply touched. She leaned down and kissed Ashley's cheek.

"I think I'd like that very much. Thank you."

A nurse entered the room and told Helen it was time for Ashley's medication and her rest time was crucial. Helen bid her friend goodbye and promised to visit again later that evening. She found Daniel in the waiting room browsing a magazine; he stood as she approached. "Daniel, thank you again for everything. Really."

"Think nothing of it. It's just wonderful to see you again." He glanced at her bandages. "Are you sure you're okay?"

"Just a few scratches, really. It's a long story. Ashley is sleeping now."

"Oh well, that might be my cue to catch the bus."

"Which way are you headed?" Helen asked.

"Well, I was planning on heading downtown to go the markets."

"That's where I'm heading too. I feel like a shop, and it's a beautiful day. How 'bout I give you a ride?"

"That'd be great. Maybe we could grab a coffee somewhere too?" he suggested.

"Sounds like a plan."

Soon they were wandering LA's famous fashion district. Helen loved it; and Santee Alley was always bustling and full of bargains. They strolled together, stopping at shops and stalls, and she began browsing the dresses and was quickly smitten with a lovely white number. It was perfect and summery, just what she wanted.

After a while, they sat down for a coffee break. Helen liked the way Daniel looked. He was overweight in a cuddly kind of way. His hair was thinning on top, with some silver frosting around his ears. He had lovely, friendly hazel eyes.

"I couldn't help but notice your Hollywood memorabilia collection when I was in your house Helen. It's remarkable, just amazing."

"Thank you. My mother and aunt started the collection before I was born, and I caught the collecting bug from them. I've almost run out of room to place things, but I'll always collect. I just adore the old movies. I have hundreds of them."

"I'm quite the old Hollywood buff myself, you know. I rather think I know my films quite well too. But I'll bet you're quite the expert. What can you tell me about the Hollywood Sign's history?"

"Erected in 1923, it originally read "Hollywoodland." Its original purpose was as an advertising gimmick to sell land. It was shortened to just Hollywood in 1949. The entire sign was replaced and rebuilt in 1978. It's been renovated several times, and it's been a global icon ever since."

"Wow, you are an expert."

"No expert," Helen laughed. "But I think I'm reasonably knowledgeable. After all, I've been living under that sign all my life; you tend to learn about your surroundings. Are you from LA originally, Daniel?"

"No, I moved here from San Francisco not long ago. I left a bad marriage, and now I'm following a dream, moving out here to Hollywood. I'm renting a place in Laurel Canyon."

"It's a nice spot."

"It is indeed."

They chatted away like old friends and finished their coffees, then continued shopping. Helen truly enjoyed having Daniel by her side. He even gently took her hand as they strolled around, and Helen loved it; it felt right somehow, like he belonged next to her.

The rest of the afternoon was wonderful. Helen bought two new dresses and treated herself to a new pair of shoes.

She wasn't sure what it was, but she felt a new confidence about herself. Perhaps the whole Lillian experience had left something behind after all—not something bad, but something good.

There was a new woman in Hollywood. She had always been there; she'd just been in hiding for a long time. Helen Elliot was back. And she felt completely happy and at peace with herself.

They wandered into a little perfume store. *Ah, yes*, a new fragrance would be just perfect. She decided on her mother's favorite brand. After a little more shopping and browsing, Helen and Daniel headed back to her car.

* * *

Karson was exhausted. Following the shootout at the restaurant, he had been under intense media pressure for a comment. The press had gone insane over the incident. It was the story of the decade. The police station was besieged by journalists, and the call center was swamped. The chief of police and the mayor had been breathing down his neck for answers.

The trouble was, he didn't seem to have any yet. The one thing he knew for certain was that he had to find Lillian Kelly, and by God, he would, and he didn't care how long it took him. But the only person who knew where she might be was lying in a hospital bed.

* * *

Carlo Genisi looked and felt like death warmed up as he lay in his private hospital room. He'd been awake only a few moments, dazed and groggy. An EKG machine sat next to his bed monitoring his heart rhythm, and an IV unit was hooked up to his arm. While nasal tubes fed him oxygen.

A bespectacled middle-aged doctor leaned down close to him. "Mr. Genisi, I'm Doctor Vincent. You've had surgery to remove two bullets. Everything went well, and you should make a full recovery, but for now you need to stay here in the hospital and rest. Do you understand me, Mr. Genisi?"

Carlo grunted.

The doctor turned to Sebastian and an intense-looking man in a sharp black suit standing next to him, Jack Thorn—Carlo's lawyer. The doctor nodded, giving him permission to speak to Carlo.

"One minute only." He left the room.

Thorn leaned down to Carlo. "Hello Carlo. You don't need to speak. Just listen. Don't say one word to anybody about anything that happened, especially the police. Not a word, okay, Carlo?"

Carlo gave a feeble nod.

"Don't worry about a thing. I'll take care of this; that's what I do. You just rest now."

Sebastian then leaned down to Carlo. "Hello friend. I'm so glad you're going to be okay."

Carlo's lips parted slightly. "Lillian," he croaked.

"Carlo, don't worry about her. Nobody knows where she is.

And it doesn't matter. Just rest, go to sleep. Jack will take care of everything."

Despite everything that had happened, Carlo knew that somehow, at least on some level, he still loved Lillian. And when he was well enough, he would find her.

He closed his eyes and fell asleep. Sebastian and Jack headed out past the uniformed cop who was guarding Carlo's room. After all, he was currently suspected of attempted murder. They stepped into the corridor to see Doctor Vincent speaking to Karson.

"Definitely not, Detective. Not for at least another few days. Mr. Genisi is still very weak."

Karson nodded and turned to Thorn, who he'd recognized from dealings in the past. "I'll be needing to speak with Mr. Genisi as soon as possible."

"When the doctor says he is able to and certainly not without me present," Thorn shot back sharply. "I'll call you when Mr. Genisi is well enough to speak."

Sebastian and Thorn headed for the elevators.

* * *

In an intensive care unit in the same hospital, Cliff Summers also lay in a bed, his face partially covered by an oxygen mask. Tubes were inserted into his chest, and a central venous catheter was inserted into his neck. Cliff felt numb all over. Bronwyn and two doctors stood at his bedside.

One doctor leaned down to Cliff, whose eyes were barely open. "Mr. Summers, you're going to survive, and I believe you'll make a full recovery, but it's a very serious injury, and it could be weeks before we can release you. Fortunately, the bullet missed your vital organs, but the damage is going to take quite some time to heal. Please just try to remain calm and get some rest."

Cliff stared up at the ceiling. He could feel practically nothing, could hardly move his fingers. He remembered snippets of what had happened at the restaurant: people screaming, Carlo pointing a gun at him, the cracking sounds like fireworks, the ambulance ride to the hospital…He knew he had been shot, he wanted this to be a bad dream, but he knew it was real. The media would have a field day, and filming of his upcoming movie was now put off for who knows how long. And would he ever be the same again? He'd been shot in the stomach for Christ's sake. Even in his groggy, numb, and shocked state of mind, a surge of sinister anger pulsated throughout him. He decided right then and there if Carlo Genisi was still alive, he would do…and pay, whatever it took to have that son of a bitch killed.

* * *

Karson headed back to his office via the back way to avoid the media crowd outside the station, salivating for a comment. He made himself a coffee and sat at his desk. He still had a lot of work to do on his official statement about the shooting at the restaurant. He checked his inbox and noticed an email from a tobacco store. It was the one at the Hollywood shopping center, right on Hollywood Boulevard. He remembered it clearly.

He opened it; the shopkeeper had remembered something unusual. He'd sold a tin of Vanilla Dove cigars weeks before to a woman he'd known for a long time but had never known as a smoker. She had gone missing recently, and she also worked in the same shopping center. Karson read the name, Helen Elliot. Alarm bells rang—he knew that name, but from where? He typed Helen's name into the police database, and up came the missing person's report Ashley had filed. Karson scrolled down and saw a photograph of Helen's face. He stared in disbelief as it all came back to him. This was the missing woman he had seen on flyers posted along Hollywood Boulevard. He even recalled seeing one outside the tobacco store itself. Going by the report, she was last seen leaving the store she worked in at the very same shopping center. His eyes widened, and his heartbeat accelerated. He checked the date of purchase the shopkeeper had supplied; it was the same day she had vanished, which also happened to be the day before the young girl was found with her wrist slashed in Peter Jameson's apartment. This was no coincidence, Karson could feel it. He brought up Helen's home address, and moments later he was in his car, headed straight to Beachwood Canyon.

CHAPTER 42

FINDERS KEEPERS

Old Ethel pushed her shopping cart along the sidewalk in Beachwood Canyon. It rattled and shook with all her meager possessions inside it. She had been going through dumpsters and trash cans all afternoon. She smelled awful and she knew it, but she just didn't really care anymore. She'd been looking for things to sell and trade, but she hadn't really found much: a hair dryer, a pair of sneakers, some sunglasses—just some odds and ends she hoped to get a few bucks for.

She knew she had no chance of making it back to Hollywood before nightfall with her bad hips, and she'd have to find somewhere close by to sleep tonight. Anywhere would do if she could curl up out of sight safely, or as safely as a woman her age could be sleeping on the streets.

A gentle breeze caressed her face, carrying a peculiar but pleasant smell, like the rich, sweet after-scent of a forest fire. It was enticing enough to draw her to a white picket fence across the street. She hobbled over and peered through the fence. She spotted the remains of a fire, a small but thick pile of ashes. It looked as though somebody had been sitting in a chair in front of it underneath the deck that extended out from the rear of the little house.

The fading sunlight sparkled on something half-buried in the ashes. Ethel ambled along the fence line to an old gate that looked as though it hadn't been used in many years. With a good firm tug, it opened, and Ethel stepped silently into the yard. As she approached the remains of the fire, she saw the sparkling object peeking out from the ashes again. She knew she was trespassing, but she figured she would be concealed by the deck overhead. Besides, it looked like nobody was home. She knelt down slowly and began blowing the ashes away. And she was amazed to see a small cluster of…diamonds? Lord, how they sparkled!

No…they cannot be real. She scooped them all up and quickly tucked them into her pocket. There were two large ones and a whole bunch of smaller ones. She blew more ashes away—now what? Gorgeous ornate little silver knobs and handles. Goodness.

Why on Earth would anyone try to burn things like these?

Ethel scooped them up and placed them in another pocket. After a few more minutes of sifting through the ash, she was satisfied there was nothing else to find, when suddenly her hand struck something small and strangely cold. She picked it up and with her coat wiped away the black soot covering it.

It was a tiny perfume bottle. She stared at it, awestruck at the dazzling crystal, and the sparkling silver base and lid. She held it up high. It was magnificent.

Even in the fading afternoon light, she could see a very small amount of red liquid inside it. Delighted with her find, she began searching through the ashes again, just to be sure there were no more treasures.

* * *

After dropping Daniel off at his house, Helen was pleasantly surprised to receive a gentle kiss on the cheek. She got home, still smiling, and locked her car in the garage. Daniel had asked her out to dinner later in the week, and she was very much looking forward to it. It was wonderful to be back. She took her new items down to her bedroom and began putting them away. She scooped up Shadow and cuddled him. "It's lovely to be with you again, my baby boy." Helen had been feeling guilty about the young women Lillian had murdered, and even though she knew it was Lillian who had killed them, and there was nothing she could have done to stop it, she still felt dreadful about it all. Even if she had gone to the police and told them what had really happened, she knew they would likely have her thrown into an asylum. Who in the world would ever believe her? She knew soon, though, that she would have to go the police station and tell them a story she had concocted, that her being missing had all been a big misunderstanding, and that she had actually been away on vacation in Santa Barbara. She was not looking forward to that one little bit, but she knew it had to be done. She began preparing some food for Shadow in the kitchen when there was a knock at the front door.

Helen opened it, and saw a tall, handsome, but very stern-looking man standing there in a dark-gray suit. His green eyes stared back at her in surprise.

"Helen Elliot?"

"Yes, I'm Helen."

He held up a police badge. "I'm Detective James Karson. I'd like to speak with you."

Helen's stomach did backflips and her fingers trembled, but somehow, sooner or later she had known this was coming. And she knew she needed to talk to this man. She took a deep breath and gestured him inside.

"Yes, please come in, Detective. We'd better have a talk, but I warn you…you're going to think I'm crazy."

Karson gave her a puzzled look, then stepped inside.

* * *

Satisfied there was nothing else to find, Ethel tucked the perfume bottle in her inside coat pocket and left the yard as quickly as her tired old legs would take her, closing the gate behind her.

Her heart raced with excitement. Could the diamonds be real? And surely she could sell the little perfume bottle. Although nearly empty, it would certainly fetch her a few dollars at least. It looked like an antique. And somebody would want the little silver knobs; they were quite exquisite.

She was very happy she had ventured out of Hollywood Central to the outer areas to try her luck for a change. This lucky break had made it all worthwhile. Tomorrow, she would make her way back to Hollywood Boulevard, back to where she knew the alleyways and the places she could go to have a wash in a public bathroom and get herself a nice hot bowl of soup. Then she would try selling or trading her newfound treasures.

She headed off with her cart toward Beachwood Drive and chuckled aloud at the thought of herself having the diamonds valued by a jeweler. She would never be that lucky, though; good luck just never came to her, never.

It was late in the afternoon, a cool breeze filled the canyon, and Ethel caught a whiff of her own scent. *Lord, I smell a fright.* She hadn't washed in days. She patted her inside breast pocket where she had placed the tiny perfume bottle. *If I don't find somewhere to have a wash tonight, there might just be enough left in there to spray on myself. Besides…it's been years since I've worn perfume.*

She pushed her cart along the sidewalk with a smile on her face, as the sun began sinking slowly down over Los Angeles, and the Hollywood Sign towered on the mountain behind her.